Gone

by

Karyn Good

The Aspen Lake Series, Book 3

Gone

Cover Art by *Kim Mendoza*

The Wild Rose Press, Inc.
PO Box 708
Adams Basin, NY 14410-0708
Visit us at www.thewildrosepress.com

Publishing History
First Crimson Rose Edition, 2019
Print ISBN 978-5092-2549-1
Digital ISBN 978-5092-2550-7

The Aspen Lake Series, Book 3
Published in the United States of America

The music still played, but no one listened. They were too busy trying to talk at once.

Mike settled in beside her, and his disapproving green eyes scanned her face. He lifted the cloth covering her knee and winced. "You okay?"

Grace flinched as his fingers did a gentle probe. "Welcome to the party."

"Seems we were a little late getting our invitation." His expression turned serious. "This may need medical attention."

"It's just a scratch." She tamped down the gooey need threatening to overtake her. Tried to remember it didn't pay to get sentimental over this particular man.

Her reassurance didn't stop him from carefully dabbing at her cut. Or from leaning in to get a closer look. "I don't see any glass, but that doesn't mean there isn't any in there."

"I'm fine." She braced her hands on the floor, ready to lift herself up, having had enough attention and being at the center of it.

Mike put his hand on her shoulder and coaxed her back down. "There's no rush. Take a moment."

She warmed under his touch and the tender concern she'd secretly, and not so secretly, yearned for since he'd arrived in Aspen Lake two years ago.

Praise for Karyn Good and...

BACKLASH
"Ms. Good sure spins a tale of deceit and a trail of clues that lead right to a climax I never imagined."

~Sunflower, Long and Short Reviews

OFF THE GRID
"Sophie and Caleb have astoundingly good chemistry. The plot rushes ahead, almost without them being able to catch up, and in the end, they are firmly together in a whirlwind of tension, romance, and potential disaster."

~Unabridged Andra's Book Reviews

Dedication

To Edwin and Audrey
for all your unconditional love and support

Chapter One

Grace Bighill hustled to wipe down the recently vacated table and pocketed the ten-dollar tip from a forty-dollar tab. Waitressing at the Back Forty, Aspen Lake's version of a dive bar, was demanding work, especially on a Friday night during tourist season. She spared a second to catch her breath, but the stink of body odor and beer mixed with the August heat didn't provide a lot of relief.

Unnoticed by patrons who swayed to country music blasting from ancient speakers, she slapped her rag down. The dim lighting and neon bar signs gave the illusion of a good time waiting to happen. For the patrons, anyway.

A college-aged kid knocked into her on his rush by, hand pressed to his mouth. She really hoped he made it all the way to the toilet, or there was a mop bucket in her future. Tourists. You had to love them, unless you were serving them or cleaning up after them. Then you kind of hated them. Take the guy at the pool table looking to sink a solid in the right-hand corner. He ordered drinks like it was his job to make her run and fetch things.

Then there was Ms. Do-You-Serve-a-Decent-Cabernet perched at the bar flashing her platinum credit card and boobs at the guy more interested in his phone then her D cups. Didn't stop Grace from rooting for her.

She tipped an extra fifteen percent when she got lucky.

But if one more hipster in skinny jeans ordered some complicated cocktail, she was going to flip a shingle. The Back Forty was a bar in the middle of nowhere. They served cold beer, cheap wine, and free peanuts. The bartenders might be persuaded to toss a celery stalk in a glass of vodka and tomato juice. Unless they were out of celery.

Seriously, people.

The locals were out in full force, too. Laughter drifted over from a bunch of ladies toasting a tiara-wearing bride-to-be and her fist full of darts. They signaled for another round, and Grace gave them a nod. But the second she dropped the bowl of complimentary peanuts down on the almost-clean table, the chairs filled with a group of young people.

"Going to need to see some identification, folks." Even though it wasn't necessary. The other nine months of the year, Aspen Lake was a small town. She knew everyone, which was not always a check in the plus column.

With a huge grin, Dixon Sawyer handed her his driver's license. "There you go."

Grace pretended to inspect the plastic card proving he had indeed reached the province's legal drinking age and tried not to feel every one of her thirty years. "Look whose nineteenth birthday it is."

His smile was so broad she could have counted each individual tooth. "Yep, finally legal." Dixon held out his hand to take back his license.

She pulled it out of his reach. "You sure this isn't fake?"

"No, ma'am." His fair skin was no match for his

adorable blush.

She cocked a hip. "Did you just ma'am me, Dixon Sawyer?"

"No—" His flush deepened. "Miss Bighill."

She handed him back his identification. Made a show of looking at the licenses of his buddies, Chris Donaldson and Jordan Lowe, in case she was wrong about ages and birthdays. Last but not least, she held a hand out for Mandy Trent's ID, glanced at it, and handed it back.

"So what'll it be?"

Drink orders taken, Grace leaned down to brush a strand of blond hair off the birthday boy's forehead. They were a decent enough group of kids who came from salt of the earth, hardworking folks, but holy crap, they had a knack for finding trouble, and she was not in the mood to put up with any mischief. "Behave yourself in here, young Dixon, and we'll get along fine."

Jordan gave her a wink, then elbowed Dixon in the ribs. "How about a kiss for the birthday boy?"

Yep, definitely in the mood to stir things up.

Dixon punched Jordan back. "Shut up, jerk."

Grace took pity on him and kissed his cheek, which encouraged a round of clapping and another blush. "There, that wasn't so bad, was it?"

"No...Miss Bighill."

"Seeing as you're nineteen and all, you can probably call me Grace. And remember, behave." She left them to their teasing and stopped at Ian Connelly's table. They lived off the same grid road, and Ian had ploughed her laneway clear of snow more than once after a winter blizzard. "Get you another?"

"Thanks." He didn't smile often, but he always had

one for her. "You're a good sport, Grace. Made that boy's night."

Grace picked up Ian's empty glass. "I'm sure he's forgotten me already. What is it with you men?"

Ian pushed back a length of salt-and-pepper hair. "Many a good woman has slipped through a stupid man's fingers."

Grace couldn't remember the last time the quiet man had slung so many words together. She risked a peek at the tattoos covering his arms, the top of his hands, and his fingers. Some of them in color, others jailhouse rough. "Truer words, Ian."

He squinted up at her. "How is the old place?"

Grace rented the house Ian's parents had once owned. After their son had gone to prison, they'd sold the farm and moved farther west. "Nothing a handy woman like myself can't fix. Be right back."

Every door and window in the bar was propped open to entice a non-existent breeze into the overheated room. The locals knew better than to call attention to the sticky heat or the spotty cutlery. The Back Forty put up with tourists, but it catered to the locals. If you kept your mouth shut, you paid a dollar less for drinks.

Scott Walker strolled in and straddled a chair at a table full of guys. Her nephew, Levi, spent Friday nights with Scott's parents. She didn't begrudge Scott some adult time, and his folks loved their grandson, but Levi didn't like to spend a lot of time with them. Generational divide aside, Grace suspected there was a fair amount of trash talking going on behind her absent sister's back and to Levi's face. To spare him, she spent as much of her free time as possible with him. Not a hardship. She loved her quirky nephew to bits.

Grace added doing laundry at Scott's to her mental to-do list as she hip checked her way through the throng of patrons lined up at the bar to where Brittney Moore, university student and summertime bartender, poured and mixed drinks. As usual, her sexy bartender act attracted plenty of attention. Tonight it was a couple of determined twenty-something-year-old guys with tousled beach hair, hoping to arrange some one-on-one time once the bar closed.

Grace rattled off her drink order and waited while Britt worked her magic. She rose to her tiptoes to yell over the din. "Mandy's the designated driver at table twelve. Keep an eye on her for me?"

Britt gave her a thumb's up.

Grace heaved up her full tray. "Coming through."

She delivered drinks and laughed with customers. Thankfully tonight's crowd was a happy one. Not to mention generous. And when a couple inquired after Grace's sideline knitting business, she slipped them a card.

Her euphoria lasted a whole sixty minutes until four men from Glenville swaggered through the door. Any hope Grace harbored of an uneventful end to a very long shift died.

Every small town had a neighboring rival, and the adversarial relationship wasn't confined to school grounds. Considering the Aspen Lake Mooseheads had trounced Glenville's butt in baseball last week and the identity of the men walking through the door, Grace wasn't predicting a good outcome to their late-night visit.

To prove her luck was on the downslide, the group from Glenville settled at a table in her section. She set her tray down on the bar with a thud and raised a brow at Britt. "Great. What do I do with these guys?"

"Watch out for Mason." Britt swiped at hair damp with sweat and hard work. "He didn't appreciate you putting him out at second last week. Twice."

In the background, she heard Mason holler. "How about some service over here?"

Grace picked up her tray. "Is it possible for his mouth to get any bigger?"

Britt winked. "I say we spit in their drinks."

Grace grinned back. "What's a little saliva between enemies?"

Grace plastered on a fake smile and headed in their direction. The locals shifted in their chairs. She caught sight of more than one phone coming out and aimed in their direction. That was all she needed, a video going viral with her in the leading role.

Didn't stop her from cocking a hip, or the taunt from coming out of her mouth. "The bar full in Glenville?"

Mason Pearce, a big bear of a man with an unruly beard and no filter, gave her an insulting once-over. "Well, look who we have here. It's the pretty little second baseman with the foul mouth."

Grace gave her shoulders a cautious, calming roll. They'd won. She could afford to be gracious. "Stopping in for one? I hope."

"I could find a better use for that mouth." He slapped Carter Smoke, Glenville's own second baseman, on the shoulder. "Bet that sister of hers gave her lessons."

The rush of murmurs buzzed in Grace's ears as people shifted in their seats. Her fingers tightened around her tray. Everyone within a hundred kilometers had heard the rumors of her sister's alleged affair with an oilrig worker who'd long since up and left. Grace knew her sister. Hope might have a wild streak, but she wasn't promiscuous. Reality didn't matter to those who'd branded Hope Bighill-Walker a slut. To add insult to injury, Grace was pretty sure she was facing down the man who'd started the rumors in the first place, although she had yet to figure out why.

Grace huffed out a hearty laugh like she found Mason's insult the funniest thing she'd heard all night. "Anyone stupid enough to volunteer for that nasty job would have to find it first."

He spread his legs and grabbed his crotch. There was no need to raise his voice in the sudden hush of silence. "Doubt that would be a problem for you, sweet-cheeks."

Behind her, a chair scraped across the floor. She didn't look back. Grace didn't need or want anyone coming to her rescue. What she lacked in height, she made up for in grit. "Might be a good idea to skip the drinks and make your way home."

Mason lifted his chin. "And maybe we won't."

Whatever was happening in the background had Carter bracing for impact. "Dial it back, Mace."

Grace stayed focused on Mason. "Be smart and listen to your friend."

"Why don't you fetch us a pitcher of beer?" Mason sneered up at her, then he slapped her ass.

Hard.

A rush of movement ended with her brother-in-law planting Mason's hairy face into the table. "Apologize, asshole."

Too bad Scott lacked the extra fifty pounds and the necessary extra inches to keep the big man down. With a growl, Mason reared back and brought Scott with him.

Everyone close to the table scrambled back as the two men faced each other, fists raised and breathing hard. Grace did a frantic search of the onlookers, looking for someone capable of running interference.

"Hey, asshole." Dixon shouldered his way through the inner ring of the crowd. "Don't you have your own bar?"

Definitely not the solution she had in mind. "Get back, Dixon."

"Yeah." Carter moved to flank Mason. "Mind your own business, kid."

Scott pointed at the exit. "There's the door. Use it."

Mason sneered. "The Bighills always been trash, always gonna be trash. When you going to figure that out, Walker?"

Scott swung, and Mason stumbled into the table behind him. Glass shattered. Others squared off. Soon taunts and jabs joined the reek of slopped beer in the air.

Mason gained his feet and punched back. Scott ducked. Grace struggled to get out of the way only to slip in a puddle of beer and land hard. Pain radiated from her kneecap, making her eyes water.

Rough hands yanked her to her feet. Ian gave her a push. "Move."

Grace stumbled into Scott and knocked him sideways. It saved him from a right hook. Ian wasn't so lucky. Mason's fist caught him square in the mouth. In a blink, Ian snapped Mason's head back with a mean jab that froze Grace in place.

Ian shoved her out of the way of another swinging fist. "Head down."

In a deep crouch, she searched for a way out, but twisting bodies and pummeling fists blocked her exit. Ian grabbed the back of her shirt, and the worn fabric gave way. She made a frantic attempt to hold the edges together as he dragged her out of harm's way.

"Grace, over here." Britt struggled to hold out a hand as the crowd continued to shift around her.

Grace spotted her serving tray and scooped it off the floor to use as a shield. Wayne, the bar owner, announced he'd called the police, for all the effect it had, which was none. A bald guy with a sunburn toppled into her, and she staggered to the left. Only to be shoved back by Carter.

More than done being surrounded by idiots, Grace brought her tray down on the side of Carter's head. Carter retaliated without looking.

Next thing she knew, she was on her butt in a pool of beer and peanut shells, the continuing fight on mute and a little out of focus.

"Jesus, are you okay?"

She blinked up at Carter.

Britt loomed over her. "Her leg."

"Grace, you okay?" Ian pushed Carter to the side.

"Not quite sure." She put a hand to her aching cheek to check for blood and found none, then brushed at her knee. Her hand come away bloody. "Oh, crap."

"Stay put." Ian laid a hand on Grace's shoulder. "Britt, grab a clean cloth."

There was a disturbance by the door. "All right, fun's over."

She had no problem identifying the voice. Constable Mike Davenport was not happy. "You, stand over there. You, opposite wall. Go. Now."

Mason's response suggested he wasn't on board.

"Over there. Now." A person with any sense at all would have obeyed. So it wasn't any big surprise Mason paid no attention. Mike's voice rose. "If I have to repeat myself, I won't be happy."

Britt handed Grace a wet cloth. "For your knee."

Grace held her breath as she pressed the warm rag against the inch-long scrape under her kneecap.

With every light in the place on, the illusion of a good time was shattered. The music still played, but no one listened. They were too busy trying to talk at once.

Mike settled in beside her, and his disapproving green eyes scanned her face. He lifted the cloth covering her knee and winced. "You okay?"

Grace flinched as his fingers did a gentle probe. "Welcome to the party."

"Seems we were a little late getting our invitation." His expression turned serious. "This may need medical attention."

"It's just a scratch." She tamped down the gooey need threatening to overtake her. Tried to remember it didn't pay to get sentimental over this particular man.

Her reassurance didn't stop him from carefully dabbing at her cut. Or from leaning in to get a closer look. "I don't see any glass, but that doesn't mean there isn't any in there."

"I'm fine." She braced her hands on the floor, ready to lift herself up, having had enough attention and being at the center of it.

Mike put his hand on her shoulder and coaxed her

back down. "There's no rush. Take a moment."

She warmed under his touch and the tender concern she'd secretly, and not so secretly, yearned for since he'd arrived in Aspen Lake two years ago.

"Is she okay? I tried to stop—"

Mike shot to his feet, plenty of menace where there was usually cool confidence.

Carter backed up, palms out. "I'm sorry. I didn't mean to hit her. Honest. I would never hit a girl—woman...whatever. I wouldn't. At least, not on purpose."

"Carter's telling the truth. Besides, I hit him first." Grace struggled to her feet with the help of a reluctant Ian. "Anyway, I've gotten worse sliding into home."

A muscle worked along Mike's jaw. "You don't look fine to me."

"Always with the flattery." She noted a funny kind of breeze where there shouldn't be one. She twisted and found the long, gaping tear where the side seam of her shirt had given way, and she fisted the edges together.

His eyes narrowed at the sight of her wrestling with her torn shirt. "Brittney, find Grace a shirt."

Britt hustled to do his bidding. His voice had that kind of power. Grace was very careful never to reveal her urge to comply, but it was getting harder the more he fussed over her. She didn't get a lot of sweet. And never from him.

"Constable Davenport, I could use your help over here."

Mike's partner, Constable Chase Porter, was no slouch in the ass-kicking department, but he did, indeed, have his hands full. Scott was trying to get at Mason, who was too stupid to shut up. Dixon was there, too young and too rash to know when to fade into the background.

Ian pressed in close to her other side. "We've got her."

Britt arrived with a shirt and Nancy Boedel. "There's a group of nurses here. Stagette. Nancy will check her out."

"There's no need to fuss. I said I was fine. But someone should look at Ian's lip." She tried to take a step and damned if her knee didn't betray her by buckling.

"Don't bother about me," said Ian, forced to accept a stack of napkins from Britt.

"Sit." Mike righted a chair for Grace, and then he stepped back to give Britt space to drape a hoodie over her shoulders.

Ian gave Mike a curt nod. "She's in good hands."

"She certainly is." Nancy, a nurse with the regional health unit, shooed Mike out of the way.

"I'll be back. In the meantime, cooperate." Mike gave Grace a last warning look and moved off.

Grace saluted his retreating back.

Nancy held up a hand in front of Grace's face. "How many fingers?"

She'd served Nancy three rum and cokes. Grace should be the one asking her. But it was pointless to argue with the mother of six. "Four."

Nancy carried on with her probing, taking inventory while Ian lurked nearby, having appointed himself her unofficial guardian. Any residual adrenaline drained away, leaving her painfully aware of her hot and tender cheek. She doubted swollen and bruised was a good look on her. Not that it mattered. On a good day, no mirror was going to proclaim her fairest in all the land. A bruised cheek and a scrape on her knee were minor inconveniences. She'd suffered worse. Much worse.

****

Constable Mike Davenport unwrapped a stick of gum and shoved it in his mouth, hoping the burst of flavor would help him focus. He never lost his temper. Rules and upholding them kept him grounded. But Mason Pearce's malicious tirade against Grace, and the inhabitants of Aspen Lake in general, inched him closer to a line he refused to cross.

Summoning his limited supply of goodwill, Mike held up a hand, warning Mason to stay put, and used the other one to hold back Scott Walker. "Who started the fight?"

Blood dripped from a cut near Mason's right eye and his Beer O'clock T-shirt was shredded at the shoulder. He thrust a thick finger in Grace's direction. "It was that bitch's fault. She's fucking crazy, just like that old man of hers."

Mike's carefully guarded objectivity packed its bags. "Keep pushing. I'm more than happy to escort you to jail for the night."

"Okay." Chase stuffed his notebook and pen away. "Let's all take a breath."

"Mace, let it go." It was clear Carter was losing patience with his burly friend. The other two men with them had already apologized and offered to help pay for damages.

Mason ignored his friend's advice, and his finger swung in Scott's direction. "And I want Walker charged with assault."

Scott struggled to get around Mike. "Nobody gives a shit what you want, asshole."

Leaving Chase to deal with Mason, Mike braced a hand on Scott's chest and pushed him back. "Knock it off."

"Ten bucks says he's screwing her," Mason tossed out from behind them. "Couldn't wait for that wife of his to be gone so he could get it on with the sister."

"Enough." Chase's growl and the scuffling behind them had Mike once again pushing against a protesting Scott.

"Yeah?" Scott shoved off Mike's hand with a sneer. "How's your wife doing these days? Dished out any more black eyes, you piece of shit?"

Mike had zero respect or sympathy for Mason, but he wasn't a big fan of Walker's either. He didn't like how Scott watched Grace, relied on her, how she laughed at his jokes or dropped everything to help him out. It was a pleasure to manhandle him into an empty corner of the room.

"Cool off," he ordered.

"Every person here will tell you that asshole started it." Blood leaked from Scott's split lip, and his Walker's Plumbing and Electric shirt was missing a pocket.

Mike swiped a napkin from one of the few upright tables and offered it to Scott. "So he attacked you first?"

"Not exactly." Walker snatched it and dabbed at his bloody lip.

Mike raised his brow and waited.

Scott's snort left little doubt as to his opinion of having to spell things out for Mike's benefit. "He verbally attacked Grace, and then he hit her."

To hide his less-than-objective reaction to the thought of someone assaulting Grace, Mike pulled out his notebook and gave his wad of gum a workout while he recorded the details of Scott's side of things. Walker might be a little too fond of Grace, but he was as honest as they came. He believed Walker's story. He might even have felt a drop of gratitude for his defense of Grace.

Somewhat mollified by Mike's no-nonsense approach, Walker settled down. "I need to leave. Go pick up my kid."

If Walker had one thing going for him, it was his parenting skills. He tried hard to do the right thing for his child. Mike did a quick survey of the room. "A lot of damage done here tonight."

Scott crumpled the soiled napkin into a ball and shoved it in a pocket. Guilt roughened his voice. "I'll talk to Wayne tomorrow. We'll work it out."

Mike didn't doubt he would. Walker was a believer in an unwritten small-town code of ethics Mike would never understand. "See that you do."

Walker wasn't a fan of taking orders, especially from Mike. "I'll just go collect Grace, and we'll be out of your hair."

Mike was only too happy to enlighten him to the contrary. "Grace is my business tonight."

"You might want to check with Grace over that one." Scott offered a smirk. "Constable."

Mike planted his hands on his hips and purposefully took up more than his share of space. "I'm not required to check-in with anyone."

"Okay, then." Walker shrugged and let out a laugh.

"It's your funeral."

"It's my job." Mike was done. "Go home."

Walker crossed his arms. "As soon as I collect Grace. I gave her a lift into work, and I'm taking her home."

The day Mike let this man get the best of him was the day he rethought his career path. "I'll make sure she gets home safely. You're free to go and pick up your son."

Walker yanked a ball cap from his back pocket. "I don't need you to tell me how to take care of my family."

"Except you didn't take such great care of your wife, so I'm not sure why I should believe you about Grace." It was a low blow, and they both knew it.

"Go to hell, Davenport." Walker moved to swing around him.

Mike grabbed Walker's arm. He didn't raise his voice. Didn't need to. He'd been raised to remind others of their lower status, and there was enough of that man left in him to want to put Walker in his place. "I'm not telling you again. Go home, Scott."

Walker wasn't getting near Grace. She deserved one night to recover in peace. Walker yanked his arm free and opened his mouth.

"Be very careful what you say next." Mike blocked Walker's path and waited. He couldn't decide whether he was relieved or disappointed when Walker managed to remain silent. "You've got five seconds to make your way out the door."

Walker gave Mike a hard, scathing look. "I'll be checking in with her tomorrow."

Mike stepped back, knowing he'd already given

too much away. "You do that."

"You do anything to make this night worse for her, you and me are gonna have words."

Parting shot delivered, Walker headed for the door. He stopped to accept a couple of backslapping congratulations from a small group who had volunteered to stick around and help Wayne clean up. Then he was out the door and gone.

Mike shook his head. He had a decent enough relationship with the people of Aspen Lake and the surrounding area. For the most part, they were good folks. But he wasn't one of them and never would be, not in the way Chase was, having grown up here. Or even their friend, Seth Stone, who had taken to small town life like he'd been born to it. Mike had no desire to stay. The opposite, in fact. He wanted a city, restaurants, cinema, and anonymity in his off time.

"Can we *pleeeeease* leave?"

Mandy Trent was wrapped around Dixon Sawyer. Dixon's swollen nose sported wads of tissue and complemented his black eyes. He wasn't going to forget his nineteenth birthday anytime soon.

As part of his policing duties with the Aspen Lake detachment, Mike was the high school liaison officer. He knew these kids. They didn't look for trouble, but it usually showed up. Beside Mandy, Dixon vibrated with righteous indignation. "Mason Pearce started it. He was disrespecting Miss Bighill."

Mike pinched the bridge of his nose. "Mandy, you're the designated driver?"

She gave an eager nod.

"Take them home. I mean it. I don't want to see any of you out cruising later." He gave all four of them a stern look. "You hear me?"

"Come on—"

"Home. We'll talk about how you're going to pay for your share of the damages tomorrow at the station." He worked hard to develop a connection and a sense of mutual respect with the town's youth, wanting them to see the police as an ally, not the enemy. But he also never gave the impression he was anything other than what he was—the law.

"Yes, sir." Dixon's resigned tone matched his slumping shoulders. His parents were solid, hardworking ranchers. Any money Dixon needed to pay for damages, he'd earn the hard way.

Mike ushered them out, waited while they piled into Mandy's battered two-door sedan, then he headed back inside where the rank and file had grown to include Constables Deke Kowalchuck and Cal Bartlett. "How are things going in here?"

Pearce hadn't calmed down any. "There was no reason for the police to get involved. No reason at all. Police brutality. That's what this is."

Deke crossed his massive arms. "Do yourself a favor and stop talking."

"We're working it out." Chase motioned Mike to join him off to the side. "Got your end under control?"

"Walker is on his way home, and the younger crowd has been ordered home to bed. We'll hit the usual party spots later to see if they actually listened."

"Grace caught a ride to work." Chase narrowed his eyes. "Why don't you give her a ride home while we finish up here?"

"Sure. No problem." It saved Mike from having to insist. His partner, being a smart guy, knew it, too.

Grace was capable of finding her own way home. Ian or Britt would be happy to take her, and Grace wasn't going to thank him for his highhandedness by insisting it be him. Mike generally avoided alone time with Grace. He had his reasons. He was making an exception tonight.

On his approach, Grace lowered the ice pack onto her lap, more than a hint of wariness in her pretty eyes. He crouched down in front of her.

She lifted her chin in Mason's direction. "Guess he's not signing up to be president of my fan club, huh?"

Mike eyed the stark white bandage on her knee. He knew better than to touch her, but he was unable to stop his hand from making contact with her warm skin. "Ignore him."

"I think this is one of those easier-said-than-done situations." She huddled farther into the overlarge hoodie and gave his hand, still resting above her knee, a cautious glance.

He was too concerned with her pallor to appreciate her attempts at sarcasm. "Ready to go?"

She shifted in her chair, and his hand slipped off her leg. "I can find my own way home."

"I can drop her off on my way." Ian stepped forward, reminding Mike they had an audience.

"Thanks for the offer, Ian." Mike didn't take his eyes off Grace. Not even to question why the usually reticent Ian had bothered to stick around. "I'll see her home."

"Guess I'll be heading out." Ian put a hand on Grace's shoulder. "Take care of yourself."

"I don't care who takes her as long as she gets

there sooner rather than later." Nancy pointed a stern finger at Grace. "Take some pain meds, keep icing your cheek and your knee. Get some sleep. Nurse's orders."

Mike stood. "Let's get you home."

She ignored his outstretched hand. "I didn't break a leg."

No, it was only bleeding and swollen. He let his hand drop.

"Stupid fuel pump," she muttered.

Nancy sighed. "Just go with the nice police officer."

"Sheesh. I'm going." She pulled the hoodie close and stubbornly got to her feet unassisted.

"That's the spirit." Nancy winked in his direction. "There are worse things."

To lighten the mood, Mike winked back.

Grace rolled her eyes. "We can go out the backdoor. I'll grab my things on the way."

"Grace." Wayne paused in his mission to re-right chairs. "You're officially off the schedule tomorrow. Paid leave."

She all but stomped a foot. "I'm not dying."

"I can see that." He bent, picked up another chair, set it down. "Still don't want to see you in here tomorrow."

"Fine. Thanks." She wrapped her arms around her middle, her voice dropping to a frustrated whisper. "For nothing."

Mike caught the defeat in her voice. It was so unlike her he forgot himself and tucked a few dark strands of loose hair behind her ear. She flinched, and he dropped his hand. "He's worried about you."

"Sorry. It hurts." She laid a gentle hand over her

cheek. "And it's making me feel like a wimp."

God, he wanted to kiss it all better. So badly. He ached with holding back, but further contact was a terrible idea. To distract them both, he opened the Staff Only door for her. "I'll wait out here while you collect your things."

A moment later, she limped out of the office toting a bulging bag with knitting needles poking out the top. She knit the craziest blankets, all kinds of colors with no rhyme or reason to them he could see. They resembled her life—busy, chaotic, and bright.

There was no room in his life for chaos. All of a sudden, he didn't want to be alone with her. When he'd first arrived in Aspen Lake, those extraordinary eyes had invited more than friendship. But he hadn't wanted to want her. He liked her. Admired her. But to crave her, too? The last time he'd felt those things for a woman, he'd lost a piece of his soul. And so much more.

****

Grace climbed into Mike's police cruiser and winced at the pain the movement caused her knee. Mike was busy stowing her bag in the back seat and didn't notice her discomfort, which was a good thing. He was taking the whole business of her getting hurt a little too personally. Not that his light touches and obvious concern for her welfare weren't appreciated. They very much were, and that was a problem because he'd made it clear he wasn't interested in any kind of physical or emotional relationship.

The interior of the cruiser was an excellent reminder Mike's insistence on seeing her home was professional not personal. He was dedicated to his job, a career cop. She clicked her seatbelt into place, sat back, and waited while he made his way to the driver's side.

Two years of knowing each other and they'd only been alone together one other time. Shortly after his arrival, they'd both attended a New Year's Eve party and had found themselves alone in the kitchen at midnight. They'd kissed, as expected. But their lip lock had gone on to include a bit more tongue than necessary and significantly more groping than required to ring in the New Year. Shored up on yuletide cocktails, she'd let him know she wouldn't mind continuing things at her place.

Big mistake.

Huge.

His clumsy rejection had stung, almost as much as his continued avoidance. The cruiser shifted as Mike settled into the seat beside her. She sat up straighter. When they didn't move, she waved her hands in a forward motion. "Anytime you're ready."

"You should press charges against him." His hands curled around the steering wheel.

"Carter?" She dropped her head back against the headrest, wishing she were already home in bed. Or anywhere but trapped in a car with Mike. She let her eyes drift shut. "He apologized. It's done. Moving on."

"No, Pearce."

Her eyes snapped open. "What? No."

He twisted in his seat. "He assaulted you."

The atmosphere in the vehicle thinned as his words bit chunks out of the air. Gone was the staid and steady cop, his tone no longer professional. Or neutral.

She didn't need or want him running interference

for her. She'd done a decent enough job of looking after herself for the last seventeen years, after all.

"Leave it be. Please." She caught and held his gaze. "I don't want to make things worse for his wife. He'll only take things out on her."

His brows lifted. "You telling me how to do my job?"

"Amanda works two jobs and has three kids." It was no secret Amanda Pearce's life was difficult. Grace had no intention of making it harder.

"How is it you know everything about everybody?"

"I work in a bar." She was tired and not in the mood to answer probing questions about her motives, which were none of his business. He'd made that perfectly clear. When he remained silent, she sighed. "People tell me things."

"What kinds of things?" he asked.

She frowned. Polite Mike kept her at a distance. Polite Mike never asked her personal questions. Tonight's inquisition threw her off. "I can't tell you. What kind of secret-keeper would that make me?"

His gaze slipped to her mouth. "People trust you."

Warmth spread through her at his unexpected compliment. "I guess."

He brushed his knuckles along her uninjured cheekbone. "They do because you've proven you're loyal. To them. To this place."

It was the sweetest thing he'd ever said to her.

He dropped his hand. "You're a good friend, Grace. To us all."

Friends.

Right.

It wouldn't do to forget it. Her cheek muscles

protested the effort of offering a beaming smile. "I'm all about being a good friend."

He twisted the key in the ignition. "I should get you home."

"It's been a long day," she agreed, desperate to get them moving.

When was she going to accept he was the exact wrong type of man for her? Sure, those broad shoulders looked like they could carry a lot of weight. And he was irritatingly calm, tonight's reaction being a rare exception. He was also articulate and thoughtful, as well as annoyingly honest.

Goodness gravy, why couldn't she be one of those women who craved bad boys? There were plenty of those lounging around, surrounded by a litter of crushed beer cans and broken motorcycle parts. And lucky her, most of them were single.

The crunch of gravel under tires filled the sudden silence inside the cruiser. They left town with only the dispatcher's voice and the odd beep disrupting the awkward quiet. When they pulled up to the little farmhouse she rented, she was more than ready to get out. But she paused when she noticed the spill of light coming from the kitchen window. Lights she'd left dark. A figure crossed in front of the window.

She leaned forward. "What the heck?"

"Do you have someone staying with you?"

She squinted harder. "No."

She did a quick check of her yard and spotted an unfamiliar vehicle parked off to the side.

Mike put a hand on her arm. "Stay here."

He walked up the front steps and knocked on her door. She worried her fingers across the blunt end of her ponytail. Her view was blocked by six feet of police officer. She was all too aware a uniform and a vest of soft body armor didn't make him invincible. The door opened, and her sister's face peeked out from around Mike. The rest of her followed, an apron tied around her waist. Her very pregnant waist.

Grace hustled her butt out of the vehicle. The last time they'd heard from Hope, she'd been in Calgary. She'd managed quick phone calls home to let them know she was alive, that she was figuring things out, and she asked after her son.

"Tell Levi I love him."

Grace had relayed her sister's messages. But ten-year-old Levi hadn't wanted to listen. And who could blame him?

Mike cast a wary look back as she hobbled up the worn porch steps and passed the ancient wicker rockers. She spared Mike a spot of sympathy. The unfortunate man was about to get a glimpse of Bighill drama.

Her sister spread her arms and offered a nervous smile. "Surprise."

Hope might look like a blonde, blue-eyed angel, but she possessed a wild, restless heart. They were nothing alike in looks or temperament, but she loved her sister. When she didn't want to throttle her.

Grace didn't smile back. "Gee, Hope. Long time no see. Missed you at Christmas. And Easter. And all the other holidays."

Hope dropped her arms, eyes widening. "What happened to your face? Oh, my God, your knee?"

"Bar fight." Grace waved off her sister's concern. "What are you doing here?"

Hope's expressive eyes widened even farther, and

she risked a furtive peek at Mike, who was very obviously in uniform and on duty. "You didn't start it, did you?"

"No, I did not." Grace resisted the urge to stomp her foot. "And quit stalling."

Mike moved in next to Grace, his warm hand coming to rest against her lower back. His fingers flexed, and she wanted his arm to slip around her. She wanted to lean into him. To tap into his quiet strength so she wouldn't be quite so tempted to open her mouth and scream. She wasn't a fan of either screaming or leaning.

Instead, she stepped away from his comfort. "Thanks for the ride."

Mike glanced at Hope. "Can I have a minute with Grace?"

Before she could explain how very unnecessary his continued presence was, Hope slunk back into the house and closed the door. The traitor.

Mike hovered at her side. "Are you sure you want me to leave?"

Just doing his job. That's all his concern meant. "My sister's not going to hurt me."

"Not what I asked. And for the record, not what I was thinking."

"Well, excuse me for not being psychic." God, she should stop talking.

"I was thinking you might need a friend."

If he said the *friend* word one more time tonight, she was going to lose her mind.

He fixated on the bruise blooming across her cheek. "You're losing weight you can't afford to lose. There are shadows under your eyes. You're worn out."

She resisted the urge to smooth a hand over her messy hair, to adjust her soiled and torn clothing. She refused to give one single sign that his words had cut deep. "Thank you so much for the flattering assessment."

He didn't get the hint. "Pretty sure I'm not the only one who's noticed you're spreading yourself too thin."

She was so done with him. It felt amazing to look him in the eye and know it was true. "Goodbye, Mike."

He narrowed his eyes, like he was having trouble understanding what had just happened. "I didn't mean it as an insult."

She reached for the door handle. "Consider your job done here. See you around, Constable."

"I don't think of you as a job. I—" He put his hand on her elbow, and his touch stopped her cold. He stepped closer and lowered his eyes to her lips for the second time that night. Then his baffled look disappeared, and the cop was firmly back in place. His hand slipped away. "You're right. It's not my place."

He backtracked down the porch steps. Scooby brushed up against her leg with a meow. She dropped down to pick up her cat, eager for something to hold. Mike paused, and for one tense second, she thought he might come back. She waited, but he continued to his vehicle, retrieved her bag, and retraced his steps. He set her bag down next to her. When he straightened, his withdrawal was complete.

"Take care of yourself, Grace."

An owl hooted in the distance, and she snuggled her cat closer until Mike's tailgates glowed red in the distance. One problem solved, one to go. Grace stalked into her kitchen. Boxes littered the floor. Some waited for attention, and others were open and trailing their contents all over the small room. Hope turned from unpacking what looked like a brand-new stand mixer.

Scooby scrambled out of Grace's arms and disappeared out of the room.

"Make yourself at home."

Hope braced her hands over her belly, protecting her precious cargo. "I can leave and go to Dad's, if you'd rather I didn't stay here."

Their father's house wasn't an option.

Hope served up the same sweet, dimpled smile she always used to soften Grace up. "Please, don't make me go to Dad's."

A couple of suitcases waited in the hallway. "Looks like you're planning on staying a while."

Hope's hands twisted into her oversized shirt. "I'm back for good."

She might be frustrated with Hope, but she'd missed her. Hope was the only other person on the planet who knew what it was like to be the daughter of Martin and Cissy Bighill. She was happy to have her back, even if her return was going to cause problems on a bunch of different levels.

"What do you want to cover first? The baby bump? Or the kitchen store robbery?" Grace pulled out a chair for Hope, and then she snagged a bag of frozen peas from the fridge freezer. She plugged in the kettle on her way by.

Hope picked at the hem of one of Grace's homemade, cherry-red placemats. "I didn't know I was pregnant when I left, I swear."

Grace paused with the bag of peas halfway to her aching face. "Don't make me ask."

"The baby is Scott's."

"Does he know?"

"No." Hope closed her eyes and lowered her head. "I didn't know how to tell him. Any of you."

Grace pressed the frozen vegetables to her face. "And if Scott doesn't believe you?"

Hope's head snapped back up. "I didn't cheat on my husband."

"He thinks you did."

"Because he chose to believe the lies of a jealous asshole."

Grace sighed. "You both let the gossips win."

"I get that you're a fan of the rubber-versus-glue theory to life, but some lies are a little harder to shrug off than others."

Grace opened her mouth, but she didn't get very far.

"And it's even harder when the ones who are supposed to love you and have your back choose to believe the worst."

"You coming back pregnant is only going to add fuel to those lies." The kettle whistled, and Grace limped about getting the tea things ready. She set a mug in front of each of them and hoped the soothing effects of chamomile would take the sting out of her next question. "And Levi? Is he supposed to welcome you back with open arms? Like the last eight months haven't happened?"

Hope wrapped her hands around her cup. "I want to make it up to him. And to Scott. I want us to be a family again."

"So all the unhappiness, the dissatisfaction, the disillusionment, I believe you called it. Poof. Gone."

"I went for counseling. Sort of." Hope lifted her mug to her lips. Her eyes pleaded for understanding over the rim of her cup. "Long story, but I found a purpose, Grace. I found me."

Grace nudged her cup to the side, no longer in the mood for tea, and braced her arms over the table. "Well, good for you."

Hope reached for Grace's hand and held on when she tried to pull away. "I know I have a lot of atoning to do. A lot of gaining back the trust I've lost, but I'm willing to put in the work to make things right with my family."

We're family, and family sticks together.

It had been her mother's favorite saying when times got tough, as they so often did.

"The spare room is yours for as long as you need it." But giving her sister a place to stay didn't mean Hope was getting a free pass in the reckoning department. "I'll call Scott first thing in the morning and ask him to come over. The rest is up to you."

She saw her sister to bed, then ignored the drag of her tired, aching body and tidied the remnants of their tea party. She paused in front of the fridge decorated with Levi's drawings. Her finger traced the careful lettering of her name where his mother's should have been.

There was no way Hope had missed seeing the picture. But Grace wasn't about to apologize for stepping in and doing what needed doing. She loved her nephew. These last months, she'd been Levi's shoulder to cry on when things got tough. She was only too happy to spend time with him. Sure, she spent less time focusing on her knitting and creating desperately needed opportunities for herself, but Levi was worth the sacrifice.

Family came first.

Always.

Chapter Two

Grace's beloved pineapple-shaped cookie jar was pushed aside to make room for Hope's shiny, new stand mixer. Yesterday Grace had a productive Saturday morning all planned out, with a checklist of a dozen things she needed to get done. She touched a hand to her aching cheek. Twenty-four hours later, all she wanted was to spend the day in bed with her knitting.

Grace folded a piece of packing paper and added it to a growing pile. Hope's frenzied tidying had proven infectious and about as welcome as an airborne virus. "Scott's not even going to notice."

Hope grabbed the stack of newsprint and stuffed it out of sight. "I want things to be neat."

"Well, mission accomplished." Grace's kitchen was gleaming. "He's going to walk in and think he's in the wrong house."

"Thanks." Hope winked at her, dimples denting her cheeks. "By the way, when was the last time you cleaned?"

"Ha, ha." She was tempted to slap back with the list of things she'd been doing to help out Scott and Levi, therefore neglecting her own place, but she didn't have the energy. Also, she was nervous. Things with Scott were getting a little…weird. Grace checked her watch. "Levi's art lesson was at ten, so Scott should be here any minute."

"We'll get everything out in the open." Hope reached for the dishrag and wiped her hands. "It'll be good."

Grace admired her sister's confidence, but she wasn't about to bet money on her being right.

They jerked at the sound of a truck door slamming shut. Grace hurried to meet her unsuspecting brother-in-law at the door. She'd only asked him to come over, hadn't mentioned why, not wanting to tell him about Hope over the phone. Scott grinned, despite his split lip, and offered her a to-go cup of steaming black coffee.

"Thought I'd bring some joe." He dug the keys to her vehicle out of his pocket. "New fuel pump is in. I can take you to pick it up, if you like?"

"Not right now." She rubbed the back of her neck. *Levi.* She was doing this for Levi.

Scott dropped her keys into her hand. "No problem. Whenever you're ready, it's sitting in my driveway."

Grace shoved her keys into the pocket of her shorts, all but forgetting the careful mental script she'd worked out about moving forward and keeping an open mind and possibly something Oprah said. "How much do I owe you?"

"No charge, remember?" He frowned. "Got the parts off the Jeep Dallas totaled last month."

"Right." Grace didn't know what to say or how to look him in the eye.

"Is something wrong?" Scott tilted his head. "This isn't about last night, is it? Don't worry about Mason. I'll make sure he's not a problem in the future."

Grace placed a hand over her cheek. She'd forgotten about the achy bruise. "Come on inside."

His smile disappeared, replaced with a sympathetic wince as he squeezed into her miniscule entryway. "How's the face? Oh, man, so glad I got a couple of good shots in."

"No worse than yours." She wasted a few seconds praying for the right words.

His eyes narrowed. "You're starting to worry me, Grace."

Like ripping off a bandage. "Hope's back."

Scott snorted out a laugh, but his eyes went cold. "Not funny."

She agreed. Nothing about this was fun. "She needs to talk to you."

"Damn it, Grace." He lifted his ball cap off, then immediately twisted it back into place.

"I'm sorry." She sensed his retreat and moved to block his exit. A splash of hot coffee hit her wrist. She switched hands and flicked the pain away, like she wished she could do for Scott. For Hope. And most especially for Levi. "I didn't know how else to do this."

"She's not my problem anymore."

"You have a child together." Two, as it turned out.

"And she abandoned us, along with any claim to Levi. He's mine. I've got nothing to say to her." Scott screwed his eyes shut. "I cannot believe you blindsided me like this."

"There's something you need to know." She put a hand on his arm. To keep him there. To calm him. As an apology for everything, but most especially for what was coming next. "Promise me you'll listen to her."

He rolled his shoulders, readying for a fight. "I don't have to do anything."

His denial was bravado because he would listen.

He loved his little boy and would do anything for him. She swallowed her regret at manipulating him. "For Levi's sake."

Scott hung his head. She had to dip her own to catch his next words. "Grace, he's finally starting to settle."

"I know." Her heart ached for Levi and the pain her sister's return would cause her nephew. But she also knew what it was like to lose your mother and wonder why she'd left or what had happened to her, and she didn't want that for Levi. She tugged Scott into the kitchen. "But you don't have a choice."

Hope bumped back from the table and gained her feet.

Scott stopped dead at the sight of his wife's bulging stomach. "What the fuck?"

Grace rescued Scott's forgotten coffee cup when it tipped and leaked coffee to the floor. "Listen to what she has to say."

Stiff with his sense of betrayal, he refused to look at either of them.

"I'm sorry," Grace whispered, when Hope remained mute.

"So fucking typical." His arm swept out, toward Grace then Hope. "You're the one apologizing, and she stands there like nothing's happened."

"Scott." Hope's fingers plucked at the edges of her maternity shirt. "I can explain—"

"See you around. Good luck to the new guy, whoever he is." He lifted a hand in farewell and headed for the door.

Hope smoothed hands over her belly and spoke to her husband's retreating back. "This baby is yours."

Karyn Good

He jerked around. "You think I can't see your traps coming a mile away?"

"It's true," insisted Hope.

"Like I'd believe anything that came out of your mouth."

Hope flinched. "I've made mistakes, it's true. We both have. But I've never lied to you, not at our worst. Not now."

"After the dust settled, there was a part of me that thought that son of a bitch was lying." He shook his head. "I'm such an idiot."

Grace gritted her teeth. "Your wife is telling you this child is yours. You do not get to dismiss her if there's a possibility it's true."

Scott's mouth worked, bunching and fighting to remain shut. His internal struggle lasted only seconds but seemed like a lifetime. "She gets five minutes."

Grace offered Hope an encouraging nod. "I'll just go outside and—"

Scott grabbed her hand. "You're not going anywhere."

She freed her fingers. "It's really not my business—"

"We all know he's more your son than he is hers."

Hope's face paled, and she dropped into her seat.

"That's not true." Grace rounded the table to crouch down in front of her sister. "Hope, it's not. Are you okay?"

"Oh, please, don't tell me you're falling for her poor-me act."

"Scott, lay off." Grace rose and grabbed a glass and filled it with water. "Here. Drink."

Hope sipped, set the glass down, and met her

husband's fuming glare. "I screwed up. I know asking for a second chance is asking a lot of Levi, of both of you."

Scott crossed his arms. "No."

Hope braced her hands against the table and surged to her feet. "He's my son, too."

"Not anymore. You abandoned him, remember?"

"I explained about—"

"Seriously? Do you think a couple of quick phone calls made everything okay? How delusional are you?"

Hope took a deep breath. "I'm asking for a chance to make it right. With both of you."

Scott dipped his head back and spoke to the ceiling. "This can't be happening."

"For our son's sake."

"The best thing for Levi would be for you to turn around and go back to wherever it is you came from."

Grace resisted the childish urge to cover her ears. "Guys, let's just take a minute."

"I need to make things right with my son. You might not think I deserve that chance, but he needs to know I'm willing to try to make amends. That I'm here for him when he's ready." Hope straightened her shoulders. "And I'm here because this baby needs to know her father."

A stifling silence crept in to gag them all. Scott broke the spell with a shattered laugh. "How could I have been so fucking stupid? God...*Levi*."

Grace flinched at the heartbreak in his voice.

Hope moved toward him. "We'll make it okay for him. It'll be—"

"Make it okay for him?" Scott looked like someone had punched him in the face.

Grace put out a hand in warning. "Scott."

He wasn't done. Not by a long shot. He spewed the rest of his resentment all over his wife. "Is that what I'm supposed to tell him? That everything is going to be *okay*. Like the last eight months haven't happened? As if he hasn't suffered? But you wouldn't know that because, as usual, you caused a whole bunch of shit, then were unavailable to deal with the fallout."

Hope's chin wobbled. "That's not fair."

"But you know who has been here? Me. And Grace. We've dealt with his nightmares, his troubles at school. Things are finally settling down." A sheen of tears brightened his eyes. "And here we go again."

"I'm sorry."

"You don't get to fucking tell me you're sorry." The tears he refused to shed ground his voice to gravel. "Do. Not. Even. Try."

Grace didn't know who to go to, who needed contact the most. They both looked broken. Defeated. Done. But Scott wasn't finished making Hope bleed.

"And if this kid is mine, and I guess she's a girl, thanks for telling me in the shittiest way possible, you're not getting anywhere near her. Full custody goes to me, for both of them. Feel free to leave town after that happens." Scott scrubbed his hands over his face, erasing any evidence of tears. "I'll figure out what to tell Levi. Before anyone sees you and talk spreads. So he's prepared."

Hope swiped at the dampness clinging to her own cheeks. "I want to see him."

Grace put a hand on Hope's shoulder. "Maybe it's best if we take this one step at a time."

"No." Scott headed for the door. "It's not

happening at all."

"Scott. Please." Hope hurried after him. "Let me see him."

He stopped but didn't look back. "That's his call, not mine. I'll look into the paternity thing."

When Scott was gone, Grace turned to her sister and tried to assess the damage. "Okay, so that was bad."

Hope closed her eyes. "He's never going to forgive me."

"How is it you've forgiven him?" Not like her brother-in-law was perfect. Far from it.

Hope opened damp eyes. "I love him. I've finally figured out how to honor what I feel, and now I'm going to lose him."

Grace didn't get it. Not at all. Some days they'd done more fighting than loving. "There's a lot of bad history between you two."

"A lot of good, too. But if he doesn't want me in his life, I'll deal. Levi is my first priority."

"I want to believe that, Hope…"

"My son's hurting because of what I've put him through, and he's going to hurt worse because I'm back. But Grace, I have to believe that disappearing out of his life for good won't be better for him in the long run. You and I know that better than anyone. If he decides on a future without me in it, at least it'll be his choice. And I'll accept that."

Her fierce look, the raw emotion in her sister's voice, almost convinced her. "That's very mature of you."

Hope managed a shaky laugh. "I lucked out in Calgary. Got a job as a companion to a retired psychologist. She helped me find the answers I was searching for."

Her sister's newfound enlightenment sounded good in theory, but Grace wasn't sure how to put it into practice. "So where do we go from here?"

Hope surprised her by mustering a smile. "Cookies."

Grace blinked. "Cookies?"

"I love to bake. In a huge way. Like I could turn it into a business kind of thing. I even have a name—Homemade by Hope."

"Bake? Like with flour and an oven?" The revelations were coming so fast Grace couldn't keep up. She did know one thing—her mom would have loved the idea.

"I'm planning to whip up a few batches. Thought tomorrow I'd take some to Dad and Pops." She tried to look innocent, but a flash of dimples gave her away. "Maybe you could take some to Levi?"

Levi's sweet tooth was legendary. "Woo him with baking. It's a good place to start."

"I didn't come home without a plan. Or thinking it would be easy." Hope's dimples disappeared. "But I'm going to need your help."

Grace didn't have a lot of time or energy to spare, but the earlier fight had brought out her protective older sister instincts. "You have it."

"Do you still have that box of Mom's things? I think her recipes are in there."

"In my closet." Grace motioned for her to follow.

It took her a moment to retrieve the battered box from the back of her closet. Their father had squirreled away most of their mother's belongings, but they'd managed to rescue a few of her things for themselves. She pulled out the stack of old-fashioned recipe cards covered in her mother's careful script and handed them to her sister.

Hope pressed them to her chest. "Thanks."

She gathered Hope in for a hug they both needed. "Make me a list of what else you need. I'll get a ride into town later to pick up my Jeep and anything you need."

"Thank you. For everything." Hope gave her an extra squeeze. "Oh, I forgot last night. There was an envelope stuck in the door when I got here yesterday. I put it, along with some other papers, on the coffee table in the living room."

Grace left Hope sifting through their mother's recipes and hunted down the mystery correspondence. She recognized the return address of her landlord. Short and to the point, the letter stated he had sold the parcel of land her house stood on and the new owner would be in touch soon. However, there was a number to call if Grace needed anything in the meantime.

News of the land sale wasn't exactly a surprise. The property had been on the market for a couple of weeks, but Grace hadn't expected the land to sell so quickly. There was no indication as to the new owner's plans, so she tossed the paper back onto the pile for not so safekeeping. That's when the other letter spilled to the floor. The one she'd gotten two days ago.

We regret to inform you…

It wasn't a big deal. Couldn't be a big deal. Certainly not as big a deal as homelessness. But that didn't stop her heart from hurting. The job would have been perfect for her. More stability, better benefits. She put a hand to her cheek. Safer. Necessary. Even though it had involved a commute and a cubicle, she'd still wanted it. But they hadn't wanted her.

****

Mike eased open his living room blinds and squinted into the afternoon sun, thankful he'd managed to catch a few hours of sleep after a busy night. Besides the bar fight, they'd handed out a DUI, a couple of speeding tickets, and a drunk and disorderly in the campground over a missing twelve pack. But he'd take a hectic shift over a deadly one any day or night of the year.

He rubbed at the rumble in his stomach. The fridge didn't yield much in the way of inspiration. One sniff of the leftover ham and cheese sub and he tossed it into the garbage. He reached for the orange juice carton.

Empty.

Likely drained before stumbling into bed this morning. He grabbed his keys. Mary's Café on Main Street served excellent coffee and all-day breakfast. He usually kept his morning routine simple and healthy, but today called for sausage, eggs, and a couple of Mary's famous Saskatoon berry muffins.

Maybe stuffing his face would ease the need to call Grace. He'd almost kissed her. Had wanted to so badly. But he refused to complicate her life. Or mislead her. Small towns weren't designed for avoiding people, but he'd given it his best shot for the last two years.

In a couple of weeks, he was joining an organized crime unit in Toronto. He'd worked hard to move the next step up the law enforcement ladder, doing his time in remote posts where he'd gained experience working on a variety of files in a hands-on environment. His ambitions didn't stop with a gang unit in one of Canada's major cities either, but ended with him as the Commissioner of The Royal Canadian Mounted Police. He wouldn't be satisfied until he'd climbed to the very top of the law enforcement mountain.

A knock on his door had Mike expecting to see his neighbor from across the hall wringing her hands over her perpetually lost cat. But the woman standing there wasn't elderly. Or kind. And he hadn't spoken to her more than a handful of times in the last seven years.

"Mother."

"Michael." She made every one of the seven letters of his name sound like a reproach. Helen Alton Davenport didn't kiss his cheek, extend a greeting, or smile.

He swallowed, then remembered his manners. Manners were important to her. Using them made dealing with her easier. He backed up. "Please, come in."

She wasn't alone. There was movement at her side, and too late Mike noticed Elizabeth.

She stepped into the void and offered her cheek. "Michael, how are you?"

Politeness and shock had him brushing his lips over her cool skin. It marked the first time he'd touched her since Justin's death, her perfume as familiar to him as rain in spring.

"Is everything okay?" he asked. Their intrusion into his everyday life was at best alarming, at worst terrifying.

His mother, cutthroat criminal lawyer, in clothes that had corporate corner office woven into the fabric, stepped into his apartment. "We have things to discuss."

Elizabeth slipped in beside her. Her lavish curves disguised by a severe suit, and her blonde hair tamed and hidden in a sleek roll. Gone were the dangling earrings and the flowing skirts of the girl both brothers had loved. One of them in public. The other in private.

A necklace circled her throat. He'd given it to her after a particularly sordid encounter in a dirty alley behind a five-star restaurant. Inside—a function attended by everyone they knew, outside— the smell of garbage and damp rain. Pigeons had cooed and things had scurried.

Afterward, Justin had asked where they'd disappeared to.

Mike's stomach rolled, and self-loathing clawed its way up his throat. Showing weakness in front of his mother wasn't an option. Not at five years old and not at thirty-two.

"Sit. Please." He escorted them to the couch, then adopted the pretense of waiting. There was no rushing Helen Davenport. She'd let them all stew until she was ready. It amused her. The power she wielded over the rats in her maze.

So he gave her a moment and took one for himself. Elizabeth's eyes were soft and full of apology. He looked away.

"The anniversary of your brother's death is in October," announced his mother.

Like he didn't know. "I'm not likely to forget."

The rebuke slipped out, but much like affection, sarcasm bounced off her, repelled by the stern lines and her severe style.

There wasn't so much as a hint of warmth in her

stare. "I'm starting a foundation in his memory."

Elizabeth fidgeted in her seat.

He choked on more bile and guilt.

His mother flicked an imaginary fleck of fluff from her skirt. "There will be a ceremony followed by an announcement. You're expected to give a speech."

A speech.

"You'll write it. I will review it and make any changes needed."

Because he couldn't be trusted to honor his brother's memory. He might tell the truth. A story of dishonesty and betrayal. She would never risk exposing cracks behind the powerhouse synonymous with the name Davenport.

He turned to the woman perched at the edge of his ratty second-hand sofa. "And your part in this?"

Elizabeth met his look, apology swimming in her wary eyes. "Justin would want me involved."

His mother sat still as stone. "I expect you to cooperate. You will be the face of the foundation, and Elizabeth will manage it."

Panic was swift and immediate. "I don't think that's a good idea."

"What you think is irrelevant." Distaste created wrinkles in skin pulled taut by the best plastic surgeon in the country. "It is the least you can do for your brother. For your family."

For disappointing her.

He had never lived up to her expectations, while Justin had exceeded them. The death of her favorite son, the way and the why he'd died, had solidified her disenchantment. Her chastisement had been immediate. She'd given Mike's corner office at Alton and

Davenport to someone else.

Kicked out.

Disinherited.

He'd lost his upscale condo when he couldn't afford the mortgage, had his Porsche reprocessed, and lost his country club memberships.

All of his privilege vanished when Helen Davenport had waved her wand in punishing retribution. In retaliation, he'd done the one thing guaranteed to piss his mother off. He'd become a cop.

She stood. "After which you'll be reinstated at the firm. Someone from Human Resources will arrange it."

Having delivered her edict, she didn't wait for him to refuse. She opened the door and paused, one foot out. "I'm done with your sulking. It's time you got back to work."

Her departure left him weak with relief.

"I'm sorry we surprised you." Elizabeth put a hand on his shoulder.

He pulled away.

"Michael…"

He closed his eyes. "I'll write the damn speech. Send it to her."

Her palm pressed against his cheek. "Michael, we need to talk."

He'd ignored her recent attempts to reach out, but there was no putting it off any longer, and he needed the sense of closure. So he could start a new life with a clear conscience. He removed her hand. "You're right. We do. But not here."

Not in his dank apartment, colorless and boring and full of thrift store finds. But who cared? Certainly not him. He'd put zero effort into it. All he'd required was a place to sleep. That would change once he was settled in Toronto. New job, new city, new life.

For the last seven years, he'd restricted himself to monkish behavior within the cloistered rural environments he'd been posted to, but it was time to move forward. And he couldn't do that until he severed all ties to the woman who linked him to his past.

****

Grace pushed her sunglasses into her hair and scanned the booths for her coffee companions. In an era of deluxe coffee grinders and skilled baristas, Mary's Café was a dinosaur. Coffee was served black in thick ceramic mugs. In a place of honor, on an antique cake stand, sat Mary's famous double fudge chocolate cake. As delicious today as it had been when she and Hope had often shared a slice waiting for their mother to finish her shift.

Kate Logan, former model and childhood cohort in all things ill advised, waved at her from a back booth. Grace wove her way between the tables but was unable to resist the urge to stop and kiss retired teacher, Mrs. Williams, on her powdery cheek.

And because Grace remembered her former teacher's offerings of ham sandwiches, sweet pickles, and books about an orphaned boy wizard, she spared a couple of minutes to learn about the icebergs and bald eagles she'd spotted on her last cruise.

When Grace finally reached Kate, she was freeing a fretting two-month-old Chloe from her bucket seat. Grace dropped onto the faded red bench across from her with a wince. Kate definitely didn't have a bruised cheek, or a hole in her T-shirt, or worn Chucks on her feet. The only concession Kate made to motherhood was a lighter shade of lip-gloss.

"Alaska this time, wasn't it?" Kate grimaced. "Give me Paris or London any day."

Grace tugged on the hem of her T-shirt, ensuring the hole was out of sight. "I don't know. Snowcapped mountains, whale watching, I can see the appeal."

"Liar. You live for sunshine and the beach." Kate nuzzled the top of Chloe's head. "Lily's running late."

Lily Porter, high school teacher and fierce advocate of the underdog, was the third of a triad formed in kindergarten. Oh, the trouble they had caused.

"No problem." Grace wiggled her fingers at Kate. "Hand her over. I need my fix."

Once Chloe was settled in her arms, Grace rested her cheek on her tiny head and inhaled her clean baby smell.

Kate's eyes narrowed in sympathy. "Your poor face. I heard what happened."

Grace shrugged off her friend's concern. "It looks worse than it feels."

Kate raised a brow. "Thank God, because it looks pretty bad."

No amount of makeup would have covered the evidence of last night's bar fight, so she hadn't bothered. "I'd like to say the other guy looks worse, but it would be a lie."

"Ladies." Mary Bennett, proprietor, didn't ask them for their drink order. She filled two mugs with coffee as dark as night. "Heard about the kafuffle last night and that you'd taken a spill."

"It was nothing." Grace reached for the sugar, ignoring Mary's snort and pointed look at her cheek. "I'm starving. So I was thinking turkey club. Pretty please?"

Mary scratched her pencil over her pad and nodded her head in approval. "Need to put some meat on those bones."

A breathless Lily, red curls bouncing, squeezed in beside Grace. "Coffee, please. And cake. I need cake."

"Uh-oh." Kate picked up her cup. "Problems in paradise?"

"Leaky bathroom. Which is now torn apart." When Mary paused with the coffee pot hovering over her cup, Lily fanned her flushed face. "Lemonade, please. Thank goodness you called and gave me an excuse to ditch a grouchy husband who expects me to know one wrench from another."

Kate relaxed back against her seat. "You remodeled the entire bathroom in your old house. You do know a thing or two about wrenches."

"Dad did most of it. Thank you." Lily beamed at Mary when she returned with her drink. "And working with him did not make me want to hit him over the head with said wrench."

Grace snuggled Chloe closer. "Scott does good work, and he's pretty reasonable."

Lily slapped her hand against the tabletop. "That's what I said. Instead, I have a hallway full of bathroom parts and a husband who insists he can do it all himself. But enough about my plumbing problems. Give us last night's grizzly details."

They pulled the particulars out of her, excluding the part about Mason suggesting she should suck his dick in front of the whole bar.

Mary set an impossibly huge sandwich in front of Grace and a massive slice of cake between Lily and

Kate. She held out her hands for her great granddaughter. "My turn. She needs showing off."

Once Chloe and Mary were on their way, Lily picked up a fork. "Is there any chance Mason is not going to be a jerk about the whole thing come next game day?"

"I wouldn't bet good money on it." Grace picked up her sandwich.

Kate frowned as she broke off a crumb-sized piece of cake. "That's next week. Is your knee going to be all right to play?"

"More than. And I hope Mason knows it." Grace had the turkey on rye halfway to her mouth when the little bell over the door chimed, and she caught sight of Mike escorting a beautiful blonde to an empty table. She sat up a little straighter, craned her neck a little more, and wished she hadn't bothered when Mike looked right at her then away.

"What is it?" Kate twisted in her seat, and Lily leaned forward to get a better view. Kate's voice dropped to a whisper. "Who do you suppose that is?"

"No idea." Grace slid down the bench seat, hoping to stay out of sight. "And stop staring."

Lily gave her a wary look. Grace bit off a mouthful of sandwich and hardly noticed the bacon-flavored mayo or the taste of homegrown tomato. She chewed like her life depended on grinding the bread to paste.

"Guess we know who's not helping fix your bathroom." Kate twisted back around for another quick look.

Lily shushed her. "Maybe she's a real estate agent? Or...or a life insurance rep?"

Kate raised a brow at Lily. "She's wearing a Greta

Constantine."

"A who?" asked Grace.

"Her dress. It's designer."

"Just because she spends a lot of money on clothes, doesn't mean there's anything romantic going on," insisted Lily, loyal to Grace's unrequited crush and her husband's partner.

"How much money?" The words slipped out before Grace could stop them. Her entire outfit, if she were generous enough to label her T-shirt and cut-off shorts an outfit, was worth less than her sandwich.

Laughter, soft and sexy, drifted over, and it was impossible to miss Kate and Lily's sympathetic looks.

"Hope's back." Grace's deflection worked. There were gasps and exclamations, followed by questions and her quick explanations. And while she hadn't forgotten Mike sat three tables over, she regrouped enough to remember why she shouldn't care.

"Are you buying Hope's transformation?" asked Kate.

Grace shrugged. "We'll see. Honestly, she seems different. I don't know…more settled? Reasonable? It sounds crazy, but I'm hoping her good intentions stick."

Lily beamed at her. "And you get to be an auntie again."

The blonde stroked Mike's arm. A violent desire to bend the woman's fingers back until they snapped came out of nowhere. She pushed her plate aside. "Auntie Grace. Yes. Can't wait."

With her usual perfect timing, Mary appeared at their table with a full pot of coffee.

Kate crossed her arms. "Um, where's my baby?"

Mary refilled her cup. "Sunni's next door at the

drugstore showing her off."

With that, she moved off, and Grace was left with a clear view of Mike and his companion deep in conversation. "I was thinking I should go on a date. With someone. Maybe."

Lily carefully rearranged her glass, while Kate eyed her with concern. "Do you have anyone in mind?"

Grace lifted a shoulder. "Someone nice."

"Nice?" clarified Kate.

Lily covered Grace's hand with her own. "Sweetie, you've been going non-stop for months. Maybe what you need is a holiday."

"I'm not looking for anything complicated, just a little bit of fun."

"Okay. Um…" Lily snapped her fingers. "How about Deke?"

Kate, clearly suspicious of Grace's announcement, hesitated. "I don't know…"

"Why? What's wrong with Deke?" asked Grace. "He's a good guy and a heck of a pitcher."

"There's nothing wrong with Deke," insisted Lily.

"She's not mountain man's type."

Lily shot Kate a not-helping glare. "What about Canyon Bear? He's adorable. And funny. You like funny, right?"

Didn't matter if she did or not. "And dating Ashley Wilson."

Kate leaned in, a hint of excitement easing her worried frown. "How about Garrett Eberle?"

Lily managed to get in a sip of her lemonade. "Only if you can get him to dump his boyfriend."

Kate's eyes widened. "Since when?"

"Since forever." Grace laughed. "Pay attention."

"Sorry, busy being an entrepreneur and birthing a baby." Kate raised her hand. "What about Garrett's brother?"

"Damian," Grace and Lily sighed in unison.

The laugh bubbled up, and releasing it eased some of Grace's tension. She caught sight of Mike watching her. When he didn't look away, stubbornly neither did she. He nodded vaguely at something his companion was saying. The blonde turned her head.

Sunni blocked Grace's view. She handed a squirming Chloe over to Kate. "She's done with me."

Kate settled her fussy baby into her car seat and cooed at her. "Is it time to go?"

"My turn to pay." Grace dug some bills out of her pocket.

"Until next time." Lily checked her phone. "Errands to run. Husband to avoid."

After Grace finished at the cash register, Mary pulled her off to the side. "Tell your sister if she's looking for a job to come see me."

"How did you—?" But Mary was off, coffee pot in hand.

Grace pushed open the door to find Kate and Lily waiting. "Big Brother has nothing on that woman."

"Big, who, what?" asked Lily.

"Nothing." Grace bent to tuck in the receiving blanket dragging out of the back of Kate's massive bag. "Geez, did you leave anything at home?"

Kate struggled to balance Chloe and her enormous bag. "Yes. The potential for disaster."

Lily put a hand on Grace's arm. "Are you sure you're okay?"

"Why wouldn't I be?"

Lily wasn't one for letting things go. "It's just…you know, with the fight, and your sister, and this dating idea?"

Grace sighed. "What's wrong with wanting to go on a date?"

"Nothing. But I wasn't kidding earlier when I suggested a holiday. You've got a lot on your plate. And you're only one person. A week on some faraway beach wouldn't be a bad thing."

Mike and the goddess picked that moment to stroll out of the café. There was no way for them to avoid each other.

Lily unpacked her perkiest smile. "Out for coffee, I see."

"A last-minute thing." Too polite to keep walking, Mike paused, then cleared his throat. "This is…Elizabeth."

Lily thrust out her hand. "Lily, and this is Kate and Grace."

The goddess's eyes widened for the briefest second when she noticed Grace's bruised cheek, but she quickly regrouped, clearly taken with Chloe. "What a beautiful baby. What's her name?"

"Chloe." Kate preened, immediately turning traitor.

Chloe started to fuss, and Kate offered an apologetic grimace. "Nice meeting you, Elizabeth. Time for us to make our way home." She gave Grace a searching look. "I'll call you."

Grace never should have brought up the stupid dating idea. Thank God she'd left out the part about being next to homeless and having been rejected for the half-time executive director position.

Their little party whittled down to four, Elizabeth

smoothed a hand down Mike's arm and ended the caress by twining her fingers through his. Claim staked.

Lily's phone rang, and she rolled her eyes at the screen. "Sadly, I also have to go."

And just like that, Grace was left alone on the sidewalk with Mike and Elizabeth.

Fan-friggin-tastic.

Elizabeth pressed closer to Mike. "Perhaps we should be on our way."

Mike disentangled his fingers. "Give me a minute, then I'll walk you to your car."

Generally speaking, Grace was a firm believer in standing her ground. But not today. "Unfortunately, I have to go. Nice meeting you, Elizabeth."

She turned to make her escape and almost ran over her grandfather.

"There you are. Can you believe that goddamn drugstore won't give me any more of my pills?" His eyes narrowed, and he leaned in for a closer look. "Christ Almighty, what happened to your face?"

She fished her sunglasses out of her hair and slid them on. "Nothing."

"Those bruises are a damn sight more than nothing."

"You mentioned your pills?" she asked, hoping to distract him. "I just filled your prescription last week."

It worked. He waved a hand. "Well, they disappeared. Probably stolen. Can't trust a single soul in that loony bin of a retirement home. Now tell me whose ass I have to kick."

He wasn't kidding about the ass kicking. Grace sighed and did her best to sidetrack him again. "Come on, I'll give you a ride back to your place, and I'll help you find them."

Mike moved in beside her and extended his hand. "Mr. Bighill, nice to see you."

Pops latched onto Mike's hand. "Constable Davenport, isn't it?"

"Yes, sir."

Pops couldn't help but notice Elizabeth, who stood behind Mike maintaining her smile with the zealousness of a game show model. Her grandfather held out his hand to her. "Who do we have here?"

Elizabeth placed her hand in his elderly one. "Elizabeth McCray."

"Well, aren't you a looker."

She blushed prettily, then worked at reclaiming her hand, which was still firmly enmeshed within Pops' rheumatic fingers.

Grace gave him a warning nudge. "Pops."

"How about I help Grace get you sorted out." Mike turned to Elizabeth. "You don't mind finding your way back to your car from here, do you?"

Elizabeth looked like she very much did mind, and Grace didn't need help handling her grandfather. "Don't bother with us. We're fine."

Pops pointed a frail, bent finger at her. "I'm still waiting on that name."

Elizabeth laid a hand on Mike's cheek and brought his attention back to her.

Grace didn't wait to see any more. She steered Pops in the direction of her Jeep. "Let's get a move on, Pops."

He shuffled along beside her, both of them making quite the pair as they limped along. "Can you make me one of those grilled cheese sandwiches?"

"Sure." Pops lived on white bread and cheese slices. She made a mental note to check the contents of his fridge. After she hunted down his missing pills.

Mike appeared at Pops' other side, taking on the brunt of Pops' weight. "Where's your vehicle?"

"Right there." Grace peered around Pops. "Only half a block away. I'm pretty sure we can make it unassisted."

"I'm happy to help."

She refused to engage in a tug-of-war over her grandfather in the middle of Main Street. Once they had Pops safely seated in her vehicle, he looked past Mike to Grace. "Cheese sandwich?"

"Just like I promised."

Her grandfather grinned. "Cross your heart?"

It was an old game. One they both loved. She crossed her eyes. "And eyes."

"Fingers." Pops held up fingers swollen at the knuckles.

"Toes."

"Tap you on the nose." He reached out a shaky hand and brushed the tip of her nose. "Love you, Jellybean."

"Love you, too, Pops."

Mike cleared his throat. "I should get going. I'm on shift in a little bit."

She shut Pops' door, a wave of relief washing through her for having made it through the whole awkward encounter pride intact. "Thanks for your help."

"You're good with him."

Compliments of any kind made her uncomfortable. "He did his best to look out for us for a lot of years."

"How are things with Hope?"

She waited for a couple to wander past them, compelled, for some reason, to answer honestly. "They're not horrible."

"Good." More awkward silence. "About Elizabeth."

Grace shook her head. Nope, not going there. "No explanation necessary. See you around, Constable Davenport."

She absolutely did not want to know anything about his relationships. She had to feed Pops, get Hope her supplies, and then get to work on a new custom order. Just reciting the list exhausted her.

"Grace, I can take him home and make him a sandwich. Take some of the load off."

"No." She tempered her abrupt refusal with a shrug. "I can handle it."

"You shouldn't have to. Not all on your own."

"He's family. My family. Go find Elizabeth." And why was she bringing her up if she didn't want to talk about her? But there was no stopping the words tumbling out of her mouth or the bitterness giving them momentum. "She's gorgeous. Ideal. Just your type."

He got in front of her, blocking her critical escape, doing the unthinkable and slipping her sunglasses off. "You mind explaining that last part."

She helped him out. That's what friends did, after all. "I think she went the other direction. You'd better hurry. You might lose her."

He crowded her in against her Jeep, his expression no longer blank. It was hot and heavy and filled with a warning given too late to make a difference. The noise of the street disappeared. All she could see were his eyes. Some said the mysteries of a person's soul were hidden there. But with Mike it was more of a haunting.

"I don't have a type." His angry whisper kissed her ear. "But if I did, it would be dark hair and dark eyes on a woman too stubborn to accept a little bit of aid when it's offered."

She remained mute, soaking up the heated metal at her back and the press of warm, affronted male to her front.

"You think you've got me figured out?" His lips were warm against her neck. "If you did, you wouldn't give me the time of day."

He shoved away from her, pushing her sunglasses into her hand, and stalked across the street. It was probably the first honest thing he'd ever said to her. And he was right. She didn't know him. How he'd lived his years beyond the two he'd spent in Aspen Lake had never come up. But she'd caught the hint of trauma in his green eyes. He was broken, like her.

****

Mike paused at his apartment door, aware Elizabeth was closing in on him. He tried to regroup, but he had that silly rhyme of Grace and her grandfather's stuck in his head. She made him cheese sandwiches. He called her Jellybean. They loved each other. Had forged a strong bond, despite hard times and unimaginable loss. He had never experienced a moment of the family connection she had with her grandfather. He never would.

"Michael. Wait."

"I thought you were heading back?"

A strand of her hair escaped its careful knot. Her uncertain look more than familiar to him. Once upon a time, she had excelled at gauging his moods, anticipating his wants, smoothing out his anxieties. "I wanted to make sure you were all right."

His days of longing for her quiet ministrations were long gone. The last thing he wanted was her back in his apartment, but there were things that needed to be said, and the hallway was not the place to do it.

He ushered her inside. "Why wouldn't I be?"

"I know you well enough to know you're upset." She set her purse on the counter. "I'm sorry we surprised you with the idea of a memorial. But I did try to get in touch with you. When you didn't respond, you left her no choice but to come to you."

He rubbed at the ache between his eyes. "I'm not coming back to Alton and Davenport."

"Don't you want your life back?" She cast a disbelieving look around his dull apartment.

All of a sudden, he was drowning in memories of unrelenting rain, the crush and curl of bending metal, the unstoppable spill of blood. He had begged Justin to hold on, bargained with God when it became clear Justin didn't have the life left to answer him, had heard Elizabeth's screams as she slid down next to them in the mud.

Tears gathered in her eyes. "Before Justin found us, you asked me something important, and I begged for more time. Because I was scared. Had I known—"

"It doesn't matter. Not anymore."

"Afterward, you didn't give me a chance to explain." She spoke long and slow like she was explaining to a child. She pressed in closer. "You ran."

"I didn't run. I reevaluated."

"You quit a job you said you loved, left a life you

Gone

said you wanted, and joined our national police force."

"Quit? I don't know what she told people, but she kicked me out. That life?" He snapped his fingers. "Gone when I lost the roof over my head, never mind the rest of it. I had no choice but to make a new life for myself."

His move to Toronto was the accumulation of hard work and perseverance. He was never going back to the old one.

"You could have talked to me, and we could have worked it out together."

"We did discuss it." And she had rejected him.

"No, you presented me with the facts." Her throat worked to clear her tears. "I was hurting. Grieving. We both were. It wasn't the time to make major life decisions. I thought you understood that."

"There was no going back. Not for me." He had loved her for all the wrong reasons. None of them noble. Perhaps it was fate she was here on the cusp of his departure.

He asked the question that had haunted him for the last seven years. "Why did Justin go directly from the airport to the cabin?"

What had prompted his brother's silent trek to the bedroom where he'd found them?

Elizabeth turned away. "What does it matter now?"

"Someone told him about us."

"No." She turned back around, gave him a beseeching look. "It was just tragic timing."

Mike wasn't buying it. "He knew he'd find us there before he walked through the door."

"I had no idea he was coming home. As far as I knew, I was picking him up the next day, like we'd

61

arranged." She shook her head, and more of her hair tumbled from its knot. "I swear to you, I had nothing to do with Justin coming out to the lake that night. I would never have chosen that way to tell him about us."

He could think of only one person who would have done the unimaginable, thinking to manipulate them all. But until today, he hadn't realized he'd needed confirmation, had needed to hear Elizabeth deny having any part in the fated outcome of that tragic night.

"Neither of us would have." His own throat ached until he thought he'd choke. Because he believed her, he couldn't deny either of them the comfort of wrapping his arms around her.

"I miss you," she whispered, her arms slipping around his waist. He tried to pull away. She held tight. "Enough time has passed that no one will question us being together."

He unwound her arms and stepped back. "Seven years is the magic number required to gain respectability?"

"Your mother has hinted her approval. Your inheritance would be reinstated. You can take your place at Alton and Davenport. Everything we planned, dreamed of, can still happen."

He shook his head. "I'm not going back to that life. Ever."

She did a desperate scan of his living space. "I know you want more from your life than this. You can't have changed that much."

He made his way to the window and the light. "I've changed more than you can imagine."

She came up behind him. "I know you well enough to know you feel something for Grace Bighill. I didn't think trailer trash was your thing."

He didn't rise to her bait. "That was beneath you."

"You're right. It was uncalled for. I'm jealous. I admit it." It was so like her, a flash of anger, a quick apology, followed by a natural, compelling honesty. A beguiling mix of exactly what was needed to appease him.

And she didn't move him anymore. "It's none of your business. Not anymore."

"I'm asking for a chance to change that." She coaxed him around to face her.

"Elizabeth…" He hesitated when he didn't feel the least uncertain. It was instinct to protect her, one he couldn't seem to ditch.

"You dreamed of a life in the courtroom and possibly politics. You were made to argue hard cases. Built for it. Michael, you could still—"

"Enough." His harsh rebuke hung in the air between them. But he wasn't about to apologize, and he was done explaining. "I have to get ready for work."

Elizabeth dipped her head, and he gave her a couple of seconds to gain her composure. When she stepped away, it was to find her purse. She drew out an envelope.

"Some details about the foundation and Justin's memorial, as well as the gathering afterward." She lifted sad eyes to meet his. "I need you there. I can't do this by myself."

"I said I'd be there."

"And the town hall meeting I mentioned over coffee? I would consider it a favor if you attended. In his last cabinet post, Kevin Hunt was the federal Minister of Public Safety. Since you are an RCMP officer, it's good publicity to have you in attendance."

"I'll think about it."

"If not for me, do it for your career." She spared one last glance at his sparse furnishings. "Despite what you say, you want more than this."

There was no doubt about it. "Goodbye, Elizabeth."

"Until next time, Michael." The door clicked shut after her.

He walked into his bedroom and dropped onto the edge of the bed. He was over her. Didn't want to go back there. No desire at all. But he'd loved her once. He pulled open his nightstand drawer. The velvet box mocked him.

Why did he still have it?

He flipped open the lid. The platinum-gold, emerald-cut, diamond engagement ring winked at him. He slipped it from its perch and read the inscription: *Beth*. It was worth five figures but had cost him so much more.

He kept the ring as a reminder of why he'd sentenced himself to celibacy in reparation. Which hadn't been much of a hardship at first. Too grief stricken and too overwhelmed by his new job, his sense of real sacrifice hadn't begun until his transfer to Aspen Lake. His penance had started in earnest the moment he'd met Grace.

Mike tossed the tiny box back into the drawer. The best-laid schemes of mice and men often go awry, or so Burns wrote.

He'd worked hard, and his endgame was in sight. His future days and nights would be filled with a demanding job, new city, a new life. But not for the first time did he wonder if he was leaving behind something, or someone, irreplaceable.

Chapter Three

The dry August heat had Mike sweating in his regulation boots and haunted him with each plodding step. The hiking trails of Burning Bush Provincial Park were extensive and some of the best in the province. He'd spent many free hours exploring them. The trek was far less enjoyable when you were dressed for duty. He chewed harder on his gum and ignored the discomfort, but the revelations of the day dogged him harder than the mosquitoes.

A memorial.

His mother's sudden interest in honoring his brother shouldn't surprise him and was a fine idea. But her iron fist decree he scurry back to Alton and Davenport, like he'd indulged in a teenage temper tantrum the last seven years, infuriated him. He supposed in some far away place he had feelings for his mother. He might wish things were different. That she was different. But he was done competing for crumbs of her affection. And he refused to be her Plan B.

He concentrated on putting one foot ahead of the other as Chase led the way up a well-hidden path broken down by decades' worth of teenage feet. Hook-up Hill, which veered from the main trail by some 500 meters, provided a remote place for teenagers to drink beer and get laid.

"This way is faster." His partner knew enough

about this area, having grown up in Aspen Lake, to lead them on a short cut. Chase shoved a branch aside. "It's probably an animal."

Mike caught the swinging limb in time to save himself from a leafy whack in the face. "Watch it."

"You seem pretty bitchy for a guy who had a hot coffee date this afternoon." Chase poking at him was a sure sign his partner knew bad things were coming down the pipe.

Mike rolled his shoulders. He'd rather dance naked in poison ivy than rehash his previous relationship with anyone. "It's complicated."

Chase snorted. "What, are we on social media now?"

The fiery glow of the sinking sun broke through the umbrella of greenery. "It's code for drop it, I don't want to talk about it."

"That ship has sailed, pal. Next time take your date somewhere my wife won't see you." Chase slapped a hand over the back of his neck. "Fucking mosquitoes."

"It's a long way to haul a couple of cases of beer. And it wasn't a date." Mike braced his hands on a fallen branch and jumped over. "Elizabeth was in town on business. I didn't invite her."

"Doesn't explain how you ended up having coffee together." Chase kicked some broken brush aside. "I spent all day in a cramped bathroom. Why couldn't they be partying in someone's air-conditioned basement?"

"Getting old?"

"No doubt about it." He scowled over his shoulder at Mike. "I also have to report back to my wife in the morning with, and I quote, 'the scoop on the mystery woman,' so give me something besides it's complicated."

"There's nothing interesting to tell." He caught a whiff of smoke. "Don't those idiots know there's a fire ban in effect?"

"Another thing I'm going to bust their asses over."

"Not like they don't deserve it." Mike swatted aside some low hanging leaves, grateful for the change in subject. "How do they make their way out of this in the dark?"

"Probably some patron saint of teenagers. So they can live to be a pain in my ass the next day, and the day after that. Takes me back though."

Mike bet it did. Chase and Lily had been high school sweethearts. "St. Aloysius Gonzaga."

"What?"

Mike squinted into the lowering dark. "Patron saint of teenagers."

"Have you been watching Jeopardy again?" Chase executed another insect. "You need a life, my friend."

Mike pulled out his flashlight as night settled around them. "You bring Lily up here?"

"More than once."

Mike heard the smile in his partner's voice and shook off the sense of loneliness that dogged him constantly these days. "Being a teenager was a lot more fun than tracking them down in the damn woods."

"Let's just hope it's all for nothing," muttered Chase. "So…her name's Elizabeth?"

There was no denying Chase when he was on the hunt for information. "We used to be involved. A long time ago."

"What happened?" Chase forged ahead, his casual

tone not fooling Mike.

Mike caught another swinging branch before it took out his eye. He never mentioned his past. Didn't want to go there. But seeing his mother and spending time with Elizabeth had thrown him. The darkness encouraged confession, and he was too tired of keeping secrets to resist the pull. "I asked her to marry me."

Chase stopped in his tracks. "And?"

"Obviously, she said no." Mike pushed him forward.

The sound of stumbling footsteps reached them, and Dixon Sawyer sprinted into Mike's beam of light, tripping over his feet in his haste to reach them. "Over here. This way."

Mike put a hand out to steady him. Dixon's wide-eyed sense of panic didn't do good things to Mike's insides. The kid's decision-making skills might need fine-tuning, but he wasn't one to overreact.

"Bones...down in the gully..." Dixon bent and braced his hands on his thighs.

Mike crouched down to eye level. "Take a deep breath."

Dixon swiped a hand over his battered, pale face. "I swear to God...they're human. There's a skull."

Mike gave the young man a few seconds to steady his shaky composure, then guided him upright. "How about you show us where you found the bones?"

"This way." Dixon sprinted off.

"Jesus, was it only last night this same crew helped start a bar fight? What is it going to be tomorrow night? The beginning of the apocalypse?"

"Let's hope not."

Chase's sigh was full of foreboding. "Farm kid like

Karyn Good

him would know the difference."

Mike agreed. "Time to find out what we're dealing with."

Dixon halted a couple of feet in front of them and waited until they caught up. He babbled all the way back to the popular clearing where a rustic circular fire pit dominated the glade. Its ashes sizzled, and the air reeked of the beer they'd used to douse the fire. Like there wasn't a creek a stone's throw away.

Beer wasn't the only thing Mike smelled on the air. But he put his lecture on hold to study the five other young people huddled together on the far side of the clearing. Whatever they'd found was keeping them as far away from the opposite edge as possible.

Mike and Chase followed an impatient Dixon to the ledge and peered down the steep slant, which led to a shallow creek below. Their twin beams of light searched the darkness. It didn't take them long to spot the battered remains.

Erosion and time had done their work, but there was no mistaking it for an animal, despite the significant amount of decomposition.

"Christ." Chase brushed a hand over his eyes. "I hope that isn't who I think it is."

Chase's distress matched his own. "You okay?"

"Yeah." He shook his head at Mike's questioning look. "Just a bad feeling."

Mike had plenty of suspicions of his own. "Call it in, start processing the scene. I'll see the kids back to the parking lot and take their statements."

Chase gave him a tight nod. Mike crossed the clearing. The kids scrambled to talk at once. He held up a hand. "Calm down. One at a time."

70

The group looked to Dixon, whose arms were wrapped around Mandy Trent, the young woman from last night. "We weren't doing anything wrong."

They never were. "Two of you are underage, and I smell beer and pot."

They all attempted some wide-eyed version of "Who? Us?"

Mike wasn't in the mood. He counted the infractions off on his fingers. "Open liquor $250.00, underage drinking $360.00, providing liquor to a minor $1,050.00, and then there's the drugs."

"Come on, man." Chris Donaldson pushed forward. "We did the right thing and called you. That's got to count for something."

"That's Constable Davenport to you." His tough tone silenced their mutters. He'd yet to make up his mind regarding clemency. "Let's get you back down the hill. Follow me."

The march back to the parking lot took forever. Mike was forced to stop for a pee break and two bouts of vomiting. How many times had he talked to these kids about drinking and drugs? Eventually, they made it. There wasn't much to tell, and it wasn't long before they were arranging for rides.

Mike got ready to educate the next generation on the perils of breaking the law. He wrote up the appropriate violations to moans and groans about fairness and hadn't they cooperated, yada yada. Mike wasn't in the business of handing out merit badges. He wanted them to be safe, stay safe, and have a future. And if that took tough love, so be it.

When the last vehicle left the rutted parking lot, Mike grabbed the necessary gear from the back of the cruiser and began the long trek back up the hill.

Chase met him at the edge of the woods. "The coroner is on her way, but it's going to be a wait."

Mike nodded. "Jordan went over the bank on a dare and managed to dislodge the remains when he tripped."

"Consistent with what I saw." Chase crossed his arms, his eyes searching the dark. "Of all the missing-persons reports ever filed, only one individual has never been located."

Mike had familiarized himself with that particular file for reasons he refused to name. And although it didn't pay to make assumptions, neither did he discount probabilities. "Cassandra Anne Bighill."

"Most everybody assumed she'd taken off. Left her family for a better life." Chase scrubbed a hand over his jaw. "Gone somewhere she wasn't married to the town joke and stuck waiting tables."

"Doesn't mean it's her." Mike looked to the stars, chose one, and prayed it wasn't, despite the odds not being in their favor.

Chase didn't bother debating Mike's doubtful optimism. "Let's get to work."

They did what they could to record the scene by way of photographs, notes, and sketches while they waited for the rest of the team to show up. Removing a skeleton from a wooded area in the pitch dark took time, and the sun was rising before the coroner was done overseeing the removal of the body.

She approached them. "Here's the last of the evidence. Found this underneath the body. We'll need dental confirmation, of course. But otherwise…"

"Thanks." Inside the bag were the contents of a

wallet, including Cassandra Bighill's driver's license.

"Guess we have our answer." Chase's usual cocky façade had dissipated hours ago.

"You knew her. Grace's mother?"

"Hope resembles her most in appearance. But Grace inherited her personality. Always smiling even when there was little to smile over." Chase's voice grew distant. "After my mom died, she used to drop food off at our house. There were always cookies. One time she came, I hadn't eaten in two days."

There wasn't a lot Mike could say. "I'm sorry."

Chase dipped his head. "Damn."

Mike thought of Grace and what the news was going to do to her. He swallowed back the protective instinct he had no right to feel. The best thing, the only thing, he could do was his job. "It's obvious she wasn't up here alone."

Chase's face settled into a hard mask. "Shallow grave in a spot you'd only find by accident, for all that it's a popular location. During the day, it's hikers. At night, teenagers. A high traffic area. Stupid and risky."

"Useless to speculate on whether it was an accident or a homicide. We'll have to wait and hope the autopsy can tell us something."

"You're right. She disappeared almost twenty years ago. My memory of that time is sketchy, at best." Chase swung his flashlight across the clearing a final time. "Whether it was an accident or worse, someone buried her up here."

"And left her family to wonder."

Chase growled. "We're going to find out who."

Mike's hands curled into fists. "Damn right we are."

It was time to head back down. At the bottom of the hill, shrouded in the pinking dawn, Mike finally gave a voice to the dread battering his insides. "Hardest part comes next."

"No doubt about it."

"If you want, I can handle telling the family." It eased Mike's conscience, if not his anxiety, to make the offer. He dug out his keys. Grace's father wasn't the most stable of men. He'd never heard any mention of violent tendencies, but that didn't mean it never happened. "I want to see Martin Bighill's face when he hears the news."

Chase nodded. "That makes two of us."

****

Grace scooped the cardboard box containing brownies, butter tarts, and the promised cookies out of the backseat. Ahead of her, Hope juggled an iced angel food cake and a plate of sandwiches. Her sister was banking on sugar and flour to ease her reentry into their father's sheltered world. Grace doubted Hope's confection, worthy of a pastry shop with its careful swirls of frosting, would have any effect on their father.

These days Martin Bighill ate to survive and not a mouthful more. Hope didn't need a cake baked at an obscenely early hour to gain absolution for her missing months. Grace doubted their dad was aware of his daughter's absence most of the time. He would be overjoyed to see her, insist there was nothing to forgive, and welcome her back with open arms.

Hope paused with one foot up the stoop and waited for Grace to catch up. "Why wait to tell me the fight started because Scott was defending your honor?"

Hope had managed to ferret out the details of the

bar fight. Stupid social media. "Right, and it had nothing to do with your husband being a hothead."

"Impulsive, maybe." Hope dipped her head to hide a secret smile.

Grace rolled her eyes. "It's not an attractive quality."

"Didn't say it was," offered Hope, who had perfected the wide-eyed innocent look by the time she was ten.

It drove Grace nuts. "You didn't have to. You went all swoony-eyed."

"You also failed to mention Mason Pearce slut shamed us in front of the whole bar."

"Who cares what that jerk says." Grace pushed past her and shoved the door open.

"I care. He was the one who started the rumors about my so-called affair and almost cost me my marriage."

Almost? "Didn't mean Scott had to believe them."

"True." Hope placed her precious cake on the counter and lifted her arm to cover her nose. "Holy crap, what died in here?"

Grace nudged dirty dishes aside to make space for Hope's goodies and cranked the kitchen window open. "With any luck, not Dad."

Hope went to the fridge to unload her plate of sandwiches. "Very funny."

"I wasn't going for funny." Grace grabbed the can of ground coffee, measured out the appropriate amount, and got some much-needed caffeine perking. Then she climbed up the first of the narrow steps leading to the second story. "Dad! Where are you?"

Like she didn't know.

Hope got busy filling the sink with soapy water. "Good to know things didn't get crazier while I was gone."

"Sarcasm. Helpful." Grace threw a stack of newspapers into the empty recycling bin. She blocked the memories of Sundays as a child, pancakes before church and lunch at Mary's afterward. She tossed in a pile of junk mail. Those days were long gone.

Hope slapped a rag against the counter and scrubbed. "Yeah, well, you're the perfect child. Not me."

It was too early, and Grace wasn't in the mood to let the familiar taunt slide. "What's that supposed to mean?"

"Nothing, forget it." Hope picked up the shepherd's pie Grace had dropped off two days ago and scraped what remained into the trash. The casserole dish hit the sink bottom with a clang. Hope braced her hands against the counter. "Don't you get tired of it? You've been looking after him since you were thirteen. It should have been the other way around."

Grace rescued the broom from the corner and swept over the ancient linoleum. "Right. I should have been more concerned with staying out late and partying, pretending I didn't have a family."

"Better than hiding out here. Same as him." Hope punched a hand in the direction of the stairs. "Drowning in grief."

Seventeen years of scar tissue didn't protect her from Hope's jab. Grace's hands tightened on the broom handle. "So...what? I'm supposed to apologize for being sad?"

"No." The fight drained out of Hope. "I'm saying

we each dealt with her being gone in our own way."

Grace pushed back her hair, the strands clinging to her neck in the stifling, airless house. "I don't want to talk about it."

"You never do." Hope turned back to the sink.

Grace abandoned the broom and stomped over to the stairs. "Dad!"

Hope went to war cleaning food off plates. "He needs help, Grace. Professional help."

"He has to want it." Grace tied an overflowing garbage bag shut.

Hope bowed her head. "I can't imagine what Levi thinks of all this."

"Scott won't bring him by anymore." Grace heaved the trash out the back door, along with all the accusations she wanted to fling at her sister. Like how it was a little late to be worrying over Levi's sensibilities. Or preach about professional help. Like they hadn't tried to get her dad to see someone. Anyone.

Hope was full of remorse when Grace stepped back into the kitchen. "You've been dealing with this all on your own for so long."

"It's fine."

"No, it's not. But I'm back, and I'm going to do my share of the caregiving." She sighed when the only response Grace gave was silence. "I know what you're not saying. I haven't been a lot of help in the past. But I want to do better. I *will* do better."

A shuffling noise from the stairs interrupted the awkward quiet. "Gracie, I didn't know you were stopping by. I would have cleaned—" He froze in the kitchen doorway. "Hope?"

"Hey, Daddy." Hope opened her arms.

Martin Bighill smoothed a hand over his thinning gray hair but remained where he stood, neither in nor out of the room. He was only fifty years old, but his face was etched with deep lines and framed by sagging skin. For once he wasn't in his usual sleep pants and shaggy robe, but the jeans Grace had laundered and the flannel shirt she'd hung in his closet. He put a hand to his mouth, his eyes damp with love and confusion.

Grace's frustrations fizzled. He was so broken, so vulnerable and the urge to protect him, as always, overwhelmed her.

"Hope?" he asked again.

"It's me. I'm back. For good." Hope put a hand on his elbow and guided him to the table. "I brought you some goodies."

Like Grace had predicted, he hardly glanced at her peace offerings. "To stay?"

Hope's smile was gentle. "To stay, Daddy. I promise."

"So like your mother." He allowed Hope to usher him into a chair, his surprise replaced with a distant look. "She loved to bake. Do you remember?"

Once their kitchen had smelled like cinnamon and vanilla instead of defeat and rotting casserole.

He reached out a tentative hand to Hope's stomach but stopped short at the last second. "Another brother or sister for Levi?"

Hope didn't hesitate to press his hand to her baby bump. "Only one more month to go."

No counting on his fingers to determine dates, only genuine amazement. "A September baby. Like you."

Hope's birthday month was May. Grace's was September. But neither of them corrected him. They hadn't bothered to point out his memory lapses in a long, long time. His apologies were always immediate and heartfelt, followed by a sadness and self-recrimination that lasted for days.

They weren't going down that path this morning. Grace pulled out a chair and motioned her sister into it. "Let's get some breakfast into both of you."

Hope rattled on about her time away as Grace served sandwiches and coffee. She left them to eat and finished the dishes. She was drying the last of the plates when there was a knock at the front door. She motioned at Hope to stay put and dried off her hands.

Mike and Chase stood on the other side of the door, both in uniform. Neither of them returned her smile.

"What's wrong?" She tossed the towel on a nearby bench and ushered them into the tiny entryway.

Mike's strong face was soft with apology. "We need to speak to your father."

She knew their news was bad. Could sense it. Smell their remorse. "I don't understand. What's going on?"

Mike put a hand on her arm. "Grace, we'll explain everything, but your father needs to be there."

Explain everything?

"He's in the kitchen." Grace put one lead foot in front of the other and led them into the kitchen.

Mike's green eyes were stark as he guided her to the table and pulled out a chair. "Why don't you have a seat?"

"I prefer to take my bad news standing." Her hand shook as she lifted it to her mouth. "Is it Pops? Is he okay?"

"No, it's—"

Hope jerked out of her chair, eyes wild, one hand protecting her stomach, and the other braced against the scarred tabletop. "Oh, my God, Levi?"

Chase laid a hand on her shoulder. "I'm sure they're both fine."

Mike, face stoic and tight with pity, faced her silent father, whose eyes already brimmed with tears. "Mr. Bighill, we're here to inform you that a body was discovered last night, and we have reason to believe it might be your wife, Cassandra."

A brutal stillness followed Mike's staggering revelation. Grace latched onto the back of a chair. Seventeen years of waiting...

"You found her?" she whispered.

The fearful anticipation of this moment had lessened somewhat over the span of time. But Mike's announcement closed the gap of years, and she was a thirteen-year-old girl waiting desperately for news of her missing mother. Praying it wouldn't be the worst kind, as she had continued to pray every day since.

For naught.

"Human remains were found outside of town last night on provincial park property." Mike cleared his throat. "Due to the amount of...decomposition, it will take some time to conclusively identify the body."

A dizzying amount of blood drained from Grace's head. She reached over to clasp her dad's hand. On the other side of him, Hope did the same.

His palm twitched in hers a second before quiet sobs racked his body. Chase continued where Mike had left off. She zoned in and out of the next part of the conversation, catching phrases like *evidence at the scene, we can't say for sure foul play was involved,* and *forensic autopsy.*

"We're sorry." Mike's voice came from impossibly far away. "We know how hard this must be for you."

Grace focused on the tabletop where she'd glued and colored, had done her math homework. Where the waiting for news had begun. And where their vigil had ended.

"Yes, there will be an investigation," assured Mike.

Her dad must have managed a question.

She forced her way back to the conversation.

"We'd like to ask you some questions."

Chase's voice snapped her head up.

"Why?" Hope demanded, in a tear-stained voice Grace barely recognized.

"It's okay, sweetheart." Her dad let go of their hands and stood. "Follow me."

Hope struggled out of her chair. "Dad, wait."

Grace reached out to hold him back. "Dad, maybe now's not the best time…"

He slipped past his daughters. For a man who'd moved through the last seventeen years in slow motion, he took the steps leading up to his 'evidence' room with manic ease.

When she would have followed, Mike put a hand on her arm. "It might be best if you stayed down here."

"Best for whom?" She searched for a hidden agenda but couldn't see past the burgeoning panic tightening her chest.

"We won't be long." His hand, warm against her skin, traveled up the length of her arm and back down. With one last apologetic look, he followed Chase up the narrow stairs.

Hope shoved her forward. "Move."

She twisted around. "Didn't you hear him?"

Hope gave her another push. "All the more reason to follow them."

"They wouldn't...they don't think...they know him." But she knew what they'd see once they reached their destination.

Hope's eyebrows levitated to her hairline as she pointed up the skinny staircase. "He's not thinking like a boyfriend. They're here to figure out why a woman was buried in the middle of nowhere."

"He's not my boyfriend." Although why that distinction was important in the moment, Grace had no idea. Except she couldn't think straight, couldn't decide on the smart thing to do, never mind what was necessary. All she pictured was her mother buried in the woods. Dead. But found. And lost to her forever.

"All the more reason to get your butt up those stairs."

Another massive shove jolted her up the first step. She braced her hand against the wall. But momentum overrode her inertia, and she stumbled up the next step, and the next, until she was sprinting up the stairs, racing to protect the parent she had left.

Grace catapulted into the small room where seventeen years' worth of notes and photos clung to walls, pinned in place by a varied collection of tacks and nails. Her father's reasoning tracked by meters worth of yarn. Much-traveled pathways that made little sense to anyone but her father.

"The answer is here. Somehow it's here." Martin faced his cluttered collage, shattered but determined, pushing aside clippings, rearranging notes. "The answer to what happened to my wife."

Neither Mike nor Chase spoke, but Grace didn't miss the look they exchanged. She cringed. Her father was at his most vulnerable in this twelve-by-twelve room where his obsession was bottled up like the few remaining jars of her mother's special sauce.

Grace moved to protect him, but Hope grabbed her by the elbow. Grace tried to shake her off. "What?"

Hope doubled over. "Just give me a second, okay?"

Alarmed by her sister's hunched back, Grace paused. "Are you okay?"

"I'm fine." She straightened, only to slump over instantly. "Took the stairs too fast, I guess."

Grace didn't think so. Hope's tight lips suggested more than a need to catch her breath.

"You should lie down."

Hope winced as she massaged her side. "I'm not going anywhere. Not until they leave."

Grace was desperate for them to go, too. For an entirely different reason than a moment ago. Hope gasped and rubbed a hand over her bulging belly. Grace forgot about the men in the room. "What's happening? Is it the baby?"

"No," insisted Hope, but she leaned into Grace.

"Let's get you downstairs." And then to the clinic and away from the crazy plastered around the room.

"You stay here." Hope's lips settled into a thin line, and she grabbed Grace's hand. "Someone needs to make sure Dad doesn't incriminate himself."

There was no arguing the fact that after years of vying for law enforcement's undivided attention, her father was taking advantage of their interest. He wouldn't, or couldn't, shut up about his evidence, as he called it.

Grace knew her father hadn't killed their mother. Knew it in her heart and down to her bones.

A door slammed on the main floor.

"Marty," Pops called up the stairs. "Good news, son. I think they found your wife."

Grace closed her eyes. *Not now, Pops.*

Hope clutched her belly and moaned. Grace forgot everything else and put her arms around her sister. "A little help over here?"

"I'm fine."

But the hiss aimed at Grace's ear missed as her sister's knees buckled. Then they had everyone's attention. Mike all but carried Hope down the stairs, and Grace might have spared a brief nanosecond to swoon if Chase hadn't barked at her to fetch a glass of water and blankets. Her dad rushed down the stairs ahead of her, faster than she'd seen him move in years, and into the living room where he swept his varied collection of junk from the couch onto the floor.

Pops wandered in eating a cookie and lifted his chin in Hope's direction. "When did that one get back?"

Grace pushed him back into the kitchen. "Not now, Pops."

Mike paused at the side of the ancient, sagging sofa, concern deepening the grooves in his forehead. "I think we should get you to the clinic."

"I'll bring the truck around." Her dad pushed past them and grabbed his keys.

"Grace, where's that blanket?" demanded Chase.

She glanced at her sister's pale face. "Coming."

The water, the blankets, the hovering, did no good, and Hope reluctantly allowed Grace to drive her to the closest healthcare facility, which involved a police escort, while her protesting dad was tasked with hunting down Scott.

With Hope safely ensconced in one of the small patient cubicles, Grace searched out a chair in a less-crowded corner of the waiting room.

A cup of coffee appeared in front of her. "Sweet, the way you like it."

"Thanks." Grace wrapped her hands around the warm cup.

Mike settled into the chair beside her. "Is Scott on his way?"

"Nope." She lifted her phone, showing him Scott's blunt refusal. She ignored the frustrated shake of his head. "Things seemed to settle down a bit on the way here."

"I'm sorry about your mother. Sorrier still I was the one to have to tell you." He laid a hand on her thigh, the warmth from his palm seeping into her chilled skin.

"That part's hardly your fault." His calming touch stilled the restless bounce of her knee. She was powerless to resist the urge to lean against him, to rest her head against his shoulder. She didn't want to think about her mother, buried all those years so close to home. Didn't want to give voice to the guilty sense of relief at knowing her mother hadn't abandoned them. Sleep was easier.

"You probably have to get back to work."

"I'm off duty." He put his arm around her shoulders and gathered her close. Her eyes were already drifting shut when he gently lifted the coffee cup out of her hand. "And there's nowhere I need to be."

The next thing she knew, Mike was nudging her awake. A nurse waited for Grace to follow her. There was a brief press of his lips to her hair, and then he was gone.

The doctor explained Hope had pulled a muscle. They listened to his instructions about staying put for a couple of days. There was no attempted conversation during the long ride home, only a silent processing of the devastating earlier news.

Grace tucked Hope into bed, rearranging pillows and covering her with a mermaid blue and green blanket, one of the first she'd knitted. She set a steaming mug of chamomile tea on the nightstand.

Hope offered a tired smile. "Thanks."

Grace lowered herself onto the edge of the bed. There was no more avoiding it. "What was she doing up on that hill?"

"God, I feel guilty for even asking." Hope struggled to sit up. "But an affair, maybe?"

"No. She wouldn't." But what did Grace really know of her parents' relationship?

"At least, we can lay her to rest." Hope closed her hand over Grace's. "We can have closure."

Grace dropped her head. "She was here the whole time."

"Seems that way." Hope yawned. "Damn it. Why am I so tired?"

Grace wrapped a blanket over her own weary shoulders and carefully settled in beside her sister. She clasped Hope's hand. "I'm glad you're here."

Hope squeezed back. "Me, too."

Grace jerked awake when her phone vibrated in her pocket. Scott's number flashed on the screen. Hope was still sound asleep, and Grace crawled out of bed as carefully as possible and made her way into the hall.

She hadn't forgotten his abrupt texts of earlier, and she didn't bother to hide her irritation. "What?"

"Levi is missing."

"What?" Grace moved farther away from the bedroom door. "For how long?"

"Couple of hours." His voice was full of worry and frustration. "He overheard me talking to your dad about Hope. I hadn't gotten around to telling him about the baby. Only that she was back. I was trying—it doesn't matter. He took off while I was still on the phone, and now I can't find him."

She leaned back against the wall, letting it support her. Jeez, could this day get any worse?

"Shit, Grace. Why do I keep screwing up?"

"Give me a second." She made her way to the front door and peered through the screen on a hunch. There he sat, his narrow shoulders curved, and his arms hugging his knees.

"Oh, Levi," she whispered.

The crunch of tires on gravel had them both lifting their heads.

****

Mike was only checking in. She'd had a rough day, and they were friends. Friends looked out for each other, especially friends who shared the experience of losing someone close to them. And because they did, staying away wasn't an option.

Mike didn't notice the young boy sitting on the steps until Grace sat down beside Levi and hugged him. He parked his vehicle, an old four-door sedan he detested as she kissed the top of Levi's head. Her nephew swiped a fast hand over his cheeks. A painter might have done the pretty picture justice, but Mike was no artist. He did his best to commit the details of the moment to his long-term memory bank.

He exited the car, and Grace leaned in to whisper in Levi's ear. His narrow shoulders lifted, then fell. She tried again and got another shrug. She raised her head, and the appeal in her eyes had Mike crouching at her feet. It wasn't intruding if she wanted him there, and even though he didn't know what was wrong, it was clear something wasn't right.

Her teeth kept catching and releasing her bottom lip, and her lashes fluttered like they did when she was thinking deep. He knew every one of her tells. He pretended he'd earned the right to give Levi an uncle-like nod of encouragement.

Seven years ago, he'd been one of those guys who dreamed of fast cars, pitching in stadiums, or brokering big deals. These days, his fantasy was in front of him. A family who believed in unconditional love and support. He ached for it like a drunk craving booze.

Grace smoothed back Levi's hair. "You can talk to me about anything."

The last thing he wanted to do was make it harder for Levi to unload what was weighing him down. He was also loath to leave Grace to deal with another difficult situation all on her own. He kept his tone light but firm. "What's going on?"

Levi pressed tighter into Grace. "I ran away from home."

Grace lifted Levi's chin. "Your dad's worried about you. We all are."

Chin quivering and dirt streaking his face, Levi blinked up at Grace. "Is it true? Is she back?"

On second thought, maybe he wasn't cut out for all

this togetherness. He had no idea how Grace was able to hold it together in the face of Levi's wretchedness.

"Yes, she's back." Her dark eyes were ripe with understanding. "But you don't have to see her if you don't want to."

Levi's face crumpled. "I wanted her to stay away."

"If it helps, she seems better. Calmer. But sad that she hurt you."

"Do you believe her?" whispered Levi.

Despite knowing a thing or two about being a ten-year-old boy with parent issues, Mike kept silent and followed Levi's example. They both looked to Grace, trusting her to give an honest answer, to guide them toward the next step.

"I'm beginning to, but you take all the time you need to figure out if you believe her." Grace's tone was as gentle as the hand she used to smooth Levi's hair. "She's the one with something to prove. Not you."

Levi ran his arm under his nose. "I guess."

It was Mike's turn to step up and save Grace from having to say the obvious. "But you know what's not okay to do?"

The kid hung his head. "Run off?"

Mike patted his knee. "Right."

Grace gave her nephew another reassuring squeeze. "You could have gotten lost. Or hurt. I'd be so sad if that happened."

He burrowed into his aunt. "I wish you were my mom."

With her cheek pressed to his hair, she squeezed her eyes shut, her anguish hidden but not gone. "Then we're a fine pair because I wish I were, too."

"Really?" His head butted against her chin.

Mike was pretty sure Levi's infatuated gleam was reflected in his own.

"Absolutely. Who wouldn't want to call you their own? And in a way, you are my kid. You always will be. And I'm not going anywhere." She looked him square in the eye even though you didn't have to be looking at her to know she was serious. The absolute certainty was in her voice. "I'll always be here for you. *Always*. You need to remember that."

Levi's relief was a live thing pulsing in the air, and Mike bent under the weight of it.

She wouldn't leave.

And he couldn't stay.

This was it. His fork in the road. Attraction pulled him in one direction and ambition in the other. He'd learned to honor the latter at his mother's knee. The other was a persistent beguiling whisper he was finding harder and harder to ignore.

The speeding crush of tires had them all looking toward the road. Until the screen door swung open behind them and drew their attention to Hope limping out onto the front porch. She froze when she saw her son clinging to Grace.

Mike pushed to his feet. "Why don't we give them a minute?"

"Levi." Scott rushed up and gathered his son into a crushing hug.

Hope took a step toward her son and husband.

Mike blocked her way and held out his hand. "Let's give them some space."

When they managed a decent amount of distance, she pulled free, the short walk having winded her. "I don't need a lecture. I know he doesn't want to see me."

"I don't think he knows what he wants. You need to give him some time to figure it out." Levi was here after all, at a place he knew his mother was staying.

She thumped a fist against her chest. "Everything in me wants to do the opposite."

The scene on the porch was impossible to ignore. Scott had his arm around Levi, likely reinforcing how wrong it was to take off. Grace rubbed each of their backs, and Mike went cold. Next to the overflowing planters on the quaint porch, the three of them made a pretty picture.

Levi said something, and Scott ruffled his hair. Grace kissed Levi on the cheek before smiling at Scott. They were family, and it wasn't much of a stretch to think of them as a unit.

Hope stiffened, then turned away. He didn't want to feel sorry for her. She'd taken off. Left her family behind. She had to have known Grace would step in, do whatever it took to make things easier for Levi, and by association, Scott. She'd likely counted on it.

Careful what you wish for.

As if sensing discord, Grace left the porch.

Hope held up a hand at her approach. "He needs to deal with this. With me."

"He doesn't want to talk to you. You agreed to give him some space. Are you going back on that promise?"

Mike placed a hand on Grace's lower back in solidarity. "Seeing you in person was enough of a step for today."

"Make no mistake, I am going to put my family back together." Her warning was clear. "Whether it suits you or not."

Lines creased Grace's forehead as she watched her sister hobble off in the direction of the yard's outbuildings. "What the heck was that about?"

The chummy scene between Grace and Scott had done a number on him, too. "Maybe from back here that scene on the porch looked a little cozier than it should have."

Grace narrowed her eyes. "What scene? What are you talking about?"

Shut up, Davenport. "Between you and Scott. And Levi, of course."

She tilted her head. "You had better not be implying what I think you're implying."

"I'm not implying anything. I'm just saying it looked a tad…intimate."

She stabbed a finger into his chest and sent him back a step. "Are you accusing me of putting the moves on my brother-in-law?"

"No." And he wasn't. But he couldn't say the same for Scott. He rubbed at the sore spot in the center of his chest. "I'm not accusing *you* of anything."

"That he's putting the moves on me?" She shook her head, and he was pretty sure he glimpsed disappointment in her tired eyes before she shut down.

There was no forcing a denial out of his mouth. It was obvious Scott had feelings for his sister-in-law, and who could blame him? She'd stepped in when her sister had bailed. She'd been Scott's rock. The truth of that, as it always did, made Mike a little crazy. Made him want to remind Walker he already had a wife and maybe, just maybe, he should leave Grace alone to enjoy two minutes of peace.

"Is that what you think of me?" Her lip curled.

"That I would do that to my sister? Have an affair with her husband. I would die first."

He choked on the images flashing in his brain: a bathroom stall in an out-of-the-way dive bar, an even seedier motel room, the woods behind their family cabin with his brother drinking beer not fifty meters away. Some, but not all, of the times he'd betrayed his own flesh and blood.

What had his mother said to him the day of his brother's funeral? *A piece of trash disgrace.*

Grace grew tired of his silence. She smacked her forehead. "I'm finally figuring it out. And why should you be different than the rest of the guys around here? It's easier to believe the worst about my family. About me."

She didn't understand anything. When she looked at him, she saw a man with honor. He was the worst kind of coward to want to keep it that way. "I just...I want you to be careful. I wouldn't want your good intentions to be misconstrued by a guy who doesn't have his head on straight right now. That's all."

"Goodbye, Mike."

What was it about this woman that turned him into a blubbering idiot? He reached out a hand and caught hold of her fingertips. "Grace, I didn't mean that the way it sounded."

Her fingers yanked free of his. She didn't stop until she got to Scott and Levi. She gave each of them a hug and a kiss, nothing more than a peck on each cheek, but he got the message loud and clear. He was outside of that circle of caring and trust. Looking in. Always, looking in.

Scott and Levi strode in his direction. When they

reached him, Scott squeezed Levi's shoulder. "Go on and get in the truck."

Levi scuttled off to do as he was told. Scott avoided his gaze, choosing to focus on the vast wandering field behind Mike. "Hurt her one more time, Davenport, and I'll make sure you regret it."

Because Mike was teetering on the edge, between the man he'd become and the one who had never backed down from anything, he met Scott toe to toe. "You better be able to back that talk up, Walker."

Scott smirked. "Well, look at that. The Tin Man has feelings after all."

"How about you concentrate on your wife and child? Work on getting your own life straightened out." He knew he was giving too much away, handing emotional ammo to a man who wouldn't hesitate to blow Mike out of the water. He didn't care. "Stop relying on Grace for every little thing."

Triumph curved the other man's lips. "We're family. We rely on each other. Something an outsider such as yourself wouldn't understand."

Mike knew nothing of familial solidarity, but he had plenty of experience making other men squirm. "That implies a mutual give-and-take. Remind me again, what does Grace get in exchange for washing, cooking, mothering Levi, and generally making your life easier?"

"You really don't know shit about her life, do you?" Scott ticked the list off on his fingers. "Picking up groceries, a ride to work, runs into the city to pick up that special yarn of hers, and any other damn thing she needs done."

Things she would never ask of Mike. He might

wish her load was less, but he hadn't done anything to make it happen.

"You want to treat her like some kind of wounded bird, go ahead. She won't thank you for it." Scott's shoulder connected with Mike's on the way by.

Guilt had him staggering back. He didn't bother retaliating but stayed where he was until the dust of Scott's exit choked him as surely as the truth. A curtain moved inside the house, and he caught sight of Grace haunting the window. Then she slipped away.

If she'd had intimate partners during the two years he'd been stationed in Aspen Lake, he'd never heard a word in a place where word got around. She didn't hook up. Didn't do casual.

His feet itched to march up the porch steps, his hands clenched with the need to knock on her door, his mouth filled with words of want. And he did want Grace. Desperately. But relationships meant something to her. And integrity had come to mean something to him.

Chapter Four

A few minutes short of eight o'clock Wednesday morning, Mike pulled up in front of Stan Knight's rambling ranch-style home. The wide veranda and rustic surroundings suited the gruff former head of the Aspen Lake police detachment. A man he considered a friend and a mentor.

He'd left Grace's front steps with Scott's condemnation ringing in his ears, determined to do the right thing. Mike had settled on a plan to give Grace a sense of closure. He wasn't naïve enough to believe answering the questions surrounding her mother's death would solve all of Grace's problems, but he had to believe his efforts would mean something to her.

He sucked at relationships, but he excelled at drawing sound, logical conclusions, and his success rate at solving cases proved his ability. His problem with Cassandra Bighill's case was the distinct lack of evidence and the passage of time.

He'd barely knocked when Doris Knight beamed at him from the other side of the screen door. "Mike, what a pleasant surprise."

"Sorry for the early hour."

"Pfft." She swung the door open. "No need to apologize."

Mike stuffed nervous hands in his pockets. "Is Stan around?"

She ushered him inside. "He was up with the birds and driving me crazy by seven."

The inside was as welcoming as the outside. Every available space was crowded with photos and souvenirs from Doris's sojourns to Graceland. There were paintings on the wall. A small sculpture of Seth Stone's rested on a piece of lace in what Mike assumed was a place of honor.

"Do I hear company?" Dressed for the day in a short-sleeved, button-up shirt and pressed blue jeans, Stan ambled out of the kitchen with a sandwich in his hand.

"Stanley Garrett Knight, you just finished breakfast." Doris confiscated the stacked bun and inspected it. "Is that mayonnaise? And where ever did you find salami?"

"One sandwich isn't going to kill me." He reached to retrieve it, and despite his barrel-chested height of six feet, failed.

Doris kissed his cheek. "Your cardiologist disagrees."

She retreated, and Mike heard the trashcan open, then close. Stan balled up the empty napkin and shoved it into his pocket. "Take my advice, son. Don't ever get married."

Doris's voice drifted in, sunny and sweet. "I love you, too."

Stan shook his finger at Mike. "Laugh and I won't help you with whatever it is you've come to pick my brain over."

Mike smothered his grin, which was easy in light of the sobering questions he intended to ask. "You heard about the body found in the woods?"

Doris stuck her head back in. "That's my cue to leave. I'm heading into town for a meeting. If you're feeling brave, Stan's got coffee on."

"I heard. It's all anyone's talking about." They stopped to fill hefty pottery mugs with Stan's legendary coffee made from beans he ordered online, then double brewed. Stan glared at the silver trashcan. "Waste of a damn fine sandwich."

Mike knew better than to comment and followed Stan into his den, shelved wall to wall with the crime novels he favored.

Stan motioned him into one of two overstuffed armchairs. "It's Cassandra Bighill, isn't it?"

"Looks like it." Mike wasn't surprised by Stan's accurate guess. As he'd mentioned, gossip was flying, and that the remains were Cassandra Bighill was the obvious assumption.

"Those poor girls. Always knew there was more to her disappearance. Kept inquiring in my spare time. Never did a damn bit of good."

Every cop had one case he couldn't let go of. "You were on the job then?"

Stan grunted. "For all of three weeks. Had other good cops looking into it, but with no evidence of foul play, no one who'd seen anything suspicious, and plenty of rumors, we got nowhere fast. Kept hoping she'd turn up one day, alive and well. But somehow I knew that wasn't going to happen."

"What made you think there was more to the story?" Mike braved a sip of coffee.

"The evidence and the rumors made sense yet didn't add up. Was it possible she'd taken off? Yes. Was it probable?" Stan's curt words accompanied a quick shake of his shorn head. "Depended on who you talked to. Was she happy? Yes. And no. Depending on who you talked to. Was she scared? Acting strange? Same split."

Mike recited what little he knew. "Her car was found abandoned behind Aspen's Gas and Go."

Stan indulged in a healthy swallow of coffee. "Right where you'd expect it to be if you're going to catch the Greyhound bus out of town."

"But she didn't buy a ticket that day?"

"Doesn't mean she didn't have one," Stan countered. "And we didn't know for sure she hadn't gotten on the bus."

"No one remembered seeing her?" Mike didn't doubt his superior's detective skills, but he had to ask the questions.

Stan sensed his unease and waved off his discomfort. "No, but it was a Friday afternoon in July. Along with tourists coming in and heading out, a group of local ladies were bussing it to an agricultural conference in the city. She could have boarded the bus without anyone noticing."

In a small town fuelled by curiosity? "Without being recognized?"

"She could have worn a disguise, which would have made sense if she was planning on disappearing." Stan shrugged. "Or more likely, she may have met someone, and they headed out of town together. No need to take a bus at all."

Mike thought back to the file he'd pored over. "No evidence found in her vehicle?"

"Only what you'd expect to find in a family car. Hadn't been wiped clean either."

Mike sat forward and cradled his mug. "Here's the thing I don't get. If she was found on Hook-up Hill, how did her car end up behind the gas station?"

"Back in the day, a lesser known hiking trail behind the Gas and Go looped its way up there. The provincial park closed it a few years ago due to a property dispute between the neighboring landowner and the provincial government. No one uses that trail anymore, not even trespassers. Barrett Crane's as prickly as razor wire when it comes to policing his speck of land."

Mike was aware of Crane's reputation. Officers were dispatched to his ranch a couple of times a year for various vigilante infractions. "No drained bank accounts either."

"Nope. Then again, there was no cash to take." Stan rubbed his neck. "They were worse than broke."

Mike sensed Stan's hesitation. "What else?"

"You've read the file, so you know a week before she disappeared, Cissy reported a possible stalker. She was nervous, scared, and I believed her."

"Kevin Hunt." The man's name was popping up everywhere these days. "A decorated veteran and respected politician, with no criminal history."

But that wasn't the only information Mike had found on Hunt. He and Hunt had more than knowing Elizabeth and an interest in politics in common. They'd both lost a brother in the prime of their lives.

Stan took another swallow of coffee before continuing. "In those days, Kevin Hunt was fresh back from a peacekeeping stint in Bosnia and campaigning for a seat in provincial politics. He was in the area running his campaign. But nothing suggested he'd been following Cassandra. Doesn't mean it wasn't happening."

"What was your take when you spoke with him about it?" There was something lurking at the back of their conversation, something Stan was holding back.

"He was conveniently forthcoming and at the same time convincingly confused as to why she would accuse him of stalking her."

"He had an alibi for the day she disappeared."

"A woman. They had been holed up together at a rental cabin for the weekend. People reported seeing him around town but weren't certain about times." Stan rolled his shoulders. "His companion wasn't particularly helpful but was happy to claim they'd spent most of their time inside."

"What did Martin Bighill think of his wife's concerns regarding Hunt?"

"Cissy was adamant Martin know nothing of her coming to the police."

"Did she give a reason why?"

"Only that she didn't want to worry him if it proved to be nothing. Said her husband had enough on his mind. She admitted they were in danger of losing the farm. Being the new guy, I was unaware she had other reasons for not wanting to mention Kevin to Martin. Not until I dug a little deeper." Stan sighed. "Are you familiar with what happened to Kevin Hunt's brother, Gregory?"

"Ian Connelly served a manslaughter conviction for causing Gregory's death."

Stan settled back in his chair. "Martin Bighill, Cassandra Bighill—Popescu at the time, as they weren't yet married—Stella Donaldson, and Ian

Connelly were best friends back in the day. Rumor had it Martin and Ian were closer than brothers. Their group often included Gregory Hunt, who had an on-again, off-again relationship with Stella. They were all there the night Ian stabbed Gregory.

"Kevin's made no secret of the fact he's not fond of his brother's former friends. Cissy was concerned the possible stalking had to do with the past, and she didn't want to get Martin all stirred up." Stan shook his head. "I have a feeling that Martin was already suffering from mental health problems, and she didn't want to make matters worse."

Mike pushed back thoughts of what life must have been like for Grace and concentrated on what he remembered of Martin's murder board, which had made little sense. "If Martin and Ian were so close back then, why are they so at odds now? Did they have a falling out? Does he suspect Ian?"

Stan gave him a look Mike failed to decipher. "We talked to Ian, but he had a solid alibi for the weekend Cissy disappeared. Last minute shift change meant he was working instead of off fishing."

Mike waited, sure there was more to come.

Stan set his cup aside. "It wasn't until years later that I suspected the real reason those two are no longer on speaking terms."

Mike wasn't a strong believer in a sixth sense, however much his gut cramped. "Which is?"

"I won't be doing you any favors by telling you." Stan stared him down, his expression sympathetic but resigned.

Mike squared his shoulders. "I need to know it all."

Stan acknowledged Mike's determination with a

nod of approval. "A few years ago, the last time she was back before she passed away, Stella Donaldson was in town to celebrate Aspen Lake's centennial. A few drinks in, she said something that got me thinking. Something like 'Babies shouldn't have to pay for the crimes of their fathers.' Grace and Hope were sitting at the next table over. I remember Stella's sister trying to quiet Stella down." Stan gazed out the study window, lost in thought. "I remember thinking it was a little harsh. Martin might be sick, but he wasn't a bad guy, and in my opinion, not a criminal. But when Hope left the table, she kept staring at Grace."

As revelations went, it landed pretty flat.

The line between Stan's brows deepened. "Stella was sitting next to Ian. She patted his arm. And the look she gave him? It was off. Next thing I knew, Ian was escorting her home. For no good reason, I couldn't get that conversation or her look of pity out of my head."

Mike still wasn't seeing the problem.

"I went back. I checked court records and visitor logs from Ian's arrest and time in remand. I dug up the marriage certificate. Cissy married Martin in a private ceremony two days after Ian entered a no-contest plea to manslaughter charges. Besides his court appointed lawyer, he had one visitor, Cassandra Bighill."

Mike closed his eyes.

Stan delivered his closing salvo. "Ever seen Grace and Ian side by side?"

Mike thought back to the night of the bar fight. Ian's concern for Grace. Him kneeling down beside her. Two dark heads.

His fists clenched. "Grace has no idea."

"Not to my knowledge."

Mike wanted to go back in time and change his mind. He didn't want to know this thing that couldn't be kept a secret any longer. Not if he truly had her best interests at heart. He wanted to laugh, except he wasn't amused. He wanted to throw something, except he didn't have the strength. Instead of handing her answers, he was going to rip her world further apart.

****

Grace flicked a piece of lint off the extra-strength ibuprofen she'd stashed in her apron pocket and swallowed it dry. Across the room, a drunken tourist hoisted an even drunker woman onto the bar and poured a shot of tequila into her bellybutton. The resulting squeal had Grace's temples constricting. She snapped her fingers at one of the newly hired bouncers and received a quick nod.

It had been one very long week, with Hope treating Grace to the silent treatment, her dad barely able to function, and Pops coming down with a chest infection.

Here it was Saturday night, and the Back Forty was at capacity with a line-up to get in. Grace's hair clung to the back of her neck, and her arms ached from balancing trays of drinks. But her mom had taught her to count her blessings, and she supposed zero time to stew over her personal life qualified as a check in the plus column.

So, okay, Scott was becoming a bit of a problem, which was an easier issue to tackle than the rumors flying around about her mom and her family. She was certain telling him to stop being an idiot was all that was needed to end his ridiculous crush.

She hoped.

Grace stopped at a table close to the open door

where Ian Connelly and Stan Knight sat huddled together. "Another round, boys?"

Ian pushed back in his seat, his split lip thin with disapproval. "Doesn't Wayne give his employees a break these days?"

She gave a quick obvious glance around the bar. "Sure. When the place is empty."

Ian stood and offered his chair. "Take a minute. Catch your breath."

His surprising demand had her faltering. "Hard to make tips sitting down."

Ian was about to say more, but Stan put a hand on his arm. "Another round would be great. When you get a chance."

She frowned as Ian sat, muttering about finding Wayne and talking to him when a well-dressed older man eased his way past the bouncer. His gray hair was carefully combed, and his clothes were upscale. Grace rolled her eyes when he paused like he was waiting to be seated. "Any place you can find a seat is good."

The man surprised her by holding out his hand. "Kevin Hunt."

Grace didn't have a hand or a second to spare for chitchat. "Good to know."

The man blocked her path and dialed up his squinty charm. "I wonder if we might speak for a moment."

Grace raised her brows at his absurd request. "My boss doesn't pay me to fraternize, so I'm afraid I'll have to decline."

When she went to move past him, he put a clammy hand on her arm. "I was sorry to hear about your mother."

He and everyone else. Regulars had been

expressing their condolences all night.

Kevin did a casual turn at the sudden sound of chairs scrapping back. When he noticed Ian and Stan, his gentlemanly manners disappeared. "Thought this was a spot for decent folk."

If Grace hadn't been four hours into the shift from Hell, she might have mustered a little more patience. "Don't like the clientele, the door's behind you."

"It's been a while, Kevin." Stan stepped forward and offered his hand.

"Too long." Kevin lifted his chin at Stan's welcome, but his attention remained focused on Ian, who hovered in the background.

Kevin's sneer erased the last pretenses of charm. "Heard you were in the middle of some trouble here the other night."

Ian crossed his arms, tattoos rippling. "Yeah?"

"My constituents like to keep me informed of their concerns."

Ian, a bantam-sized rooster of a man, ruffled his feathers. "Good for them."

"It's lucky no one was seriously hurt." His lips curled into a snide smile. "Or died this time."

And that's when Grace made the connection.

Holy crap.

Stan nodded in the direction of the bar. "Kevin, how about I buy you a drink?"

"Take the table. I'm leaving." Ian tossed some bills down, then shocked Grace by pulling her over to the side. "Stay away from Hunt. Your mother wouldn't want you to have anything to do with him."

What would Ian Connelly know about her mother's wishes? Before she could ask, he was gone, squeezing past a couple rushing in.

Two tables over, a guy whistled to get her attention. Effing whistled. She held up a finger, not her middle one like she wanted but a respectable one suggesting she was on her way. Twenty minutes later, she was still trying to process Ian's strange demand when she cruised up to a table surrounded by Lily and Chase, Seth, and Mike.

Before she could open her mouth, Lily asked, "What happened? What's wrong?"

"Nothing." Grace had no desire to get into why she was distracted. Not in the middle of a crowded bar when she was supposed to be working. "Weird night. Can I get you guys another round?"

Seth tapped his phone. "Just got word Chloe's asleep and Kate's turning in. So absolutely."

"Someone's got to keep the young one company." Chase wrapped an arm around Lily, who snuggled in next to him.

"Ginger ale." Lily beamed up at Chase.

With Seth sending a final text, Chase and Lily making mooneyes at each other, Mike was the only one left to order. She tapped her foot. "I'm not getting any younger."

"You're sure you're okay?" he asked, his concern heavier than her tray of empty glasses.

"Yes."

"You don't look it."

"Always so quick with the compliments." Like she needed confirmation she looked old and tired. Again. "Are you ordering, or not?"

He stood up. "Take a break. You're exhausted."

"So...nothing to drink, then?"

"Take one, or I'll talk to Wayne and see that you get one."

She was soooo not in the mood. "Go ahead. You don't make the rules here."

Half an hour later, after Wayne ordered her to take a break, she slammed out of the back door designated Staff Only and braced her shoulders against the rough brick exterior of the building. She was so tired she was nauseous. All the same, she didn't appreciate the forced break. A break meant a chance to think. Thinking made her sad. She pulled out her phone and checked the time. Still thirteen minutes left, and Wayne had warned her not to come back until she'd taken at least fifteen.

He was all shadow when he rounded the corner, but she still recognized him. "I don't think you want to be around me right now."

Mike shoved his hands into his front pockets. "I saw you talking to Kevin Hunt earlier."

She pushed away from the wall. "It's what I do to put food on the table. Talk to people. Serve them drinks."

Mike tilted his head. "What did he say to upset you?"

"What did he say to upset me?" Her laugh was supposed to sound mocking, distant. Not betrayed and vulnerable. "What about what you said to upset me? How dare you go behind my back and talk to my boss?"

He moved closer, his voice low. Earnest. "I didn't talk to him. Apparently, even Wayne could see you needed a bit of peace."

She swallowed down his explanation and closed her eyes in resignation. "He mentioned my mother. Which people have been doing all night, so big shock, but something about his tone—I don't know, it was weird."

"There's more. Talk to me, Grace." His words were more plea than command.

"Then Hunt saw Ian, and things got even more awkward." She didn't want to think about it, so she cocked her hip. "Then I went back to work."

"Wayne needs to hire more staff."

"I sense we're coming to the part where you repeat I look like crap."

"Never." He lifted a hand to her bruised cheek. "Doesn't mean I can't tell you're exhausted."

Surprise had her freezing in place. "Same thing."

"To a woman, maybe." His hand dropped away. "You're sure that's all that happened?"

Her cheek still tingled from his touch, but she shrugged her shoulder with a nonchalance she was far from feeling. "I handled it. Well, Stan handled it, but…whatever."

"Don't get between those two. Promise me."

She didn't know Kevin Hunt. She barely knew Ian. "Am I missing something here? Why would I?"

"Promise me," he repeated.

"I don't make promises without knowing the details." Math wasn't her strong suit, but she was capable of adding two plus two. "Is this about my mother? You'd tell me if it was, right?"

"I said I'd keep you informed, and I will."

But he wasn't looking her in the eye. He was focused on her mouth. Confusion outweighed the instinct to wet her lips. She grabbed onto his shirt. "Not good enough."

"There will always be bad blood between the two

of them." He surprised her by pressing her hands against his chest, trapping them there. "Nothing we do can change the past, no matter how much we wish we could rewrite history."

His heart beat out a quick rhythm under her palms. She didn't want to think about slick politicians and crusty ex-cons. Not when she had his undivided attention. His focus was back on her mouth. His breath brushed her cheek. She slipped a hand around to the back of his neck and tugged until his forehead rested against hers.

"Whose past are we talking about?" she whispered, certain his answer was the key to breaking through his careful reserve and finding out more about the man he'd allowed her to see that afternoon on Main Street.

His body changed shape under her hands. Went from stiff and immobile to softer and inching closer. His hands came to rest on her upper arms. He brushed his lips over hers. Their contact hardly rated as a kiss. But it had potential. So much potential.

Laughter echoed in the background, and a car door slammed. His lips dipped one more time but didn't quite meet hers. Already closed, his eyelids squeezed tight. He backed up, his hands slipping down her arms until he was only grasping her fingertips. He opened his eyes, and the bleakness chilled her to the bone. "You don't want to know who I was before I came here. Trust me."

She tried to strengthen their tenuous grip, wanted to argue he was wrong, but he slipped free of her clinging fingers. She followed his hurried steps and saw only his shadow, a thin, gaunt wisp of a thing slinking after him as he slipped around the corner, the harsh lights of the parking lot keeping it alive. Nothing of it reminded her of the man she thought she knew.

Chapter Five

With the custom-ordered, green-and-pink dorm blanket finished and carefully wrapped in tissue paper, Grace rummaged for the shipping labels she'd printed off earlier and stuck them to the box. Her mind played a running loop of Ian's warning, Kevin Hunt's request, and Mike's veiled references to his past. But none of those strange happenings were loud enough to stand up against the passive-aggressive banging and clanging of pots coming from the kitchen.

So…first thing's first.

She rescued the box of her mother's things and lugged it into the kitchen. Hope gave her the briefest of glances, then went back to her kneading. Grace went ahead and unwrapped a tiny figurine and set it on the window ledge in front of Hope. "Mom loved this little fairy."

Grace crossed her fingers as Hope draped a towel over a bowl of dough, then washed her hands and wiped them dry. She picked up the tiny ornament. "She definitely had a whimsical side."

Sensing her sister softening, Grace swallowed her pride. "I didn't mean to overstep with Levi. It's just…"

"I get it." Without meeting Grace's look, Hope set the fairy back. "You were here for him when I wasn't. I'm grateful. Truly."

Grace put a hand on her sister's shoulder, relieved

when she didn't pull away. "With Levi...the longer you were gone, the easier it was to pretend he was mine. Spending time with him, with them, filled this void that's dogged me lately."

Hope frowned. "Void?"

"It wasn't all out of the goodness of my heart." Grace chuffed out a breath. "Kind of selfish, huh?"

"Yeah, you're the poster girl for self-indulgence."

Some said confession was good for the soul, and Grace guessed she was about to find out. "Because, maybe, I've been feeling a little stuck lately."

Hope's eyes softened. "What do you mean, stuck?"

"Like *stuck*. I don't know how else to explain it." Grace bent over the box and searched for another distraction, already regretting saying anything at all.

For once, Hope sensed her reluctance and didn't push. "We're quite the screwed-up pair, huh?"

"We didn't used to be."

Grace liberated a silver-framed photograph of her and Hope at the beach, lake water glinting in the background. She was ten years old again with the sun kissing her skin and ice cream dripping onto her fingers.

Hope pressed a cheek to Grace's shoulder. "There were happy times."

Outside the window, the stubby grass needed mowing and the birdfeeders swung empty. Chores she had little interest in doing. Grace dipped her head. She might as well finish what she'd started. "It seems like everyone else is moving forward, going through all these life-changing events. I guess I'm feeling a little left behind."

Hope gave Grace a squeeze. "What was that saying

Mom loved? Something about joining the dance?"

"Good in theory." Grace lifted a greeting card out of the box.

Hope confiscated the card, laughing when she opened it to find her childish scrawl inside. "She was such a great mom."

"She was." Grace picked up a yearbook covered in the Aspen Lake school colors of green and silver.

"Let's look at that over tea." Hope reached for the kettle and winced.

Grace abandoned the yearbook. "Let me do that. Aren't you supposed to be lying down?"

"I'm fine. And my back can't take any more time in bed." But she stood back while Grace filled the kettle.

With nothing to do but wait for the water to boil, Grace flipped through the weathered pages until she came to her mother's class, and she realized the book was printed the year their mom graduated. Her finger traced over pictures of her dad, Auntie Stella, and Ian. All so young. She lingered over the photo of Gregory Hunt. It was surreal to know a year later he would be dead and Ian would be in jail. "Ian Connelly and Kevin Hunt were in the bar last night."

Hope shrugged. "Kevin who?"

Grace showed her the yearbook. "Ian went to jail for killing Kevin Hunt's brother, Gregory."

"Awkward."

"Don't get me started. Then Ian feels the need to warn me that Mom would want me to stay away from Hunt."

Hope bunched up her nose. "Weird."

"They were all in the same class together. Mom,

Dad, Ian, Auntie Stella, and Gregory Hunt."

"You don't say. I wonder…" Hope commandeered the book and flicked to the back and the space reserved for the signatures you collected at the end of the year. She scanned the one-line quips and tapped one in particular. "Check it out."

Grace squinted. "*A light in the darkness. Ian.*"

Hope raised her brows. "Is it just me, or is that kind of…romantic?"

It was next to impossible to connect the scribbled poetic words to the quiet, guarded man she barely knew. She tugged the book free of Hope's hands and read another one. "*Good friends. Good times. More to come. Marty.*"

"Sounds like Dad." Hope held out a hand, and Grace returned the book. "Here it is. This one must be Gregory Hunt's. *Later days! Greg.*"

Grace unplugged the whistling kettle. "Do you get the feeling he wasn't exactly a deep guy?"

"How philosophical were you in high school?" asked Hope.

"True." Grace stared down at Ian's scrawl. "Do you think Mom and Ian were more than friends?"

Hope handed her the book and poured hot water into a waiting mug. "I think it would be a mistake to read too much into teenage scribbling."

"Do you think I should mention Ian's warning to Dad?"

"He's not exactly rational when it comes to Ian." Hope dropped a teabag into her mug. "His name is all over that crazy murder board of his."

Grace couldn't explain her urge to defend Ian. She just went with it. "Ian was nowhere around when Mom disappeared. He moved back a couple of months after, remember?"

Hope wrapped her hands around her mug. "You're the one with the infallible memory, not me."

Grace got her own mug out of the cupboard and filled it. "I could ask Chase. We are entitled to ask questions."

Hope snickered as she leaned back against the counter. "Why not ask the uptight one? The one you have a thing for?"

"Oh, please." Grace risked a cautious sip of weak tea.

Hope rolled her eyes. "Like it's not painfully obvious."

Nothing like having her worst fears confirmed. She changed tactics. "Kevin Hunt mentioned wanting to talk to me."

Hope made her way over to the table and eased down into a chair, hand on her back. "What about?"

"He didn't get around to saying." She joined Hope at the table, bringing their mom's box with her. "Maybe I should get in touch with him and find out."

"Up to you." Hope pulled out a picture of a long-ago Christmas. There was a tree with presents underneath it and the two of them sitting in front of it. "I had this fantasy I used to torture myself with, of her with a new family. Living this perfect life. And all along she's been on Hook-up Hill. You know they're going to say the Hill is haunted now?"

"Yeah, they probably will." During last night's shift, Grace had experienced enough conversations abruptly ending when she approached to know gossip was swirling.

Hope set the photo down and dusted off her hands. "How about French toast for breakfast?"

Grace didn't blame Hope for wanting to change the subject. "Where is this love for cooking coming from? Not that I'm complaining."

"Kind of came out of the blue." Hope winced when she tried to stand.

"Sit. I'll make it." Grace retrieved a carton of eggs from the fridge.

Mug cradled in her hands, Hope's lips curved with a shy smile. "I'm hoping I can turn it into a business."

Torn between wanting to reassure and cautioning against moving too quickly, she reached for the bread Hope had made the other day. A knock on the door had Grace turning back. "Don't even think of moving. I'll get it."

Levi was standing on the porch, head bent, with Scott standing behind him, hands on his shoulders. Grace urged them forward, and they came through the door, all stiff movements and uncomfortable shuffles. Sunday morning breakfast was a tradition they'd started soon after Hope had left, but she hadn't expected them to show up today.

"Look who's here?" Grace cleared the nervous stutter from her throat. "Just in time for breakfast. There's a rumor of French toast."

Levi kept his gaze glued to the floor. "It's tradition, isn't it?"

"Of course, it is." Grace bent to give him a quick hug and to whisper in his ear, "Proud of you."

"We can't stay long. Levi's got piano lessons in an hour." Scott rubbed his hands together. "Then there's the big game this afternoon. We've got some payback to dish out."

Then he winked at her.

Grace ignored him and prayed Hope hadn't noticed. "Well then, let's get some food in you. Levi, why don't you feed Scooby?"

Levi grabbed the dry food container out of the cupboard and headed for the cat's bowl.

Hope touched Scott's arm and mouthed a silent, "Thank you."

Scott shrugged her off and turned to Grace. "Your face looks better."

She shoved a stack of plates at him, and he grunted in surprise. Busy work eased the awkwardness, and they all did their best to keep the atmosphere light and any sullen undercurrents hidden from Levi. The tension settled back in the moment they sat down to eat.

"I don't think I want to go to the game," Levi announced, his forkful of toast poised in mid-air.

Because he was sitting as close to Grace as it was possible to get without being in her lap, she bumped her shoulder against his. "I'll miss seeing you in the stands."

Levi slumped back in his chair. "You won't even notice."

Hope swirled syrup over her toast. "It's too bad both of us are going to miss it. I've got so much stuff to do around here I won't be able to make it either."

Scott ruffled Levi's hair. "Gonna miss a great game, buddy."

Hope added another slice of bacon to his plate. "How's Auntie Grace going to hit a homerun if you're not there to cheer her on?"

Levi straightened his shoulders and allowed a small

smile to show. "I guess I could go."

When the only thing left on their plates was syrup, Hope excused herself, citing the rule of she who cooks does not clean.

Once Hope was out of the room, Scott pulled his son in and kissed the top of his head. "Proud of you."

Levi leaned into Scott. He'd made it through breakfast, but the effort had taken a toll. Grace squirted dish soap into the filling sink and gave them a moment. When she heard rustling behind her, she broke the silence, eager to get them back on familiar ground. "You two going to help me, or what?"

Scott set a stack of dishes down beside her. "Anything to help out."

His words were innocent, but his smile was flirty. Grace spotted Levi, head tilted, eyes wide, and ears listening. She pasted on a relieved smile when she remembered Levi's piano lesson. "You're probably pressed for time. Feel free to take off. I've got this."

Coming to stand a little too close, Scott dropped some dirty cutlery into the sink. "Happy to help."

Grace elbowed him out of the way. "I don't want Levi to be late. Off you go."

He shrugged. "The world won't end if he's five minutes late."

"Levi, why don't you let Scooby out?" With Levi occupied, she did a quick scan down the hallway to make sure Hope's door was closed. She couldn't believe they were about to have this conversation. "Stop with the flirty stuff."

"Oh, come on." He gave her a nudge and a smile. "You like it."

Grace flicked her dishtowel at him. "No, I don't."

"Ow." Scott frowned and rubbed his arm.

"It all stops right now." She flicked the towel at him again. "Do you hear me?"

"Okay." He backed up a step when she tightened her grip on the towel. "Jesus, I was just playing around."

"It's inappropriate," she insisted.

"I'm sorry." He shook his head. "It's just, you're so steady. Reliable. Like…"

"Like an old sweater?" Let him carry that image around in his head for a bit.

"No. Not like that at all." But he didn't sound very sure.

Thank God.

"Just so we're clear, you're done with the flirty stuff, right?"

His only response was a quick nod and a refusal to leave until the clean up was finished. Grace waved them off from the front stoop. Hope joined her, lifted a hand, and received a slight wave from her son in return.

Grace tucked an arm around her. "You did good."

Hope rested her head on Grace's shoulder. "Long way to go yet."

"It's a start…" promised Grace.

Hope rolled her eyes. "…and you have to start somewhere."

"Another favorite of Mom's." They stayed put and watched Scott's truck disappear down the road.

They'd survived the first step. But Grace wasn't sure of the next step or what it should entail. She was pretty sure none of them did. The thought wasn't particularly reassuring. The only thing she did know for sure was that Bighills didn't give up. Not even when they were down by one at the bottom of the ninth.

Hope knew it, too. She fisted her hands to her hips. "Don't you have a baseball game to win? And an asshole to put in his place?"

Grace grinned and checked the time. "Yes, I most certainly do."

****

Blessed with an abundance of athletic ability, Mike had plenty of experience playing sports in high school, had gone on to play intercollegiate hockey. Thanks to his affluent lifestyle, he and his buddies had spent plenty of time in big stadiums watching professionals play, but none of those experiences had prepared him for small town sports.

Rural folks took their local sports *very* seriously. They fundraised, supported, and cheered until their throats were raw. People trash-talked, and tempers flared. In a professional capacity, Mike had handled disputes at hockey rinks, curling clubs, and baseball diamonds.

Didn't stop him from joining in on various teams wherever he was posted and when his schedule allowed. He was competitive and a team player by nature, if not through nurture, and it was the only time during the last seven years he felt like he fit in. Today both teams were evenly matched, evenly motivated. Aspen Lake was out to claim a win, and Glenville was determined to deny them. The bar fight had raised the stakes.

Plenty of Glenville spectators joined a larger than usual Aspen Lake crowd in the stands. He caught sight of Grace's nephew, Levi, sitting with Scott's parents. Ian stood, apart from the stands, arms crossed. Mike couldn't remember seeing him at previous games. Stan stopped to talk to him. Ian shook his head and waved him off. Mike did a quick scan for Grace and didn't see her.

Chase caught up to him, bag in hand, cap pulled low, and huge grin in place. "Perfect day for some ball."

Mike upped the ante. "Perfect day to win."

Deke appeared beside Chase. "Got that right."

Due to shiftwork, the three of them playing together was a rare occurrence. But as Deke was their star pitcher, today was the perfect day for it to happen. "Arm fired up?"

Deke cracked his knuckles. "Yep."

Mike spotted Mason and a couple of Glenville guys in the opponents' dugout pulling bats out of a gear bag. "Heard you were called out to Pearce's house yesterday."

Deke's glare of disgust confirmed it. But before Mike could ask how Deke figured yesterday's visit might affect today's game, Elizabeth stepped in front of them.

He tried his best not to flinch at the sight of her. "Michael, do you have a moment?"

He ignored his colleagues' raised brows and waved them off. "See you guys in a few?"

Chase saluted back. "Sure thing, *Michael*."

Mike waited until his coworkers were on their way. "I don't remember you being much of a sports fan."

"My presence here is work related. Kevin is throwing out the ceremonial pitch."

At the mention of Hunt's name, Mike did a search for her boss. Eyes on the crowd, he missed Grace picking her way through the curious throng of onlookers until she was almost beside them. Elizabeth's fingers curved around his elbow. He didn't misread her show of ownership. Neither did Grace. Irritated by his adolescent flush of guilt and the irrational sense he'd been caught doing something illicit, he still stepped aside to dislodge her hand.

Grace's long black hair swung from the back of her baseball cap as she hustled by them. He'd ached with the need to touch her last night in the alley. To kiss her, to hold her in his arms. He'd almost succumbed.

Almost.

Under bright sunny skies and using the excuse of the baseball game in his favor, he gave in to his urgent need to follow the woman who'd overtaken his dreams last night. "I really need to get ready for the game."

"Of course." Elizabeth bit down on her bottom lip. "I only wanted to remind you about Friday and the town hall meeting."

"I said I'd be there."

She glanced away at his abrupt tone. "Till Friday, then."

Self-reproach over his harsh wording had him waiting until Elizabeth joined her boss where he waited behind home plate. Hunt smiled and rested a hand on her lower back, drawing her into the small group. Nothing about the man's history or neat, trim appearance raised any red flags. But the warning look he gave Mike over Elizabeth's shoulder had him frowning.

He knew Elizabeth's preferences, or had, and he also knew enough about Hunt's life after researching him to know it was unlikely there was anything intimate between them. The knowledge didn't stop the spot between his shoulder blades from itching.

"You're worried about her."

Grace watched him from where she'd paused a few feet away, and he could only guess what his scrutiny of a small group of people that included Elizabeth might suggest to her. He gave a minimal shake of his head. "Not worried so much as confused."

"She matters to you."

"There's nothing between Elizabeth and I."

"But there was?"

"Grace..." But she was busy walking away.

Then Chase was beside him, putting a hand on his shoulder. "Let's play some ball."

The umpire moved into place behind home plate. Mike lined up with everyone else to watch Kevin Hunt throw the ceremonial pitch. From the first swing, tempers on both sides brewed. The tension spread to the restless crowd until it competed with the smell of hotdogs the 4H club was selling. But it wasn't until the bottom of the eighth inning things went to shit.

The score was five to four in Glenville's favor. Mason huffed and puffed, clinging to first base. Scott punched his fist into his glove and glared as he guarded first base. From her place at second, Grace prepared for a forced out. As the shortstop, Mike moved in to back her up. Chase crouched behind home plate and nattered at Seth on third. Deke bent forward, jaw muscles grinding his immense wad of gum.

The crowd leaned forward on the hard bleachers, both sides yelling encouragement. Mason crept off first and pointed a finger at Grace. The batter caught a break and hit a line drive straight at second.

The ball bounced, and Grace missed the catch. Mike dove for the ball and shot it back to her. She tagged the base and got ready to throw the ball to first. Even though he was out, Mason dropped into a slide and aimed for Grace. He took her out in a cloud of dirt.

Mason scrambled to his feet, smirk at the ready. "Gotta say, Bighill. You look better lying on your back."

Mike lost his mind. Before he knew it, his fists were full of Mason's jersey. "You son of a bitch. You're out of here."

Mason leaned in close, his lips barely moving. "Just because you're fucking her doesn't give you the right to make the rules."

"Mike, enough." Deke's arms clamped around Mike's torso, and he tried to pry him lose. Mike wasn't in the mood to let go. Out of the corner of his eye, he saw Seth restraining Scott. For some insane reason, Scott's efforts to get to Grace made his fists clench tighter.

Deke's breath heated his ear. "He's not worth it, man."

Grace was still on the ground, working at getting the air to move in and out of her lungs. Chase was hunched down beside her, encouraging her to stay calm. Mike released his grip, but Chase was already helping her to her feet.

"You okay?" he asked.

"This is why girls shouldn't be allowed to play with the men." Mason ignored the umpire's warning to be quiet and lifted his arms. "Am I right, boys?"

He didn't get much support from his teammates, disgust for Mason's actions evident in their awkward glances and shuffling feet.

"You slid into me on purpose." Grace paused from brushing the dust off her team shirt. "And *girls* have every right to play the game. You're the one who needs a lesson in fair play and human decency."

"What would a Bighill know about decent?" Mason spat in the dirt. "I doubt your mother was on Hook-up Hill playing cards."

"That's enough out of you, asshole." Once again Mike's hands clenched with the need to feel fabric bunching between his fingers.

Grace's lip lifted in a sneer. "Try something like that again, and you'll regret it."

"Yeah? You and what girl army are going to make that happen?"

"She won't need an army." Mike pressed hard against the hand Chase put out to stop his advance.

Mason threw off the hands of a concerned teammate. "You want a go at me, cop? Have at it."

"We've got a game to finish." Hands on hips and feet planted, the umpire sent the players back to their respective sides.

There was plenty of muttering as the teams got themselves sorted out. Mason walked backward toward the Glenville bench uttering threats and managed to get himself ejected from the game, which resulted in a few more minutes of terse silence as he collected his gear and slammed his way out of the opposing team's dugout.

Unable to help himself, Mike paused by Grace at second plate. "You okay?"

"Never better." Grace punched a fist into her glove and faced home plate, dismissing him.

Mike had no choice but to move on. He settled into his place at shortstop and willed his boiling emotions down to a simmer. They all did their best to win the game, but Glenville ended up scoring another run at the bottom of the last inning after Aspen Lake tied it up at the top. The earlier scuffle made for hasty handshakes and a quick departure of the other team.

It was Mike's turn to organize and store the equipment, while the rest of the team made their way to Mary's, as was the custom. He was thankful for the added time to decompress. In fifteen or so minutes, he needed to be able to sit down across the table from Grace with a casualness he was far from feeling.

"I thought maybe you could use some help."

Mike jerked around at the sound of her voice.

Grace grabbed a couple of bats and headed for an open equipment bag. "Kind of jumpy there, Constable."

She was right. He'd half expected Mason to come snooping back around, looking for someone to poke at. If that happened, he didn't want Grace anywhere around. "I'm good. Go ahead and join the others."

"That's just it. I don't think you are good." She wrapped her arms around her middle.

The moment he met her earnest gaze, he was lost. "Grace…you and me? It can't happen."

She didn't retreat. She waited.

His heart hammered, and the bat in his hand was one clammy second away from slipping free of his grasp. "I might have given a different impression last night, and I'm sorry if I led you to believe otherwise."

"You're a crappy liar, you know that? I thought a good poker face was one of the first things they taught you in police training."

His throat was swelling shut. Why else would it be so hard to manage a swallow? "I don't know where you're going with this, but…"

"Yes, you do." Her movements were precise as she pressed him back against the fence.

"We're friends."

She smoothed her hands up his arms. "We could have been friends. Instead, we chose to circle around each other, committing to nothing."

Like she could sense his resolve slipping, she pressed her hands to his chest. Decency demanded he tell her he was leaving, but he couldn't force a confession out of his dry mouth. Couldn't make that final break. "The rest of the team will be wondering where we are."

Her chest expanded, her perfect breasts rising underneath her team shirt. She ran her tongue over her bottom lip. "Kiss me."

He outweighed her, but he couldn't move. He was pinned in place by her whispered demand.

He searched for words. Smart ones. Ones capable of diffusing the situation, but a hint of moisture still clung to her lips, and all he wanted to do was taste her.

He dipped his head to brush a kiss across lips warm with summertime heat. The taste of bubble gum hit his tongue, sweet and encouraging. The tips of the chain link fence rimming the field dug into his back. And he loved that feeling best of all. Immobile. Trapped. With nowhere to go but closer, and her mouth was right there. Her hands slipped into his hair, and she held him in place. Letting him know he wasn't going anywhere. Not yet. He lowered his mouth to hers.

The pump of his blood echoed in his ears. His

mouth opened under her ministrations, his hands roamed over her back and up her spine to tangle in the dark length of her hair.

"Auntie Grace! Come on, I'm starving. Everyone wants to know what's taking you..." Running feet stuttered to a halt. "...so long."

She stepped back, letting go of his body but not his gaze. "We'll be right there, Levi."

"We're waiting for you guys so we can order." Levi's voice remained hesitant, careful, but determined to get Grace's attention.

Grace broke eye contact, slipping her hand into Mike's. "Okay, champ. How about we give Constable Davenport a hand putting the gear in his vehicle?"

He memorized the imprint of each of her fingers as they curled around his. Levi nodded his reluctant agreement, and she relinquished her grasp. There was no recovering from their kiss. No going back to the way things were. No more room for denial. As they tossed equipment into bags and made sure each dugout was tidy, Mike knew he was going to have to tell her he was leaving.

Chapter Six

His back to the wall, Mike sipped his lukewarm coffee and took stock of the room. Rows of chairs lined the gymnasium floor, and attendees clustered about the town hall meeting room. Elizabeth had done her job perfectly. A podium sat in the center of the stage with a glass of water at the ready, and posters promising progressive change were tacked to walls. Mike was in attendance, as promised. He'd kept his word, as Elizabeth had known he would, even though she knew being at a political rally would dredge up old dreams. Mike was pretty sure she counted on him remembering the plans they'd made when there was nothing between them but seedy, tangled hotel sheets.

Justin had lived and breathed the law, and as far as Mike was concerned, his brother had been welcome to Alton and Davenport. Mike had figured on five or so years at the family firm while he networked and cultivated a reputation as a man to trust. This election would have marked his first bid at federal politics.

Then Justin had died, and Mike's life had changed in ways he could never have imagined. He swallowed down another mouthful of coffee and focused on the woman who'd fallen from the golden gates of privilege alongside him.

Elizabeth moved about the overheated room, her hair carefully pulled back. The necklace he'd given her circled her throat. She smiled as she worked the room, no doubt knowing she had her work cut out for her. Not everyone was fond of Kevin Hunt's tough-love approach to revitalizing the lagging economy, including Mike.

There was no time to think of the campaign he would have run. Hope and Martin Bighill hustled by him. Hope's pinched face cast worried glances about the room, her hand holding tight to her father's arm as he all but dragged his daughter along with him. It didn't take any kind of clarity to know Martin Bighill and Kevin Hunt in the same room was a bad thing.

Mike abandoned his Styrofoam cup on a nearby table and was halfway to Hope and Martin when Grace rushed into the gym. He hadn't seen her since Sunday. Hadn't avoided her. Not really. He'd certainly relived their kiss enough times. But work was busy. An excuse he'd clung to when he thought of telling her he was leaving for good.

He remembered every word of his warning to stay away from Hunt. But here she was, hair in a messy knot on the top of her head, wisps of it escaping to frame her face. All thoughts of Hunt dissolved. Mike had a thing for her hair. The weight and length of it. The imagined feel of it against his skin.

He moved in her direction and reached the tense little group in time to see her eyes widen accusingly at Hope. "What are you and Dad doing here?"

"You shouldn't be here." Her father clutched at Grace's arm hard enough to make her wince. "Please, I don't want you to have anything to do with that man."

"No problem. We'll leave together."

Mike was prepared to do anything to erase the

concern from her pretty eyes. "Mr. Bighill, how about I help you out to your car?"

"We're fine." Hope put a protective arm around her dad and glared at Grace. "What's he doing here?"

"I don't know. I didn't invite him." Grace turned to Mike. "What *are* you doing here?"

Mike wasn't about to admit he was there because of Elizabeth. "Does it matter? I'm here to help."

People were beginning to stare, but Martin was oblivious. "You can't have anything to do with him, promise me."

Grace abandoned her close inspection of Mike's face and her search for duplicity and rubbed her father's arm. "Dad, keep your voice down."

"Yeah, people might start to think we're crazy." Hope's sarcasm did little to mask her nervousness.

Grace's eyes narrowed. "Not helpful, Hope."

Mike had plenty of experience diffusing difficult situations, but he wasn't there in a professional capacity and didn't want to give that impression. Grace had already accused him of thinking of her as a job. He put a hand on her lower back and prayed the intimacy of the act would communicate his support. "Mr. Bighill, maybe we could find a quieter place to talk about your concerns?"

"I'm pretty sure we can manage without your boyfriend's help."

Clearly, Hope wasn't feeling his good intentions. Grace shrugged her sister off. "Come on, Dad. Mike will lead the way out."

Unfortunately, they had to pass by Elizabeth. Smile pinned in place, she held out her hand to Grace's father. "Elizabeth McCray, Kevin Hunt's campaign manager."

"We were just leaving." Hope moved to push by Elizabeth.

Elizabeth cast a confused glance in the direction of the stage. "We're almost ready to begin."

"Gracie—"

She gritted her teeth. "Not now, Dad."

Elizabeth's brows drew together. "Is there a problem?"

Martin's distress escalated, and despite Hope's disapproval, Mike intervened. "We were just on our way out."

A young man appeared at Elizabeth's elbow, leaving her no time to protest. "Sorry to interrupt, but we're about to start."

"I'll be right there, David." Elizabeth turned to Mike, a plea for understanding nobody could mistake. "Won't you reconsider staying? I'd really like you to meet Kevin."

"Thanks, but no." Mike was done placating her. He gave Grace his undivided attention, not caring if the whole world deemed him rude or read too much into his concern. "Shall we?"

A hush descended over the room as Kevin Hunt, more than aware of the crowd's interest in their small tableau, chose that exact moment to approach them. Mike had no doubt the man had his timing down to a science.

Hunt managed to lift his chin and look down on Grace's father even though he was inches shorter. "Martin, I'm surprised to see you here. Rumor has it you don't leave the house much these days."

Elizabeth's eyes widened at her boss's subtle insult, but she was quick to try and divert Hunt's attention. "Kevin, I don't believe you've met Constable Michael Davenport. He's the RCMP officer I was telling you about."

Hunt extended his hand. "Always a pleasure to meet one of our hardworking members of law enforcement."

Mike was close enough to catch Hope's gritted whisper. "Can we please get the hell out of here?"

Mike put his hand in Hunt's and prayed Grace would listen to her sister.

"I had the pleasure of being a member of the provincial legislative assembly when your grandfather was premier of the province. He was a good man."

His hand still at her back, Mike felt Grace come to attention. He rarely talked about his well-known family. In fact, he'd spent the seven years of his banishment distancing himself from his Davenport roots and what it meant to be part of one of the province's most influential families.

"Thank you. My grandfather was passionate about politics." And little else. Certainly not his fatherless grandsons. Mike pressed his hand more firmly against Grace's back. "If you'll excuse us."

"Perhaps we should make our way to the podium." Elizabeth fingered the necklace circling her throat.

Grace caught his recoil, and he knew the moment she made the connection. A muscle jerked along her jawline, and then she was moving, winding her way out the doublewide gym doors.

"Thankfully, the trash has taken itself out."

Mike looked from Elizabeth's stunned expression to Kevin Hunt's smirk. He knew, without a doubt, Hunt was testing him, and he didn't care for it. Nor was he tempted to take his bait. "Good luck with your campaign."

Without looking back, he left and caught up to Grace in the parking lot. It was clear she was less than enthused to see him.

Before he could say a word, Martin twisted toward him. "You need to make sure he doesn't hurt her."

Mike was one hundred percent on board with making sure nothing happened to Grace, but Grace wouldn't thank him for leaving her without a say in the matter. However, Mike was also determined to find out why Martin was so desperate to keep Hunt and Grace apart.

Martin's shoulders sagged. "I want to go home."

Grace attempted to soothe him. "Dad—"

Martin, fixated on the notion of home, hustled toward Hope's car. Hope followed and waved when she had Martin settled in the passenger seat of her vehicle.

For no good reason, a slow flush of anger heated his skin. "Is this your idea of staying away from Kevin Hunt?"

There was a slow arching of her brow as she moved from shock at the subject change to affronted at his abrupt demand. "When did I agree to stay away from Kevin Hunt?"

He did some brow lifting of his own. "The other night in the alley?"

She cocked a hip. "You said not to get between Hunt and Ian, although I don't know why I would. And I haven't."

"It's upsetting to your father."

"Don't lecture me on what's best for my dad."

"I'm trying to help." It was a lie. One glance at her

mouth and all he remembered was the press of her lips against his. If he truly had her best interests at heart, he'd confess to his affair with Elizabeth and that it had led to his brother's death. Guaranteed, she'd walk away and never look back. But he couldn't do it.

"What does this have to do with my mom? Because that's what this is about, isn't it? Your sudden concern?" When he hesitated over her ill-timed change in topic, Grace crossed her arms. "Ian said my mom…"

Mike went on alert. "Ian said what?"

"It was nothing. Forget it."

Not likely. "If you want, I can ask Ian."

He expected her to call his bluff, but to his surprise she answered. "Only that my mom would want me to stay away from Hunt. Which seems to be a theme these days."

Her less than guarded answer increased his unease and loosened his tongue. "There's something I need to tell you."

Like the fact he was leaving Aspen Lake. Leaving her. That she was wrong to want him.

Her whole body stiffened, alerted by some sixth sense to what he wasn't saying.

"Not here." He wanted the beginning of the end to take place in private. "My place? Seven o'clock?"

"I'll see you then."

****

Grace managed to escape Hope's censure long enough to shower. She unearthed a black denim skirt and a reasonably crisp T-shirt, then she swiped on some lip-gloss and called it done. No doubt about it, she wanted a repeat of the kiss they'd shared after the ballgame. Did she believe anything intimate was going to happen tonight? Only a fool would assume much of anything when it came to Mike, and she was no fool. She swiveled in front of her bedroom mirror. She was reasonably sure she'd achieved understated casual and that no hint of desperation showed. Good enough to face whatever was coming.

Unfortunately, her departure coincided with Hope's. She attempted to breeze by her sister as she piled food into her car to take to their dad and Pops. "See you later."

"Wait a sec." Hope eyed her outfit with concern. "About earlier. I'm the last person who should be lecturing anyone on their intentions. And I wanted you to know I support whatever agenda you've got your mind set on, okay?"

"I don't have an agenda." Not one she was admitting to, anyway.

Hope stuffed a small box that smelled of cinnamon into her hands. "Right."

"I don't."

"Those are for your boyfriend. I thought cookies might put a little sweet in his stiff and starchy." Hope gave her a slow wink. "And sex would be good for you. I know I could use a good—"

"Stop. I don't want to hear it. I'm traumatized enough already." Grace held up the box. "And thanks."

"I won't wait up."

Grace rolled her eyes. "Goodbye."

She'd crossed the tracks at the edge of town before she was able to scrub Hope's words and laughter from her brain. A check in her rearview mirror showed Ian had pulled in behind her. She lifted a hand in greeting, then took the next turn and claimed the last visitor parking spot outside Mike's building.

Mike answered his door smelling and looking as delicious as the goodies Hope had insisted she bring. She offered him the box. "From Hope."

He ushered her in, pausing to lift the lid. "Smells tasty."

She surveyed his apartment. He certainly had a thing for beige. Beige furniture. Beige lamps. Beige walls. All of it pretty battered-looking for a guy who was always perfectly groomed. She zeroed in on his desk, which held a docking station with carefully labeled chargers. There was an honest to God desk blotter.

"Wow. You are really, *really* neat." She made a mental note to clean her whole house, which at the moment looked like a yarn factory and pastry shop had gone to war.

"Thanks, I think." He headed into his tiny kitchen with its beige cupboards.

She brushed a hand over her short skirt. Her multi-hued, handwoven bracelet made by Levi caught on her skirt pocket. She tugged it free.

"Can I offer you a drink? Wine? Beer? Soda?"

"Yes, please." His brows rose, and she realized she hadn't answered his question. Not in a sane way. "Wine would be lovely."

"White or red?"

She thought of all the beige and how spot removal wasn't her strong suit. "White."

A big ol' glass of white.

"So…" She wandered over to inspect the prints on the wall, encouraged by the fact that a guy wasn't likely to offer you a drink, then launch into a discussion regarding your dead mother. She hoped.

"Yes?" The cork slid out of the bottle with a little pop.

"Interesting art." It wasn't. It was boring and awful, nothing like she'd expected to find on his walls.

Mike grabbed a beer from the fridge and handed her a glass. She tipped it back and drank down a nice healthy swallow. Waited for the warmth to calm her panicky nerves and breathed a sigh of relief when it worked. The glass made a nice little click on his overly organized desk where she very carefully set it down. Because the hell with it.

She confiscated his drink, set it down beside her wine, and yanked him closer. Or she tried. He didn't budge. But forward motion worked in her favor, and she ended up pressed against him. Then she full-on-took-no-prisoners-stuck-her-tongue-down-his-throat kissed him.

Tall men were her weakness. She adored looking up while they bent to her level. For the rest of her life, she'd remember how he picked her up like she weighed nothing and pressed her back against the wall. She'd remember being eye to eye with him. And she'd remember his mouth covering hers, his warmth overtaking her, his intensity and his thoroughness.

She clung to his shoulders and wrapped her bare legs around his waist. Because *skirts*. Skirts were her new best friend and made it possible for her sensitive skin to rub against the soft fabric of his shorts. His belt scraped against her belly. It was all so delightful she thanked him by fisting a hand into his hair and twisting in encouragement. He hoisted her farther up the wall. The ugly artwork shuddered on its hooks. She sighed in complete grinding-together bliss.

His shirt was in the way, and she worked at getting one of her hands underneath the thin cotton. There was no way to yank it off him. His hands were full of her panty-clad ass, and he couldn't raise his arms. She managed to make a little headway, and his bared skin jerked under her touch. He groaned and trailed his lips along her jawline. She stretched her neck in offering.

Because yes, please.

The tiny break in contact allowed enough time for him to develop a conscience. His hands soothed rather than raced. Lips that had devoured her own a second ago, gentled. He broke off their kiss and rested his forehead against hers. His eyes were so green. So intent. So full of regret.

"We have to talk."

His words came out broken and tattered, but they still came out. He lowered her to her feet. With careful movements, he led her to his cheap couch and sat her down. Her skin scratched across the rough fabric, and her panties were literally in a bunch, but she was too embarrassed to straighten things out.

He sat down beside her, and she imagined him assuming the same position with countless victims. Asking the tough questions. Giving bad news. The worst news. As he managed the unmanageable. The frightened. The hurting. The reticent. He wrapped a hand around her cold fingers and prepared, she knew, to manage her.

She gritted her teeth. "I swear, if the next words out of your mouth are 'it's not you, it's me,' you're going to be walking funny for a week."

But she laughed like she was joking. And wasn't

this all so amusing instead of tragic. For her.

"Grace."

"Oh, my God, you are." She fell back and covered her face with her hands, her humiliation scenting the air like overripe fruit.

He tugged her hands away from her face. "That wasn't what I was going to say."

"Then just spit it out already."

She'd thought his eyes were green before? His knuckles brushed her cheek. "I was recruited by a gang unit with the Toronto Police Service. They had heard of our work taking down Raphael Tessier and dismantling the Prairie Brotherhood. They offered me a job."

"You're leaving?" His answer was written in the harsh lines of his face. She removed his palm from her cheek and very maturely settled it back onto his lap. "When?"

"In three weeks."

So soon.

"I want this job, Grace. It's what I've been working my way toward. But if it weren't this position, it would be another one. My time here is done."

If there was one thing Grace knew how to do, it was take a hit. "Time to leave this backwater, huh?"

"I've never considered Aspen Lake anything other than my home."

"*Temporary* home," she insisted. It was important to get it right, for him to admit it out loud.

His Adam's apple bobbed. "Yes."

She'd known that. She had. Police officers came and went, especially in rural areas. Unlike Chase who was happy to stay. Knowing it meant she could do dignified defeat. Be happy for him. That's what mature, adult people did.

"I'm glad for you. It's what we're supposed to do with our lives. Have dreams. Chase them."

The void she'd told Hope about earlier in the week spread a little wider, got a little darker, stole a little more of her resolve. She was so tired. All she wanted to do was crawl under the covers and stay there for a week. Or three.

He was touching her again. Her hand this time. His fingers wrapping around hers. "It wasn't my intention to hurt you. Or lead you on. That's the last thing I wanted."

"Oh, well, I think I've done more than my share of the leading. Take five minutes ago as an example." She produced an unnaturally fake laugh and withdrew her hand from his warm grasp, before she did something stupid like burst into tears.

"I've wanted to. So many times." He swallowed. "I just didn't see any way for us to work."

Wait. What?

Had she heard correctly? Was he confessing to an attraction? Now? On pretty much the eve of his leaving town?

"I have to go." She rushed for the door.

She made it as far as the door before Mike hemmed her in from behind, gently shutting the door and ensuring she failed to escape. His breath was hot against her ear. "I didn't want to be one more responsibility you had to juggle. One more reason you didn't get enough sleep. I didn't want to be another person you lost when I left. Because I was never going to stay. *I can't.*"

The last two words were ripped from him until they

hovered jagged and bleeding on the air. She forced her hand to twist the door handle and yank it open. He didn't try to stop her from rushing through it and down the hall.

Inside her car, she dropped her head to the steering wheel. She couldn't face Hope, so home was out. The beach beckoned, and she put her car in gear and made it to the parking lot, thankful to find it all but deserted in the gathering dusk.

She had enough presence of mind to grab a blanket from the backseat, then she headed for a secluded part of the beach, away from the few stragglers still walking the paths. She picked a familiar spot, one her family had favored in happier times.

Wrapped in the blanket, she hugged her knees to her aching chest and let the gentle ebb and flow of the water soothe her. Crickets rubbed out a lullaby while gulls swooped, and her phone vibrated for the fourth time in ten minutes. She ignored it, choosing to stare out over the twinkling water.

Her friends were all so dizzyingly happy, and she wasn't the kind of person who begrudged others joy. But she was tired of swimming in all that pleasure and feeling like she was drowning because she didn't have her life all figured out.

He was leaving. For good. And it was great. *It was.* One problem solved.

Her phone vibrated again.

Lily*: Are you okay?*

Obviously, Mike had given up trying to get a response out of her and had enlisted her friends. But she could not bring herself to type out a casual *yes* or *fine* or *why wouldn't I be?*

She tucked her phone away. There was movement in front of her. A couple stopped, their toes at the water's edge. The guy dropped down onto one knee perfectly content to get wet for the woman he loved. His girlfriend lifted her hands to her lips in a beguiling Hollywood movie gesture of disbelief when he produced a ring box. Her hiccup of joy ghosted over the water.

Grace lifted weary eyes to the starry sky. "Really?"

There was no way to avoid seeing the man slip the ring on his beloved's finger or the way she pulled him up and into a hug. They hadn't spotted Grace, her unintentional voyeurism concealed by shadows.

Her phone buzzed one more time. Desperate for a distraction, she picked it up.

Mike: *I just want to know you're OK.*

Alerted by her vibrating phone, the couple giggled and stumbled their way down the beach.

More texts.

Lily: *I have ice cream.*

Kate: *Here if you need me.*

She considered tossing her phone into the lake.

In three weeks, he'd be gone. Off to follow his dreams. That's what smart, ambitious people did. What would a grown man with his shit together see in a woman who was coasting along? Letting circumstances dictate her direction?

Starting tomorrow, she was getting a life, creating a solid business plan. No more stalling. She'd wanted to branch out for some time, but hadn't. She needed to update her website, but hadn't. Order supplies, but hadn't. Do more networking, look for a new place to live, but hadn't. Because she was too tired. Too busy.

Too…scared to take a chance. That changed right now.

The next time her phone rang, she answered, determined to impose some necessary boundaries. "I'm fine. You can quit calling."

"I'm relieved to hear it." The voice was unfamiliar. Male. Older.

God, what now? She struggled to sit up straighter. "Who is this?"

"Kevin Hunt."

She froze in confusion. "The politician?"

Because what the hell…

"I was wondering if we could get together and talk. Over dinner."

"How did you get my number?" She couldn't resist a nervous glance down the dark, deserted beach.

"It's important."

Well, pompous the shit out of him.

"It's about your mother." He cast his words like bait, looking to hook a flounder.

Don't engage. Don't— "What about her?"

"What I have to say is best said in person."

No one had ever uttered those words with the intention of doing good. "Then you've got a bit of a problem on your hands because it's not going to happen."

"You're not interested in the truth, Grace?"

His patronizing use of her first name infuriated her. "If you've got information regarding my mother's death, you should be talking to the police."

"Even if it's not in your father's best interests?"

It was the wrong night to play games with her. "I'm hanging up."

"I had hoped you'd be smarter than that."

The animosity in his voice was palpable. "What has my father ever done to you?"

He laughed, not kindly. "More than you've been led to believe."

She massaged the space between her eyes. "What's that supposed to mean?"

"Meet me and find out."

The guy could go to hell. "No."

"I care justice is served. As should you. For your mother's sake. Dinner. Tomorrow."

Damn him. "For a drink. Not dinner. In public."

"I'll text you the time and place. And Grace?"

"Yes." But she knew what was coming. Read the subtle threat in his voice.

"Best we keep our little get together private."

"Best for who?"

"I'm not the one with a crime to solve." He disconnected.

Her phone vibrated a few seconds later.

Hunt: *Sunday 7:00 pm @ The Pines.*

Fine by her. She'd show Kevin Hunt she wasn't as easily manipulated, or as stupid, as he seemed to think. Righteous indignation shoved thoughts of Mike and his new job in an exciting new city to the side. In order to move on, she needed to do what she could to find out what had happened to her mother and lay the past to rest.

Chapter Seven

After a sleepless night and a frustrating start to his early morning shift, Mike was more than ready to join the line of Saturday morning coffee seekers at Mary's. He did his best to dodge questions about the early morning fire that had leveled Mason Pearce's garage while he waited for Mary to fill his order. Three weeks until he'd be able to order his coffee in obscurity. Twenty-one days until he was the observer not the observed. Not that he was anti-social. But some days, like today, he wasn't a great candidate for small talk.

He massaged his stiff neck, and the scent of caffeine eased the pounding ache in his skull. His phone vibrated with another text from Elizabeth, asking to meet and discuss Justin's memorial. There was no getting around the necessity of a face-to-face meeting, so he typed back an affirmative.

The continued absence of a reply from Grace had him resisting the urge to rub at the weighty ache in his chest. It may have been years since his last panic attack, but it was easy and disheartening to recognize the return of those startling symptoms.

His first one had hit the day of Justin's funeral, and the attacks had become commonplace the first months after losing his brother. Forced to seek help, he'd given in and filled the doctor's prescription. Medication along with therapy had allowed him to manage his anxiety.

Just one more secret he kept.

A nudge brought him back into the present. Mary handed him his order. "You were a long way off."

Mike dredged up a smile for one of his favorite people. "It's been an interesting morning."

"I heard." She patted his shoulder. "Got your favorite curry chicken club for lunch special today. You come by. It'll be my treat."

He might prefer a cosmopolitan center, but he would miss the folks who gave small town communities personality and warmth. People like Mary who'd welcomed him and who would do the same for his replacement. He gave her a rare peck on the cheek. "Count on seeing me later."

He climbed into his cruiser and pried off the lid of his to-go cup. The steam of caffeine distracted from the lingering stench of smoke and wet ash. The fire had started just before sunrise, and at first glance, appeared intentional.

Pearce had ranted and raved and was quick to insist Ian Connelly was responsible. That Ian had threatened him after he'd left the baseball game. Mike pulled into the street. He doubted Ian was an arsonist, but it was the perfect reason to pay the man a visit.

With Chase off to take Lily to a doctor's appointment in the city, the timing was right. Mike hadn't mentioned the question of Grace's paternity to his partner. They were going to butt heads over Mike keeping information from him, but Mike was determined to protect Grace's privacy a while longer.

A thought of Grace, with her hair a tousled mess and her lips plump from their kiss, pushed through the barrier he'd erected. But indulging in the sexy image of her legs wrapped around his waist, of her hands fisting in his hair, when she was hurting and angry made him squirm. He had no right to replay those intimate moments for his own selfish private pleasure after what he'd done.

Soon enough Ian Connelly's ranch style bungalow loomed in front of him, a dog lazing on the wide steps. The grass was trim and the hedges clipped. Surprisingly, flowers bloomed at the base of the porch. Connelly's ancient work truck was parked in front of a doublewide garage, beside a newer, darker blue version of the same make and model. Surprise, surprise, Pearce had reported spotting an unfamiliar blue truck in the area.

Ian never had much to say on the rare occasions Mike had contact with him, and he doubted this meeting would be different. Mike exited his vehicle as the older man stepped out his front door.

Ian saluted him with his coffee mug. "Constable."

The dog greeted Mike's climb up the porch steps, and he bent to hold out his hand for the aging German shepherd to sniff. "Do you have a moment to talk?"

"Guessing I don't have much choice." Ian tilted his head in the direction of the screen door. "Coffee?"

He doubted Ian's version would measure up to the one he'd purposefully left in his vehicle, but he nodded. "I wouldn't say no to a cup."

The dog followed them inside, and Ian quietly ordered him to a bed in the corner. Once coffee was poured, they seated themselves at the scarred wooden table. Ian waited, his hands flexing around his cup, his back a little too straight.

Mike attempted to put him at ease. "I've got a

couple of questions to ask you, if that's all right?"

Ian shrugged. "Can't say for sure until you ask 'em."

Mike got straight to the point. "What can you tell me about the time Cassandra Bighill went missing?"

Ian lifted his cup, sipped, set it back down, and did his best to hide his surprise at Mike's question. "Nothing."

Mike wrapped his hands around his own mug. "Anything at all would be helpful."

Ian wasn't fooled by Mike's attempt at camaraderie. "Wasn't around."

Mike set his cup aside and leaned forward. "But you were in contact with Cassandra Bighill before she disappeared."

"No."

At the boldfaced lie, Mike squared his shoulders. "We both know that's not true."

The dog whined, got up, and put his head in Ian's lap. His owner eased his distress with a few strokes of his head. "It's okay, boy."

Mike needed to remember the man in front of him had survived ten years in a maximum-security prison. He doubted he could intimidate him. That meant appealing to his sense of honor. "I think you have information that could help me figure out what happened to her."

Ian crossed his tattooed arms over his chest, proving he knew a thing or two about intimidation. "Wrong again."

Mike tossed down his ace in the hole. "Closing this case would mean peace of mind for Cassandra's daughters. For Grace."

If he was upset at the mention of his daughter, it didn't show. "I've got work to do."

"That's not very cooperative of you."

Ian didn't smirk, sneer, or offer any kind of reaction. The man was cold-stone calm. "We're done here."

Mike lifted his chin. "I don't want to be having this conversation either, but I care about her, too."

Ian looked him dead in the eye. "Have a good day, Constable."

Mike kept his seat as the other man gained his feet. He did his best to keep any judgment out of his voice. "Ian, she deserves to know the truth."

"You can forget what you think you know."

"It's too late for that." Ordinarily, Mike lived for challenges like these. Breaking down barriers, getting to the truth, discovering a piece of the puzzle. Mike beckoned at Ian's empty seat. "Sit down, Ian. For your daughter's sake."

"Leave it be." Each word was a warning.

Looking at Ian with his dark hair and stubborn chin, Mike wondered how no one had figured out Grace was his biological daughter. "Someone buried the mother of your child in the woods. They left her to rot in the dirt. Like she was trash."

Ian's eyes narrowed the tiniest bit, but otherwise all Mike got was dogged silence.

Mike pried, searching for a crack or advantage he could use. "Why did you warn Grace away from Hunt?"

Ian's nostrils flared.

Mike leaned back and lifted a booted foot and braced it over his knee, made it plain he wasn't going anywhere. "I've read your file. Hunt made no secret of the fact he thought you should have served time for first-degree murder. Insisting you brought the knife to the bar that night with the express intention of killing his brother."

Ian's jaw worked, the muscles straining and stretching in an attempt to keep his mouth shut.

Mike changed tactics. "Were you and Cassandra Bighill having an affair at the time of her death?"

Ian's fist hit the table. "She wasn't that kind of woman."

Mike buried his flinch at the fact he had been that kind of man and concentrated on what he suspected to be the truth. "Right. You gave a woman you care nothing about thousands of dollars to keep a roof over her head."

Ian's Adam's apple bobbed.

"Sit down, Ian."

Ian's expression flatlined, but he sat.

Mike wasn't done poking the bear. "Maybe you considered the cash donation child support?"

"Don't." The man who'd stabbed another man outside a bar one dark night thirty-one years ago bared his teeth.

"What do you think is going to happen when a man who hates your guts finds out you have a daughter?" Mike let the silence stretch as thin as fishing line. "And when it becomes obvious she doesn't have a clue? He's either going to tell her and blindside her, or use the information against you."

In a flood of rippling hatred, Ian swept the contents of the table to the floor. For the first time in his career as a cop, Mike considered the possibility he might have to pull his service revolver. The dog clambered to his feet with a growl, teeth bared. Much like his owner.

"Call off your dog."

"Duke." His sharp command satisfied his dog, who settled into a wait-and-see stance.

Conscious of both man and beast, Mike met Ian's glare, relieved to find his wrath waning. "This discussion is about protecting Grace. Hunt is this close to figuring it out."

The man aged five years in the time it took for his shoulders to sag and his spine to curve. The chair met his slump downward. When his breath stuttered, he paused a moment before continuing, "He's never stopped trying to make me pay for Greg's death."

"What do you mean?"

Ian's laugh was low and mocking. "He's messed with me for years. Can't prove it's him. Don't own a cell phone, don't do email. Somehow he finds out. He screws things up at my bank. Cancels utilities. You name it. However he can. Whenever he can. But he's kept it to petty shit."

"You expect me to believe a career politician with an impeccable reputation has nothing better to do with his time than turn off your water?"

"Call it whatever you want."

"Have you reported him?"

Ian was lost in thought. "But he hasn't bothered with me since…"

"Ian." Mike called him back from the fog he'd disappeared into. "Since when?"

The grooves etched into his cheeks deepened. "The night at the Back Forty. The way he looked at her? I prayed I was wrong."

The time for secrets was over. "You have to tell her the truth. Before Kevin Hunt tells it for you."

Ian shook his head. "That's Martin's call. Not mine."

Mike's patience snapped. "Martin is ill. He's in no condition to make that call."

"I promised *her*." The agony in Ian's voice had Mike looking away.

He was more than acquainted with pacts forged in guilt. Ones born of love were foreign to him. Maybe that's why he'd always felt uncomfortable around Ian. Ian had paid the price for his part in Gregory Hunt's death. His mother had never publicly revealed his affair with Elizabeth or the details of what had happened the night Justin had died. He'd never had to face people's censure. Their judgment. Only his mother's. And his own.

"And it's admirable. You keeping your secret like you did. Because you loved her, you did the only thing you could to look after your family."

"Thanks to his brother, I don't have a family."

"You do," Mike insisted. "She lives down the road from you."

Ian braced his knuckles against the solid wood surface of the table and lifted out of his seat. "If he hurts her, he dies."

Ian may have whispered the threat, but Mike heard him clear enough. "Don't say things you don't mean."

Ian's lips barely moved. "If I said it, I meant it."

Not wanting to fuel Ian's temper but needing to know, Mike asked, "Did Kevin Hunt's sense of revenge extended to Cassandra and Martin?"

"I don't know." Ian's frustration was clear,

touchable. Penetrable.

Mike wanted him off balance. "A week before she disappeared, Cassandra went to the police, concerned she had a stalker."

Ian's mouth went slack. "What?"

"You didn't know?"

"I told you, we weren't in touch." He raised his hand and let it drop. "A school picture each year and the one request for money. That was it."

Mike was tempted to believe him, didn't mean he did. "I'm going to need a list of Hunt's harassment attempts."

"What good is that going to do, except stir shit up?"

It gave Mike another place to look. "Just collecting information."

"You're going to provoke him. How's that going to help Grace?"

He didn't take orders from civilians. He changed tactics again. "Where were you this morning, between the hours of two a.m. and six a.m.?"

"Asleep for most of it. Feeding cattle for the rest of it."

"Not going to ask why I'm curious?"

"Don't need to." Ian shrugged. "Already heard about Pearce's fire."

"He seems to think you had something to do with it."

Ian gave him a bland look and didn't offer an explanation.

"Not answering questions isn't very helpful of you."

"Not my job to figure out who burned down that

asshole's garage."

"No, it's mine. Did you threaten him on Sunday? At the game."

"Like I said, if someone hurts her…"

"You're not helping yourself here, Ian."

"I wouldn't waste so much as a match on that asshole."

"What did you say to him?"

"Friendly warning."

"Specifically?"

"Might have mentioned I'd heard he'd lost big at a poker game the night before and that his boss must be overpaying his employees."

Premonition reared its unreliable head. "Meaning?"

"It was a damn big pile of money for a man making a mechanic's wage to lose."

"I don't have time to drag the information out of you, Ian."

"Pearce is earning extra money from somewhere. Or someone." Ian ran an impatient tongue over his gritted teeth. "Hunt's real fond of his cars. Got quite the collection. Gets them serviced in Glenville. At Henley's Garage. Seems he almost always requests one mechanic in particular."

"Guess Hunt's not the only one keeping track of someone."

Ian said nothing. Still, it was quite the coincidence, considering Mike had spent a considerable portion of his morning with an angry mechanic employed by Henley.

Mike dug a card out of his pocket. "Call me if anything happens or Hunt contacts you."

Ian stuffed Mike's card in his shirt pocket. He

walked to the door and opened it. "I got chores to do. You have a good day, Constable."

Back in his cruiser, he scrubbed a hand over his face and thought about Pearce showing up at the Back Forty and going out of his way to insult Grace. Pearce targeting Grace at the baseball game. Pearce's remark about her not needing any more enemies.

He needed to look closer at Pearce and into Ian's claims of harassment. He needed to know if Hunt's vengeance extended to the rest of the group in attendance that fateful night. If it did, Grace, with her connection to Martin and Ian, was next in line to face Hunt's hostility. He wasn't about to let her face it alone.

****

Mike rattled his way up Martin Bighill's rutted driveway, not surprised to find Grace's ancient Jeep parked in the yard. He'd intended on talking to Martin in private, but if that weren't possible, he'd use the opportunity to check on Grace. He was one step away from approaching the screen door when Grace appeared on the other side.

He refused to be swayed by the aloof look in her eyes. "Is your father home?"

She slung a dishtowel over her shoulder. "Today's not a good day."

The words came out of nowhere, spur-of-the-moment and delivered without any finesse. "I'm sorry about yesterday."

"Good for you."

It wasn't the time to press her. Mike attempted a reassuring smile. "I'll do my best not to upset him."

Grace continued to block the door. "Like I said, not a good day."

She was angry. She had a right to be. But her antagonism couldn't prevent him from doing his job. "I'm not here to accuse him of anything, but I do need to speak to him."

"Gracie, who's out there?"

She didn't break eye contact. "No one important, Dad."

The fluttery warnings of an impending panic attack presented themselves. He was the worst kind of asshole. He was no good for her. For anyone. He reminded himself her anger wasn't the end of the world. That he had her best interests at heart. That he was doing the best he could for both of them. And he fought to step back from the impending sense of dread.

"Constable Davenport, is there news?"

He looked past Grace's worried frown to the haggard-looking man behind her. "Not yet, sir."

Martin gave his daughter a look of reproach. "Gracie, let the man in."

Mike got a better understanding of Grace's warning once he was inside the house. He tried to hide his reaction to the cloying scent of body odor, proving Martin hadn't showered in days.

Martin attempted to straighten his stained shirt with a hand that shook and a gaze that wandered. When he staggered, Mike put a hand out to steady him. Grace was right. He wasn't going to get answers out of Martin in the condition he was in.

Lashing out at the man for succumbing to a chronic disease was unfair and inappropriate, but that's exactly what Mike wanted to do. He relaxed his grip on Martin's arm and focused on what he could do for Grace. "Do you think you could give us a minute?"

She hesitated, clearly not wanting to indulge him.

Her father nodded at her. "It's okay, Gracie."

"Fine. I'll be out on the stoop. Doing whatever." She shoved her hands into the back pockets of her cut-off shorts and banged her way out the back door. As promised, she didn't go far.

Martin shuffled his way into the kitchen. "What can I do for you, Constable?"

He wasn't overstepping. He was doing his job by helping out a needy member of his community. Mike kept his voice low. "You'll feel better once we get you cleaned up."

He allowed Martin a brief second of bewilderment, then guided him up the stairs with a firm hand. The man was going to shower if Mike had to shove him under the water. When he was clean, he'd make Martin a sandwich, and after they'd eaten, they would talk.

Mike located Martin's bedroom with little effort and waited while Martin dug out a fresh change of clothes from a neatly packed drawer and closed himself in the bathroom. When he heard running water, he headed back downstairs.

Grace pushed in beside him when he opened the fridge door. "What are you doing?"

He grabbed a package of cold cuts and some mustard, not trusting himself to speak.

She made a move to grab the deli fixings back. "I'm fully capable of making my dad a sandwich."

"Sit down." He made no effort to soften his words. His anger was too close to the surface to manage subtleties. "I'm making your dad a sandwich. Then I'm making sure he eats the damn thing."

She gave up her tug of war over the sliced ham.

"While I sit here and do what? Give myself a manicure?"

He tossed aside the stupid ham and wrapped his hand around her wrist. He lifted her arm, bringing attention to her chapped knuckles. "Would that be such a bad thing? Taking time to do a little something for yourself?"

Humiliation flooded her lovely dark eyes, but he was too angry and scared for her to find the right words.

She yanked her hand free. "What I do in my spare time is none of your business."

He stepped back because it was either that or pull her close and never let her go. "You're right. I can't tell you what to do. I can only create an opportunity."

Overhead the shower shut off, and they both glanced at the ceiling. Her worry was a tangible thing. "I can't—"

"You can and you will."

He expected anger. He could have dealt with anger. But he was powerless against her defeat and sadness.

He tossed the bread aside. "Grace—"

"Don't."

Thank God he was wearing Kevlar because that one bitter word and its accompanying shudder were bullets to the heart. He'd never seen her looking so small. So defenseless. So closed off.

Christ, he couldn't breathe. "I can't do this," he whispered.

"Do what?" she asked. Then her hand was on his arm, and her voice was a mix of concern and frustration. "Hey, are you okay?"

Soon you won't hear her voice at all.

Again, words were tumbling out of his mouth.

"Last night. I didn't mean any of…that's not what I want. Have dinner with me? Tomorrow night. One meal. To explain."

His plans with Elizabeth didn't matter. They could reschedule. He wanted one dinner, to hear her laugh, to see her smile, to think of her as his. "Please."

He managed a weak laugh when she continued her worried inspection of his face. "But you said—"

"Forget last night. Forget everything I said."

"I-I can't. I have plans." She stumbled over her words, a guilty blush blooming across her cheeks. "A thing. With someone."

"Someone?" In his head his question came out a satisfying mix of casual and mildly confused, not broken and suspicious.

She reached out. "It's not like that. I-It's business."

"No problem." She was lying, but he didn't have the emotional wherewithal to figure out why. He backed up enough to clear her way to the door. "And you're right. It's none of my business."

The screen door slammed shut behind her. He waited for the cleansing rush of relief that never came. He braced his hands against either side of the doorframe and bowed his head. And almost jumped out of his skin when a hand touched his shoulder.

Martin staggered back when Mike spun around. "I'm sorry. I didn't mean to startle you."

"It's fine." Mike swiped a hand over his face.

"You care about her." When he remained silent, Martin clarified. "Grace."

Mike was all too aware of who he meant. So hyperaware he was ready to crawl out of his own skin.

Martin spent an extra second trying to figure out

what to do with his fluttering hands. In the end, he tucked them under his freshly cleaned armpits. "You're a good man."

Mike wasn't sure if Martin was asking, stating, or both. Mike moved past him to the counter and yanked open the bread bag.

"You might as well join me." Martin surprised him by reaching over and pulling out two more slices from the bag and passing them over. "This might go easier if we're both eating."

Once they were seated at the table and a couple of bites in, Mike broached the subject he'd come over to discuss. "Mr. Bighill—"

"Call me Martin, please."

"Martin—"

"I know how all this must look to you." He laid his sandwich down on his plate.

"Not here to judge." Mike handed his sandwich back to him. "I'm not much of a chef, but it would be a shame to waste it."

Martin managed another mouthful. "I hope you know how much my girls mean to me."

Mike set his own sandwich down. "I do."

"My wife meant a great deal to me, too. I didn't kill her. That's what you're thinking, isn't it?" He waved a hand to encompass the whole room, neater because of Grace's efforts but in a sorry state all the same. "Because of how all this looks, that I must have killed her?"

"That's not what I'm thinking. But I do have questions. Difficult ones that you might not want to answer."

He attempted a weak smile. "But you're going to

ask them anyway."

Mike grabbed a napkin and dusted off his hands. "There's no way to make this easier, so forgive me for being blunt. I know you're not Grace's biological father."

Martin's face lost what little color his reclusiveness allowed. "Grace is my daughter." He thumped his chest. "Mine."

Hoping to mollify him, he nodded. "Yes, she is. In every way that counts. But it doesn't change the fact that she's Ian's biological child."

"He swore he would never…"

"Ian didn't tell me." Mike rolled his shoulders to ease the tension and fudged the truth. "I figured it out."

"Y-you figured it out?"

"And if I did, others will, too."

He clutched at Mike's hand. "You have to keep her safe from him."

Mike didn't pretend to misunderstand. "Has Kevin Hunt harassed you in any way?"

Martin paused, then chose his words with care. "Not in a way I can prove."

That sounded familiar. "Why don't you tell me the story, and we'll worry about proving it when you're done."

"I was stupid." Martin rubbed at his ear, a little bit of embarrassed color coming back to his face.

Much like he'd done with Ian, Mike settled his arms on the table and leaned in. "I'm not here to judge."

"Years ago, weeks before Cissy disappeared, I was offered an opportunity to invest in a junior oil company." Martin shoved his plate to the side. "There was a man. He had a prospectus, geological surveys, and expert opinions. Everything checked out. There were phone numbers to call. And I did. I talked to a person."

"But?"

"Turns out the company didn't exist."

"How much money did you invest?"

"All our savings." Martin ran a hand over the scarred table like he was taking comfort from the grain of the wood. When he finally met Mike's look, his anguish was terrible to witness. "And more."

Mike crossed his proverbial fingers. "Do you still have the information?"

"Of course. I've kept everything."

Mike followed Martin up the narrow stairs to the stifling upper story and helped him shift boxes until Martin found the one he wanted.

"He wasn't the professional he claimed to be. It only looked that way on paper." He pulled out a bundle of glossy papers and handed them to Mike.

The name Prairie Gold Resources was stamped out in raised lettering. "I'd like to send this to someone in the Financial Crimes Unit."

Martin shuffled his feet. "It was so long ago I can't see how it'll help."

"It might be useful in determining if you were one of numerous victims or if you were singled out as a one-time target. Were there other victims in the area that you know of?"

"I didn't ask around." He hung his head. "It was clear enough when the dust settled who'd been behind it. I just couldn't prove it."

"Kevin Hunt has never contacted you directly?"

"All because of that horrible night…"

Despite the cloying heat of the second floor, Mike felt a chill. "Is there something else you're not telling me, Martin?"

The man blinked back into the present and was quick to reassure him. "No."

Mike didn't believe him. "Have there been other instances, other unusual circumstances?"

Martin's face twisted. "Other than my wife disappearing?"

"Which is exactly why you need to tell Grace the truth."

Martin's shoulders straightened as his spine clicked into place one vertebra at a time. "Or you'll do it for me?"

"You have a week."

Mike showed himself out.

****

Cyberstalking Kevin Hunt was boring, but it was better than wasting time regretting saying no to Mike's dinner invitation. He was leaving, after all. For good. And it wasn't Grace's problem he was second-guessing how they should spend his remaining time in Aspen Lake. Did she really want to sit across from him oozing pheromones while he scarfed down chicken and noodles and talked about the weather?

She was almost positive she did not.

"What are you doing?"

"Nothing important." Grace snapped her laptop shut. "You?"

"Same." Hope filled the teakettle. "So…ever going to tell me what happened with tall, blond, and stuck up?"

"No." Grace eased the lid off a plastic food container. Bingo. Cinnamon pumpkin muffins. Her favorite.

Hope slapped her wrist. "They're for Levi and Scott."

"With the amount of food you're shoving at them, they'll be lucky to fit through the door in a couple of months. I'll be doing them a favor by eating one." After her next dodge and grab met with success, she groaned around a mouthful of moist muffin. "Oh, my gosh, these are delicious."

"Glad you approve," Hope mused. "Pass me a mug, will you?"

Grace handed over a pretty, green one. Hope tossed a teabag in her mug and doused it with boiling water. "I'm guessing the big date didn't go so well."

"It wasn't a date." Grace crammed in another mouthful of muffin.

Hope dunked the teabag a couple of times. "What happened?"

Grace flushed a lump of muffin down with a mouthful of coffee. "Nothing. We talked."

"Well, something happened." Hope lumbered over to the table and sat down. She patted the seat beside her. "Spill."

If she was going to give accepting help when offered a try, she needed to start somewhere. Grace plunked her butt in the chair. "He wanted to let me know he's leaving town. He's been transferred to Toronto."

Hope covered Grace's hand with her own. "I'm sorry."

Grace shrugged off her sympathy. "It's no big

deal."

"Yes, it is." Hope squeezed her hand. "I can see how much you like this guy."

It was getting harder and harder to pull off nonchalant, but she tried. "His loss."

"Damn straight it is." Hope moved around in her chair, fighting to get comfortable. "You deserve a guy who wants to give you the world."

"Yeah, well, I'm not expecting some mythical wonder man to walk through the door anytime soon."

"So go out and find him. Or don't bother with a guy at all. Have your own solo adventure." Hope gripped both of Grace's hands, her face determined. "You have cared for this family for seventeen years without compliant. And I don't know what any of us would have done without you. Seriously. But it's time to pass the baton, sweetie. For the sake of your future and your sanity, you need to get a life."

"I have a life," Grace insisted.

Hope squeezed her hands. "Travel. Take some classes. Channel that *Eat, Pray, Love* woman and go find yourself."

"I'm not you. I can't pick up and abandon the people who depend on me." Hope let go of her hands and sat back. Grace closed her eyes. "That came out wrong."

"You won't be abandoning anyone. Jeez Louise, I'm not asking you to change your name and never contact us again, just take a vacation."

She was tired. Depleted. And after the last few days, more than a little sad. Hope was right about Grace needing to make changes, which meant initiating a difficult and honest discussion about a potential problem that threatened them all. "I do have something to tell you."

Hope's brow furrowed. "Sounds intriguing."

Grace took a deep breath. "Kevin Hunt phoned me and insisted I have dinner with him."

"The politician?" Hope wrinkled her nose. "Why?"

"Says he has information about Mom. And he insinuated things about Dad." A sense of foreboding raised the skin on her arms, despite the warm, cheery brightness of her kitchen.

"You told him to go to hell." When she hesitated, Hope gave her a stern look. "Right?"

Grace sighed. "Not exactly."

"You cannot seriously be thinking of meeting this guy."

"It's not like we don't have questions."

"You're not going."

She ignored Hope's strict order. "Aren't you even a bit curious about what he has to say?"

"It's creepy. I don't like it."

"I doubt he's dangerous." Grace opened her laptop, found the link, and pushed it over to her sister. "The guy's an actual hero. He rescued a woman and her young son after a car bombing in Bosnia. Was awarded the Cross of Valor."

"Don't care." Hope barely glanced at the screen. "But if you insist on going, I'm coming with you."

"Because a hugely pregnant woman is so intimidating."

"Take Scott with you, then."

Grace shook her head. She'd already decided the less time she spent alone with Scott the better for future family relations. "No."

"They can call that guy a hero all they like, give him medals up the wazoo." Hope tapped a finger on Grace's laptop. "But there's something not right about this guy, and you're not going alone."

"It's only a conversation."

"Yeah, and it's only a drink unless it's got a rufie in it."

"Are you suggesting Kevin Hunt is going to try and drug me?"

"I'm saying I don't trust his motives. And you shouldn't either."

"I don't." She gathered up her hair, slipped an elastic from her wrist, and twisted the strands into a messy bun. "But I also want to hear what he has to say."

Hope braced her elbows on the table. "And if he's bluffing and he's really a creepy old man trying to get in your pants, then what?"

She had a wealth of experience dealing with those men. That situation she could handle. "We need answers, Hope."

"Then we have to tell Scott." Hope stopped her with a fierce look. "I'm done keeping secrets from him. We'll grill burgers and corn on the cob tonight. Have an old-fashioned picnic outside, less claustrophobic for Levi, and have us a Bighill plotting session."

"You promised not to push him, Hope."

"If he doesn't want to come, he doesn't have to. Deal?"

Hope's reasonable compromise secured, Grace went to work and left Hope to handle the details. For once, she didn't give what was happening at home a thought. A little after six and fresh out of the shower, she was carrying a stack of plates and a basket of cutlery to the picnic table when Scott and Levi arrived.

With Hope busy at the grill, Grace waved them over. "Hey, guys."

Usually Levi would have scampered to Grace, eager to tell her his latest video game news, but he hung back, sticking close to his dad. Scott shrugged at Grace's silent question and bent down to whisper in his son's ear. Levi nodded but didn't look up. She was on her way to rescue him when he straightened his narrow shoulders and followed his dad over to Grace.

Scott held out his hands for the plates. "We're here. What gives?"

She kissed the top of Levi's head, then handed him the cutlery. "Food first."

Hope set a heaping platter of burgers and grilled corn on the red-checked tablecloth. "Cheeseburgers anyone?"

Scott studiously avoided looking at his wife and ruffled Levi's hair. "Ready to dig in?"

Levi gave a faint nod, and Scott swung a leg over the bench. Levi nested in beside him. Grace followed their example on the other side. "This looks delicious."

"Wait till you taste the double fudge brownies I made for dessert."

Grace winked at her nephew. "My favorite."

A hint of the dimples he'd inherited from his mother made an appearance as he reached for a bun. "Mine, too."

Scott reached for the corn. "So what's the story with this Hunt guy?"

"Is that the guy Grand-Pops says is a no-good, bloodsucking son of a bitch?" asked Levi, ketchup bottle paused in mid-squeeze.

"Language." Scott dumped a cob of corn on his son's plate.

Grace pointed her fork at him. "Word of advice, never quote Pops. All it'll get you is trouble."

Hope laughed in agreement. "Remember that time he told us Father Francis was an exiled Russian spy who spiced the communion wine with mind-altering drugs?"

"Super funny until you share it with your fellow third-graders during circle time."

Levi snorted out a laugh. "That is so lame. I can't believe you fell for it."

Her chest loosened at the sound of her nephew's laughter. Grace picked up her water glass. "It's lame until you're standing in the corner with your nose pressed against the wall."

Hope's dimples flashed. "Which is where your Auntie Grace spent a considerable amount of time."

Grace stuck out her tongue at her sister. "Unlike the time he told you his dog, T-Bone, turned into a werewolf during the full moon."

"He had a dog named T-Bone?" Levi doubled over laughing and almost toppled off the bench.

"Your mom refused to go near him unless she had garlic in her pockets."

Levi rolled his eyes. "Mom, everyone knows that's vampires."

Hope froze for a brief second at Levi's use of the word mom. "Yeah, well, I wasn't taking any chances. That dog was mean enough on a good day."

Grace smirked in Levi's direction. "He was the size of a teacup."

Hope pointed a pickle in her direction. "Sure he was, didn't stop the whole neighborhood from being terrified of him."

Scott reached for the pitcher of iced tea. "Moral of the story? Do like Auntie Grace says and never repeat a word of what Pops says."

More stories ensued, and by the time Hope started to gather up the plates, the sun was setting. "Brownie time."

Grace nudged her sister back into her seat and poked at Levi. "Come on, help me carry these in, and we'll dish it up."

"I don't mind." Hope lifted out of her seat again.

"She who cooks does not clean."

"I'll help," Scott offered.

"Sit." Grace shot him a warning glare. "Guests don't clean either."

"Hey." Levi stuck out his lower lip. "I'm a guest."

"Yeah, but you're short." She motioned at him to get moving.

"Fine." He shot a smug look over his shoulder. "But I'm making my piece extra-large."

"I knew a smart guy like you would figure out an angle."

Grace dragged out assembling the dessert plates as long as possible while spying on her sister and brother-in-law through the window.

"They're not fighting, are they?" Levi elbowed her aside.

"No." Grace pulled him away from the view of his parents' awkward-looking conversation.

"Weird."

"But good weird." Grace cut the first row of

brownies. "Right?"

"If you say so."

She put an arm around him. "She loves you."

He shrugged. "I guess."

Not for the first time, she wished she had a degree in psychology. She bent down, looked him in the eye. "What's wrong?"

"Why do I have to come here tomorrow night? Why can't I go with you and Dad?"

She brushed a strand of his hair aside. "You don't have to come over if you don't want to. I'm sure your dad would understand and make other arrangements."

"He said I should give her a chance. Since it doesn't look like she's going anywhere for a while." He scratched his head. "Tonight's a trial run."

Grace worked to keep her smile in place. "Fair enough."

"Grandma Walker called her a piece of trash." Levi swiped his finger through the bowl of honest-to-goodness real whipped cream Grace pulled from the fridge. "That Dad should take the new baby when he comes, and we should all go live with her and Grandpa."

Grace shuddered at the thought of her sensitive, vulnerable nephew living under the restrictive, uncompromising rule of Melinda Walker. "She said that? In front of you?"

Levi managed another swipe of cream before Grace moved the bowl out of reach. "Not exactly."

At his careful admission, she lifted his chin. "Have you talked to your dad about this?"

He shook his head.

"Try, okay? You'll feel better." She recognized the

glazed look of emotional overload clouding in his eyes. "Hand me that tray, and let's take this outside."

His eyes pleaded with hers. "Can I eat mine in here? I brought my iPad, and I got a new game."

"Sure." She offered him a plate but held on when he tried to tug it free. "If it makes it easier, you're getting mac and cheese and meatballs for supper tomorrow."

He lifted a shoulder, let it drop. "A new video game would probably make me feel even less sad."

"Uh-huh, nice try." She gave him a gentle push in the direction of the living room, then gathered up the other dessert plates. Hope had lit the candles in the middle of the table, and the tiny flames flickered in the twilight. Not that the romantic lighting had eased the tension.

She handed out the brownies. "Levi's eating his dessert inside."

Scott pulled his plate in close. "What time are you meeting this Hunt guy?"

"Seven." Grace scooped up a spoonful of brownie, caramel, and whipped cream. A second later, she went limp from the chocolaty goodness melting in her mouth. "This is the best thing you've made yet."

"It's not bad." Scott shoveled in another mouthful. "Is someone going to fill me in as to what's going on?"

Grace swallowed another mouthful of heaven and related what she knew about Hunt and the events preceding his invitation.

"So this is about your dad." His flat tone implied it was always about her dad.

She'd take his disapproval over his flirting any day of the week. "That's not fair. None of this is his fault."

Gone

Scott shoveled in another mouthful. "You're too soft on him."

"Scott." Hope shook her head in warning.

He shrugged and wiped his mouth with a napkin. "You know I'm right."

Hope sighed but didn't disagree.

Grace wasn't about to take crap over how she cared for her parent. Not from these two. "You know what, I think it's better if I go by myself."

"Don't be like that." When her only response was a glare, Scott lifted his hands in apology. "I didn't mean to make it sound like you're a…"

"Pushover?"

"You're not going by yourself." Hope gave up on her dessert. "If you won't ask the cop, then Scott's going with you."

At the mention of Mike, Scott balled up his napkin and tossed it on his plate. "I'll pick you up at six fifteen. That will give us plenty of time to get there, and then we'll find out what this asshole has to say."

Hope rubbed her arms. "I still think I should come."

"You and Levi are staying here where I know you'll be safe." An awkward pause followed his revealing words, and Scott cleared his throat. "Grace should stay, too. I'll meet with him. I guarantee he'll no longer be a problem."

Hope's focus wandered to the bird feeder swinging with customers enjoying the replenished supply of seed. "First Mom's body turns up. Now this guy is blackmailing you into meeting with him? It can't be a coincidence."

"Blackmailing is a strong word."

175

Hope gave her a fierce look. "I don't like the way he looked at you the other day, and neither did your cop friend."

Scott frowned at his wife. "Looked at her?"

"Like a man waiting for his steak to fight back."

Grace sighed. "That's a tad dramatic, even for you."

"Promise me you won't underestimate this guy." Hope licked her spoon. "And if he suggests another meeting over fava beans and a nice Chianti, get the hell out of there."

Scott rubbed away the smile curving his lips. "No one's going to mess with my family."

"With *our* family," corrected Hope.

"Better together," agreed Grace, raising her glass.

Chapter Eight

Grace smoothed down the sides of the black dress she usually reserved for funerals and gave her name to the hostess. If you had a desire for fancy food, you came to The Pines. Two brothers had converted the historic building, built and abandoned by French aristocrats in the late nineteenth century, into a first-class steakhouse famous for its cowboy cuisine. Nothing said let's put a ring on it like popping out a jeweler's box over The Pine's blackened bison steak strips. Or so they said.

"Follow me," murmured the hostess.

Staff clad in clichéd white shirts and black pants eased about the room balancing plates. She failed to spot Kevin Hunt, and when the hostess led her through the dining room and down a short hallway, her burgeoning intuition fired off a warning salvo.

"Where are we going?" asked Grace. Scott came up behind her and gave her arm a discreet squeeze.

The hostess gave them both a brief once over. "The private dining room."

Scott nodded his head and detoured to the bar area.

The converted house was a maze of cozy nooks and intimate crannies. A fair distance from the kitchen and bathroom traffic, she was relieved to find the private room cloistered but not entirely closed off, its double doors wide open. She loosened her grip on her useless little clutch of a purse.

She paused at the open doors, and Kevin Hunt dabbed his lips with a napkin. His blue dress shirt was immaculate, and his thinning hair was short and neatly combed. Nothing about his appearance raised a red flag. Until he lifted his head.

"Grace." He beckoned her forward like royalty granting an audience to a peasant. "Please, have a seat."

She changed her mind about the room. Everything about the space was too intimate, from the shimmering candlelight to the elaborate flower arrangement on a side table. Their discussion didn't require china, cloth napkins, or elegantly papered walls.

"If there was one thing I admired about your mother, it was her grit."

The frowning hostess, hand clinging to the chair she'd pulled out, waited for Grace to either sit or leave. And because she was her mother's daughter, Grace settled into her chair.

Once the hostess had departed, Hunt resettled his napkin on his lap, rescued his cutlery, and tucked back into what looked like lake trout. He kept her waiting while he portioned off a piece of fish and worked at masticating the tender offering.

Grace's stomach rolled.

When he was finished chewing, he once again dabbed his lips and then set his plate of half-eaten food aside. He braced his elbows on the table and interlocked his fingers. "I thought it was time you and I had a chat."

Grace doubted their discussion would evolve into anything as cozy as a chat. She set her clutch off to the side and ignored her curdling stomach. "I'm not playing this game with you."

"As you're currently sitting across from me—" He paused, gave an elegant wave of his hand. "—I very much think you are."

He was such a clever fox. But she wasn't one to flap and squawk. Or run. She leaned back in her chair and crossed her freshly shaven legs. "Fuck you."

"Tut, tut, tut. Such language from a young lady." He lifted his wine glass and swallowed a king's mouthful. "Once upon a time, your father said much the same thing to me. Crudeness must be a genetic trait."

The waiter appeared to bus his plate, and Hunt used the awkward silence to study her. She stared back until her eyes stung with the need to blink.

"Can I get you anything to drink?"

Hunt answered for her. "Two coffees, please, Alexander. Make mine a decaf."

"Yes, sir."

She waited until she heard the waiter's footsteps echoing in the hall. "You're wasting my time."

His thoughtful examination lasted another several seconds. "Would it surprise you to know I approached your mother about working on one of my campaigns?"

Grace lifted her chin. "I'm sure there are many things about you that would surprise me."

He was unmoved by her sarcasm. "You'd be right about that, my dear."

Objecting to his familiarity would only win her more patronizing indulgences. "So…I'm guessing she said no."

He inclined his head in agreement. "She suspected me of ulterior motives."

She abandoned the fight not to fidget and nudged her knife into better alignment with its accompanying spoon. She was no good at head games, preferring a more direct approach to conflict, but she doubted she'd get away with stabbing him with her fork. "Golly, I can't imagine why."

He gave the briefest lift of his shoulder. "Or perhaps a guilty conscious was behind her refusal to what can only be described as a very generous offer. Certainly a step up from the gutter of a job she insisted on keeping."

"Are your constituents aware of what a snob you are?"

The waiter returned with their coffees. Once the overly correct Alexander had vacated the room, Hunt nudged the sugar bowl closer to Grace. "I like you, Grace. I don't want to, but I find myself charmed by your rough edges."

"And I wish I cared." She gave an exaggerated flutter of her eyelashes while silently freaking out over his knowledge of her sugar preferences, which she now felt the need to abandon by pushing the sugar bowl back into place. Feeling very Alice-like, she gave a pointed glance at the broad-faced watch on her wrist. "Why don't you get to the point you're so desperately wanting to make?"

Kevin Hunt wasn't fooled by her bravado. Not at all. "You don't look like her."

"I thought we were here to talk about my dad."

"Martin? You don't resemble him either."

She had come of age on innuendo and small-town gossip, and his insinuation wasn't anything she hadn't heard outright. Unfortunately for Hunt, she'd learned to deflect long ago. Buffeted by her mother's insistence Grace resembled her maternal grandmother's side of the family, a clan of Eastern Europeans, she left his taunt hanging. Her triumph was short lived.

"They were all there the night my brother, Gregory, was murdered. Your precious Aunt Stella." He placed a yellowed photograph retrieved from his shirt pocket on the table between them. "Heart attack, wasn't it? And taken so young? One can't help but wonder what telling lies and keeping secrets does to a person. Quite toxic to the system, I imagine."

She fought the urge to leap to her aunt's defense. He wanted her shock, her anger. Her retaliation. She concentrated on the photo. The snapshot was of three young men and two young women. From her mother's yearbook, she knew the one on the left was Gregory Hunt, beside him stood Ian, and next to Ian was her dad. Auntie Stella and her mom stood in front of them, tucked into the middle. Gregory had his arm draped over Stella's shoulder.

"Martin's changed so much, don't you think? Guilt has a way of aging a person." The lines bracketing his mouth deepened, and his nostrils flared the tiniest bit as he tapped the photo. "Connelly, of course, and your sainted mother."

Such acrimony, barely cloaked by a conservative disregard that wouldn't dupe the most gullible of fools. And Grace was no fool. "Either tell me something I don't already know, or I'm leaving."

Hunt picked up his cup and sipped. "Your mother came to see me before she disappeared."

She settled her shaking hands in her lap. "Really?"

"Your parents were on the brink of financial ruin. They were going to lose the farm. I can't imagine how much it would have angered Martin had he found out she'd come to me."

Memories flickered, of angry words, slammed doors, tears, and apologies. She kept her breathing even and got herself under control. "Don't think that because she's been gone a long time that I've forgotten her or what she stood for. She would never have gone to you and asked for money."

"So right, my dear." Hunt leaned forward, his eyes gleeful. "She came to me begging for forgiveness."

The truth staining his words made her flinch. "You're lying."

"I denied her, of course."

Grace refused to sit there, submissive, while he left expensive leather-soled shoeprints all over her. She gathered as much brashness as she could manage and met his narcissistic superiority head on. "We're done here. Don't contact me again, or I'll go to the police."

"Ah, yes, the inestimable Constable Davenport, no doubt. You've developed quite the fondness for him. Unfortunately, he's not for the likes of you."

She struggled to absorb his insult, repressing an involuntary shiver. How much did this man know about her life? "Are you stalking me?"

"I'm afraid our time is up. As lovely as your company has been, I have another appointment." He stood, fished a business card out of his shirt pocket, and held it out. "When you figure out the right questions to ask, I'll be more than happy to satisfy your curiosity."

She would never be desperate enough to fall for an offer of candy from this particular stranger. She racked her brain for a zinger, one last stinger that would go down in history as the best kiss-off ever, and came up blank. Worse, she stumbled up from her chair, her lack of finesse greasing his smile.

Then he was beside her, seizing her arm. "I'll escort you out."

The man had to be in his sixties. He looked like a stiff wind could blow him away, but her instincts warned her not to underestimate him. She jerked her arm free. "I'll walk myself out."

****

Mike was shown to a less-than-discreet table in the center of the main dining room, which suited him fine. He wasn't there for a cozy, intimate dinner in one of the many secluded corners. Bad enough the simple act of waiting for Elizabeth brought back all kinds of sordid memories as The Pines was exactly the kind of out-of-the-way place they had frequented during their affair. But a conversation about Justin's memorial had to happen, and The Pines was as good a place as any.

"Something to drink while you wait, sir?"

"Coffee, please."

"Certainly."

Justin deserved to have his life honored. He'd had a natural talent for the law. A love for it that Mike, with seven years of self-reflection behind him, could admit he'd never shared. But he had more than an aptitude for policing. In law enforcement, he'd found his calling despite his mother's frigid disapproval.

"Michael, it isn't enough to be good at something. You are capable of being the best. Do not disappoint me."

The waiter arrived with Mike's coffee and he nodded his thanks. The rich blend warmed his throat and melted some of the ice coating his stomach. He would stand at a podium beside the woman he'd once loved to honor the brother he'd betrayed and worse. He owed that much to Justin. Then he would be free.

"Michael."

Big hoops peeked out from blonde waves, and thin straps clung to bare shoulders in a dress that met the floor but hugged every curve. The platinum gold necklace of knots and diamonds he'd given her circled her throat.

"Elizabeth." He lifted out of his chair and waited for her to be seated.

Soft pink lips curved to tease. "Once upon a time, it was Beth."

She was smart, sophisticated, and beautiful. He half expected some of those long ago very complicated feelings to rush back. When they didn't, he breathed a small sigh of relief. "That was a long time ago."

"Not so very long, surely?"

The waiter appeared, offering menus and explaining the special of the evening. "Anything from the bar?"

"Vodka rocks." She tilted her head in encouragement at Mike.

He lifted his coffee cup. "No, thanks."

Pretty smile firmly in place, she reached out to toy with the cutlery. "I've missed you. So much."

"I wasn't hiding." The words slipped out, coated in resentment. He cursed himself for letting foolish pride make him sound bitter.

"No, you weren't." She glanced around the restaurant. "It's a charming spot. Justin would have hated it."

It was hard to argue with the truth. "Not nearly urban enough for his tastes."

"But places like this suited us."

Out of the way places like this had been necessary. "I'm not here to talk about our past."

"No, I don't imagine you are. But I am."

They paused when the waiter returned with her drink. "Are you ready to order?"

"A few more minutes, please." Elizabeth indulged in a small sip of her drink as the waiter moved off. "Your mother and I had an agreement."

Shock. Surprise. Disbelief. He wished he could feel any of them. Instead, he felt nothing.

"I agreed to stay away from you…" She laid a hand over the necklace at her throat.

It was a lie. He did feel something, an impatience to get this dinner over and done. Mike closed his eyes and rubbed a hand over his aching brow. "In exchange for what?"

"Her promise to do the same."

She managed to do the unthinkable and surprise him. He hid his reaction behind sarcasm. "How noble."

"You don't know the things she was threatening to do."

"Like fire me, disinherit me, make it impossible to get hired by another firm? I hate to break it to you, but all those things actually came to pass."

She laid a hand over his. "And you survived. Like I knew you would, because you were the strong one."

He swallowed the bile climbing up his throat. It hadn't been easy. Trust fund? Gone. He'd lost his penthouse overlooking the heart of the city in foreclosure. Sold his remaining possessions to pay for cadet training. No more trips to ski, golf, hike, or snorkel. His friends drifted away, and Mike had cut the remaining ones lose.

He slid his hand out from under hers. Then again, he'd deserved to be stripped of those things. He'd given them up without a fight. But he would have kept the woman across from him. "You disowned me, too."

"I bought you seven years of peace." She reached for her drink. "You may think I abandoned you. But I didn't."

The grief, the loneliness, the guilt had been almost too much to bear. "I needed you."

Her smile turned sad. "No, you didn't. You wanted me because Justin had me."

If that's how she'd felt, no wonder she'd refused to see him after the accident. "How much?"

"Excuse me?"

Her pretty blush of confusion didn't sidetrack him. "How much money did you get in return for my seven years?"

"Seven hundred thousand dollars."

He leaned in, not upset by the amount so much as his mother's scheme to set him utterly and completely adrift. "I lost everything. And believe me, money was the least of it. Honor. Self-respect. *You*."

"You don't think I realize that?" Her face settled in hard, unfamiliar lines. "It was my fault. All of it. Justin's death. Your guilt. So I bought you time to regroup. To build a life. Away from your mother's quest for complete control."

"If you're waiting for a thank you..."

Her voice dropped to a whisper. "But I misjudged."

He shook his head, not understanding.

"I thought you'd come back for me when you figured out you could live without the perks of being a

Davenport. But you didn't, and I was left honoring a promise." Elizabeth bowed her head. When she lifted it again, her eyes were wet. "Please tell me it's not too late."

An automatic apology dangled from the tip of his tongue, but he resisted the urge to offer it.

"I miss you. I miss the way things were. In time—"

"No." His refusal was kind but firm.

"Have you had a chance to look at the menu?"

Elizabeth flipped open her menu, her face flushed, her hands shaking. "The oyster mushroom gnocchi, please."

The waiter looked to him. "For you, sir?"

"The special." He swallowed back his utter lack of appetite. "Whatever that is."

"The grilled bison tenderloin with apple slaw is very popular tonight." The waiter left them in a silence made louder by the clink of cutlery and muted conversation surrounding them.

Cool fingers touched his. "If Kevin is elected, I'm going with him to Ottawa to serve as his chief of staff."

That got his attention, because despite his resolve to leave concern for Elizabeth in the past where such feelings belonged, he didn't want to see her hurt. "Are you sure about Hunt?"

Her brows gathered. "Why do you ask?"

"Nothing. Forget it." He let it go. She was an adult, capable of making smart decisions, and very skilled at looking out for herself.

"His reputation is impeccable. His list of achievements long. He cares about his constituents. He—"

"I'm familiar with his resume."

"Is this about Grace Bighill?"

"I'm not discussing Grace with you."

"You need to come to your senses, Michael. Her family is a nightmare. They haven't an ounce of decorum among the lot of them."

"Is this you or your boss talking?"

"I'll admit I did speak with Kevin after the town hall meeting. And while he does have a certain...bias when it comes to Mr. Bighill, you can't argue with the fact she and her family have created their share of drama over the years. My God, in the past two weeks alone, she's been involved in a bar fight and a scuffle at a baseball game."

"Neither of us is in a position to judge another's character or actions."

"You can't possibly think she's an appropriate choice to support you."

His numbness evaporated. "Unlike you? With your 700,000 dollar compensation package?"

She narrowed her eyes. "I know the game and how to play it."

"No doubt about that."

"I know you, Michael." She leaned forward. "You have plans. I'm guessing top brass?"

The waiter arrived with a breadboard and saved him from confirming her assumptions. He was stuffing a mouthful of The Pines famous sourdough into his mouth when Grace rushed into the dining room, followed by Kevin Hunt.

He flashbacked to Grace standing in her father's shabby kitchen and her guilty blush.

I have plans.

"She wouldn't..." But obviously she had.

Elizabeth frowned at him, then looked over her shoulder. She half rose from her seat. "Kevin?"

The space was small, intimate. People were easy to spot. Hunt scanned the room. So did Grace. Her destroyed look when she caught sight of him and Elizabeth together had him choking on his bread. He swallowed. Or tried. Hunt put a hand on her back and steered her toward them, where everything from the pristine white tablecloth, the warm light from the candle, and the tiny table screamed romantic evening for two.

Grace refused to look at Mike, her hands crushing a little purse.

"Elizabeth, what a pleasant surprise. Constable Davenport. Out for a nice dinner, I see."

Mike rose to his feet. Something was wrong. Very, very wrong. Abandoning his manners, he held a hand out to Grace. "Can I talk to you? In private?"

"No." She didn't make eye contact, only continued her extended search of the room.

"We were just catching up before discussing the details of Justin's memorial." Elizabeth's voice was soft, deflecting, conciliatory, searching for a way to save him. Just like old times, and the reminder brought a fresh wave of shame. "And you? Here for dinner?"

"No." Grace rubbed her arms and scanned the room. A second later, her body relaxed.

Until Hunt said her name, and she flinched. "Grace was kind enough to meet me for a drink to discuss a personal matter."

Scott Walker appeared at Grace's side. "Ready to go?"

Grace gave him a relieved grimace. "You have no

idea."

When she was halfway across the room, she glanced back. Gone was the woman with the wry smile, the one who coiled her hair around her finger when she was deep in thought, who teased him into relaxing, although he never let it show. This Grace looked destroyed. By him. And he couldn't let her go thinking the worst.

Mike tossed down his napkin. "Excuse me."

He rushed out the door and caught up to Grace and Scott at the second row of parked vehicles. "Grace, wait."

She prodded at Walker, who was busy scowling at Mike. When he reluctantly moved along and climbed into his truck, they were left alone in the relative privacy of the darkening parking lot.

"Let me explain." He set the matter of her meeting with Hunt aside for the moment. Even though he was worried over Walker's presence, and the fact she'd brought a bodyguard.

"Your cozy little dinner with the goddess is none of my business."

"That's exactly what it is, business."

There was no mistaking her disbelief. "Your food is getting cold."

"What did he say to upset you?" She ignored him and moved to leave, like she couldn't wait to get away from him. He blocked her exit, put a hand out. "Talk to me. Please."

There was the whir of a window gearing down and a blast of bluegrass music. "Davenport, the fact you're a cop won't stop me from getting out of this truck."

He dropped his hand and waited while she climbed

in, waited until they'd wound their way out of the parking lot, waited until they were gone from sight.

A hand landed on his shoulder, and he started. "You've got a beautiful woman waiting inside for you, son. Let that one go."

"What did you say to her?" To put that look in her eyes. That shiver under her skin that the heat of high summer couldn't chase away. It was time to let Hunt know he didn't hold all the cards. "It had better not have anything to do with Ian Connelly."

His words got Hunt's attention but didn't shake his confidence any. "What does one have to do with the other?"

Mike hadn't expected easy from a man with Hunt's history. "That's what I'm asking you."

He gave an elegant shrug. "What could I possibly know?"

Mike allowed his lips to curve and the superiority he'd once bathed in to coat his words. "Leave Grace Bighill and Ian Connelly alone."

Hunt had his own reserves of pretentious condescension. "That's a rather intrepid warning, Constable Davenport."

"I don't care how you perceive things. Just make sure you heed my...*request*." Mike indulged in a casual ignore-my-warning-at-your-peril scan of the area and left Hunt loitering in the parking lot. Inside Elizabeth had finished her meal and was sipping a glass of wine. He sat down, and immediately the waiter was back with his plate.

"I asked them to keep it warm for you."

What little appetite he'd had before had disappeared.

"Are you in love with her?"

The thought of eating made him queasy, but it was better than talking. He spread his napkin over his lap and picked up his knife and fork. "That's none of your business."

"If not in love, then on your way."

"There is no Grace and I." He shoveled a hunk of meat into his mouth, delaying the conversation while he chewed and swallowed and worked at finishing a meal he had no stomach for.

She sipped her wine. Tried to engage him in small talk. When her efforts proved fruitless, she offered him a resigned smile. "I think I'll call it a night, if you don't mind?"

He nodded, more than willing to let her go. "Take care, Elizabeth."

"Goodbye, Michael." She set a piece of paper on the table and walked out of the dining room.

He stared down at the cashier's check made out to him for the amount of seven hundred thousand dollars.

****

Grace replayed her conversation with Hunt, using as few words as possible. When she was done relaying what little she managed to get out, Scott's only reaction was to nod and turn up the song on the radio. Grateful for his silence, she rested her temple on the window glass and ignored the slideshow of pretty cottages, overflowing pots of summer flowers, and evening walkers.

She'd cyber snooped on Mike. Knew he was one of those Davenports. That's what computers were for, after all. Of course, she knew he had a dead twin brother. Was she hurt he'd never confided in her? Sure.

But she'd never pushed him to talk about his family, even though she'd recognized certain far off looks of his. Grief had a feel to it. Detectable only by those who'd experienced it for themselves.

Scott pulled up in front of her little house. She was about to jump out when he turned toward her and sighed. "For what it's worth, he didn't look like he wanted to be there."

She closed her eyes against his gruff admission. "It doesn't matter. He'll be gone in a couple of weeks. New posting."

"Can't say as that news breaks my heart." He held up his hands. "Sorry, but it's true."

She let her head drop back and groaned. "Everything is such a mess."

He put his hand on her thigh, let his fingers linger. "We'll figure it out."

She removed his hand. "Scott, don't."

Levi banged on her window, and Grace looked up to see Hope shutting the screen door and retreating back inside. Levi pulled the door open, and there was no time to chastise Scott on his overstepping before Grace was hopping out as Levi scrambled in.

"You guys take care." She waved.

She found Hope in front of the kitchen sink, up to her elbows in soapy water.

Grace nudged her aside. "Let me do that."

"I'd say no thanks, but I don't have the energy." Hope rubbed her lower back.

Grace scrubbed a pot and rinsed it off. "How did your evening go?"

"No miracle breakthroughs happened, if that's what you're asking." She filled a glass with water.

"Did it at least go okay?" Grace dumped more pots into the sink.

"We played chess." Hope swallowed down some water. "God, what I wouldn't give for a beer right now."

Grace grunted in sympathy. Levi was a huge chess fan. "I'm guessing you lost."

Hope set her half-empty glass down and massaged the spot between her brows. "Seven out of seven times, proving he's smarter than his mother and always will be."

"You're doing great. Don't give up now."

"I'm not. But seeing how awkward he is with me makes me wonder if I can ever make up for leaving him."

"He'll forgive you." At her sister's skeptical look, she dried her hands. "He will. It'll just take some time."

Hope straightened. "Enough about me. What happened with Hunt?"

Grace didn't bother to sugarcoat it. "He said Mom and Dad were on the brink of losing the farm. That she came to him begging for help. No, make that forgiveness."

"As if." Hope shook her head. "She would never air their dirty laundry like that. Can you imagine if Dad had found out?"

Grace raised a brow. "I'm pretty sure that was his point."

It didn't take Hope long to catch up. She held up a hand, eyes defiant. "No. No way."

"I don't believe it either. But one thing was very clear. Hunt is obsessed with our dad. And not only Dad, everyone that was there the night his brother died. You should have heard what he insinuated about Auntie Stella."

Hope frowned. "God, what could he possibly have to say against Auntie Stella?"

"He suggested her heart attack had something to do with her keeping secrets. And telling lies." No one ever had a bad word to say about Stella. Certainly not Grace or Hope, who'd loved her dearly. She'd been there for them before and after their mom disappeared.

Hope scowled in solidarity. "The more I find out about this guy, the more I want to meet him and set him straight on a few things."

"He's got this aura of truth about him." Grace rubbed her arms. "It's…troubling."

"Since when are you the mystic sort?"

Grace's fingers found the ends of her hair and rubbed. "There's something he wants me to know, but I'm not—"

"Hey." Hope squeezed her arm. "Don't give this guy any more mental real estate than he's already taken."

"Maybe I should talk to Dad?"

"You can't be serious." Disbelief widened her eyes. "Since Mom's body has turned up and that stupid town hall meeting, he's slipping. He didn't want you within two feet of this guy. Can you imagine what will happen if you tell him you met with him privately?"

"Ian, then."

"What would Ian know about Mom and Dad going bankrupt?"

"I don't know," insisted Grace. "But it feels like the right thing to do."

"The man doesn't put two words together at the

best of times. I'm sure asking questions about why he went to prison isn't the way to get him to open up."

Grace remembered him hovering over her the night of the bar fight. "Maybe he'll talk to me."

"Well, no one's talking to anyone else tonight." Hope stretched and groaned. "I'm dead on my feet. I say we table this discussion until tomorrow when I can think straight again."

"Good idea. Night." All she wanted was her yarn and her needles. "I'm going to stay up and get some work done."

Grace changed into yoga pants and a tank top and curled up on the living room sofa. Her love affair with yarn had begun as a way of staying connected to her mother, and for years that's all it had been, a hobby. Somewhere in the middle of her twenties, it became less about losing herself in the pattern and the colors. It became more about providing that comfort and warmth to others. But it wasn't until a request from a friend for a custom blanket that her skill with needles and yarn had turned into a cottage industry.

Remembering the vow she'd made the night on the beach, she bypassed her needles and yarn to reach for a notepad and pen. She scribbled the name Prairie Knits across the top. She'd chosen the name on a whim, but it never failed to make her smile. Before she knew it, she was sketching plans for a toque, scarf, and sock set with Christmas craft shows in mind.

She set a goal. Ten sets. To test the items popularity. Then after Christmas, more pop-up markets. For the first time in a long time, she felt inspired to create. Plenty of red, cream, some black, a touch of gray. Another more colorful set of greens, purples, and pinks.

She lifted her head at the sound of a soft knock on her front door. Grace tossed a blanket around her shoulders and tiptoed through the muted light of the kitchen. She eased open the door.

Mike stood under the dim light of the porch, hands in his pockets, head bowed to study the battered floorboards. The same collared shirt he'd worn to The Pines stretched across his broad shoulders, and the same dark denim hugged his hips.

"What are you doing here?"

He lifted his head. "Can we talk?"

There was no denying the appeal in his green eyes. She stepped out onto the porch and motioned for him to follow her around the side of the house to the firepit area. The three-quarter moon and canopy of stars provided plenty of light. Certainly enough to let her know Mike had something on his mind.

"I want to explain about Elizabeth."

His earnestness was going to kill her. It really was. "You don't owe me an explanation. We're not a couple. We're not...anything."

"Then it won't cost you anything to listen."

She inhaled the scents of goldenrod and evening primrose. And then she sat, and she waited, but he was wrong, and it cost her plenty to pretend she was immune to his presence.

He perched on the edge of the chair he'd dragged over so they were knee-to-knee. "It wasn't a date."

"Okay." One-word answers, that was the key to making this as difficult as possible for him.

He scrubbed his hands over his face. "My history with Elizabeth is complicated."

There was no way to remain impassive in the face of his ruined eyes, the messy hair he'd run fingers through, the swallow she tracked all the way down his long throat, but she did her best. "Can we hurry this along? I'm tired."

"I barely remember my father. He died when we were three. Massive heart attack." He threaded his fingers through hers and stared at their combined hands like their connection was an essential service. "I lost my twin brother, Justin, seven years ago."

She tightened her grip, hoping to infuse some warmth into his chilly grip. A haunting *whoo-hoo-ho-oo* added to the sudden eerie silence between them.

"I know. Have known for a while." She managed a whisper. "And I'm so sorry."

His fingers tightened around hers at her admission. "Here's something you likely don't know. My mother? She and I? We're not close."

She didn't know what to say. To do. "Again, I'm sorry."

"Justin and Elizabeth were engaged."

Relief rushed in, followed quickly by guilt for making assumptions. "I didn't realize…"

He let go of her hands and rubbed his palms on his thighs. "We were, um—" He cleared his throat. "She and I were having an affair at the time of his death."

"An affair?" She leaned closer, encouraging him to deny it. Because clearly, she'd misheard. He wouldn't. Couldn't.

He swallowed again, another long painful process that took forever to complete. "He loved her. He'd also won the corner office. He was getting a lot of attention. My mother hinted that a wedding, that kind of stability,

198

might mean an early partnership for Justin at my parents' law firm. He was so…*happy*."

He stumbled over the word like it was an alien concept and not to be trusted. She searched his face. The bleakness, the self-loathing she saw there hurt her heart. His lips thinned. "I didn't like it."

His face was a twist of fierce and unrelenting honesty; exposing shadows of truths she would never have thought him capable of hiding.

"We'd always been competitive. It was encouraged. That didn't change when we became adults. I made it my mission in life to get into her bed. Elizabeth turned me down. Repeatedly. After a couple of months, I gave up. Then she gave in."

Grace pressed a hand to her bruised heart. "I don't want to hear any more."

"I fell in love with her." He said it like the joke was on him. Like he wasn't ripping Grace's heart out.

"Don't do this," she whispered.

"Then Justin died. I thought I would never recover. I didn't want to recover. Then I met you." There wasn't a speck of hope or joy in his words. Nothing to suggest he was sitting across from her ready to breach a gap.

Her very bad feeling morphed into dread. "Why now? Why tell me when you'll soon be gone for good?"

"So you'll have no reason to miss me."

"Is that your plan?" Her fingers knotted in the blanket she'd worn outside to guard against the chill. "To make me hate you?"

His eyes got hard. She knew he was gearing up to hack and slash any remaining connection between them into bloody pieces. She shivered in the moist night air as he lifted his sword of truth and brought it down.

"I think that when I tell you on the night Justin died I was fucking his finance's brains out at the family cabin where he caught us in bed together, you'll get up and walk back into your house and forget all about me."

She lifted her chin. "Then you don't know me as well as you think you do."

He put a hand on each arm of her Adirondack chair, trapping her, chasing away the air. "I betrayed my brother. Because of me, he was driving in a rainstorm. Because of me, he lost control of his car. Because of me, he died on the side of the road, his blood soaking into the ground around us."

She could feel the rain on her skin. Smell the panic that had surely been on the damp breeze. The horrifying image made her desperate to cling to any hint of the man she thought she knew. "You went after him."

He let out a long sigh. "Grace, what you feel for me? I don't deserve it."

"And second chances? Those are for other people, is that it? There were two of you in that bed." His confusion gave her the courage to ask the one question she didn't want an answer to. "Do you still love her?"

He traced a line along her jaw, his eyes tracking the progress of his fingertip until he reached her chin and his hand dropped to his lap. "I'm not sure I ever knew the meaning of the word."

She pressed a hand to his cheek. Brushed her thumb over his skin. He closed his eyes, and whether he realized it or not, leaned into her touch. It wasn't fair to ask him, but there was no stopping the words tumbling out of her mouth when her heart had deemed it time to take a chance. "You could stay. We could figure out what each of us is feeling. Together."

His eyes opened, and he put his hand over hers, catching her fingers next to his skin. "I can't spend the rest of my life handing out traffic tickets and DUI's to the same people."

It was her turn to close her eyes against the truth.

"I can't stay." He gathered her close and kissed the top of her head while his hand smoothed over her hair. "Not even for you."

She slipped her arms around his waist and held on, her forehead pressed to his chest. She breathed in his scent. The temptation to suggest an alternative solution was overpowering. But she had a family who needed her. A little boy who relied on her. A failing grandfather. A mother to bury.

"I need you to do something for me."

She nodded against his chest.

His hands cradled her skull, his words brushing against her hair. "I promise you I will find out what happened to your mother. You can trust me to do that for you. You do not need to put yourself in a situation like you found yourself in this evening."

"I can take care of myself." Had taken care of herself since she'd been thirteen years old.

"I know you can. Better than most. But I'm asking you to leave Kevin Hunt to me. I will get you the answers you deserve. Tell me what he wanted."

She sighed. It was futile, and self-sabotaging, to remain stubborn in the face of his earnest intention. "He didn't say anything. Not really. He was playing with me. He made it sound like he knew things, but he didn't give me anything specific. Just told me to contact him when I had the right questions."

His keen eyes narrowed. "There's more."

She didn't know how to say what she'd learned without implicating her father.

His thumbs caressed the line of her jaw. "Tell me."

There was no resisting his plea. "He hinted my parents were in financial trouble. That my dad would have been angry at her efforts to resolve their problems. That he'd approached her to work on his campaign. Some nonsense about her wanting his forgiveness."

"For what?"

"He didn't say. But it's a ridiculous notion. She would never have gone to him for help. Even as a kid, I understood her aversion to the pity of others."

"What else?"

She bit her lip. "He told me to stay away from you."

"You should stay away from me."

Sadness glistened in his eyes, a second before he lowered his head. She held her breath until his mouth covered hers. Her hands curled into his shirt. But the warmth of his lips couldn't mask the taste of goodbye.

She shivered in the dark. He gathered her closer, his heart hammering out a beat under her fists. She smoothed out her palms. He pulled away, his forehead coming to rest against hers. He gave a gentle tug to the ends of her hair.

"I'm going to miss you. More than you can possibly know."

Then he was gone, the waiting darkness swallowing him whole. She brought her knees up and hugged them to her chest. He was more broken than she'd imagined that day on the street, but putting his life back together. He was a Phoenix rising from the ashes, strong enough to know what he needed to do and committed to making it happen. It still hurt like hell to watch him go.

Chapter Nine

At the beginning of her Friday shift, Grace informed Wayne she was finished after the Labor Day weekend. He'd wished her well, then disappeared into his office and hired her replacement. And just like that, she was unemployed. She couldn't claim it was a rash decision because she'd done nothing but pluck an infinite number of imaginary daisy petals for six long days and nights, ever since Mike had walked away from her.

Quit my job.

Don't quit by job.

Commit to a future she wanted and a vocation she was passionate about or stay the course of safe, employed, and solvent. She still wasn't sure she'd done the right thing, and all she wanted to do was panic in private, but she drove home to find Scott's four-by-four in the yard and her dad's aging pickup next to it.

Inside the house, Levi spotted her first. "Auntie Grace, you're finally here."

"When you're done, there's more to go out." Hope handed her son a stack of paper plates, some plastic cutlery, and hustled him out the backdoor.

Levi mumbled something Grace didn't catch as the door slammed shut behind him.

"Hey, Grace." Scott yanked the fridge door open. "We expected you an hour ago. Beer?"

"My shift didn't end until—"

"These need to go on the grill. Burgers first." Hope hip checked the fridge door closed and shoved a plate of uncooked hamburgers and hotdogs at an annoyed Scott.

He worked at juggling the massive platter and his bottle of beer. "I know how to grill burgers."

"Yes, you do." Hope patted his cheek and aimed him at the door.

Her dad looked up from a large mixing bowl, wooden spoon in hand. "Hey, sweetie."

"Hey, Dad." She narrowed her eyes at Pops who settled in beside her. "Since when do we have family cookouts?"

"That sister of yours threatened to have him committed if he didn't come."

"Huh."

"She also threatened to liberate the door to his office from its hinges." His arthritic fingers formed quotes around the word office. "She can be downright ornery. Did you know that?"

"He showered." While Grace appreciated the clean-shaven jaw and neat hair, she didn't quite trust the illusion. "What did she threaten to make that happen?"

Pops shuddered. "You don't want to know."

Grace blinked suddenly damp eyes. It was all so *normal*.

"Seemed like a good night to get together." Hope shrugged her shoulders in apology. For what, Grace didn't know. Being a good daughter? Mother? Knowing the right thing to do?

"Perfect." So what if Grace asked her dad over for

dinner an average of five times a month only to be turned down every single time? She wasn't going to take his acceptance of Hope's invitation personally. That would be immature. Not to mention churlish. When she'd done a considerable amount of praying for this very thing to happen.

She rubbed at her chest.

Hope comes back and everyone jumps.

An unwelcome and unstoppable laughter bubbled out of her.

Sheesh, ungrateful much?

Why were they staring?

Because you're acting crazy.

"I need to wash up." Grace rushed for the bathroom and locked the door behind her. She leaned against the sink and pointed a finger at her watery reflection. "Stop it. You don't get to do this."

But there she was, hiding out in the bathroom because things were going well with her family. Talk about a new low.

"Be thankful," she whispered.

She pushed her hair out of the way and stole another peek at her face in the mirror. Red eyes, pale skin, lips pressed thin. "This is about you quitting your job."

Her knitting business was important to her, and she wasn't going to apologize for finally making it a priority.

No, she was not.

You hear that, person in the mirror?

Hope's voice drifted through the door. "Are you okay?"

"Yep. Peachy." She rescued her makeup case from

the cabinet. "Just give me a minute, okay?"

"No problem." Long pause. "But someone's here to see you."

Grace frowned at the closed door. "Who?"

Longer pause. "The cop."

Grace yanked the door open. "What's Mike doing here?"

Hope's eyes widened. "Are you crying?"

"No. Maybe. It's nothing." Her grip on the door tightened. "Back to Mike being here?"

"I kind of invited him."

"What?" Grace demanded. "Why?"

"You've been so mopey this week. And it's his fault. I know it is." She avoided eye contact, the meddler. "I happened to bump into him in town this afternoon. Some things were said, and to make up for what might be described as a lapse in judgment on my part, I invited him for supper."

"So help me, Hope." Grace yanked Hope into the bathroom. "What did you say to him?"

"That's not really important." Hope pried Grace's hand loose. "What is important is the fact he cares about you."

Grace planted her hands on her hips to keep from wrapping them around her sister's throat. "Which still doesn't explain why he's here."

Hope edged her way back into the hall. "He may have mentioned something about making sure you're okay."

"I am okay."

"Are you?" insisted Hope.

So maybe she wasn't all the way okay, but Mike didn't need to know that. "Great. Thanks. That's not humiliating at all."

"Also, Scott thinks you invited him." Hope twirled about and escaped.

Grace slapped on the tap and splashed cool water onto her heated cheeks. She made hasty use of the cosmetics she rarely bothered with these days. Her fingers made extra quick work of braiding her hair. She detoured to her room and fished out the poppy-covered sundress Kate had given her for her birthday last year, because drastic times required drastic measures.

Satisfied she looked less like the mangled puppet of a few minutes ago, she made her way to the kitchen to find her father and Mike deep in conversation and neither of them particularly happy.

Hope swatted at Levi, who was swiping icing off a chocolate layer cake. "Stop that. You'll ruin the presentation."

He paused, finger halfway to his mouth, to stare at Grace. "What are you wearing?"

Scott pushed the screen door open. "Out you go."

Pops whistled. "Look at you."

Levi halted in the open door and wrinkled his nose. "But she's got a dress on."

Hope was all bustling efficiency as she shushed her son. "Food's ready. Everybody out."

Concern sharpened her dad's features, but Grace didn't have the energy to reassure him. She clapped her hands together. "I'm starving. Let's eat."

Scott looked from her to Mike and back to her flowery dress, his brow furrowing. Hope shoved him toward the door, then came back for her dad and shuffled him out.

"If you want me to leave, I will."

"Depends on why you're here." Grace liberated a beer from the fridge and twisted off the cap. "I'm not interested in your pity. I'm doing just fine."

There were dark shadows under his eyes and tired lines creasing his forehead. "I'm not. Doing fine, that is."

As far as confessions went, it was a doozy. She'd always thought of him as an aloof warrior, but here he was looking more the fallen knight, disgraced but still clutching his sword.

She'd done plenty of stewing this past week, trying to reconcile the upstanding, straight-shooting man she knew with the one who'd betrayed his own flesh and blood. Tried to figure out why it bothered her but wasn't a deal breaker. The answer was in front of her. He was a man bowed but not beaten, with the heart of a Lancelot and a desperate need to find his Holy Grail.

"I get it's a bad idea. Me being here. That I'm saying one thing and doing the opposite." His eyes were swirls of regret. "But I need to know if you meant what you said about second chances."

She nodded, not quite trusting his question.

"Selfish, huh?" Mike shrugged when she failed to reply. "But that's not a big surprise after what I told you."

"Mike." His name, saying it, grounded her. Gave her a sense of time and place and circumstance.

He rushed his words. "I thought it would make it easier for you to move on. But seems I've only made things worse. That's a theme with me, unfortunately."

Damn you for meddling, Hope.

"I don't know what she said to you, but…"

His lips curved. "Besides threatening to emasculate

me?"

She bit back her own smile. "She did not."

"It was sweet, actually. I think I may have misjudged her."

Scott appeared on the other side of the door, his frustration clogging the mesh of the screen. "Burgers are ready."

"Don't keep your family waiting." The old Mike was back, his guard rising, his hesitancy dissolving. "I just wanted to make sure you were okay."

Grace wanted to make one thing very clear. "You don't have to worry about me. I'm a survivor."

"I never doubted it."

"Then stay." It was more than a dare. It was a chance for him to act on everything he wasn't saying. "Eat with us."

"I'd like that."

"Okay, then."

"But I'm not sure I can leave here after having eaten with you and have it be enough." His eyes did a resolved, squinty kind of thing that had lines fanning out from his honest eyes. "I tried. I did. To spare us both a harder goodbye. But I don't think I can leave without us...without me asking for a whole lot more."

Grace understood. If it was going to hurt, it should hurt for the all the best reasons.

She tugged him outside where pretty glass traps ringed the picnic area and coaxed the wasps to them instead of the heaping platters of food. Everyone scrambled for a seat at the wooden picnic table. Hope dragged a lawn chair over to accommodate her stomach. Levi settled in between Scott and her dad. That left Mike, Grace, and Pops opposite them.

Scott signaled at Levi to fold his hands, and they waited for Pops to say his usual blessing.

"Bless this food for our use." At the sound of her dad's voice, Grace opened an eye and peeked at him. His head was bent, his eyes shut tight, fingers clamped together. "Amen."

Short, but so sweet. And the first time in years he'd spoken the short prayer they used to say before every evening meal.

Pops passed Grace the tray of burgers. "This takes me back."

"Here we go," muttered Scott, who got busy heaping pasta salad onto his plate.

"You girls remember your great-aunt Enid? She was a big fan of cookouts. Shame, she was never quite right after the last one."

"Remember little pitchers have big ears." Martin gestured to his grandson. "Pass me the salad, will you?"

Levi frowned as he struggled to hand the enormous bowl to his grandfather. "What happened at the last one?"

Pops tapped his thumb and pointer finger against his lips and puffed out some imaginary smoke. "Someone put a little too much wacky tobacco in the brownies."

Levi grabbed a bun. "Mom makes brownies."

Hope choked on her mouthful of food.

Grace managed a laugh. "Not the kind Pops is talking about."

Levi paused, ketchup bottle in midair. "What kind is Pops talking about?"

"Careful there." Martin set his fork down and confiscated the oozing red bottle. He glared at his rumpled, whiskered father. "Pay no attention to him. He's talking nonsense as usual."

Scott patted his son on the shoulder. "They're special brownies for adults only."

Grace kicked at Scott under the table. "Some adults."

Scott winced. "Jeez, relax. Not like he can arrest us for talking about it."

Hope smirked at Mike. "Sorry, we're not used to having company at the table."

"Are we talking about marijuana?" asked Levi.

Mike winked at him. "I kind of think they are."

Grace elbowed Pops. "See what you started."

"Doesn't Uncle—?"

Scott slipped one hand over Levi's mouth. "No, he doesn't."

Pops, bless his heart, piped up. "Back in the day, my dad ran moonshine. Awful stuff. Memorized the recipe. Should try my hand at it."

"No." Grace hammered him with a stern look.

"Absolutely not," echoed her father, his horrified look more of a reaction than she'd seen in a long time.

"No, it's a great idea." Scott toasted Pops with his beer. "You're always going on about wanting to blow stuff up."

Mustard and ketchup dripped from the massive burger in Levi's hands. "Cool."

Scott nudged him. "Use your napkin."

Levi set his dripping burger down. "Can I help?"

There was a collective and very loud, "No."

Mike swiped his napkin over his mouth. "My great-grandfather was a rum-runner."

Pops nodded his head in approval. "You don't

say?"

"What's a rum-runner?" asked Levi, nose bunching.

"In the early nineteen-twenties it was illegal to drink alcohol in Canada and the United States." Mike settled his fists down on either side of his plate. "But that didn't stop people from wanting to have a drink."

"Or from unruly women and priests trying to stop them."

Grace rolled her eyes at Pops, and without thinking, put a hand over Mike's. "Your great-grandfather sounds like quite the guy."

Mike turned his palm and threaded his fingers through hers. "It was his job to smuggle truck loads of Canadian booze across the border into North Dakota for a certain famous gangster. Ten dollars a trip."

Levi shoulder's slumped. "Ten dollars? Is that all?"

Mike's fingers tightened around hers when she went to tug them free. "That was quite the bundle of cash in those days."

"I saw 'Diamond' Jim Brady once. In Moose Jaw." Pops paused with a fork load of food halfway to his mouth. "He was quite the sight."

"Who was Jim Brady?" Hope swiped a pickle off Scott's plate and ran it through a batch of mayonnaise before popping it in her mouth.

Scott's lips curved before he remembered he wasn't supposed to find his wife or her pregnancy habits amusing.

"Worked for Al Capone." Pops puffed out his chest and tapped his front teeth. "Had diamond chips in his front teeth. I was just a lad, no more than five or six. But I remember the sight of him glinting in the sun like it was yesterday."

"A rum-runner risked their life to do the job. The Americans didn't like illegal booze coming across the border." Mike's thumb began a subtle rub of her hand. "You got caught, you were in big trouble."

"What kind of trouble?" asked Levi.

She left her hand where it was, and Mike continued to navigate the story and Levi's questions, making sure he didn't say too much while managing to satisfy Levi and Pops' curiosity. His manners were impeccable. He was charming. Urbane. But less cautious, more open. It was a heady combination.

"Why don't you two take a walk?" Hope hoisted out of her chair, dimples denting her cheeks. "The rest of us will clean up."

"Can I come with you?" begged Levi.

Her dad abandoned his dish-gathering duties. "I'm sure Constable Davenport isn't staying."

Grace wasn't the only one surprised at her dad's unusually curt response. Mike's face was curiously blank. "Actually, a walk sounds like a great idea."

Hope motioned their dad back into his seat. "Why don't you stay out here with Pops and Levi?"

Less than pleased with the prospect of spending alone time with his wife, Scott got to his feet. "We should probably be going."

Hope thrust an empty bowl into his hands. "I need you to catch me up on what's going to happen once school starts in a week. Levi needs supplies and clothes."

When Scott and Levi both groaned, Grace steered Mike in the direction of a forgotten cow path that ambled along the fence line.

Once they were out of sight, she stopped to gaze out over the neighboring pastureland. Her amazement hadn't waned during their walk. "You sat through a Bighill family dinner."

He took her hands in his. "The bond you have with them? That's something special. Take it from someone who's never felt that a day in his life."

The loneliness was back in his eyes, and she wanted to send it packing, if only for a night. "I am. Very lucky. We stick together. Always have, always will."

His gaze touched on her hair, her cheeks, her lips. "Come home with me?"

"Yes." Her whisper joined the slight breeze lifting her hair.

He captured the wayward strands and combed them back into place. "Be sure."

"I am."

She wasn't going to second-guess. Or tiptoe her way into his bed. She may not resemble an Amazon in height, but she would in purpose. She would sleep with him. She would claim the memory of having and holding him, and she would protect and cherish that memory for as long as she needed. Until she didn't need it anymore.

****

Grace ignored Hope's knowing smile and Scott's scowl and collected her bag. Mike followed her trail of dust all the way to town. She had enough time to smear on some raspberry lip-gloss before he opened her car door and held out his hand. Even with his support, she tumbled out, tamping down her fluttering dress and nerves.

His hand wrapped around her fingers. His other rested at her waist, like he was waiting for the music to begin. "I love the dress."

"I'll let Kate know you approve." She might even buy another one. Or three. Because truth was, she liked it, too. She felt pretty. And she was worth the effort of a pretty dress and a dab of shiny lip-gloss. "Kiss me."

His lips curved. Not a flashy grin. Or a seductive smile. But a charming lift of his lips as he brought her hand close and kissed each knuckle. His eyes, however, were much too serious. "These hands handle so much, take care of so many."

She spent a considerable amount of time hiding her cracked and calloused hands in pockets or behind the click of needles, but his awed words eased her insecurities. "Right now, all I can think about is getting them on you."

His laughter ebbed out to meet the accompanying waves of red and orange from the setting sun as they rushed into his building. His apartment door thumped shut behind them, and his mouth was on hers. Her bag hit the floor with a thud as she did her best to keep up with a kiss that threatened to incinerate her and a momentum that had her stumbling backward until the back of her calves hit something solid. She broke the kiss and looked down.

He shoved a box out of the way. "Sorry about the mess."

There were varying sizes of boxes stacked here and there. Not a surprise. He was packing. Leaving. "Moving is a messy business."

A wariness crept between them as he smoothed his hands over her shoulders. "I should probably offer you a drink."

"Maybe later. Much, much later." Her hands slipped down his chest and around his waist. She was better when they were touching. When he was pressed against her, silencing her jitters.

"Need this." His voice was wispy as smoke, and he bent to rest his forehead against hers. "Need you."

"You have me."

She found the first button of his shirt by touch. For each button she freed, he wrapped more of her hair around his fingers. She pushed the edges of his shirt apart and placed a kiss on his broad chest, traced a finger along his collarbone. So warm. So tempting.

She peeked up at him. "So tall."

His hands landed on the curve of her behind, and he hoisted her up. "Better?"

She began with small nibbles. Teasing. Retreating. A lick of his top lip. His bottom lip. The seam between them. She added a little tongue. He added the intensity along with some pressure, his hands holding her, molding her. Her fingers slipped around to the short hairs at the nape of his neck then to the longer strands at the crown of his head. When he groaned, she tightened her hold.

The shape of his mouth was intoxicating. The smoothness of his teeth, the mint taste of the gum he must have chewed and discarded during their race to town. The roll of his tongue as he captured hers.

Then it was neck kisses. And the spot just behind her ear…

"Yes," she whispered. "That feels amazing."

How was he so good at this? It wasn't only his lips or his tongue. It was his teeth that left a bit of a sting behind. *God, did he have a map?* Her thighs clamped around his waist, and she toed off her wedge heels. She opened her eyes when he stopped kissing her.

"Bed." For all his whispered urgency he wasn't asking. "I can't wait to taste all of you."

"Then you'd better get started." She shoved his shirt off his shoulders. When she slid down his body and her feet touched firm ground, it floated to the floor. They paused in the short hallway to lean against a bare wall and to indulge in more heat-seeking kisses before moving on to his bedroom.

At the foot of his bed, she grasped the hem of her dress. The fabric stroked against her body on the way up and was forgotten about once it cleared her head. The careful part of him was lost to insistence. He skimmed her panties and her bra off. She kicked them out of the way.

The expected shyness returned with the first brush of air on her exposed skin. What would he think of her pointed shoulders and jutting hipbones?

"Beautiful."

Her breath caught with each feather touch of his lips. His urgency tapered to a careful exploration of her shoulders, her collarbone, until he bent his head and pressed a kiss to her breast.

The shape of his skull was perfect for her cradling hands. "More. I need more."

"So impatient." The covers were soft against her back, his shorts rough against her stomach. She reached for his belt, the jangle of metal loud in the quiet room. The warmth from his skin was replaced with cool air. He sat back on his heels. "I love the way you look."

She curled up to bat his hand away from his zipper,

and he sucked in a breath. She pulled the fastener down and dipped her fingers inside to brush over the cotton of his underwear. She wanted him naked. Must have said the words because he complied with slow purposeful moves until he was unapologetically nude.

He pressed her back down, and his long body stretched out over her. They were skin to skin, his hair-roughened legs outdistancing her smooth ones, dampness where his cock was trapped against her belly.

"I need you to touch me."

Such anguish. She couldn't bare it. One shove and he was on his back. His ribs were firm against her straddling thighs, his chest strong and sure under her questing hands. But it was his face that captured her attention. She would never get enough of looking into those stormy green eyes. Not if she lived to be a hundred years old.

She slipped her hand between them until she reached the hard length of him. His eyelashes stuttered shut. Lines creased his forehead, and his lips broke apart on a gasp. She rewarded him with a loose slide of her fist. Up, down. Up.

"Wait. Stop." His neck stretched as his head pressed into the crumpled pillow, his throat bobbing with each swallow.

He rose to his elbows to meet her mouth. Then he twisted, and she was underneath him. His mouth settled around her nipple, and he sucked the tip into his mouth. His erection rubbed back and forth over her clit while his hands pinned her arms to the space above her head. His skin, dampened by heat and need, slid against hers, leaving her unable to do little more than spread her legs.

"You make me want to lose my mind. Don't move them." His smile turned wicked as he released her wrists to open the drawer of his bedside table. He tossed a little wrapped package onto the bed beside them.

"Always prepared."

"Nothing in my life has prepared me for you." He kissed his way down the center of her body. As he licked and sucked, she buried a hand in his hair and twisted just hard enough to get his attention.

Her back arched off the bed. "I can't…"

"Then don't." His questing fingers shot her into space. Then he was finally pushing into her, whispering to her, giving her time to catch up, adjust.

But it was too late. There was no way to go back and undo it all. It was too late to unwind her legs and her arms. To stop the pleading whispers spilling out of her mouth or the reaction of her body. Too late to wonder how she was ever going to let him go.

****

Mike shut off his alarm. Light filtered in through the thin curtain covering the bedroom window, but it was early yet. Still a couple of hours before his Saturday shift started. He wrapped his arms around Grace, the skin of her shoulder warm under his lips.

Seven years of abstinence. Over. And he didn't regret a thing. Not a touch. Not a press of his lips. Not a *please*, or a *more*.

She squirmed until her back was plastered against the length of his front. He buried his nose in her hair, finding he was more addicted than ever to the scent of coconut that clung to the silky strands. His body was quick to show its appreciation. But it wasn't only morning wood, or the promise of more sex. It was the uniqueness of the woman in his arms.

Grace stretched, and his hand curved over her breast. A slip of sound escaped her mouth, and his fingers tightened.

"Do we have time for this?" She twisted her head to look at him, her voice sleepy and teasing. "Don't you work today?"

"We've got a couple of hours." He wanted to give her a chance to catch up, to blink further awake before he sweet-talked her onto her hands and knees.

She wiggled her butt against his very hard erection. "Early riser, are you?"

He tipped her onto her stomach and grinned as she muffled a laugh. But the sass disappeared when she snuggled her cheek into the crook of her arm. Then she was all beckoning siren, the music of her quiet movements drawing him closer.

He kissed the spot in the middle of her back. "I reset my alarm after you fell asleep."

"Planning ahead," she murmured. "Very sexy."

He nipped at the skin he'd just kissed. She jolted at the hint of teeth. His fingers trailed down her spine. "You taste so good."

Her throaty hum buzzed the air. He knelt in the space between her legs and ran a finger over the tan lines riding low on her hips and kissed the one in the middle of her back. The sight of her fingers curling into the sheets caused his own to tighten, and he bent to lick the dip at the base of her spine.

His lips trailed after his hands, his thumbs running up the center of her back, pressing her into sheets that smelled of cheap laundry detergent. They should have been softer with an impossible thread count, the pillows full of feathers, the bed bigger with a creative amount of room.

Her moan was soft. "You're really good at this."

Overwhelmed by her praise, he grabbed a condom from the pile spilling across his nightstand. He'd purchased them midweek after considerable soul searching over her mention of second chances, of questioning the wisdom of ending up right where they were at this moment. The fairness of asking, if not begging her to give them both the memory of being skin to skin.

He slid on the condom with shaking fingers. Her hips were heavy in his hands, pliant, and waiting to be guided. With her weight on her hand and knees, she glanced back, eyes wide and wondering. He stole a moment to enjoy the view of her lean back and strong shoulders as he rubbed his erection along the folds of her vagina. Her slick arousal making him glide faster, clutch harder.

Then he was inside her. Her back arched as she sank down to her elbows and reached between her legs to stroke herself. The sound of skin slapping against skin had him going deeper. There was no stopping the urge to twine his fist into her hair. No denying the gratitude rushing through him.

"Yes." Her body squeezed tight around him. "Right there."

He fought to obey. To time his thrusts. To rub against the right spot. To make her tremble. Shake. To have her shatter first. Her body froze, then stuttered, her elbows and knees grinding into the sheets as she pushed back against him.

He wished they were face to face. He wanted to see her lush lips curve and her impossible eyes darken. But he was claimed by need, conquered by friction, and ruled by the shattered reactions of the woman under him. He surrendered, and it was glorious.

He pried his eyes open in time to see her push her messy hair back from a face he'd see in his dreams years from now. Her lips curved, but it turned into a wince. A stab of guilt shot through him. "Are you okay? I shouldn't have—"

"No." Her bottom lip caught between her teeth as she cushioned her cheek against her arm. "It was amazing."

He trailed a finger over the dewy skin of her shoulder. "It certainly was."

"Worth waiting seven years for?" A flash of doubt tempered the return of her cocky grin.

Too lost in her impossible eyes to police his words, they slipped out honest and revealing. "Worth waiting a lifetime for."

Her eyes widened a fraction in the muted light. He didn't regret a moment of what had happened between the two of them, but wishing for more and knowing it wasn't going to happen was too much truth to handle.

"I need a shower."

The squeak of bedsprings and her lingering concern followed him out of the room. Condom dealt with, he braced his hands on the bathroom counter and faced his reflection. "It can't change things."

His matted hair, the love marks scattered across his chest, increased the pounding ache of his heart. He fled to the shower, but he was no more successful at convincing himself with hot water warming his chilled skin. Suds ran down the drain. He gave up the pretense of getting clean and braced his hands against the tiles and hung his head. The rungs of the ladder beneath him and the ones left to climb above him led to career goals set in stone. Ones he intended to honor.

He grabbed a towel and rubbed until he was numb. He found her sitting up in bed, clutching the sheet to her breasts. Any ground he'd gained with his little pep talk in the shower crumbled underneath him as he climbed into bed and pulled her back down with him.

She settled in beside him, laid a tentative hand on his chest. "Are you okay?"

He toyed with the ends of her hair, not wanting to ruin the moment with the truth. Plenty of time for that in the coming days. "More than okay. Last night was incredible."

Her fingers traced a pattern over his skin, tiny circles widening into larger ones until his entire chest tingled. "What was your brother like?"

It wasn't a surprise she would ask, and more and more, he wanted her to know the whole story. "Justin was committed. Tenacious. Competitive. Traits we shared, that were encouraged. Rewarded."

"Were you identical?"

"No. Fraternal."

Her nose wrinkled. "Whew, because being identical would have added a whole other layer to the Elizabeth thing."

"Justin was two inches shorter than me, which he resented." He threaded his fingers through hers. "Darker hair, stockier build, wicked smart. Smarter than me, which I resented."

"And he didn't suspect?"

"I think he was so focused on creating the Norman Rockwell illusion of the young, up-and-coming couple that my mother wanted that he didn't notice how unhappy Elizabeth had become."

"My heart bleeds." She rolled her eyes. "Forget I said that."

The tanned skin of her back stretched taut when she sat up and wrapped her arms around her drawn-up knees. He placed a hand dead center of her back, claiming as much space as possible while he tried to figure out what to say next.

"For the record." She glanced back over her shoulder. "I understand leaving is something you have to do."

There was so much he hadn't told her. "I need the city. The lights. The noise. The anonymity. It's where I feel the most at home."

"It sounds kind of perfect, actually." Her wistfulness took him by surprise. Then it made him wonder. Before he could question her words, she squared her shoulders. "Are you planning on feeding me?"

Her sass had them back on familiar ground. He curled up behind her and kissed her shoulder. "I might be able to find you a couple of eggs, a slice of bread."

"I'm going to grab a quick shower." She climbed out of bed, taking the top sheet with her. She paused in the doorway and raised an eyebrow. "Just to be clear, I'm not offering to cook it, only eat it."

That was his girl. Not one for theatrics, she wouldn't beg him to stay or try to change his mind. He should be relieved. Thankful. But there was an ache in his chest he refused to name as he flopped to his back.

"Enjoy it while you got it. That's all you can do," he whispered to the empty room.

On a sigh, he got to his feet. By the time steam followed her through to the kitchen, he had some brutally scrambled eggs and burnt toast to offer her. He handed her a mug of coffee. "Just the way you like it."

"Perfect."

"Sit. Eat." He led her to a stool. "What are you and Levi up to today?"

"Not sure." She scooped some eggs into her mouth, chewed, then swallowed. "Stuff."

On impulse he lifted from his seat and dropped a kiss on her lips. He replaced the hints of egg and coffee with heat and thoroughness. The sense of time flying was too great to ignore. The question popped out before he could bite it back. "Attend Justin's memorial with me?"

She pulled back. "What?"

"Come with me." He captured her hand and fisted it against his heart. "To Justin's memorial. Spend the weekend with me. In the city."

"I'm not so sure that's a good idea."

He should drop it, take her wide-eyed wariness seriously, and never mention the idea again. But there was no abandoning his certainty that with her at his side, he just might survive it. "One weekend. That's all I'm asking for."

"And after those seventy-two hours are over?"

He was saved from replying by a knock on his door, but answering it only elevated his problems. It was six-thirty in the morning. It had been an hour and a half drive from the city, but her suit was immaculate, and her hair was styled to death.

"Mother."

"Michael."

The squeal of chair legs against tile split the air. His mother zeroed in on Grace.

He sighed. "Mother, this is Grace Bighill. Grace, my mother, Helen Davenport."

Grace held out her hand. "It's nice to meet you, Mrs. Davenport."

His mother gave Grace's hand the briefest of shakes. "I need to speak with you, Michael. Alone."

Mike rubbed at a sudden ache between his brows. "I'm busy."

"Then un-busy yourself. We have important family matters to discuss." She stepped aside, clearly expecting Grace to hustle her butt out the door.

"You should have phoned. I could have told you I'm working a twelve hour shift today and unavailable."

"Your shift doesn't start for another hour. Plenty of time for me to say what I need to." She opened her purse and extracted a set of keys and held them out. "Let me start by saying these are for you."

"I'll leave you two to talk."

"Stay." He grabbed Grace's hand and ignored the Porsche keychain. Damn her for remembering fast cars were his weakness.

Her smile was as unnatural as her penciled-in brows. "It's a welcome back to the firm present."

Some of his urgency must have conveyed itself to Grace because she paused at his side.

"For heaven's sake, Michael. If the woman wants to leave, let her leave." His mother unbent enough to tug her suit jacket a little straighter. "This discussion is for family only."

A warm hand settled against his back. The soothing circles leveled his heart rate. "I'm not coming back to the firm."

"This rebellion of yours has gone on long enough. A gang unit? I won't have it." For an impossible second, he wondered if she was worried for his safety. "That kind of work is beneath you."

Of course, she wasn't. "My career choices are no longer a concern of yours."

She eyed Grace's shower-damp hair and wrinkled dress. "You've had your fun. It's time to come home."

Fun?

She thought the last seven years had been fun for him? Her callous dismissal of his grief split him in two. "It wasn't my idea to leave Alton and Davenport. You threw me out, and then you cut me off. Remember?"

"A decision I made while grieving the horrific loss of one son and confronted by the disgraceful conduct of another."

If they were going there, they were going all the way. And Grace needed to hear it. She needed to know the whole ugly truth. Then maybe she would run as far and as fast as she could get.

"You were the one who sent Justin to the cabin that night, weren't you? Even though you knew what finding Elizabeth and I together would do to him."

She lifted her chin. "I do not wish to discuss the details of Justin's death in front of strangers."

"You could have come to me." Maybe life would have played out the same, no matter the rearrangement of the circumstances, but what if it hadn't?

"You are needed back at the firm."

"Why didn't you?" He'd never demanded much

from her, but that was about to change.

Her exasperation snapped at him. "Why didn't I what?"

"Come to me? Call me out? Deliver one of your famous ultimatums?"

"You didn't deserve that kind of consideration."

Grace gasped.

His mother scowled. "I will not discuss this in front of strangers. For now, all you need to know is that I've been approached by certain top members of the Conservative party who are seeking candidates they believe can make headway in our urban areas in the next federal election. I don't wish to leave the running of the firm to others."

"Ah." A bid for federal politics required a united family front. All hands on deck. A family rift might be cause for speculation.

Too damn bad for her.

"I need you overseeing things at the office. Ensuring the continued success of our firm."

Duty over family.

Always.

"No." She had never loved him, not like a mother should love their child. He reached for the warm, ready hand of the silent woman next to him. "I wish you and the firm well, I really do. But I'm not coming back."

Helen Davenport was a master at stoic and sedate. Neither of those standards served her now. Her face twisted. Not in disappointment. But in rage.

"What would you have done in my place? He came asking for your grandmother's ring. He was going to surprise Elizabeth. Ask her to *marry* him, for heaven's sake." Her cruel red slash of a mouth contorted. "Her pedigree was perfect. They would have made such a pair. But your pride couldn't let them be. I waited as long as I could, hoping the two of you would come to your senses."

Bile coated his throat.

Grace stepped forward. "You've said what you came to say."

"You have a debt to settle, Michael."

"With God, maybe." He was done kneeling at her feet and hoping for a crumb of affection. "But not with you."

She was back to the cold and calculating person who'd raised him. She set the keys down on the counter. "Monday morning following the memorial, I expect to see you in the office. We'll discuss the terms of your employment and the reinstatement of your inheritance. We will move forward. As a family. And we won't speak of this unpleasantness again."

His mother walked out the door.

Without having heard a word he'd said. Without offering a smile or a kind word. And he was a fool if he thought she was ever going to change.

"Did that go as badly as I thought it did?" asked Grace.

He was staring at the door, couldn't seem to look away. "I'm sorry you had to hear all that."

She was in front of him, taking his temperature as surely as if she'd put the back of her hand to his forehead. "It could have been worse."

He was forced to look at her then. "How so?"

She smiled, a careful attempt at lightening the mood. "We could have decided to eat breakfast naked."

"True." But he wasn't in the mood for jokes.

She touched his arm. "We should talk about what just happened."

He couldn't, not for all the love or money in the world. "Later."

"You can't go into work like this."

He turned away from her. "There are a lot of things I'm not capable of, Grace. But doing my job isn't one of them."

The door shut quietly behind her.

Chapter Ten

Grace and Levi played a game of chess. She lost. They built a lethal death ray machine from Lego bricks, and out of desperation for something to do, went to Mary's for lunch. Back at home, she'd purposefully lost the tablet war, and Levi was curled up on the couch playing a game. All because she had yet to come to terms with what she'd witnessed this morning.

For the first time, she fully understood why Mike was putting as much distance between him and his old life as possible. Helen Davenport would suck the life out of him given enough time and access. It was the heartbreaking truth. Love had a feel to it. As did the absence of it. Helen Davenport didn't love her son, but she had a use for him.

She checked her watch. "Time to turn it off, Levi."

His voice drifted into the kitchen, foggy with distraction. "Ten more minutes."

"Off. Now." She grabbed a pair of scissors off the counter.

Levi plodded into the kitchen, shoulders drooping from their sockets. "I wasn't done."

"We're going outside for a bit." She pushed through the screen door and waited for him to follow.

His head flopped back, his whole body slumping in misery. "I don't wanna go outside."

"The fresh air will be good for you."

"You sound like Dad."

The screen door slapped shut behind them. She handed him a clear glass jar. "Here. Hold this."

"How come you're so mad today?"

"You noticed that, huh?" She brushed at the irresistible curls framing his round face. "I'm sorry. I'm a little distracted."

He blinked up at her. "Why are you distracted?"

"It's nothing you need to worry over."

Thinking of Mike's mother made her shiver. Chances were good the woman was already busy at her cauldron whipping up a poison apple with Grace's name on it.

"What's paternity mean?"

Oh, good Lord.

Why today? When she was not at her best? Deep down, she knew why. He trusted her. She'd gone out of her way to see that he did. But there were some things only a parent could answer. "Have you asked your dad?"

"Not yet." He held the jar up to his eye and squinted through it.

She wished she'd left him to his video game.

He scratched his nose. "I don't get it. Why does the baby need a test? Is he sick?"

"No. The baby's fine." Hope had agreed to a paternity test as long as it was done after the baby was born, as it was a less-invasive procedure. Obviously, Levi had overheard bits and pieces of his parents' conversation. "But if you have questions, you need to ask your mom or dad."

He balanced the jar on the palm of his hand and watched it teeter-totter, then almost fall. "That's what

Ms. Mossbank said, too."

Hard to say what the new librarian, with a fondness for pink hair and Stephen King, had made of his inquiry. She crouched down. "Sweetie, you need to go to your parents with these questions. It's their job to answer them. They *want* to answer them for you."

Levi chewed his bottom lip. "What if I do and someone gets mad?" He shrugged his shoulders, but his chin wobbled. "And they start fighting? I don't like it when they fight."

This kid was going to break her heart. The idea of him tiptoeing around the adults in his life made her sad. She ruffled his hair. "It's also okay to tell them it makes you feel bad when they're unkind to each other."

"Grandma Walker says there are some things I don't need to know."

Grace tried for casual. "You didn't, um, ask her about the paternity thing, did you?"

Levi shook his head and bent to pick up a pebble.

"Not that you can't ask your Grandma Walker," she told the back of his head while lifting her hands to the sky in a desperate plea for help. Hope was persona non grata with her mother-in-law, who would continue the cold shoulder through eternity if Melinda found out Scott was questioning paternity.

Which wasn't Grace's problem.

Another pebble pinged against the bottom of the jar. "I'll ask Dad."

"Good idea." Crisis averted, she knelt down in front of the purple coneflowers and sunny asters. "Time to pick some flowers."

He dropped down beside her. "What are you going to do with them?"

Gone

"They're for my mom, your Grandma Bighill." She snipped off a coneflower and handed it to him.

"Because she died?" He stuffed it in the jar.

"Careful." She clipped another stem. "Yes, because she died. And because I miss her."

"Are you taking them to Grandpa's house?"

"No." She reached the asters.

"Where, then?"

She cut a couple flower stalks off and rolled her tight shoulders. "Hook-up Hill."

"Where she died? Cool." His bored expression vanished. "Can I come?"

"It is not cool." She rubbed a hand over her gritty eyes and cursed her sloppy mouth. "And no."

"Why not?" he pleaded, stabbing the flowers she handed him into the jar.

"Because your dad will be here soon to pick you up."

"You could call him and tell him you'll bring me home after."

"He'll say no."

"No, he won't." His eyes widened at her skeptical look. "He won't."

She sliced off a couple of stalks of violet foxglove.

"Please?"

His wheedling tone had her eyes narrowing in warning. "No. Case closed."

"You're the one who said I needed fresh air." His bottom lip popped out in a pout.

She handed him a pink snapdragon. "Now you want to be outside?"

His huge puppy dog eyes widened even farther. "I don't think you should go alone. It'll make you sad."

"Sweetie, this is something I have to do by myself." She reached past him and dropped another stem in the jar.

He leaned down to sniff the flowers. When he lifted his head, he had pollen on his nose. "Do you think she would have liked me? Even when I say the wrong thing?"

She brushed off the yellow dust, her heart melting. "Especially then."

The sound of vehicles approaching rumbled in the background. Scott's truck rattled down her lane, followed by Hope's car. And just like that, she was forgotten. Levi bounded over to meet his dad. Scott put his hand on his son's shoulder while Hope parked her own vehicle.

Grace wandered over in time to hear Levi ask, "Can Mom come home with us and make supper? I'm starving."

Grace didn't say a word about her nephew having inhaled an entire chicken strip meal, a chocolate shake, and a huge slice of Mary's apple pie an hour and a half ago.

Hope cast a pleading look at Scott. "And maybe do some organizing at your place for the baby?" She lifted a shopping bag. "I could get Levi's school supplies organized and packed for Tuesday."

Grace held her breath, hoping Scott would have the good sense to answer in the affirmative, and not only because his agreement meant she'd have the house to herself. He shook his head in defeat. "Whatever. I've got stuff I need to get done. He can drive you nuts instead of me."

Her sister rubbed her hands together. "Bet I can

guess what you want for supper."

Levi crossed his arms. "Cannot."

"Maybe it's my strong man spaghetti and meatballs."

"Maybe," hedged Levi. "Maybe not."

Hope tapped her nose like she was deep in thought, then announced, "I think I'll make them anyway."

"Whoopee." Levi took off at a run.

Grace called after him, "Don't forget your stuff."

Levi changed direction, the door banging shut behind him, while Scott, phone in hand, climbed into his truck to wait.

Grace put a hand on Hope's arm when she moved to follow Levi. "He asked me what paternity means today."

"Great." Hope's shoulders slumped. "What did you say?"

"I told him to ask you or Scott."

Hope blew out a breath. "Okay, we'll talk to him."

Grace narrowed her eyes. "Before he starts asking his teachers or the other kids at school."

"Today. Cross my heart."

Grace had to be satisfied with that. "How did your doctor's appointment go?"

"My blood pressure is a little on the high side, so I have to monitor it at home." Hope rubbed her belly. "Nothing to worry about yet. I don't have any of the other symptoms they look for in preeclampsia, but I have to go back in a couple of days to make sure it's not getting any higher."

Levi raced out of the house. Grace reached out to halt Hope. "Take time for a nap."

Hope nodded. "I'll be back later to hear last night's

yummy details."

Grace wasn't sharing those with anyone. "Nope."

Hope waggled her eyebrows. "Definitely."

Grace waved her sister off and went inside to collect a water bottle. Ten minutes later, she was entering the larger and more easily accessible south parking lot. A pickup truck sat in one corner, two SUVs in another, but otherwise it was empty. A blessing in the middle of the afternoon.

Halfway up, she met a group of eight other people coming down. They exchanged greetings in passing, and then she was on her own. But when Grace made it to the clearing, she wasn't alone. His back was to her, his head bowed, hat circling in his hands, but she knew him by the stoop of his shoulders and the ink on his arms.

A heaviness in the air suggested a very private moment. He hadn't even heard her approach. "Ian?"

He stiffened, and a moment passed before he turned to face her, his hat back on his head with the peak pulled low. "Grace."

"What are you doing up here?" Ian didn't strike her as much of a hiker.

He nodded at the flowers clutched in her hand. "I'll leave you to it."

Grace frowned. "I don't want to chase you off."

"You're not." There was no reason for her to want to keep him there. It was a mystery why she tried. "I don't want to pry, but I've always wondered about your butterfly."

He frowned at her.

"On your arm?" There was nothing feminine or dainty about his tattoo. A monarch resting on a beautiful daisy, it covered his entire forearm.

Ian's lips curved into a sad smile. "To remind me."

"To remind you of what?" asked Grace, before she could stop herself.

"Of someone special."

A weird tingle settled at the base of her spine.

"I should—"

She thought of her mom's yearbook and the words he'd written. "You cared about her."

Ian stopped in his tracks. "She told you that?"

"I have some of her things: recipes, knickknacks, stuff like that. A yearbook. You wrote in it, and your words..." She hesitated, but some sixth sense pushed her to go for it. "They seemed...personal."

"Right." He backed up a step. "We, ah, were in the same grade at school."

She frowned at his retreat and then gave in to the tiredness that dogged her and let it go. She checked the time. "Well, I don't want to keep you."

Ian cleared his throat. "Nice watch."

"Thank you." She shrugged. "My mom gave it to me. Told me I should look after it because it was very special."

She didn't know why she was sharing, especially when he looked away and didn't reply. It was clear she was making him uncomfortable, but her mouth kept talking. "She didn't say why, but I've always wondered."

"Wondered...what?"

"Why, I guess." She waved the conversation away and lifted the flowers in her hand. "I should probably..."

"I'll leave you to it." He dipped his head at her.

"You take care."

She frowned at his retreating back until the jar of flowers in her hand became an impossible weight. She crawled over the embankment and let the many boot prints lead her to the disturbed ground.

What were you doing up here, Mom? Were you meeting someone? Did you walk out of the house that morning knowing you weren't coming back?

She gently laid the flowers down and stepped back. "Bye, Momma. I promise we're working hard to find out what happened to you."

****

It was afternoon before Mike had a chance to visit Kevin Hunt's campaign headquarters. Tucked between a dry cleaner and a sandwich shop, it was plastered with Hunt's slogan: *Investing in Rural Life*. Inside, a young woman pushed away from a group huddled around a table and met him at the front desk.

Her confident smile was no match for her questioning eyes. "Can I help you, Officer?"

"Is Kevin Hunt around?" Mike slipped his sunglasses off. "I need to speak to him."

"I'll get him for you." She hustled off.

Mike nodded to the rest of the curious group, then moved off to study a wall of framed pictures. Photo evidence of campaign victories, completed marathons, and his military service. Front and center was a picture of Hunt being presented with the Cross of Valor. One of Canada's highest honors awarded for exceptional acts of bravery under extreme peril.

"Constable Davenport, to what do I owe the pleasure?" Hunt didn't look surprised to see him. Then again, he probably had one hell of a poker face.

Mike braced his hands on his hips. His utility belt shifted with a satisfying creak. "Can we talk in private?"

"Of course." Hunt's mouth curved in amused apology as he motioned to the group of curious onlookers. "First, let me introduce you."

Hunt's smile was easy and his voice the perfect mix of bass and treble. "Constable Davenport is an excellent example of what the future looks like for the Royal Canadian Mounted Police. Keen intelligence, strong leadership skills, and the chops to get the tough jobs done."

Mike wasn't fooled. And he wasn't impressed. "Your office?"

The door opened, and Elizabeth entered, a cardboard box in her hands. They hadn't spoken since she'd handed him nearly three quarters of a million dollars.

She came to an abrupt halt. "Michael, this is a surprise."

"Elizabeth."

She eyed his uniform, worry gathering between her brows. A man left the group and rescued the box. She smiled her thanks. "What's going on?"

"Nothing to worry about," answered Hunt. "Constable Davenport has some questions for me."

"I won't keep you, then." She put a hand to her throat, but the necklace of knots he'd given her was gone.

Hunt made a production of ushering Mike into his office, claiming his seat behind the solid wood desk, and leaving Mike to settle into one of the two guest chairs. A computer sat off to the side, and an old-fashioned day planner sat front and center flanked by neat stacks of paper.

Hunt leaned back and crossed his legs. "What can I help you with, Constable?"

Mike didn't waste time. "It has to do with Cassandra Bighill's death."

Hunt eased forward and braced his forearms on the desk. "I'm not sure I can be much help."

Mike noted a smudge of beige color at the edge of Hunt's snow-white collar. Was he wearing makeup? "Where were you the day Cassandra Bighill disappeared?"

Hunt's flicker of contempt was immediate if fleeting. "That was a long time ago. I doubt I can recall specifics."

"Why don't you humor me and try?" Mike made a show of settling back to wait.

"Remind me of the date?"

Once Mike gave him the information, Hunt tapped his index finger against his lips. "I was busy managing my first provincial campaign that summer, so I would have been around."

Mike wasn't buying his vague innocent act. He was willing to bet Hunt never forgot the tiniest of details. "In the original report, you mentioned a woman you were spending time with."

Hunt shrugged. "If I said it, it must be true. But as I've stated, I've long forgotten the details."

Time to shake this guy free of his lofty perch. "Cassandra Bighill claimed you were stalking her."

"A preposterous notion."

Hunt's unguarded, surprised response forced Mike to take him seriously. "And why is that?"

"My reputation speaks for me and is built on service to this country by way of impeccable moral conduct." A little of Hunt's casual superiority slipped away on a harsh huff of breath. "I can assure you I wasn't stalking Cissy Bighill."

"It's my job to be thorough."

"Unless that thoroughness is called into question because of your emotional attachment to the daughter of your victim."

"My personal attachments are none of your business."

Hunt sat back. "Such a lovely evening last night."

The hair on Mike's arms lifted. He narrowed his eyes. "Meaning?"

Hunt's hands lifted in appeasement. "She's a decently attractive woman, and you're a single man in a rural community. Your options are limited. Sometimes we have to make do with what's available."

There was no stopping the clench of Mike's hands into fists. "I'm pretty sure those kinds of archaic observations aren't going to win you many votes. And might lose you a valuable campaign manager."

Hunt nodded his head in apparent approval. "Now there's a woman worth your time."

"You seem oddly preoccupied with my private life."

"Apologies, my affection for Elizabeth has me crossing a line. Shall we move on to more important matters?" He didn't wait for Mike to agree or disagree. "My constituents are concerned about a garage fire that happened a week or so ago. Rumors are escalating, and folks are wondering at the lack of updates from the police as to cause or suspects."

There was no question Hunt thought of himself as the superior and Mike as the subordinate. But since Hunt had brought them around to another topic Mike had wanted to poke at, he didn't much care. "We're looking into it."

"Is there anything to the victim's claim it was deliberately set?"

"We have people on it. These kinds of investigations take time. You know that."

"Mr. Pearce is very upset. Not to mention worried for his family."

"You seem to be quite chummy with Mason Pearce."

"We're acquainted."

"Right." Mike pulled out his notebook. "Pearce fixes your cars."

Hunt's already thin lips flattened. "He's one of my mechanics, yes."

"You mean one of Henley's mechanics, as he doesn't work for you directly. Does he?"

"No."

Mike made a show of flipping pages. "According to Henley, and Pearce himself, you have quite the car collection."

"I do." Hunt's voice lowered a notch in warning. "I confess I'm at a loss as to what that has to do with anything."

Mike flipped ahead a few more pages. "Aside from the maintenance of your vehicles, you show up with coffee and pastries on a regular basis. Usually when Pearce is working."

"As you've already stated, I've amassed a collection of classic cars. They require service, and I try to support my constituents and show my appreciation whenever possible. Henley's is not the only business I call upon with refreshments."

"Right. Benson's Hardware, Pratt's Practicalities, Cordon's Beer and Bait Shop, and the list goes on."

"Is there a reason you're investigating me, Constable?"

Mike referenced his notes, and he could almost hear Hunt grinding his teeth. "Pearce is quite proud of the fact you ask for him specifically."

Hunt's jaw tightened. "Is that a crime?"

"You're no doubt aware he's accused Ian Connelly of setting the fire. He's quite adamant about it." Mike shrugged and prepared to bait his trap. "But he's off base; I've ruled Ian out as a suspect."

"Are you telling me Connelly has an alibi for that night?"

"Are you suggesting he doesn't?"

"I have good reason to doubt the man's integrity."

"Ian served his time. His prison record was impeccable. Which is why you failed to keep him there. He's turned his life around. In fact, no one seems to have a problem with him, except for you. And your buddy, Mason Pearce, of course." Hunt did his best to appear unimpressed. To throw him off, Mike changed tactics. "Have you ever heard of Prairie Gold Resources?"

"Should I have?"

"About the time Cassandra disappeared, Martin was the victim of a carefully planned case of fraud."

"You don't say?"

"We also had an interesting conversation with Ian Connelly. Seems someone has been harassing him for years. I don't suppose you know anything about that, either?"

Hunt bared his teeth in a rare show of emotion. "No idea. But if you find out a name, let me know. I'd like to thank him."

"You don't believe in second chances?" The question made him think of Grace and the scene that had transpired in his kitchen that morning. He refused to let emotion sidetrack him. "They were young. Drinking. There was an argument."

"Which doesn't make any of them any less guilty. Or bring back Gregory. I would think you of all people would know what it means to mourn the loss a brother."

Mike wasn't interested in joining a support group. "I wouldn't want you drawing comparisons between us that aren't there."

"I hear you're leaving." The air in the room shifted with Hunt's announcement. "The Combined Forces Special Enforcement Unit is a plum assignment. Congratulations."

Mike's hackles rose. "And what would you know about it?"

"Your new boss and I attended the same function in Ottawa a couple of months ago. He mentioned they were looking to fill a position, and I happened to know the perfect candidate. I put in a good word." To his credit he didn't appear smug. He was too smart for that.

"That right?" Mike was no fool, and a master manipulator had raised him. Hunt didn't know it yet, but he had met his match.

"You're dedicated with a proven record. Your work dismantling the Prairie Brotherhood speaks for itself. You're meant for better things than an out-of-the-way rural detachment. We both know it." Hunt's gaze had a microscopic quality Mike didn't appreciate. "I want you on my side, so I did you a favor. I also value the people who work for me. Loyalty and talent should be celebrated, rewarded."

Elizabeth.

Had she gone behind Mike's back and asked Hunt to find opportunities for him? Mike rose to his feet. Every drop of Davenport superiority he could muster went into his warning. "Sooner or later, people who repeatedly break the law make a mistake. Doesn't matter how careful they are. How smart they think they are. The smallest mistake can be their undoing. My gut's telling me Prairie Gold Resources is going to be that mistake. And the thing about fraud? It's an indictable offense that carries no statute of limitations."

He didn't wait for a reaction. Elizabeth was nowhere around when he got to the main area, and he wasn't in the right frame of mind to search her out. It didn't mean he wasn't furious with her. He pulled out his phone and shot her a text, telling her to come to his place after she got off work. She'd likely read more into his invitation than Mike intended, but that wasn't his problem. He'd had enough of being manipulated to last him a lifetime.

****

Grace stacked her handmade placemats into a neat pile and set a bowl of yarn on top of them. She stood back to admire her handiwork. Her house was immaculate. The entire nine hundred square feet of space, excluding Hope's room, gleamed from end to end. A second load of clothes pulsed in the washing machine while the first load spun in the dryer. Busy work to help her decide what to do about Mike's invitation to join him in October.

She picked at the edge of a mat as she remembered the scent of his shampoo, felt the press of his forehead on hers. Relived the panicked clench of her stomach muscles at his unexpected request. She picked up a ball of yarn and relished the familiar feel of it against her palm.

A weekend together and then what? She tossed the yarn back into the bowl. Were forty-eight hours of pleasure worth the pain of saying goodbye all over again?

Join the dance, Gracie.

She spied the box of her mother's things and pried off the lid. She spotted a fridge magnet made of looped yarn and googly eyes that Grace had made long ago. The words *Happy Mother's Day* were printed in childish letters along the handle.

Don't you love it, Mommy! It looks like I bought it at the store. I did such a good job. Don't you think so, Mommy!

She put the magnet and the memory aside and pulled out her mom's favorite book of poetry, worn and tattered. She flipped to a page she knew by heart, imagined her mother's hand on her cheek.

Gracie, people forget a lot, but never how you make them feel.

Cissy's knitting needles pierced her last ball of yarn and her final row of stitches. They rested next to an empty bottle of her favorite perfume. She twisted off the cap and breathed in the last scents of spice and fruit. Her dad had bought her mom a bottle every Christmas.

You smell good, Mommy.

Thank you, sweetheart. Be good for the sitter, okay?

She picked up another of her mom's favorite books. She fanned the pages, hoping to encourage another memory. Or find a sign suggesting what her mom would have advised her to do about Mike's invitation. Instead, a scrap of paper fluttered to the floor, followed by an ancient, pressed daisy.

Grace rescued the fragile flower and set it aside to pick up the yellowed slip of paper. She squinted at the scrawling words: *Meet me. You know the place. Ian.*

With a flash, she saw Ian standing at the edge of the embankment, with what she had thought was sorrow bowing his head. She dropped the paper and pressed her fingertips to her aching temples. But what if it hadn't been sorrow, but guilt?

Had Ian and her mother been having an affair? Had it gone horribly wrong? God, she didn't want to believe it. But there was a weird triangle of past relationships she couldn't make sense of, and she knew the tiny scrap of paper meant something important. She returned the paper and flower to the book to keep them safe and headed for the door.

****

Mike leaned back against his kitchen counter and ate dry cereal out of the box. Mike wanted Hunt off balance, and he was certain he'd succeeded, but he'd also picked up a vibe from Hunt he couldn't define. There was an air about him that had nothing to do with his usual superiority. Something dark, almost foul. He cleared his head of the thought. It wasn't like him to get fanciful or to speculate on people's auras. He dealt in facts.

A knock on his door caught him about to toss a sugarcoated cube of wheat into his mouth.

About damn time.

He didn't reach for the bottle of wine Elizabeth offered along with her greeting, but stepped back to give her room to enter. "We need to talk."

"Your text made that clear." She made her way to the cluttered kitchen counter, her back straight and eyes cautious.

He didn't mince words, unable to keep his frustration from overflowing. "Did you ask Hunt to look for opportunities for me?"

She confiscated a glass tumbler from a box and opened the bottle of wine. "Opportunities present themselves. Does it matter how?"

"It does, and you know it." He shook his head at her offer to pour him a glass. This wasn't a social visit. But he had calmed down enough on his way home from Hunt's office to realize butting heads with her would be counterproductive. She had the answers to some tricky questions. Anger wouldn't get him anywhere with Elizabeth. There was also the matter of what to do with a certain lump sum of money he was absolutely not keeping.

The wine bottle made a nice little click of disapproval when it hit the countertop. "That must have been quite the conversation you and Kevin had today. He's very upset."

It was rare for her to take the offensive, and it put him on guard. "Is that a yes?"

She swallowed a mouthful of wine, but her deflection did nothing to erase her guilty look. "Kevin has become more than a mentor. I'm not apologizing for confiding my hopes or my regrets to a friend."

Definitely, a yes. He left her fateful admission hanging, vowing to circle back around to her motives, and moved on. "Has he mentioned Grace?"

She concentrated on her wine, set it swirling inside her glass. "After the town hall meeting, he was curious about your relationship with her."

"What did you tell him?"

She met his glare with one of her own. "Nothing, as I'm not privy to any details."

He certainly wasn't about to provide any.

When he remained silent, she sighed. "I might have mentioned you appeared quite taken with her."

"Did it occur to you to wonder why he's so curious about a woman who shouldn't even be on his radar?" Hunt was calculated, careful, and obviously very patient. Mike still hadn't figured out Hunt's end goal, and he was running out of time. He pushed harder. "There's something about this guy that I don't like. Or trust. How did you meet him?"

"Your mother arranged a meeting. He was looking for a campaign manager." Elizabeth indulged in a quick sip of wine. "She suggested I apply for the position."

"You as his chief of staff doesn't exactly work in her favor."

"No. She doesn't want me in Ottawa any more than she wants you in Toronto. But she's also aware Kevin has to win for it to become a reality."

"And judging by the polls, that is far from a sure thing."

Elizabeth nodded her head in agreement. "We have our work cut out for us."

Mike's gut told him Hunt wouldn't be giving any

victory speeches. And likely his mother, with her network of cronies and her command of politics, had made the call long before now. Right about the time she put Elizabeth on Kevin Hunt's radar. "So she put you in my path and is counting on you to lure me back to the city when Hunt loses. And hopes a reinstated trust fund and an elevated position at Alton and Davenport will keep me there."

"She's getting impatient. She never expected you to stay away this long." She lifted her glass. "The only reason she agreed to the deal I made was her belief you'd come back on your own."

"With my tail between my legs, begging for my old life back."

"She never understood you."

He hadn't asked her over to discuss his mommy issues, which led them back to square one. "Did you ask Hunt to create an opportunity for me?"

"I did not." She'd always been easy to read, and he recognized guilt when he saw it. He only had to wait a few seconds before she relented. "But that doesn't mean he didn't take it upon himself to create an opportunity that might prove beneficial to both of us."

He frowned. "Not even Hunt is egoistical enough to assume his victory is a given."

Elizabeth lifted an elegant shoulder. "He's arranged another opportunity for me in Ottawa should he be defeated in November."

A reminder she was more than capable of looking after herself. He didn't issue words of caution. Didn't respond to the puzzled, pleading look in her eyes. He let it go. Let her go. Let the guilt go. And finally laid that part of his past to rest. "I hear it's a great city. I hope you find the life you're searching for there. Justin would want you to be happy. I want that for you, too."

There wasn't much more to say. He walked over to his desk and picked up the check he had ready and waiting. "Take it. Use it to distance yourself from everything Davenport."

She shook her head, sadness dampening her eyes. "I'll make it happen on my own."

"How about this?" Mike folded the check and held it out to her. "We donate it, in Justin's name, to his foundation."

"An excellent idea. I'll see that it gets done." She kissed his cheek and whispered, "Goodbye, Michael."

He was saved from an awkward send-off by a banging on his door. Mike found Grace on the other side tapping her foot and in a disturbing state of rumpled impatience.

"Hey." Grace pushed her hair back and stunned him by saying, "I think I know who might have killed my mom."

While he struggled to process her startling declaration, she burst inside his apartment and waved a book in his face. "A note. Written by Ian."

"That's my cue to leave." The door shut with a quiet click.

Grace wrapped her arms around her middle. "Am I interrupting something?"

"No."

"That's not the vibe I'm picking up."

"Then your radar's off."

Grace rubbed a thumb over the same cheek Elizabeth had kissed. She looked down at the red color smeared over her thumb. "Her favorite."

He snagged a piece of paper towel and wiped away the rest of Elizabeth's goodbye. "It's not what you think."

"And what am I thinking?"

"There is nothing between Elizabeth and me. There hasn't been for a long time. You know that, right? Especially, after last night, I would never—"

But of course, his history suggested otherwise.

"This isn't about whether there is a you and me and if we're exclusive. I found this." She held up the book in her hand.

"A book?"

"Read it. Not the book. This." She plucked a scrap of paper out of the book and thrust it at him. "What do you think it means?"

It was time she knew the truth, but he wavered over the best way to reveal it. "Grace…"

Her voice dropped to a whisper. "What if it was Ian?"

"Grace, he has an alibi for the weekend your mother disappeared."

"I saw him this afternoon. On Hook-up Hill." When he opened his mouth to ask what the hell she was doing there, she waved him off. "I took some flowers up there. He was standing there staring down at the spot where…you know…it happened. There was this feeling in the air. I was so sure it was grief. And not all of it mine. But what if it was guilt?"

He put a hand on her arm. "Grace, it wasn't him."

"Why did she keep it?" She pointed at the note, then snatched the book back and plucked out something else. "These were her favorite flower. Ian has one like it on his arm."

He ignored what he assumed was a dried flower. "Grace, listen to—"

"Why was he up there?"

"That's something you need to ask Ian."

"Why? Last time I looked, you were the police officer." She pulled away, stuffed the crumbling flower back into the book. "It's your job to ask him."

He tried one last time. "Grace, it wasn't him."

"Can't you see?" Her voice dipped. "If he didn't have anything to do with her death, then she meant something else to him. Something private and intimate."

She deserved the truth, and it was clear Martin wasn't going to tell her. He cupped her cheek. "I asked you once before to trust me."

She all but stamped her foot. "That's why I'm here."

He didn't want to be the one to tell her. The truth needed to come from one of the men who should have told her in the first place, and that meant he had to take her to talk to Ian. "Promise me, after you get the answers you're after, you'll give me a chance to explain."

"Explain what? What's going on?"

He brushed his lips over hers. "We're going to see Ian."

She shook her head.

"I'm asking again. Do you trust me?"

"I wouldn't have slept with you if I didn't."

He pulled her into his arms, the book, her family's needs, and his rapidly approaching departure date crushed between them. She felt so good there.

He smoothed a hand over her hair. "Then let me

take you to Ian."

Wariness lingered in her gorgeous eyes, but she straightened her shoulders and nodded. It was a silent ride to the Connelly place, anxiety and worry eclipsing the peaceful glow of early evening. Grace didn't ask questions. He didn't offer answers. He only held her hand, hoping it wasn't for the last time.

Chapter Eleven

Grace stepped out of Mike's car and studied the profusion of white and pink daises bordering Ian's veranda. Such an innocent, humble flower, but these ones reeked of secrets. Had he planted them, had one tattooed on his arm knowing they were her mom's favorite? She pictured her mother's quick smile. Remembered her many kindnesses. Often to people who didn't deserve her thoughtfulness. She wanted to remember her as loyal and true. As the perfect mother. Even as she felt those certainties slipping away.

Mike squeezed her hand. "You ready?"

She tightened her grip. "No."

Concern etched grooves into his forehead. "What he has to say won't bring about the end of the world. But it will change things."

"I don't particularly like change." And wasn't that the understatement of the decade. Wasn't she standing there in threadbare jeans purchased who knew when, a T-shirt she'd mended too many times to count, in broken down shoes she couldn't bear to part with?

"You also never back down from a challenge."

"I'm not falling for that flattery crap, so knock it off." When her death glare failed to intimidate him, she sighed. "You're going to make me go in there alone, aren't you?"

"I'll be out here. Waiting for you." His reassurance

combined with the warmth of his hand calmed her racing heart.

Ian stepped out his front door, hands twisting in a dishtowel, his dog pushing through his legs. "Duke. Heel."

"It's okay." Grace held out her hand for Duke's approval and bent to scratch behind his ears when he nudged closer.

There was no way to ease into a conversation she didn't want to have, so she didn't try. "Why were you on Hook-up Hill today?"

Ian stuffed the dishtowel into his back pocket, all his stoic animosity directed at Mike. "I told you to stay out of this."

Mike didn't back down. "It's time."

Duke whined and trotted back to his owner. Ian reached down and ran a hand over the dog's head. "It's okay, boy."

Grace forced the words out. "I'm thinking the worst, and it's killing me."

Still no answer.

"Talk to her, Ian."

"It won't help anything."

Good God, he was stubborn. She stepped away from Mike and moved toward the unyielding man in front of her. "Will it save me from wondering if you might have hurt my mom?"

Ian's shock flashed, then shattered. "Never."

She put a hand on his arm. "Ian, let me in."

"Stubborn."

There was no heat to his accusation. He led her into his neat but stark kitchen and pulled out a chair for her. He got down coffee mugs, set them on the table, and came back with the coffee pot. All without saying a word.

She wrapped cold hands around her mug and waited for Ian to add two doses of sugar to his cup. "Ian, talk to me."

He lifted his head, and it was hard to differentiate between pupil and iris, the swirl of emotion was so thick. "Your mother and I were close. Before I went to prison. We were…involved."

There was nothing especially startling about a teenage relationship. She dumped sugar in her own coffee, stirred, waited, and got nothing from the man across from her. She didn't have the rest of her life to have this conversation. "You had feelings for her."

"It's more complicated than that."

She dug deep for what little patience she had left. "So explain why it was so complicated."

"I-I loved her. But we couldn't be together." His short confession winded him.

"Because you went to prison," she prompted.

He nodded.

She flattened her palms against the tabletop, hoping to draw strength from the aging wood. "Ian, I can see that you had strong feelings for her, but I'm still not getting what that has to do with me. Or why it's such a secret."

"She was pregnant." He shifted in his seat, but his gaze never left hers. "With you. When I went away."

Denial was instinctive and immediate. Her life had never suffered from an overabundance of structure. But his confession stripped her of the one constant in her life—her identity. She was a Bighill. She felt like a Bighill, even when her name hadn't done her any favors.

"No," she whispered.

His reply was equally desperate. "Yes."

"That would mean…"

"It doesn't have to mean anything."

Well, then.

His words buzzed about the thin air, like poisonous wasps stinging her sensitive skin and bringing tears to her eyes. "Clearly, it didn't mean much to you."

Ian raised his chin, his hesitation dissolving. "That's not true."

She shoved his declaration aside for the moment. "My dad, does he know?"

"Yes." He gave a quick nod, like he'd anticipated her question and could answer this one thing with certain forthright honesty, if not integrity. "Cissy was honest with him from the start."

"Right." She swallowed hard. "Good for her."

"He loved her."

"Enough to overlook certain obstacles."

"He loved everything about her, including you."

"Unlike you?"

His knuckles, strained thin and white over knobby bone, clenched around his cup. "I wasn't in a position to look after either of you."

Screw reasonable. All those taunts in the schoolyard? The rumors hinted at by malevolent do-gooders? They'd been true. One hundred percent accurate. "Perfectly valid reason to dump us off onto someone else."

"Your mother confided her pregnancy to your father, her best friend since grade school. A man as loyal as they come. He offered her a life." He leaned forward, a quest for understanding in every stretch of taut muscle. "I went to prison knowing you were in the care of a man who would love you both."

She dusted her hands off. "Problem solved."

"Don't," he warned.

"Don't what?" she snapped back. "Don't ask why the subject of you being my biological father never came up? Not in thirty fucking years. Not after my mother disappeared? Not when you moved five kilometers down the goddamned road from me?" She hurtled the curse words she seldom used at Ian, who sat vibrating in his chair, a silent witness to a side she rarely unleashed. "Or don't ask why after I became an adult you still didn't tell me shit?"

He slapped his hands down on the table and lifted out of his seat. "Do not act like my not getting to raise you was no big deal to me."

She ignored his raised voice. "Did you and my mother pick up where you left off after you were released?"

His stood tall, his face hard as stone. "You know better than to ask that question of your mother."

Oh, no, he hadn't gone there. Hadn't taken the patronizing high ground. "Answer the question."

"No, we did not." His words, bitten and chewed over, slapped at her.

No flood of relief washed away her righteous anger. Not when she wasn't certain she believed him.

Apparently, sharing DNA did have its benefits because he read her mind. "I'm being as honest as I can here, Grace."

She looked up at him from where her own butt remained planted in her chair. "Why did you come back here?"

His head dipped, and when he faced her again, there was nothing left but total devastation.

"Ian." She closed her eyes and took a deep breath. "Sit down. Please."

He perched on the edge of his seat and wrapped his hands around his coffee mug as if he needed a concrete object to tether him to time and space.

She tried again. "The reason is important to me."

"I didn't just lose my freedom when those bars locked behind me. I lost everyone I loved. But you were safe. That's what kept me sane. When she disappeared, I knew I had to come back and make sure you stayed safe."

"Safe?" From where she was sitting, he hadn't protected her from much of anything.

"From Kevin Hunt."

"What does he have to do with this?"

"He's never forgiven me for killing his brother. When he failed to keep me in prison, he settled on harassing me, and he hasn't stopped. I did everything I could to make sure he never found out about you."

She didn't buy his reasoning. "Did it ever occur to you the truth would have set us all free? That if you'd taken away that bit of leverage, he would have left me alone? Left all of us alone."

"You don't know what he's capable of. I do. That doesn't mean I'm not sorry—" He reached across the table for her hand.

She yanked hers back and settled her hands in her lap. "Some of us value the truth more than others, I guess."

His eyes shut tight, but not soon enough to hide his

cold, stark fear. "That night at the Back Forty, he put it all together. I know he did."

She struggled to inject a sense of reality into a world turned upside down. "What difference does it make? She's gone. The truth can't hurt her."

The menace behind his growl raised the hair on her arms. "Hunt will make a scandal out of it. More gossip. People will drag up the past and twist it into something it wasn't. Hunt hates your dad almost as much as he hates me. And your mother—" He clamped his mouth shut.

She refused to be governed by his paranoia. "I'll survive it. My family, too."

"You sure about that?"

She met him glare for glare. "My dad is my problem, not yours."

"What about Hope and the reaction of that mother-in-law of hers? Levi and the kids at school?" His anger poured over her like wet cement, looking, she knew, to smother her defiance. "Martin Senior, when he finds out his son isn't your biological father?"

She resisted the hardening process. "Maybe you're the one who doesn't want people to know. Maybe you're protecting yourself more than anyone."

"What about every goddamned person in this town who has ever had a bad thing to say about your mother?"

"Stop it."

Her order fell on deaf ears. "When all of a sudden your sister's husband can't find work because Hunt has blackballed him? Or Hope can't find a job because for some mysterious reason no one will hire her?"

"Do you know how crazy you're sounding right

now?" But his mistrust of Hunt was rubbing off. The night at The Pines, she'd known something was very off about him. Had sensed he had an agenda, even though she hadn't understood his intention.

Find me when you figure out the right questions.

Ian's lips barely moved, but each word had an edge and plenty of disgust. "I'm not the one who's disturbed."

"I need time to process...all this." She glanced down at her watch. How had an hour evaporated since she'd sat down? She looked up to see him staring at her wrist. And she knew by the awful tightening of her skin underneath the cool leather of the band. "This is yours, isn't it?"

He swallowed, a long painful-looking process that raked claws down his throat from the inside. "Yes."

She undid the buckle and placed it on the table, smoothing out the straps. Then she pushed back from the table. He didn't try and stop her from leaving. She paused at the screen door. Mike was sitting on the bottom step, elbows resting on his knees, staring into space, dog beside him. When she opened the door, he got to his feet.

"Have long have you known?" she asked.

"A couple of weeks."

Weeks.

She urged her feet to move. One step at a time, much like she'd done every day since her mom had disappeared. She heard the slap of the door opening and closing, Ian calling her name, Mike cautioning him to let her go.

Five kilometers separated her house and Ian's. It was going to take her walking the entire stretch of road to work through what she'd learned and absorb the betrayal, the humiliation of being the last to know her parents' deception.

****

Mike gave Grace a couple of hours to come to terms with Ian's confession and his own withholding of information before seeking her out. He found her curled up in an ancient wicker rocker on her front porch, protected from the evening's faint chill by one of her colorful blankets and a cat in her lap. Porch light pooled on the worn deck boards and fought back the advancing darkness.

Hope met him on the top step, hands on hips, eyes hollowed out with worry. "She won't tell me what's going on."

Grace refused to meet his look. He scrubbed a hand over the back of his neck. "She'll talk when she's ready."

"Well, someone better tell me something soon." An *or else* from Hope Bighill-Walker was worth taking seriously. She stepped aside when he nodded. Waited while he crouched down in front of Grace.

The cat took more notice of him than Grace did, hopping from her lap with a glare and a twitch of its tail. "I'll leave if you want me to."

She gave an infinitesimal shake of her head, and he made a tentative reach for her hand. When she didn't jerk away, he gathered her fingers in his. He looked to their chaperone. "We're good. Thanks."

"Don't make me sorry I'm trusting you." She kissed the top of Grace's head and retreated into the house.

Grace's gaze remained fixed on the encroaching

dark, but her fingers tightened around his. "I kind of hate you right now."

Two thousand five hundred and six kilometers would separate them in less than two weeks. He tried to visualize that vast amount of space, with its time difference, his crazy work hours, and Grace's own unpredictable schedule. Even facing the reality of that distance, he found it almost impossible to imagine saying goodbye after having a taste of her in his life. He wanted the possibilities, a chance to keep her. Assuming she forgave him. And he wanted her to say yes to his invitation to spend the weekend with him in October.

"You knew. And you didn't tell me." She finally looked him dead in the eye, this woman who wielded a sword in defense of those she loved, even when her arms had to ache from the weight of it. "What if I hadn't gone to you for help?"

"I would have told you." He desperately wanted to believe it was the truth.

She gathered her blanket closer. "As a parting gift?"

"The day I came to visit your father and you were there? I gave him a week to tell you."

"Passing the buck?"

"Truth?" he asked.

She nodded.

"You're right. I didn't want to be the one to tell you." With his thighs burning from his crouched position and his heart breaking, he dropped to his knees. "I wanted to be the one you came to when you found out. The one you leaned on, took comfort from.

"You were already dealing with the discovery of

your mother's body." The scent of flowers he didn't know the name of wafted around them as she sat in a picture-perfect spill of light. "Finding out about Ian was going to be another blow, and I didn't want to be the one to deliver it."

He waited for a forgiving look or touch, a reassurance things were okay between them. But all he got was her sigh of resignation.

"You not telling me hurt, and don't go thinking I've forgiven you, but that's not really the point. Ian not telling me isn't the point either. My parents should have told me."

Her cheek was as soft as a whisper under his fingertips, fragile, unlike the woman. "They likely planned to tell you when you were older, but…"

She finished his train of thought. "My mom vanishing turned our world upside down."

"Martin could still be planning to tell you at some point."

"It's a nice thought." She let go of his hand and wrapped her blanket tighter around her shoulders. He gained his feet to clear her path to the porch railing. "After she disappeared, I would lie awake at night, waiting until I heard the door of that stupid room close. I would listen for the creak of the stairs. I'd give him a few minutes to settle, then I'd go downstairs to where he slept on the couch, never their bed, and cover him with a blanket. He'd pat my hand and say, 'Thanks, Gracie.' He'd close his eyes and pretend to go to sleep."

Careful not to crowd her, he braced his hands on the railing beside her. "It's obvious to everyone that he loves you. Very much."

She searched the dark, leaned into it as it pressed

against her. "He never treated me any differently than he did Hope. There were rumors, sure. But I never put any stock in them. I never suspected they were true, *not once*. Knowing where—who—I came from was the one thing I was sure of."

Surprised by her mention of rumors, he didn't show it. "You're his daughter. In every sense that counts."

"Do you think Ian made the right choice? Is that what you'd have done?"

He wished he could claim hero status for her sake. "The person I was at nineteen would have considered an unwanted pregnancy a problem. I would have found a way to make that problem go away."

She flinched. "Gee, way to sugarcoat things."

"Grace, baby, he was a teenager." He couldn't stand the non-contact any longer. He wrapped her in his arms and whispered the rest into her hair. "And he wasn't the only one involved in that decision. They were two desperate people with very few options."

Her hands slipped around his waist and twisted into the back of his shirt. She nestled her cheek to his chest. "She loved my dad. I know she did. I felt it."

What was there to say? He rubbed soothing circles over her back as moths flirted with the light and coyotes yipped in the distance. A shadow appeared at the window, then disappeared.

They stayed twined together until she pulled away. "But I think, maybe, she loved Ian, too. And neither of those men chose to tell their daughter the truth."

"Ian kept your paternity a secret to protect you. Martin, too. Like your mother kept it." He ran a hand over her sleek hair. "Kevin Hunt has never forgiven Ian for killing his brother."

She pulled away from him, and once again her focus centered on the darkness of the yard. "The night I met him at The Pines, he kept mentioning my father. Insinuating at something I didn't understand. He said to come to him when I knew the right questions to ask. I'd say the secret of my parentage isn't much of a secret. At least, not to Hunt."

He dampened the instinct to take her chin in his hand and force her attention back to him. She wasn't a willful child, and he wouldn't treat like one. "Promise me you won't underestimate him."

"Do you think Hunt killed my mother?"

"I don't know," he admitted. "There's no evidence to support that conclusion. Doesn't mean he didn't make things difficult for her. For your family." It was time for him to come clean on another issue. "Did you know your parents were in financial trouble?"

She surprised him by nodding. "Hunt mentioned it."

Was it proof Hunt had firsthand knowledge of the scam? "When?"

"The night at The Pines, he said she came to see him, not to ask for money but for forgiveness. Which is weird. Not to mention absurd. I mean, what's one got to do with the other?"

"From what I can piece together, your dad, Martin, invested in a high-risk venture capital scheme managed by someone who pretended to be affiliated with a legitimate start-up fund. Because of it, your parents were facing foreclosure."

Grace's brows wrinkled in confusion. "But it never happened."

"No."

He knew the instant she made the connection. "Ian."

"Yes."

She bowed her head.

"Hey." He bumped his shoulder against hers. "You're allowed to be pissed at him and entitled to stay that way for a while. Just be aware, Hunt is irrational when it comes to the people who were there the night his brother died. I think he's the one who engineered the scam."

"I knew there was a reason the guy gave me the creeps."

"I'm looking to see if there's any kind of paper trail that leads the scam back to Hunt." But now he couldn't help but wonder if Cassandra Bighill had put it all together and gone to Hunt to see if she could reason with him. Or worse, accuse him.

"God." She laid her head on his shoulder.

He kissed her temple. "You're amazing, you know that, right?"

She snuggled closer. "Is amazing code for exhausted?"

He tugged her with him as he sought out the old rocker and coaxed her into his lap. "So take a nap."

She was asleep in seconds.

Fifteen minutes later, Hope delivered a glass of lemonade and a couple of cookies. To thank her for her peace offering, he offered a quiet smile. "No one's ever brought me cookies on a pretty plate before."

She narrowed her eyes.

He lowered his guard a fraction more. "My mother didn't believe in offering children treats, unless it was their birthday or an important holiday."

She didn't so much as blink. "That explains a lot."

He was already regretting making the effort. "It happens to be true."

"You're a funny guy." She gave his shoulder a tap. "I'm off to bed."

He nodded in relief and shifted Grace to ease some of the ache out of his arms.

"Will you stay?" Her voice was foggy with sleep.

He imagined saying yes to the bigger question she wasn't asking. "What? You thought leaving was a possibility?"

"I don't want you to think you have to. Stay, I mean." She tilted her head back, eyes heavy with the vulnerability she was trying hard to hide. "I'll be fine."

His heart stuttered, then knocked so hard he was pretty sure she could feel the haggard thump. "I'll stay the night. That way we can make sure we're both fine."

She slid off his lap and held out her hand. He ignored it and scooped her up into his arms.

She latched onto his neck. "Don't you dare drop me."

"You mean like this." And he let her slip a couple of inches before tightening his hold again.

She squealed and held on tight. "Stop it."

His chest rumbled with unexpected laughter. He was so damn thankful to hear her giggle after the hit she'd taken earlier.

Grace ran a light finger over his lips. "You should laugh more."

There had been many times in the last seven years when he'd been sure joy and spontaneity would never find him again. "It's easy to do around you."

She raised her brows. "I amuse you, do I?"

"You entice me. Everything about you."

She tugged his head down, and her mouth opened under his. When the kiss was over, the slow slide of her body down the length of his was a sexy tease of things to come.

"Please, tell me your bed is nearby."

She took his hand and led him to her room. Her private space was a revelation, and he drank in the colored order. Drawings by Levi mingled with sketches done by Seth. A desk sat underneath them. Wall hooks held knitted scarves and bags. Her bed hosted heaps of pillows.

She slid her hands under his shirt. "I'll give you a tour later."

He reached back and grabbed a handful of his shirt and tugged it off. He shed his pants while she lost her T-shirt and shorts. She was reaching around her back to release her bra when he stilled her hand.

"Let me." He picked her up and laid her on the bed.

She stroked his cheek as he bent over her. "I love your growly noises."

He hadn't realized he was making them. It reminded him they weren't alone in her cozy little house. "I hope your sister is a sound sleeper."

She grinned up at him. "I guess we'll find out."

He dropped a sweet kiss onto her lips. She chased it, tried to deepen it, but he lifted his head. "Are you sure you're up for this? It's been a long day."

Her eager hand found its way to his aching groin. She palmed his erection. "I am kind of tired."

He was powerless to stop the need to rub against her curling fingers.

"Fragile little me should probably get some rest." Her hand slipped beneath the waistband of his underwear to his cock. "You definitely shouldn't put your hands on me. Or your mouth."

"Very bad ideas, considering." He traced the curve of her breast with his tongue. She arched underneath him. He slid the strap of her bra over her shoulder and kissed a path along her collarbone.

She pushed at his underwear. "Off."

Her bra and panties followed his boxers to the floor. "Remind me again. Where should I put my mouth?"

Her hands roamed up his ribcage to curl around his shoulders, and her nails dug into his skin. "Getting bossed around in bed turns you on, huh?"

"Apparently."

The more she twisted under him, the harder he tried to catch his breath. Desire warmed her skin. The sheets rustled as she spread her legs. He lost himself in her reactions, making sure his fingers didn't dig too deep. That he didn't push too hard, too fast. That he gave more than he took as desire guided them the rest of the way.

It was still pitch dark when the buzzing of his phone woke him. He fumbled around on his bedside table, but everything was out of place. Then he remembered whose bed he was in and that his phone was in his pants, which were on Grace's floor. He squinted at her bedside clock where the red numbers announced it was 1:48 a.m.

He slid out of bed and located his phone, kept his voice low. "Davenport."

"Thought you were smarter than that."

Recognizing the voice, Mike shouldered his phone against his ear and yanked on his pants. Her bedroom door closed behind him with a soft click. "Yeah, why's that?"

"Thought I could trust you."

"You can." He heard a motor running in the background and guessed he was in his truck, likely nearby. Guided by the light of the moon, Mike made his way to the window with a view of the laneway.

"She needs people around her she can trust."

"You're not planning anything stupid, are you, Ian?" Mike heard the pull of a cigarette. The faint sizzle of burning tobacco. The inhale and exhale of smoke.

There was another long moment of silence. "I was too late to save her mother. I won't let anything happen to her."

Mike eased out of the house onto the front porch. "Nothing's going to happen to Grace."

"Not sure why I should take your word for it."

"Don't know why you wouldn't." Mike scanned the road for signs of a vehicle sitting in the dark.

"If she ends up hurt, I swear to God…"

Mike didn't care for the threat in Ian's words. "Ian, don't make me—"

But Ian disconnected, and vehicle lights flickered far down the grid road. He shoved his phone in his back pocket and dialed Deke, who was on duty. He didn't need Ian going vigilante on him. Deke promised to keep an eye out for Ian. It was the best he could do, as it was a busy night.

Grace had claimed the entire bed in his absence. For someone who didn't reach much past five feet, she took up a lot of room. He slid back in, careful at first not to awaken her, until he realized he'd have to set off a bomb to make it happen.

He gathered her up close. Strands of her hair caught between his fingers, silky soft and tempting. Sensing warmth, she burrowed closer. In no time at all, her leg settled over his, and her arm draped over his chest. She didn't stop until she was half on top of him, holding him in place. He wrapped his arms around her in relief.

Chapter Twelve

The annual Labor Day barbecue was tradition, held on the Saturday evening of the September long weekend. People came and went, though most stayed, and a favored few held out until the sun rose the next morning. Grace had every intention of watching the sunrise, but she'd be taking it in from her own porch with a blanket and Mike wrapped around her.

Enjoy him while you can.

Grace hoisted the gigantic bowl out of her backseat and tried not to get potato salad on her newly purchased top. She was going to live the heck out of tonight. Because, hey, she had a date, even if he was coming late. That meant skinny jeans, impossibly pink nail polish, and a fresh coat of lip-gloss on her lips.

Music poured out of Kate and Seth's backyard, a country song about picnics, blankets, and a meadow out back. Fairy lights glittered in welcome. Citronella torches and gossiping matrons rimmed the perimeter of the yard.

"Oh, wonderful. Your mom's potato salad. People have been asking after it." Sunni rushed to greet her. "Let me take that for you."

"Thanks, Sunni."

"Kate's over there, feeding Chloe." Hands full of salad, Sunni bent her elbow toward a corner of the yard.

Seth manned the enormous grill rented for the

occasion, and the scent of burgers and hotdogs made her mouth water. She stopped by the drinks table to grab two glasses of lemonade.

"Fabulous job. I'd say the bar has officially been raised. So thanks for that." She stuck her tongue out at Kate and set the glasses on a small plastic side table.

"Your turn next year." Kate, blanket draped over her shoulder, cuddled a nursing Chloe. "But I can't take all the credit. Sunni and Mary have been here all day helping out."

The sun dipped, and a pre-autumn chill slipped in, making Grace glad she'd packed a sweater.

Kate shifted Chloe and adjusted her shirt. "Haven't seen or heard much from you the past week. How are you doing?"

"Me? I'm fine."

"A few steps up from fine." Kate raised a brow. "You're glowing."

"Oh, my gosh, your outfit. I love it." Lily dropped into a patio chair on the other side of Kate. "Haven't seen you much lately."

"Things are a little crazy right now." She was tempted to announce she'd worked her last shift that day, but she hadn't mentioned quitting her job to anyone yet. Or what she'd learned of her parentage. And both those things came in a sad second to her ache over Mike's looming departure.

"Did you hear about the crash?" asked Lily. "Thank God there were no fatalities, but still plenty awful."

She also knew, as did Lily, that Mike and Chase had been first on the scene. She could only imagine the memories attending a scene like that brought to the surface for Mike. She wanted to hold him, to comfort him, like he'd done for her.

"Are you okay?" asked Kate.

Grace clapped her hands together and forced a smile. "Never better. Let's get this party started."

Kate patted Chloe's back. "I don't think you're okay."

Grace didn't want to answer any hard questions. Not tonight. "Why wouldn't I be okay?"

Kate was unusually careful with her answer. "With Mike leaving so soon, we thought you might be feeling a little down."

"I was thinking we should go somewhere next weekend. Get away. Have a little girl time." The pity in Lily's eyes made Grace's stomach roll.

Grace didn't want to think about Mike leaving, let alone talk about it. She didn't want to explain she was spending the weekend with him in a couple of weeks. They'd be excited she was stepping out of her comfort zone. Then they'd want to know what came next. And she didn't have an answer to give them. Or herself. "I'm starving. I think I'll go get something to eat."

Kate put a hand on her arm. "Grace—"

"Not now." Because she couldn't. She just could not. "Okay?"

Kate let her go. "But soon."

Grace piled her plate with a burger, pork and beans, and enough side salads to keep her mouth busy with eating instead of talking. Round tables were set up on the patio, and she joined a group of other Back Forty employees, refusing to feel guilty about avoiding Kate and Lily. She was tossing her empty plate into the trash when Scott cornered her.

"Grace, I need to talk to you."

She tamped down her frustration. "Sure, what about?"

"Not here."

"Okay, but—" He was already dragging her down the path leading to the lake's shoreline. She stumbled over a rock, regained her balance, all without Scott noticing a thing. She yanked her arm free. "Jeez, I'm coming. Slow down."

They stopped as abruptly as they'd started. "You have to get her to let up."

She could play dumb with the best of them. "Who?"

Scott glared at her. "Hope! Who do you think?"

Grace shrugged. "Let up about what?"

"Me." He ran a hand through his hair. "Us. She's always around. Feeding us. Cleaning. Organizing."

"You poor thing." She was so done getting caught in the middle of her sister's marriage. "I can see how you'd be upset over her getting her act together."

"It's not funny."

No, it wasn't. It was getting old. "Is it Levi? Is he upset? Confused?"

"No." A muscle jumped along his jawline. "He's coming around fine. He likes having her around."

She spread her hands. "Then I'm at a loss here, Scott. What exactly is the problem?"

And how had she gotten into the habit of solving those for him?

His voice dropped. "She wants us to get back together."

Grace stared at him. "And this is a shock because…"

"It. Can't. Happen." He punctuated every word with a huff of breath.

She waved her hands in an abort-mission kind of way. "I already know too much about your relationship. This is for the two of you to figure out."

"It can't happen because I have feelings for you."

Whoa.

And hell, no. They were not going there. She deliberately spun his claim in a different direction. "Of course you do. I'm your sister-in-law. We've got each other's back—"

Then he kissed her. Like really laid one on her. His mouth on hers, his hands grasping her arms. *Cripes, was that his tongue?*

She slapped at his chest and gained an inch of space. "Let me go."

"You heard her, Walker."

Mike stood behind them, his hair damp from his shower, and no less a threat for his casual attire.

Hope huddled beside him, a shattered expression on her face.

Scott backed up but not far enough. She gave him another shove. "It's not what it looks like."

Said every last guilty person ever.

Mike crossed his arms. "Explain yourself."

It took Grace a second to realize he wasn't demanding an explanation from her.

Scott wasn't as quick. "She doesn't owe you an explanation."

"You're right about that, she doesn't. But you owe one to your wife."

"None of this is any of your damn business."

Grace smacked Scott on the arm. "Stop it."

"I'm making it my business."

She pointed a finger at Mike. "Not helping."

A hint of temper showed in his face. "He kissed you."

She let out a squeaky, guilty laugh. "It wasn't really a kiss."

"Yes, it was," insisted Scott.

She hit him again. Harder this time.

"Jesus." He rubbed at the bright red mark on his arm. "Ow."

"Don't make me do it again," Grace warned.

"I'm not standing here or listening to another word." Hope stumbled her way up the path.

Mike advanced. "Way to upset your pregnant wife, Walker."

There it was. Irritation and a little bit of what he'd been through that day. She gave him a look. "Mike, easy."

But Scott was oblivious to all but his own problems. "What's it to you?"

In that moment, she officially and unequivocally reached the end of her rope. She was done. "You know what? Knock it off. You're panicking because things are going great. You love pretending it was all Hope's fault your relationship went south. But it wasn't. It was just as much your fault. She's stepping up to the plate, and it's freaking you out because you know it's up to you to do the same. Stop being an ass, go after your wife, and stop dragging me into the middle of your marriage."

Mike opened his mouth.

She jabbed a finger in his direction again. "Not another word out of you." She turned to Scott. "Tell me this, did the earth move? Did you get butterflies? Cramps? See stars? Be honest."

"It's not that simple."

His hedging took some of the fight out of her. "Yes, it is. Go talk to your wife. She's the one who churns you up. Stop lying to yourself about what you want and go fix your marriage."

When he hesitated, she pointed in the direction Hope had disappeared. "Go."

When Scott stomped off, she rubbed a hand over her aching forehead. "Crap."

Mike definitely had the right idea, new life in a new place. Visit family on holidays and special occasions. A little distance wouldn't be the end of the world, and she might even gain some much-needed perspective.

"Did the earth move for you?" asked Mike.

It was impossible to ignore the hint of vulnerability he was working hard to shrug off. She closed the gap between them and wound her arms around his neck. There was resistance in his stiff muscles, and his hands were slow to circle her waist. She met his question with the truth. "I've felt the earth move all week."

He linked his hands at the base of her spine, urging her closer. "Glad to know it's not just me who's unsteady on their feet."

She attempted to smooth out the furrowed lines of his forehead. "I heard about the crash."

"Everyone's going to be okay." His mind drifted, and he was no longer looking at her but through her.

"Thanks to you." To distract him, she tugged his head down.

His lips were warm against hers. Slow, thorough.

Her fingers teased at the short strands of hair at his nape. He smelled so good. Felt so solid.

He smoothed back her hair. "Let's go be sociable for a while so we can make a scandalously early exit."

She tried to memorize the way his eyes crinkled at the corners, the unhurried curve of his lips. She wanted to attend his brother's memorial with him. Visit him in Toronto. Say yes to possibilities. Adventure. Love. Later tonight, in bed, she'd tell him, and then she'd show him.

He growled low in his throat. "Unless you want to leave now?"

She hated to remind either of them of her brother-in-law's stupidity, but she had no choice. "I have to find Hope. Make sure she's okay."

"Come find me after you've smoothed things over."

The breeze coming off the water caused a shiver. "Promise me you'll stay away from Scott. Even if he's being an idiot."

He rubbed her arms. "Don't worry, I have no intention of going anywhere near your brother-in-law."

Despite the hard edge to his voice, Grace trusted him not to make a scene. Which was more than she could say for Scott. But she refused to waste another minute worrying over a kiss that hadn't meant anything to either of them. Not when her sister was hurting.

They hiked back up the path. Grace linked her hand with his, a silent announcement, a way to say they were a couple, even if it was temporary.

****

Mike choked down a swallow of warm cola. He was too churned up to eat, and alcohol was a definite no-go when he was rattled. He'd learned that the hard way the first few months after Justin's death. He liked alcohol just fine, but he knew his limits and when to leave it alone. Tonight was definitely one of those times.

Scott was hanging out with a couple of friends on the other side of the party. With Grace and Hope nowhere in sight, he was tempted to break his word and corner Walker. Warn him to keep his hands and his mouth off Grace. So yeah, it wasn't smart to indulge in something that would only make it easier to cross the space separating them.

Chase wandered up beside him. "I don't know what Walker did to piss you off, but you might want to dim the death glare."

Mike grunted in reply.

Chase jabbed an elbow into his ribs. "Loosen up, pal. It's a party."

He blinked out of a very satisfying fantasy where he handed Walker his ass on a platter. "What is it about that guy?"

Chase lifted his beer. "Could it be his overprotective attitude to a certain dark-haired gal we all know and love?"

Mike ignored the love reference. "Grace can take care of herself."

"Well, obviously."

Walker wasn't the only thing on Mike's mind. He waited a beat, suddenly wishing he'd gone for the beer. "It's been a bad week in Toronto. Tensions are escalating between two rival gangs, and my new boss wants me there yesterday."

"When the call comes, you gotta go."

"A week sooner than expected."

Chase put a hand on his shoulder. "It's not going to be any easier to leave seven days from now."

No, it wasn't. But he'd figured on more time to plead his case, to convince Grace to take a chance on him despite the terrible timing.

Seth strolled up with Chloe in his arms. "Hey."

Mike had never given serious thought to having kids, but he couldn't help but be enchanted by the tiny little person snuggled into the crook of his friend's arm. "She gets cuter every time I see her."

"Thanks." Seth's quick grin disappeared as fast as it appeared. He did a check for eavesdroppers. "Heads-up, Kate and Lily are planning on having a *talk* with you."

Chase groaned in disgust. "I thought we agreed to stay out it."

Seth, with his chill vibes, was a master at ignoring Chase's surliness. "If it was me, I'd appreciate the heads-up."

"They care about her, and they're concerned. I get it." Mike was going to miss the closeness of their little group in a way he'd never have imagined possible. "But I also consider them my friends, too. I think the feeling is mutual."

Seth shifted a wiggling Chloe to his shoulder and rubbed circles over her back. "And if you think your friendship with the two of them trumps their friendship with Grace, you're delusional."

"God help me, I understood that." Chase pinched the spot between his eyes.

"Mike." Kate stepped in beside him and slipped an arm through his. "We were looking for you."

Lily flanked his other side, and her bright smile dimmed much of Mike's concern. They really were friends. "Great party, isn't it?"

Kate batted her eyes at Seth. "I'd love a drink."

Lily cocked her head at Chase, who held his hands up in surrender. "Going. Come on, young one."

"But—" Seth added a bounce to comfort his daughter who seemed as anxious to be on the move as Chase.

"Unless you want to stay and be part of this conversation." Chase dropped a kiss on his wife's cheek. "You. Play nice."

It was hard to laugh off both Chase's warning and Kate death grip on his arm, harder still when Lily dropped her usual sunny expression the moment Chase's back was turned.

"Why don't we take a walk?" asked Kate.

They herded him in the direction of the lake, along the same path that had led to the scene with Walker. A few meters from the water, he called a halt. Thinking to save them all some embarrassment, he leveled a directive of his own. "I'm not talking to you about my relationship with Grace."

Lily peered around him at Kate. "That's promising. He's calling it a relationship."

He wasn't stupid enough to roll his eyes, but he came close.

Kate smoothed her hands over her hips. "Also, points for sounding noble."

Their barbs didn't sting. Much. He braced for more of the same. They cared about their friend. Something he not only understood but was counting on. Didn't mean he was going to cooperate with their inquisition.

"If you're worried about Grace, you should talk to her."

"Like we haven't tried that." Lily's exasperation was undercut with more than a hint of worry. She slipped into the good-cop suit like it was tailored for her. "You're leaving, and she's upset. We get that. But she's more than distressed. She's sad. And we don't like it when our friend is sad."

Kate, born to play the bad cop, didn't spare his sensibilities. "And we want to know what you're going to do about it."

"Are you asking what my intentions are toward Grace?" He injected a hint of humor, unwilling to betray Grace's confidence, certain Grace's upset had more to do with Ian revelations than his departure. When she wanted her friends to know about her paternity, she would tell them.

"This is us asking if you're going to break our friend's heart. Or if you're going to step up and do the opposite."

Mike reined in his temper. "Okay, you've had your fun."

"Fun?" Kate's eyes widened, and her brows rose, never a good sign. "He thinks this is fun for us."

"How is it men know exactly the wrong thing to say?" Lily's lush lips narrowed into a thin line. "Do you have feelings for Grace?"

"Of course I have feelings for her." It was enough. Too much, actually, to have them interrogate him over his feelings for Grace, when *feelings* was so inadequate a word.

"Hallelujah." Lily's head fell back, and she lifted her palms to the sky. "Finally."

Mike gritted his teeth. He didn't go around wearing

his heart on his sleeve. Didn't mean his insides weren't slowly eroding, the direct result of feeling too much.

"Have you even entertained the thought of asking her to come with you?" asked Kate.

Only every minute for the last week. "No. Of course not."

"Why?" demanded Lily.

"Why?" he echoed.

"Yes. Why?" seconded Kate.

How could they not know their friend better than to suggest she would abandon everyone? "Because this is her home. Her family is here. Her friends. Her life."

She couldn't leave. She'd made that very clear.

"I think she'd like Toronto," stated Lily.

"Toronto would be good for her." Kate brushed her hands off like her job was done and the rest was up to him.

Lily's smile was light, but her suggestion wasn't. "You should ask her."

"Probably smarter to act like it was your idea." Kate patted him on the cheek before turning to Lily. "Help me bring out the cake?"

"Sure." Lily linked arms with her friend. "It looks delicious."

"Of course." Kate nodded. "It's Mary's double chocolate fudge."

Who cared about the goddamned cake? "Grace would never leave Aspen Lake."

There was nothing soft or vague about the hard lines of Kate's face. "If you don't ask her, you'll never know for certain."

Lily gave his arm a friendly, reassuring rub, but her set face told a different story. Disappointment. In him.

It hurt to think this strong, resilient woman, who he considered a friend, thought him a coward. Off they went arm in arm like they hadn't turned his world upside down.

Because, damn it, was a future together even possible? Grace was reluctant to commit to a weekend. He'd tried a couple of times during the week to bring it up, but she'd shut him down. And if she wasn't willing to commit to forty-eight hours, how the hell was he supposed to broach the possibility of more?

Behind him the music suggested *the stars were meant to be wished on*. There was an abundance of them illuminating the lake, and he eyed the brightest one. He couldn't bring himself to wish she'd choose him over family. He just wanted her to be happy, however that played out, and he promised to be content with that.

Mike made his way back up the path and spotted Grace helping Lily and Kate hand out pieces of the promised cake. People laughed at whatever jibes Grace served along with the chocolate fudge. She had a way with people. She had a way with him. Life was brighter with her in it.

Ask her.

Someone jostled him from behind. He forced his feet into action. "Hey."

"Hey back." She offered him a slice.

"Looks delicious." Out of the corner of his eye, he saw Lily give him an encouraging thumbs up. If she wanted to think she had played a hand in forcing his, so be it. He plucked the plate out of Grace's hand and tugged her out from behind the table. "Dance with me?"

Her pretty lips parted in surprise. He led her to a

makeshift dance floor with dim lights and slow music. Two other couples swayed and shuffled their way around the tiny space. Mike escorted her into the mix. With her hand in his and his palm settled against her lower back, her hair, left long tonight, brushed the back of his hand.

"People are staring." She dipped her head, but not before he caught the trace of shyness darkening her eyes.

Thanks to his mother's insistence on dance lessons, he was familiar with step, touch, and glide. He wasn't above showing off his technique to impress her or press against her. "Let them."

The singer crooned about blue skies and sun-kissed skin, and he lifted her hand and encouraged a spin.

Twirl complete, she beamed up at him. "Constable Davenport, you are full of surprises."

"Because I'm a great dancer?"

She waggled her eyebrows. "Dancing is just one of the things you're great at."

His ears heated at her flirting, which was crazy for a man who'd spent as much of the last six days in bed with her as possible. He was as intimately acquainted with every part of her as she was with him. "It's been a while, but I guess you never forget the moves."

She took a deep breath, let it out in a whoosh. "I'll come to your brother's memorial and spend the weekend with you."

Full of gratitude, he brought her hand in to settle against his hammering heart. There was so much he wanted to say and no privacy to say it in. "Let's get out of here."

Their departure was preceded by an interminable,

long list of goodbyes and an even longer drive to Grace's house. A place void of packing boxes and the reminder he was leaving sooner rather than later. They tiptoed through her cinnamon-scented house, the moonlight encouraging whispers even though they were alone. At the door to her room, Grace paused and turned to face him. He took her face in his hands. Didn't crowd her, grab, or push. Only waited while she lifted her face to meet his kiss. He was beginning to learn sweet had a taste all its own.

She reached behind her back and located the knob by feel. He made sure it shut with a quiet hush as she made her way to the bed. Her bedside lamp snapped on, and he blinked against the sudden glow of light to see her crook her finger and beckoned him toward the bed.

Four steps later, he gathered her in his arms and didn't resist the urge to wrap her hair around his fist and tug until the long, clean lines of her neck were exposed.

Some of the man he'd buried alongside his brother rose from the dead. The confidence he'd lost sparked in his chest, and it ignited a desire he was no longer desperate to banish. "I've never wanted anyone the way I want you."

"And how do you want me?"

"So many possibilities." He gave her hair another slight yank and tickled the sensitive skin behind her ear with his tongue. "All of them involving your legs wrapped around me."

She shivered. "I'm good with that."

Her whispered consent made him hurry, and that encouraged little stumbles and hushed laughs, but they didn't stop until their clothes and underwear were a heap on the floor. He swept the pile away with his foot and tossed the rescued condom onto her bed.

She brushed a chunk of hair off his forehead. "If I forget to say it later. This has been the best night ever."

He placed a kiss in the center of the palm that had lingered at his cheek. "Can't wait to get my mouth on you."

A breathy laugh escaped. "Not about to stop you."

He bent down and scooped her up. Her legs wrapped around his waist, and she was all dampness and need. The press of her desire matched his own. The bed protested at the sudden press of his knees and their combined weight. His body missed the warmth of hers the second he laid her down. But it was a small price to pay when her whole body quivered as one of his fingers traced a line down her center and ended up between her legs.

He was done with sweet. Didn't mean his breath came any easier or that it didn't stutter in his chest when he knelt between her hips and yanked her toward his lap. With her legs spread and the rest of her one lean line, he leaned over to circle one pink nipple with his tongue. She arched into his mouth, and he dialed back the enticing suction, intent on banking the tension. When she settled back against the sheets a few seconds later, he circled her wrists and held them to the bed.

"Your turn to take orders." He let go of her hands and grabbed a pillow. "Lift up, baby."

Once she was propped up, he looked his fill at her trim thatch of hair, the inside of her thighs, the curve of her waist. He ducked his head and kissed her trembling stomach. The sheets rustled beneath her restless body, and the air heated with their combined desperation. He steadied them both by putting a hand on her hip. All too soon, her siren sighs had him settling his other palm over her mound and against the sensations hidden underneath her skin.

The commands that had come easily to his mouth years ago slipped free of their chains. "Play with your nipples."

He wanted to see her touch them. Squeeze them. She drew it out, taking forever to brush her fingers over her breasts, her eyes dark with longing as she watched him.

As she dared him to take things further. "That can't be all you want."

She was right about that. "Make it hurt, just a little."

Her nipples tightened under her touch into taut, hard little knots that demanded she keep at it.

"That's it, baby." His fingers got back to work.

But she stilled. "No. Use your mouth."

His tongue replaced his fingers. When he eased back a third time, it was for his benefit, the weight of his own desire reaching its limits. He concentrated on her trembling legs. His hands traveled the inside length of them. When neither of them could wait a second longer, he reached for the condom. He wanted slow, sweet torture for them both, and he rocked his pelvis against hers, nudging at the most intimate part of her.

Every one of her responses brought him closer to the edge. Made him want to go harder. Faster. The sheets bunched under her clenching hands and slipped from the corners of the bed. It wasn't enough. He settled his mouth over hers and begged for more without saying a word.

He relished the moment her muscles tightened, and she bore down, reaching toward the end. He fought as hard as he could to check his orgasm while her body clenched, froze, and then loosened under his. But there was no avoiding the climb to the inevitable.

His satiated brain was no defense against the leap to love, his mouth moving against her hair uttering the words before he could call them back. But the only reaction to his confession was soft puffs of breath that brushed against his hypersensitive skin. His hand skimmed her arm, testing how deep she'd slipped under. She didn't even twitch.

The silence left him time for regret. He'd made little headway on her mother's case. They were waiting for further forensic reports, but a cold case wasn't about to inspire anyone to jump the evidence up the line. His buddy in financial crimes was swamped, so same story. He and Chase had split the questioning of banks and utility companies on Ian's claims of harassment, but so far no one remembered much. Kevin Hunt was proving smarter than Mike had given him credit for.

The sense of failure ate at him. He checked Grace's bedside clock. Inside of forty-eight hours, he'd be in Toronto. And he'd be leaving Grace behind to face Hunt's vendetta all on her own.

Chapter Thirteen

Grace stuffed her phone into her back pocket and reached for her coffee. Her third cup. If she continued at this rate of intake, she'd vibrate through the arranged visit with her dad. She'd chosen to trust his promise to come right over, proving she was quite the optimist today. No more dragging her feet. She needed the upcoming conversation over and done.

Earlier that morning, when Mike had confessed he was leaving earlier than expected, she had wanted to hang onto him and do the selfish thing and tell him not to go. But that wasn't what was best for either of them, and knowing that had fostered her growing need to put things in order.

Hope waddled into the room, bags under her tired eyes. Grace plugged in the kettle for tea. "Didn't sleep well, huh?"

"About as well as this little one will let me." Hope sank into a chair. "Also, you ever notice how thin the walls are in this place?"

Grace hadn't heard her come in last night. Then again, she'd been a bit preoccupied. "Sorry. Not sorry."

Hope dropped her head back and groaned. "God, I miss sex."

Grace would be thinking the same thing before too long. It was amazing how quickly one could become addicted to pleasure. She waited for the whistle of the kettle, then poured hot water into a cheery red teapot and brought it, along with a selection of teas, to the table. She needed to concentrate on something else, anything other than Mike's looming departure. "Isn't today your due date?"

"Yes." Hope lifted her crossed fingers. "And I don't want to alarm anyone, but I think it's going to turn out to be an accurate estimation."

"Do we need to call Scott? Or do you want to head straight to the hospital?" Grace grabbed for her keys.

"Time yet for both those things. Just experiencing a few tweaks." Hope rubbed her belly. "I'm waiting for a bit more confirmation."

"You should probably know I asked Dad to come over this morning. But I can call him and postpone."

"Don't." Hope picked out a packet of green tea and ripped it open. "The sooner you talk it out the better."

Grace was still tempted to pick up her phone and put off her dad. "Did you check your blood pressure this morning?"

"First thing. Doing okay. And as a precaution, since it's Sunday, I phoned the hospital earlier and gave them the heads-up the baby might come today."

They'd settled things between them last night, but Grace wanted to make sure they were okay before the baby came and complicated things further. "About Scott…"

Hope dipped a teabag into her steaming cup of water. "I don't want to talk about him, except to say the man's an idiot."

Grace put a sympathetic hand on her sister's arm. "But he's your idiot."

"I suggested we go for counseling."

"And?" Grace held her breath.

Hope wrapped her hands around her mug. "He said he'd think about it."

Grace hated the defeated look in her sister's eyes. "I know that sounds lukewarm, but from where I'm sitting, the fact you're both contemplating it is a miracle."

"I want my family back. I want to build on the promise that was there in the beginning. Before the rumors started and everything went to hell."

Grace had definite reservations. Hope's optimism was seeing her sister through a serious case of resistance on Scott's part, but Grace was less than certain of a positive outcome. "Scott's a great guy, don't get me wrong. But with all this new-found wisdom you've accumulated, maybe you've outgrown your first love?"

"Relationship advice." Hope saluted her with her cup, damp teabag string clinging to the side. "From the woman who's in love with the cop and is going to let him leave without telling him. Where is he, by the way? I expected him to be here."

"He's wrapping things up at the detachment, saying some last goodbyes, and then I'm meeting him for lunch." And for some more alone time. At least, that had been the plan this morning. "But I think I'll just hang out here, with you."

"No. You will not. Having you mope around here will be bad for the baby."

"Hope, I can't leave you here by yourself."

"Dad will stay with me."

"Dad? You can't be serious."

"Why not? He's done this twice. Technically, he

has more experience than you."

Grace didn't have the energy to argue, and the sound of tires on gravel meant she didn't have to.

"That will be Dad." Grace gripped the edge of the table and waited for him to walk into the kitchen, mentally rehearsing what she wanted to say.

Hope gave her hand a quick squeeze. "It's better to have it all out in the open."

Another knock followed the first. Grace frowned. None of them stood on ceremony, usually coming and going unannounced. Forced to go to the door, she found Kevin Hunt inspecting a pot overflowing with sweet alyssum.

Her hand tightened over the doorknob. "Lost, are we?"

"Grace." He tucked his sunglasses away. "I hope you don't mind the impromptu visit."

"It turns out, I absolutely do, *Kevin*." She checked for signs of her dad. He'd be along soon, and she didn't want him coming face-to-face with Hunt.

"Unfortunately, I must insist as we have business to discuss."

"Sorry." Grace rolled her eyes. "I can be too subtle sometimes. I meant go away."

His lip curled the tiniest bit. "Charming as ever."

She released a beleaguered sigh. "And I'm sick of your passive-aggressive crap. Whatever you've come to say doesn't interest me."

She was about to slam the door in his superior face when he stumbled. He immediately righted himself, but his pale face had Grace wondering if his lurch might actually be genuine.

Hunt pulled a handkerchief out of his pocket and

mopped his forehead. "Forgive me, I seem to be coming down with a summer cold."

Grace caught sight of beige smudges on the square of cloth wedged in his hand, suggesting his ill health was something far more sinister than a simple cold if he took such extremes to camouflage the symptoms.

"Perhaps a drink of water?" He clutched at the door for support.

She wasn't a monster. "Fine. I'll get it for you. Stay here." Grace went in search of a glass.

Hope looked up from sipping her tea and sucked in a breath. "What the hell is he doing here?"

Grace whipped around to see Hunt settle into a chair at the table. She squared her shoulders, determined to get him out as swiftly as possible. "He needed a glass of water."

He stuffed his handkerchief away while he eyed up her kitchen. "How…eclectic."

Grace set a glass of water down in front of him. "Drink it and get out."

He attempted to hide a catch of breath behind an unsteady hand, but his slight cough morphed into a hacking fit that went on and on. Grace gave him a quick thump on the back, not knowing what else to do. Hope lifted her hands in a silent *what now?* Grace didn't have a clue.

When the fit finally subsided, Grace shoved the glass of water into his hand. But Hunt only dabbed at his face. More traces of makeup wiped away, causing him to age ten years in twenty seconds.

"Trust me, this part wasn't planned." His feigned politeness was as creepy as his blotchy face.

"Now that you're feeling better…" Grace nodded

her head in the direction of the door.

He straightened the collar of his starched shirt. "Always in such a rush."

She needed him gone ASAP. "Things to do. People to see."

Hunt's only response was to pull a letter from his pocket and place it on the table.

"What is that?" asked Grace.

"An eviction notice."

Her skin goosed over. "You're the new owner?"

"What's he talking about?" asked Hope.

"The place was sold, but I didn't know to who."

"And you didn't think to tell me?" demanded Hope.

"I suppose the decent thing would have been to inform you that night at The Pines. But I've found decency has little to do with this situation."

Hope stiffened and put a hand on her belly.

"Is it a contraction?" Concerned, Grace reached for Hope. Her doctor had warned Hope to avoid stress, and they were notching up stress points like it was a competition. "Here. Sit."

"I'm fine," insisted Hope.

But Grace didn't care for the way her eyes clouded over or her sudden pallor. She pulled out her phone. "I'll call Scott and tell him to meet us at the hospital."

Kevin Hunt cleared his throat. "As charming as this familial display is, I need a moment of your time."

"I don't particularly care what you want." Grace didn't bother looking up from her phone but gave her sister's arm a reassuring rub. "Are you feeling dizzy? Nauseous?"

"Hang up the phone, Grace."

"Screw you," she murmured, not bothering to look up.

Hope's fingernails dug into her skin.

"Easy, Hope. Try not to draw blood. I promise, I'll get you there."

"No. Him," whispered Hope.

A ringing phone stuck to her ear, Grace shifted her attention back to Hunt. It was perfectly normal to have to look twice, to make sure she wasn't imagining things. To doubt what she was seeing. Because no way was Kevin Hunt pointing a weapon at them.

Answer your damn phone, Scott.

The gun in his hand wobbled. "Hang up, now."

She shielded Hope as best she could but let the phone continue to ring.

"Put some water in the sink. Drop your phone in."

Scott. Pick. Up.

"My hand may not be as steady as it once was, but it would be impossible to miss at this range."

She remembered the research she'd done and that they were dealing with a decorated former soldier. She flicked on the tap. Her phone made a fatal little swoosh when it hit the water.

There was nothing left to do but stand her ground. "You really had me fooled. I never once suspected how batshit crazy you clearly are."

"Your family has gotten away with far too much for far too long. It's not insanity to want to see justice done. To finally expose decades' worth of lies." He set the gun down, leaving his hand to rest atop it. "Some might see that as honorable."

"Yeah, I'm sure that's the dictionary definition. Barge in, wave a gun around." Grace snorted.

"Honorable, my ass."

"That smart mouth of yours might be appealing to some, but I find it tedious. Perhaps you could do us all a favor and keep it shut."

Grace started at the slam of a car door, followed by rushed steps up the porch stairs. Someone pounded a fist against her door. Then Ian shouted her name.

"Fate does have a way of providing." Hunt pointed the gun at Hope, and her sister flinched. "Answer the door, Grace."

Ian burst into the room before she made it a step. "Grace, are you all right?"

"Oh, shit," whispered Hope.

Hope was staring at the floor, and when Grace looked down, there was a small puddle of water at her sister's feet.

Ian made it to Hope first, bolstering her upright when she stumbled. "Hang in there. I'm going to get you both out of here."

Grace kept her voice low. "He won't let us leave. He's got a gun."

"Lurking around corners again, are we?" Hunt pushed out of his chair. "Why don't you all sit down?"

Ian's voice was hushed but insistent. "Do what I say."

Hunt tsked. "I don't think so."

Grace faced the lunatic across from her. "You have Ian. You have me. Let my sister go."

"I'm afraid she stays. For now."

Ian secreted a set of keys into her palm and whispered, "When I nod, the two of you move. Fast as you can."

Alarm bells went off deep in her belly, but before

she could protest, Ian gave her a sharp nod. Out of the corner of her eye, she caught sight of Hunt reaching for his gun.

"Go." Ian pushed Grace in the direction of the door. She grabbed Hope by the hand and made for the door.

A deafening bang stopped Grace and Hope in their tracks. It was like nothing she'd ever heard before or wanted to hear again. Plaster rained down on them from the ceiling as they both stumbled to find cover. Ian faced Hunt and shoved Grace and Hope behind him. Ears ringing, Grace blinked dust from her eyes and wrapped her arms around her sagging sister.

When the veil of dust dissipated, Ian braced for a standoff. Hunt faced him, equally determined. They stood, two aging enemies with a hatred for each other so deeply rooted it had a personality all its own.

"No one is leaving. Any phones need to go in the sink." The gun was still in his hand, his finger on the trigger. "I won't ask twice."

Hope pulled a hand away from her ear to yank her phone out of her back pocket. It disappeared under the water. "That was a new phone, asshole."

Hunt cocked his head at Ian. Ian growled back. "I don't own a fucking cell phone."

Hunt smirked. "No one to call?"

Grace grabbed the back of Ian's shirt when he stepped in Hunt's direction, and whispered, "Don't."

Don't get yourself shot and leave me to deal with this madman.

She'd read people's emotional energy had an aura. Ian's rage was so intense it shimmered as he struggled to keep his voice reasonable. "I'm the person you want.

Let Grace and Hope go."

A quick, muted knock sounded at the front door, and seconds later, Martin wandered into the kitchen. He stopped short when he saw Ian and Hunt. "What the hell is going on?"

"Ah, Martin." Hunt waved him in, his warm welcome provoking shivers. "This just keeps getting better and better."

Martin, his sense of betrayal evident, turned to Grace. "What's he doing here?"

Hope moaned and doubled over, and Grace had her hands full holding her up, praying they both didn't hit the floor.

Martin rushed to his daughter, confusion etching lines in his forehead. "She needs to get to the hospital. Why are you all standing around?"

Grace cautioned him with a look. "Dad, listen to me—"

"Let me catch you up, Martin." Hunt waved his gun in the air. "The reason they're not on their way is because we're going to play a little game first."

Whether her dad didn't understand the seriousness of their situation or he chose to ignore it, Grace wasn't sure. He latched onto Hope. "Move out of our way."

"Take another step, Martin, and one of your daughters will die. The pregnant one, in particular, is testing my patience."

Ian scrambled to nail himself into the space between them and Hunt. "Listen, you bastard—"

"Why are you doing this?" Martin pushed his way forward.

Ian thrust out an arm to stop him. "Be quiet."

Martin shoved Ian's arm aside but thankfully

stayed put. "He needs to answer the question."

"Winston Churchill famously said, 'It is not enough that we do our best; sometimes we have to do what's required.' " Hunt's gestures and easy smile suggested he, at least, was enjoying the show. "I've done my best all these years to see that the people responsible for my brother's death paid the appropriate price, and it isn't enough. Not when you are free to live your lives, to love your children, your grandchildren."

"None of it is their fault." Ian lowered his voice. "Let the girls go."

"No one is leaving." Hunt wiped at the sheen of sweat dampening his brow. "Grace, please seat everyone."

Behind her, Hope whispered a curse and gripped the back of Grace's shirt, pushing into her as she bent forward.

"It's okay. I've got you." Grace did her best to hold Hope upright. "I need help getting her to a chair."

Ian all but carried Hope to a seat, while Grace hustled her dad into one of the chairs beside Hope. Grace sat next to her, and Ian slammed into the chair beside Grace. Under the table, Grace laid a cautious hand over Ian's bouncing knee.

Hunt surveyed the group and lifted the corners of his lips in sickening anticipation. "Who's up for a little game of truth or dare?"

****

When Mike's third call to Grace went unanswered, along with several texts, he tried not to think the worst and went back to packing up his personal belongings. She was sleeping, in the shower, knitting. Any number of things could have kept her from checking her phone.

There was no reason for the sick fear he couldn't ditch.

He had come to work early to pack up his stuff and say his goodbyes. The rest of the day would be spent convincing Grace a long-distance relationship was worth the work. He'd rehearsed all the ways to say Toronto was a great city with lots of potential for someone as creative, smart, and determined as Grace. His phone vibrated. He crossed his fingers and checked.

Elizabeth. Again.

He let her call go to voicemail, unable to shake the sense that something wasn't right.

"Problem?" Chase paused in his ritual of hunting and pecking out reports to scowl at Mike.

"No." Mike gripped the back of his chair, then dropped his head. "Yes."

Chase's chair groaned with his shift in position. "Don't really have time for twenty questions this morning."

Mike abandoned his death grip on the chair to scrub his hands over his face. "I don't know, I can't shake this sense—"

Another call. Elizabeth. Her fourth. He ignored it.

Chase raised his brows. "Are you sure you don't want to get that?"

"It can wait." Mike pinched the bridge of his nose. "Grace isn't answering her phone or replying to my texts."

Chase pushed out of his chair and laid a hand on his shoulder. He tilted his head in the direction of the door. "Go, get out of here."

All of a sudden, it was hard to get his feet to move. Chase was the first friend he'd risked making since losing Justin. "I'm going to miss your surly attitude."

"Damn right you are." Chase, his voice gruff, gave his shoulder a punch.

Mike's throat tightened as Chase's hand dropped away. One more piece of business. "You know how much I wanted Cassandra Bighill's file closed before I left…"

"We'll take care of it. And Grace."

Mike acknowledged Chase's promise with a tight nod. "Thanks."

His phone vibrated. Elizabeth texting.

It's important.

A curse slipped out. Mike gave in and dialed. "Elizabeth, hey."

"Oh, my God, Mike." Her tumbled rush of words escaped, breathy and panicked.

Premonition pimpled his skin. "What's wrong?"

"You were right."

He didn't have time for this. "About what?"

Elizabeth inhaled, and it lasted forever, followed by an excruciatingly long exhale. "Kevin's ill. Pancreatic cancer."

"Hunt has cancer?" Mike switched to speakerphone, not liking where her agitation was leading.

"It's advanced." Her disbelief was quiet, shocked.

He reined in his temper. "I get the news is upsetting for you. But it's not really an emergency."

There was a little catch of breath. "His desk was clear this morning, except for two things: his Cross of Valor Medal and his will."

His anxiety blistered into dread.

She was back to live stream consciousness. "The person he's supposedly meeting this morning just called to set up an appointment, so I went to check his calendar. He's such a Luddite, refuses to use his phone or his computer. For much of anything. He's a freak about his personal privacy."

He channeled all his impatience into one word. "Elizabeth."

Her voice dropped to a whisper again. "The last couple of days...It's like he's not planning on coming back. And he's named me the executer of his will. Me. Why would he do that?"

It wasn't the tears or the tremor in her voice that scared the shit out of him. Hunt was unaccounted for, and Grace wasn't answering his calls. "Start at the beginning. You arrived at the office..."

"I was supposed to be out until late this afternoon, but I needed to stop by and pick up a box of campaign supplies I'd forgotten. Otherwise, I wouldn't have checked his office." She cleared her throat. "I couldn't help myself. I read his will. He's left strict instructions for his several holdings, but there is one property in particular, for which he gave very specific and concerning directives. The tenant is to be evicted, the buildings torn down, and the land sold. The money from the sale of that property and his other liquidated assets are to be used to start the Gregory Hunt Scholarship Fund."

"What specific property are we talking about?" But he knew, and he was already halfway out the door when Chase caught up to him.

"A property he purchased a month ago." Elizabeth's voice wavered. "It was weird enough to have me doing a quick search. The former owner is part of a corporate farming operation based out of Alberta who had previously rented out a small section of the property to Grace Bighill."

It was a punch in the gut to have it confirmed. He climbed into the passenger seat of their cruiser, leaving Chase to drive. "We're going to check things out. I need you to stay at the office. I'll be in touch."

He disconnected and dialed Grace's number again. Nothing. Guilt chased the realization he'd left her unprotected after deliberately antagonizing Hunt. Taunting him over Prairie Gold Resources.

Elizabeth had said Hunt had created an opportunity for her in Ottawa in case he didn't win. More like he was confident he was going to lose. The undertone of viciousness Hunt protected so thoroughly had slipped past Mike's radar. Most likely he wouldn't be found on Parliament Hill come fall session because he had an altogether different agenda. One he wasn't likely to survive. Revenge.

Chase's hands gripped the wheel. "For years, that land belonged to the Connelly family. Hugh and Nancy Connelly sold the property after Ian went to jail."

"Drive." Mike's heart pounded, his lungs expanded, and his senses sharpened, but he refused to let the rush of adrenaline take him for a ride. "I'm trying her landline."

****

The ringing of the landline jerked Grace to attention. No one dared answer it, and the wall clock ticked away the seconds until the ringing stopped.

She clung harder to Hope's hand. "I'm not playing some stupid game. You have something to say? Have the guts to say it."

"And I don't believe I'll be taking orders from a

girl too stupid to see what was right in front of her face."

Ian's fist thudded against the table. "You want to play with someone, you son a bitch. Play with me."

For the first time, she understood the distance people kept from Ian. His fists were anchored to the tabletop and had the resting quality of a coiled snake. "But Grace and Hope walk out the door first."

"It wouldn't be much of a game without them." Hunt swept an elegant hand in Grace's direction. "Truth or dare?"

Hunt's eerie singsong delivery was proof the snapping of one's mind had a tone. Grace was sure his final break with sanity was buried under that stupid question. There was no way to evade, no place to hide, no reasoning with him. The decorated soldier and career politician was gone, leaving an empty shell of bitterness and grief behind.

She wiped damp palms over her thighs, but her mouth refused to open.

Cooperate. Don't say or do anything rash.

Mike's voice was in her head. Firm. Calm. So real she feared she was the one losing her mind.

Hunt attempted a smile, a failed stretch of lips in his gaunt face. "Perhaps some incentive. There is a prize. Keep that in mind before you refuse to play."

"The truth?" demanded Ian. "When have you ever been interested in the truth?"

Hunt's ugly laugh echoed around the room. "This from a man who has lived a lie for thirty long years."

Ian snarled back. "You don't know a thing."

Hunt pointed his weapon, aiming for Ian's puffed-out chest. "Don't I?"

Ian nodded at the gun. The faint tremor of Hunt's hand was obvious to everyone. "If you had the balls to pull the trigger, you'd have done it years ago."

Hunt hunched forward in his chair. "You have no idea what I'm capable of."

Martin straightened his shoulders, and there was a firmness to his voice Grace hadn't heard in years. "As far as the rest of the world knows, you're an honorable man. Why not keep it that way?"

"I'm merely evolving with the circumstances."

Ian affected a sneer. "Do us all a favor and drop dead already."

Kevin Hunt pulled the trigger. Once again, Grace's ears rang with a pain so sharp and extreme it was like a kick to the back of the knee.

Hope cried out as Ian jerked back. Grace added her own scream when a second later Ian toppled to the floor.

She jerked out of her seat. "Oh, my God, Ian."

Hunt swung the gun her way. "Sit. Down."

A firm hand landed on her shoulder. Martin urged her back into her chair. "I'll see to him."

With no memory of having moved, Grace plopped down. Everything was muted: sound, movement, vision, dulled by the pealing ring of bells in her ears.

"Get him back in his chair," ordered Hunt.

Martin hunkered down next to Ian, only to be pushed aside as Ian gained his feet; one hand wrapped around the upper meaty part of his other arm. His mouth worked to remain shut, but his distress was obvious to everyone. Grace tried to gauge his wound's severity by the blood leaking through his fingers. It didn't appear alarming, but what did she know about gunshot wounds and vital arteries? His weight hit the chair, and it squealed back a couple of inches.

"A warning." Hunt shook his gun at Ian, like a teacher cautioning a disobedient student. "Next time, I aim for your heart."

Mike's voice was back inside her head.

Stay calm.

She closed her eyes against the sight of blood seeping through Ian's fingers.

Think it through.

A narcissist like Hunt required flattering, liked his ego stroked.

Don't react. Respond.

She eased her eyes open. "You're a smart guy. We know we can't fool you. Just tell us what you want to hear."

"I want the truth." A bout of shaking forced him to lay his gun on the table, but his gaze never wavered from Grace's. "And I want Cassandra Bighill's daughters to know what really happened that night."

"You son of a bitch."

Grace put a steadying hand on Ian's arm as a warning to keep quiet. *Negotiate. Keep him talking. Keep him calm.* "Then why play games? Tell us. Get it off your chest."

He nudged the barrel of the gun so it was pointing at Grace. "Let's start again, shall we? Truth or dare?"

When she hesitated, he picked up the gun and pointed it at Ian.

Grace latched onto the edges of her chair. She crushed the instinct to lash out. "Truth. That's why we're all here, isn't it?"

Hunt smirked in triumph. "How long have you

known Martin wasn't your father?"

Her dad twisted in his seat. Grace spoke to him but kept her gaze locked on Hunt. "He always has and always will be my father."

"Unless you need a kidney. In which case, you'll need your biological father's assistance. Contaminated as it's sure to be."

Martin rounded on Ian. "You told her?"

"Dad, I figured it out. I went to Ian."

"To him?" He grabbed a fistful of his shirtfront, each of his words an arrow to Grace's heart. "But not to me?"

Hunt sat back and smiled.

"Contraction." Hope's nails dug into Grace's leg.

Ignoring the sting, she brushed the hair away from her sister's face. She had done an admirable job of staying as silent as possible, doing nothing to draw Hunt's attention to her. Grace wanted to keep it that way, but Hope's eyes told her the baby situation was frantic. "Make your point. Unless you know a lot about delivering babies."

"Not a thing."

Grace wanted to slap the smug, unconcerned expression off Hunt's face, but she swallowed her pride. "You've outsmarted us all. The three of us will stay, but please let Hope go. There's no reason for her to be here."

"Do you know much about your pancreas?" Hunt shook his head before anyone could force out an answer. "Me either, until it was too late. Stage IV cancer and that nosy boyfriend of yours means I'm running out of time."

Grace didn't need a psychology degree to know a

man living with a death sentence and holding a gun meant bad things for every person trapped in the room with him. She barely gave thought to the words murder-suicide before vomiting became a real possibility. Heaven help them all if that was his endgame.

"I served my country as a soldier. I buried a brother. I sat as a member of parliament. I have kept to a strict code of conduct in both my professional and personal life." A mask of confusion rearranged his features. He zeroed in on Ian. "And I'm the one dying."

Giving in to panic wouldn't do any of them any good. Grace bit down on the inside of her cheek to chase it off. Beside her, Ian's chest heaved with pain and a fair bit of rage. She gave his knee a warning nudge. "I'm sorry for what happened to your brother. We all are."

Martin stuck out his whiskered chin. "My daughters have no part in this. Let them go."

Still holding his gun, Hunt crossed his arms over his chest. "What pathetic excuse of a human being takes on the spawn of a murderer?"

Ian lunged across the table for Hunt or his gun. It could have been either, and it hardly mattered. She grabbed at Ian, hoping to force him back into his seat. Her efforts were wasted. Hunt, quicker than expected, aimed at Grace, leaving Ian sprawled in a smear of his own blood.

Hunt's face contorted. "My brother was a good man."

Ian's laugh promised retaliation as he slid back into his seat. "Your brother was a sadistic piece of shit."

The gun trembled in Hunt's hand. "He was a good man who would have went on to—"

Martin's fist pounded against the tabletop, and Grace jumped. "Your brother raped Stella."

"That's a filthy lie." Hunt scraped up a snarl, but the accusation barely caused a flinch, and it was obvious it didn't take him by surprise.

Ian sneered. "Is it?"

Martin gained a couple of inches of height. "Greg wasn't supposed to be there that night. Wasn't supposed to be anywhere near Stella, at all. We warned him, damn it. But he showed up half drunk, demanding Stella leave with him."

Hunt lost what little color he had left. Martin ignored Grace's whispered caution. "Greg followed us out. Stella was terrified."

Ian cut him off. "What does it matter? I'm the one who killed your brother. Let them go and finish what you came here to do."

Ian was not sacrificing himself to save the rest of them. Grace tightened her grip. "I'm not going anywhere."

"How touching." Hunt sneered at Martin. "That must hurt. Hearing how close they're becoming."

"This divide-and-conquer strategy isn't going to work." Tension rose, heating as it expanded. But she wasn't about to let Hunt spark an explosion.

He pulled out an old-fashioned recording device, held it up like evidence in a court case, then placed it on the table. "Guess what's on here? Hope?"

"I have no idea." Bent over, arms wrapped around her stomach, Hope gave him a tired look. "But I'm betting you're about to tell me."

"The last moments of your mother's life." He hit a button, and her mother's voice flooded the room.

"Please. Just leave us alone." Her mother's pleading voice, familiar and unfamiliar at the same time.

Hunt's voice. *"I want the truth about that night. Every detail."*

"Mom." Grace's hand reached for the unreachable.

"Oh, God." Hope rocked back and forth in her chair, her tears running unchecked.

Ian's fist pounded against the table. "Shut it off. Now."

"It was an accident." Cissy's muffled voice. *"I swear…"*

"You bastard," whispered Ian.

Her mother's voice faded like she was backing up, while Hunt's became sharper, more accusatory. *"Accident? My brother died. Because of some twisted vendetta."*

"And we've paid for it. Ian went to prison. Stella never got over what happened. Martin and I are in danger of losing everything… What more do you want?"

"I want the truth."

There was a gasp and a rustling in the background like her mother was still moving but Hunt was getting closer. Stalking her.

Grace covered her mouth with both hands, stifling a useless warning. It was too late to save her from the coming fall. To save them all from losing her. She squeezed her eyes shut.

Her mother's voice was frantic. *"Stella was so messed up because of him. And he wouldn't stop…"*

Hunt shut the device off. The silence was devastating, as painful to her ears as the gun blasts earlier.

Ian thundered to his feet. "You left her there."

But it was Martin's hushed voice that captured Grace's attention. His brows were furrowed, and his gaze drifted but never settled. "Cissy was only protecting her friend. Greg was obsessed with Stella."

Protecting her friend?

Grace shook her head.

No. No, no.

"Liar." The last of Hunt's eerie affability dissolved with his spitted accusation.

Ian braced bloody hands against the scarred tabletop, his forearms bunching. All his rage, every drop of it, landed on Hunt. "I don't give a shit if you're dying, I'm going to kill your sorry ass."

Martin's cloudy puzzlement evaporated. "Greg had to be stopped. Any one of us would have…"

Ian swung in Martin's direction. "Not another word."

Her mother hadn't—

She stuttered over his name, finally getting it right. "Ian."

He dropped his head.

She laid a hand on his arm, tendons, muscles and bone impossibly hard. "What did you do?"

She tugged harder, and he turned his head. "What needed doing."

In the stinging moment of silence that followed Ian's declaration, they all heard the approach of a vehicle.

"Grace, please close the kitchen curtains."

Hunt's command, though unwelcome, gave her the opportunity to move away from Ian and his festering revelation. She shuffled to the window. The usual view greeted her. Idyllic, sunny, calm. No visible fracturing fault lines out there. It was only inside the house where the stresses had caused the ground to fissure and shift under her feet.

"Grace," warned Hunt.

She reached for the curtain panel as a police cruiser pulled to a stop. She thought she could make out Mike's face. She blinked and half expected the mirage to disappear.

She glanced back, but Hunt was focused on her dad. Was there some kind of SOS she could send? Maybe she could—

She managed to yank the curtain, to wave it back and forth. She pretended to stumble to hide her odd movements and gave the faded fabric a couple more yanks.

"Is there a problem?" asked Hunt.

"No. Just stuck." The room grew dim as she jerked the curtains closed and they lost the sunlight. There wasn't much more she could do to warn them from inside the house. She squared her shoulders. Help had arrived. She only had to keep everyone alive until Mike figured out how to get them out.

****

Mike dipped his head down to get a better look. His view through the windshield was unhindered. He saw the house clear enough, felt the unnatural stillness surrounding it. He'd caught a brief glimpse of Grace before the kitchen window curtain of the old clapboard house fluttered, then shut.

"Did you see that?" asked Chase.

"Yeah. She's inside the house." To cover his

reaction, Mike dug out his gum and stuffed a piece in his mouth. Plenty of time for guilt later, once Grace's safety wasn't in question.

"You up to this?" asked Chase. "You're not exactly objective, and no one would blame you if you took a backseat on this one."

Mike chewed harder and forced his brain to override the clench of his muscles. "I'm good."

Chase studied him for a long second, then nodded his head. "Let's get to work."

A quick survey of the vehicles in the yard created an unknown. He didn't recognize the newer silver crossover. "Run the plates. Find out if the SUV is Hunt's."

Busting down doors might make great television, but in reality, those types of hasty actions led to fatal conclusions. There was procedure to follow and containment to initiate. He would not risk any of the lives inside the house any more than he'd jeopardize the lives of any professional gathering outside it.

Keeping his voice steady and firm, Mike got on the loudspeaker and followed procedure. "This is the Aspen Lake police. Please come to the front door."

The door remained stubbornly shut.

"This is the police. We're concerned for your safety. Come to the door and let us know you're okay."

No response. Not that he'd expected one.

"Call the boss. Tell him we have a possible hostage situation and may need a crisis negotiator and an emergency response team. Once we gather more information, we'll confirm." Mike wasn't taking any chances. If he was wrong, and in his gut he knew he wasn't, he'd answer for it later. "Get the EMTs here."

The familiar task of unloading equipment from the trunk of their vehicle helped solidify his objectivity. When Deke and his partner, Cal, arrived, he filled them in and gave them tasks.

Chase pushed forward. "The SUV is Kevin Hunt's."

Deke put his hand on Mike's shoulder. "I'm going to start digging a little deeper into Kevin Hunt."

"Talk to Elizabeth McCray. She's his campaign manager." He rattled off her number. "And get someone up on the road directing traffic."

He motioned at Deke's partner. "Cal, scout the property. We need a view inside."

"Done."

Beside him, Chase waved the incoming ambulance over to the designated area. "I'll catch them up."

Mike faced the house. Hunt wasn't impulsive. The man was smart, educated, and thorough. He hadn't wanted to get caught until today. But he was running out of time.

Mike wasn't the reckless sort, either. He needed to get them past the alarm phase of the first hour when emotions ran high, adrenaline pumped hot and furious, and fear ruled. He'd do whatever was needed to keep a level head and see that everyone else kept theirs.

He dialed Grace's landline again. *Answer the damn phone, Hunt.*

To Mike's relief, Hunt picked up. "I see the cavalry has arrived."

Mike's grip tightened around his phone, but he kept his tone level and impartial. "You want to tell me what's going on in there, Kevin?"

"I'm just wrapping up a few loose ends." There

was a brief pause. "I'd invite you in, but the guest list is quite specific."

"Mind telling me what the meeting is about? Maybe I can help."

"All in good time."

Hunt might be educated, patient, and meticulous, but he was also human and gravely ill. Desperate men made desperate decisions. Hunt might sound calm now, but Mike would make certain he stayed that way. "I want you to remember I'm here if you need me, Kevin. I want this to be easy for you. Why don't you come outside, and we'll discuss how to resolve your problem?"

"We both know that's not going to happen."

"Then explain to me what is happening. This isn't like you." There was no reply from Hunt. Mike knew the passage of time reduced stress levels. He kept talking. "I'm worried about you. So is Elizabeth. She says you haven't been feeling well lately."

"As it turns out, I do have a problem. A fly in the ointment, as my daddy used to say."

"Why don't you tell me what your problem is, and we'll go from there."

Hunt's disgust was as scathing as his words. "The one called Hope insists on bringing the next member of this morally deficient group into the world."

"Hope Walker is in labor?" Mike faced the assembled officers.

"It would seem so."

"There's an easy solution, Kevin. Send her out. It'll relieve the tension inside the house and make things easier on you."

On all of you.

A long-suffering sigh followed. "I'm inclined to agree with you. But she's the only one allowed to leave. The rest of us have business to finish."

"Then send her out."

"Pity, she'll miss the grand finale."

At the words grand finale, Mike's heart stuttered. "I'm not sure what you mean by grand finale. Why don't you explain it to me?"

Hunt scoffed and Mike sensed he was preparing to end their connection.

"You can trust me. Just like Elizabeth trusts me." Mike kept his voice even, striving to make a connection. "You wouldn't have offered her the job as your chief of staff if you didn't trust her judgment. She's worried about you. We all are."

"I wonder what the little woman across from me would think of your praise for my lovely campaign manager?"

Mike ignored Hunt's smug satisfaction, thankful for the opening. "Why not let me talk to Grace? So I can find out for myself?"

"You need to remember, I've read the playbook you're reading from, son. The obvious isn't going to work on me."

Mike felt Hunt's withdrawal, and he thought fast. "I know what it's like to lose a brother. If this is about Gregory—"

"The pregnant one is coming out."

An abrupt dial tone signaled the end of their interaction. Hunt's matter of fact announcement tested Mike's scrabbling restraint to its limit, but he waved the other officers into position and motioned the EMTs to get ready.

The door to the farmhouse opened. Hope Walker hobbled out of the house apparently under protest. He caught sight of Grace all but shoving her sister out the door. Then she closed both the screen door and the solid wood door behind it.

Officers in tactical gear surrounded Hope, inching her forward. As soon as she was within reach, she grabbed for him.

"He shot Ian."

Jesus—

"He's okay, but—" She stopped to clutch at her stomach and pant.

"Take it easy." Relief was slow to surface as he did his best to hold her up. He shook his head at the EMTs, and they were forced to wait. "Can you tell us who is in the house? Where they are? How many weapons?"

"Hunt, Grace...D-Dad..." Hope tightened her hold on him and tried to breathe as her body contorted. "Ian. Kitchen. One gun that I know of."

"Good. That's good. Let's get you to the hospital." He nodded at the EMTs.

Tears squeezed out of her closed eyes. "Holy fuck, he shot Ian."

"We've got you. You're safe now."

"No. There's something you should know..." Another pause, another round of panting as she slapped away the EMTs' efforts.

"Hope, you don't want to have this baby in the middle of the yard."

One of the EMTs pressed closer. "We need to get her out of here."

Hope refused to let go of him. "He's got a recording. Of Mom. He was there when...when she died."

Her eyes rolled back, and she collapsed. Luckily, they caught her before she hit the ground. He stepped back giving the EMTs room, his blood pressure tripping and his mind spinning.

Settle down.

Chase arrived and drew him over to the side. "Elizabeth was right. Hunt's dying. Pancreatic cancer."

"How much time does he have left?" He tracked the flashing emergency lights down the lane.

Chase's expression reflected the seriousness of Hunt's condition. "Not much."

"Shit." The ache between his eyes increased. "He shot Ian. Hope thinks he's okay, but it would be impossible for her to know for sure."

"He's got nothing to lose."

"But something to say. Hope said he has a recording of Cassandra Bighill's death."

"He was there?"

"According to Hope. At this point, there's no way for us to know if the recording's legitimate." They crossed the short distance to the command center. "Hope says everyone is in the kitchen."

Chase tugged at his vest. "We've got some visuals of other rooms, but nothing inside the kitchen."

They ran through the information from the file. Mike rubbed at the damp collecting at the back of his neck. "Stella Donaldson is gone, but Stan mentioned something about a sister. We need to contact her and see if Cassandra Bighill confided anything to her best friend."

"On it."

Deke rushed up. "This is what we've got so far,

and it's not much. Hunt's got an uncle and extended family in British Columbia. An ex-wife from a brief marriage when Hunt was in his thirties. She hasn't spoken to him in years. None of them were aware he was sick. Elizabeth is putting together a list of close associates. But it seems the guy was quite the loner outside of work. I'm going to go take a look at his office."

"Go." Mike faced down the house. Grace was trapped in there. Waiting for him to get them all out.

Deke pressed a hand to his shoulder. "We'll get them out of there."

Chase answered his ringing phone, then stuffed it back into his pocket. "Crisis negotiator is on her way, so is an emergency response team. But it's going to take them some time to get here."

Before he got the last word out, Chase's phone rang again, and he stepped off to the side.

Mike might not possess the official title of hostage negotiator, but he knew the basics: show empathy, concern, and compassion; build a sense of trust with the hostage taker. He was also trained to know what was going through the hostages' minds: helplessness, acute stress, fear of death. When people were barricaded in together, emotions ran high. Tempers flared. It was his job to maintain control.

And that's exactly what he was going to do.

Chase appeared at his side. "I talked to Stella's sister. Seems Stella was a psychologist specializing in domestic abuse."

"Did she know of any secrets Cassandra might have shared with her sister? Or if Stella had problems with Hunt before she died?"

"Oh, she had plenty to say, including the claim that Gregory Hunt was abusive to her sister and that Ian Connelly should never have gone to jail. And I quote, 'However Gregory died, he deserved what he got.' "

"However he died?" repeated Mike.

"Her exact words. She refused to say more. I've arranged for an officer from her local detachment to talk to her in person."

"Curious turn of phrase." Mike frowned. "Especially when there's no doubt as to the circumstances surrounding Gregory Hunt's death."

Chase reached for a tablet. "An abdominal knife wound, serious but not necessarily fatal. He died from blunt force trauma to the back of his head when he hit the pavement during the fight. Connelly was taken into custody at the scene. He pled guilty. Witnesses all told the same story."

"I want to talk to these other witnesses."

"That's going to be hard to do. Cassandra Bighill and Stella Donaldson are dead. That leaves Martin Bighill. Various customers rushed out of the bar and reported seeing Ian standing over the victim holding a knife, but they didn't witness the actual stabbing or Gregory falling."

Mike stared at him. "You're telling me the only two people left who know for certain what happened outside the bar that night are in that farmhouse? With Grace?"

Grace, who was connected to both Martin and Ian in a way Hunt would find impossible to forgive.

****

Grace gagged on the smell of blood, sweat, and plaster dust. The longer they sat in the hot, airless room the harder she fought to remember there were people outside working to free them. The distance from where they sat to the front door and freedom was not measurable by feet and inches but by the will of a mad man. But Hope was safe. They'd gotten her out. And Grace clung to that victory like a nun to her rosary.

Ian, his forehead a clutch of deep grooves, was as pale as Hunt. He pressed the towel Grace had been allowed to fetch him against his leaking wound.

"Are you sure you're okay?" she whispered. It was a stupid question. None of them were okay.

"I'm fine," he grumbled, swatting her hand away with a shaky hand. To Hunt, he presented a stone-cold determination that raised bumps on Grace's skin. "You've got five seconds to get on with it, or I'm coming for you, old man."

"Ian," she cautioned, all too aware of the gun resting under Hunt's hand. Hunt had calmed down some after playing his twisted recording, satisfied he'd devastated them with the sound of her mother's voice.

But it was the information that had come to light before she'd heard her mother's voice that had Grace questioning everything she knew about her gentle-minded mother, the woman who had cautioned her against striking back at the kids who were unkind to her. She'd also been fiercely loyal, and if Gregory had hurt Aunt Stella, then...

Hunt ignored Ian's threat. "Martin. Truth or dare?"

Ian straightened in his chair and leveled a glare at Martin. "Don't say a damn thing."

Hunt's eyes narrowed, and the corners of his mouth curved. "Play along, Martin. And I'll let Grace go."

Grace's stomach rolled at his oily words. "Don't

trust him, Dad."

Martin latched onto Grace's hand. The apology in his touch matched the regret in his eyes. "Truth."

Hunt's laugh was mocking. "You must have realized that she never loved you. That you were simply a means to an end."

"He wasn't there. He doesn't know what your life was like." Grace thumped a fist to her chest. "She was happy. I know she was."

Her dad's hand tightened over her fingers. "Always the peacemaker."

She pitched her voice so low her dad had to read her lips. "She loved you."

"Grace needs to hear exactly what type of woman her mother was."

"Why? What difference does it make now?" Ian barked.

Grace was exhausted, thirsty, and sweaty with fear. "Neither of you need to protect her anymore."

Ian lifted his head, and his anguish was heartbreaking. "I'm not protecting *her*."

"And I appreciate it." Grace reached for his hand, linking the three of them.

"How touching. But how else would the daughter of a murderer react?"

Hunt's taunt shattered Ian's brittle desolation. "Says the brother of a rapist."

A little of Hunt's precious control slipped. "A dirty, filthy lie the four of you concocted to discredit Gregory and reduce your jail time."

"You want to shove the truth down our throats? Choke on some of your own." Ian let go of Grace's hand and pressed the flat of his palm against the table.

"He busted Stella's arm when he raped her. Bet you didn't know that."

"Liar." Spittle flew past Hunt's thin lips.

Martin sagged in his seat. "We took her out to celebrate getting her cast off, even though Stella didn't want to come. Wasn't ready. But Cissy was so worried about her. She pushed her into coming along. Stella had refused to press charges against Greg, although she threatened to go to the police if he came near her again. We all hoped it would be enough. Then he showed up at the bar that night."

Martin shifted in his seat. Grace's shaking fingers tightened around his hand, but there was no dragging her father out of his confession. "Stella brought the knife with her out of the bar. Cissy convinced her to give it up. Then Greg charged out of the bar, right for Stella. She was only protecting her friend."

It was an eternity before anyone spoke. Then Hunt raised his wobbling chin in Grace's direction. "Quite the pedigree you've got."

"Are you satisfied?" Martin slumped in his chair. "Did you get what you came for?"

"Almost." Hunt dropped the recorder to the floor, and the last piece of her mother was crushed under the heel of his shoe.

He set the gun down and pushed it to the middle of the table. "You'll never know if she stumbled down that embankment or if I pushed her. Or who she called for at the end, and you can wonder for the rest of your miserable lives."

Grace fought to hold Ian back. But it was Martin who reached the gun first. Martin who fingered the trigger. Martin who issued orders. "Call your young man, Gracie. Tell him Hunt is going to explain how my wife died."

Grace was scared to touch him. Didn't want to jar him. "Dad, put the gun down. I can't lose you, too."

"Pull the trigger, Martin." Hunt puffed out his chest. "For once in your miserable life, have the guts to get the job done."

"Dad, don't," whispered Grace. "He's not worth it. Please."

"Gracie, make the call."

His grim confidence had her unraveling her fingers from the back of Ian's shirt. Grace crossed the small space and lifted the receiver off the ancient wall phone, terrified to take her eyes off her father and Ian. Terrified that between the two of them they'd do the unfixable.

****

Mike adjusted the peak of his cap against the cruel brilliance of the noonday sun. The yard was a mess of trampled grass and flowers, but a perimeter was established, information gathered, and officers were in place and ready to move. Their efforts still weren't enough for Mike.

The ringing of his phone stopped him cold. "Constable Davenport."

"It's me."

Thank God.

"Grace."

Her tone concerned him, but it didn't surprise him. "Tell me what's happening."

She sniffed, then coughed to cover up her distress. "Things have kind of taken a turn in here."

His mind raced with the awful possibilities. "What

kind of turn?"

There was a pause, too long and censored to end with the truth. "Please, don't hurt him."

"Grace, I need you to tell me exactly what's happening." He kept his tone firm. "Hurt who?"

Chase got ready to move and signaled for the others to do the same.

"Grace, talk to me," Mike ordered.

"My dad. He got his hands on Hunt's gun."

"Your dad has a gun?" Not the scenario he'd envisioned, and he rapidly recalculated. He and Chase made eye contact. They both knew what needed to happen if the situation escalated.

"Please, don't hurt him."

He wasn't there as her lover. He had a job to do, but never before had the strain of carrying out his duties physically hurt.

"We're going to get everyone out of there. Tell me exactly what's happening."

"I've already told you. Dad is pointing a gun at Kevin Hunt." Grace's voice rose with her loss of patience. "Hunt is taunting him, trying to get Dad to shoot him. You need to get in here. Now. And Hunt shot Ian. He seems to be okay, but I don't know…"

"The EMTs are here. They're going to take care of everyone." Voices rose in the background. "Talk to me, Grace."

"My dad wants Hunt to answer questions about Mom. I-I think Hunt killed her. He has a recording. Had a recording…"

He shut his eyes at the pain in her voice. At the notion of her in her cozy kitchen traumatized and scared. "Grace, I need you to open the curtain. Can you do that for me?"

"I don't think he's going to hurt anyone, he just wants answers."

"I believe you." And he did believe her, but he wasn't sure it was going to matter. "We need to see what's going on in the kitchen. Please, open the curtain."

She hung up the phone before he had a chance to tell her to stay on the line, to stay with him so he could talk her through the next part. The curtain cleared the kitchen window.

Deke's voice sounded in his ear and gave him a detailed account of who was where. Mike briefed his team and gave the signal to move.

Chase came to stand beside him. "You doing okay?"

"Yeah." And he prayed it was true. "I think we're over the worst of it."

He prayed that was true, as well.

Chase turned to face forward. "Gonna miss this. With you."

No eye contact was needed. "We make a hell of a team."

Chase straightened his vest. "Let's go."

Guns drawn, they moved up the porch steps and approached the door. Mike raised his voice. "It's the police. We're coming in. No one move."

More team members moved in to back them up. They heard Grace's voice urging them to hurry. Mike and Chase braced, but what they saw when they entered the kitchen was exactly what Deke was relaying to them. Martin Bighill was pointing a gun at Kevin Hunt.

Ian clutched his bleeding shoulder. "Don't be an

idiot, Martin."

"Dad, please." Grace stood off to the side, out of the way, pale and shaking.

"Martin, put down the gun," ordered Mike. "Do it. Right now."

The gun wobbled in his hands. "He killed my wife."

Hunt sat slumped in his chair. Exhaustion painting dark circles on his transparent skin under his eyes, his mouth was stretched taut. He was in far worse shape than the man he'd allegedly shot. "Even now, you don't have the balls."

"Keep your mouth shut," ordered Chase.

"Dad." Grace wrapped her arms around her middle. "Let the police handle it. Please. For me."

Mike kept his voice low but firm. "Listen to your daughter, Martin. Put. The. Gun. Down."

"Coward." Hunt gurgled out a snort. "Pull the damn trigger."

"We'll help you figure this out. I promise you." Mike edged closer. Martin's hand continued to shake, his finger resting against the trigger. "Put the gun down, Martin."

Kevin Hunt lunged, desperation giving him momentum. But he was too weak to get far, and he landed on his hands and knees in front of Martin.

"Come on, Martin. Hand over the gun." Mike inched forward. "Do it for your daughter."

"Dad, *please*."

Martin shut his eyes, his head dipping, his shoulders hunching. "She was my whole world."

Mike held out his hand. "Nothing he can say will bring her back."

Ian's voice was gravel. "Don't let him take the easy way out, Martin."

Martin lowered the gun. Mike moved in and confiscated the weapon. Chase was close behind him, and he dealt with Martin, saving Mike from having to handcuff him in front of his daughter. Grace remained where she was while Ian stood stoically at her side. She turned into him and hid her face from view. Martin offered little resistance, unlike Hunt, who struggled to gain his feet only to collapse. Mike stood guard while the EMTs secured him and took him out.

He hoped his apology was written on his face, word for desperate word, as her father was led out of the house in handcuffs. Ian whispered into her hair. Mike forced his attention back on the job and followed Martin out.

Grace wrestled to get close to Martin as Mike settled him into the back of a cruiser. Mike's arms ached to gather her up. Instead, he was forced to pry her away and force her back.

"Grace, let us do our job."

Her wounded look made his gut clench. She lifted her chin. "Hunt had a recording device with him. He destroyed it, but it has information on it. About the day she died."

"We'll collect all the evidence, I promise. We'll see what we can do with it." Everything he needed to say was saved for a time when he wasn't in uniform and there weren't witnesses. "You need to get checked out. I'll have one of the officers take you to the clinic."

"What? No. I'm fine. My dad…"

"Grace, please."

"No. I'm coming to the station."

"Okay." He risked putting a hand on her arm, knowing it was useless to argue. "We'll get your father…settled, then I'll take you to see Hope."

He waited while she struggled to process everything he wasn't telling her. He wanted to check his watch. The time. To see how much of it he had left. His panicky response left him shaken, and he signaled at Deke. "Take Grace to the station. I'll be there as soon as I can."

When she was safely headed down the road, Mike headed for the side of the house and braced his hands on his knees. The fear he'd managed to tamp down for the last few hours rose up his esophagus and spewed over a trampled patch of flowers.

A shadow came up behind him. Mike righted himself, and with nothing at hand, made a discreet pass over his mouth with his arm.

Chase slapped him on the back. "Love will do that to you."

Chapter Fourteen

Grace pushed the stale ham and cheese sandwich to the side in favor of the lukewarm, extra sweet coffee Mike had brought her. Though she was free to come and go, she preferred the sparse furnishings and soft lighting of the small room Mike had ushered her into upon arrival. A quiet room, Mike had called it. Where countless others had sat wondering what was happening with their loved ones, devastated by circumstances there was no way to prepare for, and only a box of tissues for comfort.

The door opened, and Mike slipped in. Her hands tightened around her mug, but there was no warmth to glean from the cooled stoneware. He claimed the chair beside her. It groaned under the weight of six feet of concerned cop.

She'd gotten periodic updates, along with the coffee and the sandwich. Quick stabs of information, short on detail and long on awkward reassurances he was doing everything he could to help her dad, letting her know Ian had been treated and released. That Hope was fine. And so was her brand-new niece.

"Your dad—Martin," he clarified, like her allegiance was now in dispute, "has been charged with simple assault, which is a summary offense. Likely, all he'll receive is a fine."

He paused, clearly waiting for his good news to

offer some relief.

"Okay." And she was thankful. She really was, but she'd learned the lesson of caution a long time ago and waited for the coming *but*.

"He'll have to spend the night in jail, and then he'll appear before the judge tomorrow morning. He's been in touch with the lawyer you contacted."

There it was, the picture of her dad alone in a cell, reeling from the details revealed at her kitchen table. Crushed, vulnerable, and grieving.

His fingers worked to free hers from the death grip on her cup. "He won't be left alone. We'll take good care of him."

He didn't have to say the word suicidal. It was in the press of his hand, the way it curled and held on.

"Got it."

"Grace—"

There was no way for her to give in to his comfort and stay strong enough to ask questions. "Can you fix the recording?"

"It's doubtful. But we'll try."

She cleared her clogged throat. "We're never going to know what really happened to my mom, are we? Hunt will take the last seconds of her life to his grave."

He shook his head, and she wasn't sure if he was disagreeing with her, preparing her, or just so damn sorry he didn't have words.

It was her turn to clutch harder, and her fingers bit into the flesh of his hand, pressing him to say something. Anything. Because she couldn't force any more words out of her dry mouth.

When he finally spoke, his words were full of apology. "Hunt's condition is advanced. I doubt he has the time or the conscience to come to terms with what he's done."

Her shoulders slumped, unable to support the weight of sadness pressing in on her. She dropped her head. A sob rent the air, and it didn't register as hers until Mike gathered her up and ran his hands over her hair, her back, every piece of her he could reach.

"She's really gone," she whispered into the comfort of his chest.

"I know, baby." He coaxed her out of her chair and onto his lap, wrapped his arms around her. "I've got you."

She burrowed into him. This man who was intimate with the shape and feel of grief. Who knew what it took to absorb it, reach past it. Who understood what it meant to age alongside it.

"I love you." But her whisper was lost, along with her tears, in a sinkhole of shifting muscle and bunching fabric. She hung on, concentrating on the thump of his heart as he sheltered her head against his shoulder.

"Better?" he asked.

"Better," she lied.

She was done talking about Kevin Hunt and the damage he'd done to her family. Not over it. But done rehashing it for the moment. She had the living to worry about. Her dad was beyond her reach until tomorrow, but she needed to see Hope. "If we're done here, I need to get to the hospital."

He did a quick inspection of her features. What he found there calmed the worry she saw in his eyes. "Give me a minute to change?"

She slipped off his lap. "Any chance you have a brush you can lend me?"

He got to his feet, hand extended. "Come with me."

Once they were cleaned up and in his car, Mike turned the radio down low. Lulled by soft jazz and sunshine, her eyelids dropped. The next thing she knew, Mike was nudging her awake. She opened her eyes to find they were parked outside the large, city-sized health center they'd transported Hope to instead of the smaller local one.

She rushed to the information desk and was directed to the maternity ward where Scott met them in the hallway holding his daughter, Rebecca Anne Walker.

"So sweet," she murmured, trailing a finger down one pink cheek. Her tiny fingers and rosebud mouth a reminder life moved on.

Mike glanced over her shoulder. "She's beautiful."

"No doubt about that." Scott barely lifted his head, only having eyes for his daughter.

"How's Hope?" she asked.

"Sleeping. It got a little intense there for a while, the stress of the situation and all, I think." He rocked his squirming daughter. "I know I should ask how everyone else is, but I don't much care at the moment."

"Levi?"

"At my parents'. They're bringing him up this evening."

Grace made googly eyes at Rebecca. "He's a big brother."

"Yeah. He is." Grace was happy Scott was done denying it. Unimpressed, baby Rebecca whimpered. Her dad cuddled her close. "I'm going to take her back and see how Hope is doing."

Grace put a hand on his arm. "Your wife was amazing today."

Scott finally met her searching look. "In more ways than one."

She tucked Rebecca's blanket in around her dimpled chin. "Be good to Mommy and Daddy, okay?"

Her niece yawned in reply.

Back in the car, exhaustion pulled her under again, but she blinked awake when Mike parked, not at all sad to see the sun setting and the long, awful day coming to a close. The door on her side of the vehicle opened, and Mike offered his hand. It was a silent walk to his apartment door.

Mike tossed his keys onto the counter and took her face in his hands. His intense gaze heated her cheeks. The sweet caress of his thumbs along her jawline had her seeking more contact. "What do you need most, food, shower, or sleep?"

"I could really use a shower."

"I'll…um…just unpack some towels for you."

Right. Leaving.

His stark eyes stared down at her. "Scared me today."

"I was plenty scared myself."

His lips brushed against hers, soft and sweet. Her eyes drifted shut, and she could smell the remnants of the day on him. He'd cleaned up at work, but the soap he'd used didn't mask the underlying musk of sweat or conflict. She imagined she smelled worse, and she needed the few moments of alone time a shower would provide to pull herself together. "I won't be long."

"Go ahead. Wash the day off. I'll shower after you." He brushed a hand over her hair but didn't let her go. His forehead wrinkled in uncertainty, only to clear a second later. "Then I have something I want to ask you."

She made quick use of Mike's body wash, then lowered her head and watched the soapy swirls disappear down the drain.

No one had died today.

That was all that mattered. She'd deal with the rest tomorrow. She shut off the water and grabbed the towel Mike had brought in without her hearing him. When she stepped out of the bathroom, the apartment was silent. She headed for Mike's bedroom and found him searching through a box.

"Hey." She clutched the skimpy towel closer to her chest.

"Hey," he echoed back, a folded T-shirt limp in his hands.

His obvious appreciation of her damp presence eased the restriction in her throat. She held out her hand for the shirt. "That for me?"

"Here you go. I won't be long." He turned back at the door. "I know someone else who was pretty damn amazing today. More than amazing, actually."

Then he was gone, and the shower kicked on. She slipped into Mike's T-shirt and crawled into his bed. Mike had brought her purse in from the kitchen, and she dug out a bottle of moisturizer. When she finished rubbing comfort into her skin, she wrapped her arms around her shins and rested her chin on her knees.

There was nothing else she could do today, and that left a lot of hours to fill until her dad appeared before the judge in the morning. She checked out the clock on Mike's bedside table. Too early to sleep. She spotted a small ring-sized jewelry box hiding behind the lamp. Heart pounding, she checked the empty doorway.

Something I want to ask you.

Her hand shook as she picked up the box, testing its weight. Maybe it was only something that fit inside a ring box?

She set it back down. But not for long. There was no ignoring the expensive logo. Her fingertips brushed across the velvet lid.

Don't.

But before the intention even registered, she'd flipped it open. Her breath caught. The ring was beautiful. Even her untrained eye sensed the quality and cut were superior. In awe, she lifted the teardrop diamond engagement ring out of the box.

At the sound of footsteps, she looked up and found Mike frozen in the doorway, clad in sweatpants and nothing else.

"It's beautiful." She bit down on her lip to keep her smile at a low beam.

"Grace…"

If there was ever a Jesus-take-the-wheel moment, this was it. Fate was testing her to see if she really intended to follow through on all the life-affirming vows she'd made while she'd waited in that desolate room at the police station. It was time to join the dance. To take a risk.

She smiled in apology. "I didn't mean to spoil your question."

He didn't smile back, and she ignored the shiver of premonition as she bent her head to read the inscription. One word. She squinted at the tiny letters.

Beth

Beth?

It took her a second, but she figured it out. Short for Elizabeth. She carefully settled the diamond back on its cushion. Her fingers lingered over the cold metal as the bottom fell out of her world.

He still hadn't moved, and when he did manage to put words together, it hardly mattered to her what they were. "Grace, it's not what you think."

How would he know what she was thinking? He didn't know anything. Or have a clue. About anything.

"I can explain."

"Explain what? That this isn't happening?" She set the box back on the night table, despite wanting to fling it at him. "There have been some strong contenders for worst day of my life. But this one? Hands down the winner."

"It's from years ago. When we were together." He moved in her direction. "I was planning to get rid of it."

She scrambled off the bed, out of reach. "Good for you."

He changed course to follow her, lifted a hand to stroke, to soothe.

"Don't touch me," she ordered.

He jerked back, and his battle for composure ravaged his face. "It doesn't mean anything to me. Not anymore."

"I can tell by how you've held onto it all this time."

"I couldn't just toss it out." His frustrated reasonableness stabbed her in the heart.

"No need to explain." She pasted on a toothy smile, desperate to sell the illusion she was perfectly intact. "I have to go."

"But I should have dealt with it a long time ago."

His confession did nothing to silence her hurt. "Sold it."

Well, duh!

She whirled around. "What's a guy to do when the woman he loves rejects him? Perfectly normal to hang onto an inanimate object worth, God, I can't even guess how much, for all eternity."

"It was a reminder of what I'd lost." He scrubbed a hand over his jaw in frustration. "Not Elizabeth. But my brother. My family. My career. Everything. And how I didn't want to be that selfish and conceited person anymore."

His explanation sounded reasonable, believable. But she wasn't ready to let go of the humiliation of almost saying yes to a non-proposal of marriage.

"Don't let this be the end. Please. Spend the weekend with me in October. Come and visit me in Toronto." Not a request, but not a demand either. "After I'm there, I'll have a better idea of my schedule…"

"And when you can fit me in?" She'd been about to say yes to his proposal of marriage, and he wanted her to visit him?

"We could try."

"What? Dating?" God, a parrot had better conversational skills.

"I want more than a casual relationship with you. A lot more. You have to know that."

She grabbed up her bag and clutched it to her chest. Too late, she remembered she didn't have her vehicle. Or want to go home. She didn't even have her phone.

His earnestness was replaced with desperation. "Don't leave. Not like this."

She headed for the bathroom and her clothes.

"Don't do this, Grace." His tortured plea came

from behind her.

She ignored him and shut the door. God, she was such a fool. Her mad scramble into the awful clothes she'd worn through the whole terrible day had her tripping in her haste to finish and get out.

Mike was waiting for her in the kitchen, looking as devastated as she felt. She didn't want to leave him. Didn't want this to be goodbye forever. "Today was hard. So hard."

"I'm sorry about everything. About leaving you alone this morning. For underestimating Hunt. For keeping the stupid ring."

"I know you are. But that doesn't make me feel less wrecked. Less humiliated."

"I want to make things right between us." He moved toward her. "Before I have to get on that plane tomorrow."

"I was going to say yes," she whispered.

"I know," he whispered back.

His hand covered his heart. A fallen knight protecting, and at the same time, offering the one thing of value he had left to give.

And she softened, just a little, enough to ask, "What solution could we come to in twelve hours?"

"We could have a conversation about the future. About what you want, and your plans for it."

She wanted to believe it was that simple. She really did. But she was so tired, and her exhaustion had pride and fear winning the battle over faith and intuition. "I can't do this right now."

"Then when?" He blocked her retreat. "I'm trying here, Grace. Begging for a chance. But you have to meet me halfway. You have to want to."

Easy to say yes. To agree. To have this whole horrid conversation end with her slipping her arms around his waist and pressing into him.

"Say you're still coming to Justin's memorial." He must have sensed her hesitation because he brushed his knuckles over her cheek. "I don't think I can face it without you."

His stark honesty deepened the color of his eyes to a beseeching green. No manipulation. No games. And his truth gutted her. His fingers uncurled and caressed her cheek.

She couldn't look away. "That's not playing fair."

"Maybe not." His lips curved the tiniest bit. "But it's true. And something else that's true? I want the chance to love you, Grace. I can't lose you. What happened today? Jesus, I almost lost you."

"Damn you, Mike."

"Damned until I met you. I want to spend my life with you." He took a deep breath. "And if that means coming back to Aspen Lake, I'll make it happen."

That he would give it all up for her meant everything. "No."

"No?" His hand dropped from her cheek.

She rescued his dangling hand. "I hear Toronto's a great city."

"It won't matter where I am if you're not there with me. I'll be alone. And lonely. Missing you. Only you."

His lips met hers, and for a moment, time stopped. A wondrous kiss involved more than lips. A keeper knew what to do with his hands. And Mike definitely knew what he was about with his as they smoothed back her hair and mingled with the strands at the back of her neck. He kissed her like there was nothing more important than their connection and there was nowhere else he'd rather be than there with her.

It was the kind of kiss you looked back on and said that was the moment. The moment she chose to dance.

She eased back. "I love you, and I would never ask you to sacrifice your dreams for me. I've spent enough time setting aside my own, putting myself second. I'm not sorry for it. I love my family, and they needed me. But it's time to concentrate on me, on what I want. And I want you. I want a fresh start in a new place."

"I love you." She was back in the circle of his arms, pressed close to his heart, his lips brushed against her hair. "I want you to be happy. I want you to be sure."

"I've never been more sure of anything in my life."

****

Grace ached in all the best places. And some not so good places. Her dad wasn't doing well and continued to pose a threat to himself. Come morning, the judge ordered a psychiatric assessment. Mike arranged to catch a later flight and stayed as long as he could, done what he could to move the process along, but in the end, she all but shoved him into the gifted Porsche he'd driven to the city. He planned to leave it in the Alton and Davenport parking lot. From there, it was a cab to the airport.

The day had gone downhill from there. Life. It definitely had a way of forcing you to live it. But finally a physician assessed her dad and signed the medical certificate they needed to have Martin deemed an involuntary psychiatric patient. By then, all she felt was a sense of overwhelming relief. It meant fourteen to thirty days under the care of knowledgeable doctors and staff.

When Ian opened his door, Grace set her suitcase down on the porch. "Do you have time for a drink?"

He raised a brow at her luggage. "Not ready to go home, huh?"

"Nope."

"Come on in." He beat her to her suitcase and ushered her inside.

"Thanks." She followed him in. "They're admitting Dad."

"Best thing for him." He reached into a top cupboard and pulled out a bottle of whiskey. "Doesn't make it any easier to see done. This do?"

"Perfect." She crouched down to greet Duke's searching sniffs.

"Ice?"

She shook her head. Her first swallow burned all the way down. She glanced around the room. "Forgot to mention it the other day, but the early '80s look suits you."

"We gonna talk about my décor?" He downed a sizeable gulp of his own drink.

She lifted her glass and followed suit. "I don't know where to begin with the rest of it."

He leveled her with a look. "For starters, you can let me know if I have to kick that cop's ass."

A surprised snort escaped, and there was no stopping the immediate swell of warm fuzzies, which had to be a result of the whiskey. She tossed back another swallow. "No one's ever offered to kick ass for me before."

Ian chuckled. "I came damn close a couple of

times."

Caught of guard, Grace searched for clues he was kidding and found none. "What times?"

He tipped his glass at her. "Danny Ross, for one. Jeremy—"

"Okay, point made." The thought of either one of those men in a showdown with Ian had her lips curving. She held out her empty glass.

He poured another couple of fingers of amber liquid into her glass and topped up his own. In an instant, the affable man of a moment ago disappeared. "I'm sorry for how you found out. About me."

"Not going to lie." She swallowed back a heated mouthful. "Pretty much sucked."

"The deal was they'd tell you on your eighteenth birthday. But everything went to shit when she disappeared. Tried to talk to your dad about you once." He threw back a swig, and his mouth tightened around a hiss of breath. "Didn't go well. That was pretty much the last time we spoke to each other."

She swirled the whiskey around in her glass. There was no ignoring how differently her life would have turned out had Ian been a different kind of man and her mother had been arrested. "You went to prison for her."

He shrugged.

"Was it hard for you? In prison?"

"It wasn't a picnic." He lifted a hand, stopping any further questions. "That's all I'm saying about those years."

She reached for his hand. "Thank you."

He squeezed back. "I'd do it again."

"Well, let's hope it doesn't come to that." She went to release his hand.

He didn't let go. "If things had been different, I would have been damn proud to be your father."

"Well." She blinked back tears. "Good. Because you're stuck with me now."

"It'll be hard on Martin. People knowing."

"Seeing him today was heartbreaking. I don't know if he'll ever be okay again." The hostage taking had rocked their small community. Rumors were rampant. Journalists were calling. When Mike had suggested she hole up at Ian's for a couple of days, she'd packed a bag, more than ready to agree. There was no telling how her dad would deal with the onslaught of attention.

"He'll get through this. He'll come around."

"I pray you're right."

"He's tougher than most people think." He rose and retrieved an object out of one of the cupboards and handed it to her. "Here."

She strapped the watch onto her wrist, comforted by the wrap of leather and the steel backing. "I missed it."

He pushed back the sleeve of his T-shirt to reveal a tattoo on the upper fleshy part of his arm, the one without the bandages. Her name was written in bold script. "Not a day went by I didn't think of you."

"You're determined to make me cry, and I've done enough of that for one day."

He reclaimed his chair. "You ready to talk about what happened with the cop?"

"He left for Toronto."

"So that's it?" he asked, crossing his arms.

She studied her glass. "Not exactly. We did come to an understanding."

"Meaning?"

Gone

She edged her fingertip around the rim and eased the words past her lips. "He wants me to come to Toronto."

His voice softened. "Hear it's a nice city."

Tiredness dug down into her muscles and scraped at her bones. She didn't want to admit to the second-guessing she'd done once Mike's plane was in the air. "I can't just up and go to Toronto. Especially with how things are right now."

"Why the hell not?"

As if he didn't know. "Because my life's kind of a mess."

"No. Your life's complicated. Whose isn't? Do something for yourself. For once." It came out like a demand, more angry than encouraging.

She straightened her spine. "It's not that easy."

"Yes, it is."

Stubborn man. "If you'd seen Dad today…"

He scrubbed at the back of his neck. "Do you love this guy?"

"I might."

"Then you should go."

"I want to. But…"

He indulged in a healthy swig. "You don't have to leave tomorrow. Do the face-talk thing. Meet halfway a couple of times."

Hope had said much the same thing. She rubbed her aching forehead. "I can't think straight. I need sleep."

He sighed. "I'll show you to your room."

"Ian?"

He retrieved her suitcase and waited.

"Thanks for putting me up."

"Anytime."

She followed him down a hallway lined with a collection of school pictures. It was like walking back in time. Kindergarten through grade seven, when they ended. Photographic evidence of bad haircuts, gap teeth, braces, blemishes, and dated outfits. That he'd framed them, hung them, had her stopping and fighting back tears.

He paused in the doorway of a room, and there was a sheen of tears in his eyes, too. "You were right about the truth setting us free."

She didn't overthink. She just walked up to him and put her arms around him. "Thanks for being here for me."

His arms were slow to follow suit, but eventually she was engulfed in a warm hug. "You need sleep. Time enough tomorrow to talk more."

"Tomorrow." Suddenly, it was full of possibilities.

Grace made quick work of her bedtime rituals and burrowed deep under the covers, grateful for their warmth and comfort. It didn't stop her from feeling the kilometers of separation between Aspen Lake and Toronto or from counting the days until they were together again in October.

He'd hated leaving her, and she hadn't wanted to let him go. But being in Ian's house made her realize she needed some time with him, to get to know him, before she moved so far away. Between packing up and settling things for her dad, it looked like she was going to get that time. Didn't mean she wasn't missing Mike something awful. She picked up the new phone Lily had insisted on arranging for her. Her thumbs couldn't help themselves.

I miss you.

His reply was quick. *Miss you, too.*

Her lips curved, and she nestled farther into the reassuring warmth of the sheets. Then she noticed one of her blankets sat on a chair in the corner, that there was a fuzzy rug on the floor, and that pink, fluttery curtains matched the quilt covering the bed.

It was her room. He'd come back for *her*. Stayed. For her.

Her phone vibrated.

Mike: *Sold the ring.*

Mike: *Online auction house.*

Grace: *Not going to lie. I'm glad.*

Mike: *I love you.*

Funny how those three little words made the most difficult of circumstances tolerable.

Love you, too.

Warm and safe, she let her eyes drift shut. She concentrated on the crickets and the night birds and the crisp breeze floating in from the window. She would miss those sounds when she left Aspen Lake. But there was no going back. Only forward. She wanted love. She wanted adventure. And she wanted those things with Mike.

Epilogue

Prodded by an excited Grace, Mike yanked open the door of Homemade by Hope and filed in after her. The bakery wasn't officially open yet. Not for another couple of weeks.

"They're finally here!"

People rushed them from all directions.

"Gracie." Her dad, tool belt around his hips, gathered her into a hug, then turned to shake Mike's hand. "Congratulations."

Martin was doing okay. Better than okay. His treatment plan was working, and they were all diligent about seeing he kept to it.

One dad down, one to go. They were meeting Ian for lunch. He'd been the one to help Grace pack up. Then he'd driven her and her stuff to Toronto. To say they'd bonded was an understatement.

"Let me see it, let me see it." When Grace held out her left hand, Hope latched on and lifted it to eye level. "It's beautiful."

Grace bounced up and down, her grin infectious, and her eyes shining. "I know, right?"

There was color in his life now. Every direction he turned. Everywhere he looked. There it was. Grace filled his life with sass and laughter, with plans and projects, love and passion. He was so deep down thankful he wanted to weep.

Hope elbowed Mike in the ribs. "Good job. It's perfect for her."

"Thanks." He'd picked out the vintage-looking ruby cluster engagement ring himself and had slipped it on her finger a week ago with the sun setting over the Caribbean Sea. The first of many holidays together.

Pops wandered in from the back. "Shoot anyone lately?"

"Thankfully, no." He greeted Grace's grandfather with a fierce hug. Secretly, Pops was his favorite of Grace's relatives.

"Too bad."

The door banged open. Levi flung his backpack into a corner. "Auntie Grace, you're back."

Grace gathered up her nephew and squeezed. "I missed you."

Hope ruffled her son's hair. "Guess who's got a girlfriend."

"Mooooom."

"What?"

Scott lugged a car seat through the door. "Dropping Becca off, saying a quick hi, then I gotta get back to work."

"Dad, tell her that kind of stuff is private."

Hope offered her cheek for Scott's quick peck. "Everything's in order for tomorrow?"

The next day was baby Becca's christening, and he and Grace were standing up as godparents.

"Mom says to call her." Then Scott grinned at Grace and opened his arms. She walked into them with a smile on her face. "It's good to see you."

Her arms wrapped around her brother-in-law. "You, too."

There was no denying there was a special bond between them, and there always would be, even if it made Mike grit his teeth.

Then again, they were a messy bunch. But he wouldn't trade them for anything. Grace had not only gifted his life with light and love, but she'd given him the family he'd waited his whole life to find.

A word about the author...

Karyn Good grew up on a farm in the middle of Canada's breadbasket. Under the canopy of crisp blue prairie skies, she read books. Lots and lots of books. Eventually, she migrated to the city, fell in love, married, and started a family. Occasionally, she picked up a pen and paper or tapped out a few meager pages of a story on a keyboard and dreamed of becoming a writer. One day, she knew without question the time was right. What to write was never the issue—romance and the gut-wrenching journey toward forever.

Visit her at:
http://www.karyngood.com

Thank you for purchasing
this publication of The Wild Rose Press, Inc.

For questions or more information
contact us at
info@thewildrosepress.com.

The Wild Rose Press, Inc.
www.thewildrosepress.com

To visit with authors of
The Wild Rose Press, Inc.
join our yahoo loop at
http://groups.yahoo.com/group/thewildrosepress/